CARLOTTI

DAVID DALRYMPLE

DRD CREATIVE, LLC

COPYRIGHT

This is a work of fiction. Names, characters, businesses, places, events and incidents are either the products of the author's imagination or used in a fictitious manner. Any resemblance to actual persons, living or dead, or actual events is purely coincidental.

Author Portrait by Robert Neumann, Big Event Studios, Grand Rapids, MI

Cover Design by Peter O'Connor @ Bespoke Book Covers

PROLOGUE

Come into the light.

She'd heard people after near-death experiences describe a radiant, white glow and a voice from within, beckoning them to draw near and live forever. That fleeting thought flashed to the forefront of Liza's mind before she pressed her foot to the gas with a primal instinct to survive. This light was no friend.

High beams glared from behind. Shifting her gaze, she reached to adjust the mirror. The trailing vehicle rammed the bumper of her silver BMW 325i. Liza's head whipped back against the headrest. The violent impact forced the air from her lungs. She gasped. "No! Please, no!"

A vicious thunderstorm blackened the streetlights along the northbound Schuylkill Expressway out of Philadelphia. The winding road blurred behind torrential sheets of rain as Liza struggled to focus on the faded white dividing line. Jagged streaks of lightning shot across the sky.

Tightening her grip on the steering wheel, she caught her breath and accelerated to seventy-five miles per hour. It put distance between the two vehicles. The faster she drove, the less she could see, the windshield wipers unable to keep up.

Liza fought to stay between the white lines as her car weaved from the concrete median to the shoulder's loose gravel. The pounding of her heart seemed to echo in her head as the pavement's sharp edge grabbed hold of her tires. The car pulled hard to the right. She yanked the steering wheel to the left as her tires struggled to climb back to the road. The steering wheel shuddered in her hands. The expressway ahead brightened as the street lights flickered back on.

From the corner of her eye, she glimpsed her ivory rosary beads swinging wildly from the rearview mirror. "God, please!"

The headlights again grew large in her mirror. Liza strained to keep one eye on the road while reaching for the cell phone on the passenger seat. Frantic, her hand grasped blindly over the seat's smooth leather. She turned her head for a split second toward the phone's dim blue light and snatched the phone as it slid toward her. The car veered. Her gaze cut from the road to the phone and back again. She pressed speed-dial for 'Nick.' A sudden swerve toward the guardrail forced her to drop the phone to the floor just as Nick answered.

"Mom?" Nick's muted voice emanated from the blackness at Liza's feet, "Mom . . . Mom?"

Liza slammed the gas pedal to the floor, accelerating to ninety miles per hour. The trailing vehicle matched her move, closing to within inches of her bumper. With a metallic thud, it made contact. The steering wheel slipped through her hands. The car fishtailed.

"Lord, no!" she screamed. With an abrupt turn to the left, the car struck the concrete median head-on and rolled. Sparks and flames lit up the darkness.

The next couple seconds played in slow motion, the metallic crunch of car on concrete ringing in her ears. A sea of sparks, like a million lightning bugs, danced around her head. Everything went black.

~

LESS THAN AN HOUR before the crash, Liza Carlotti stood at a white linen-covered bistro table with a well-known politician who, during his tenure as district attorney, had pledged to put an end to organized crime in Pennsylvania. Quite an odd meeting given that Liza's husband was Philadelphia's most infamous mafia capo, Tony "Rock" Carlotti.

The yearly fundraiser, held at the Philadelphia Museum of Art on February 22, 1997, supported a fine-arts scholarship fund. Liza sat on the museum's board of trustees. She loved the arts and their power to convey thoughts, emotions, and meaning through the printed word, musical notes, or strokes of a paintbrush. Liza both spoke and understood the language of the arts.

She stood out in a crowd without gaudy jewelry, big hair, or excessive makeup. Her elegance came with genuine modesty, rare for a woman of her means and social position. Most people wouldn't have guessed her parents were first-generation Italian immigrants by her flowing chestnut hair, soft hazel eyes, and fair skin, but the city of Varese was much closer to Switzerland than Rome.

Local painters, writers, actors, musicians, and other artists, as well as a few dignitaries, including the mayor of Philadelphia and Pennsylvania State Senator Lloyd Mays, attended the event. Mays wasn't on the original guest list. A fellow board member had informed Liza earlier in the day that Mays' assistant had called to thank them for the invitation, noting the senator had been a long-time contributor to the museum and a supporter of fine arts colleges in and around Philadelphia. The board member didn't know who'd put forth the invitation but had let Mays' assistant know they were glad the senator would be joining them.

Was a genuine appreciation of the arts the impetus for his attendance? Liza wasn't so sure. Mays' presence made her uneasy.

Liza did her best to quell her apprehension as she spent the early part of the night conversing with donors. She strolled down the East Wing's second floor and noticed an elderly woman admiring one of her own favorite pieces, "The Allegory of Faith" by the Dutch painter Johannes Vermeer. "He captures simple people in everyday life with exquisite colors and depth, don't you think?" Liza asked.

"Indeed," the woman said.

The painting depicted a young woman reclining before a magnificent image of the crucifixion. Holding her right hand over her heart, she gazed adoringly at a gold crucifix like a modern-day schoolgirl infatuated with a pop star.

Liza surveyed the painting as she'd done a hundred times, but for some reason she couldn't stop staring at the bloodied snake crushed beneath the large slab of stone; an image of Satan under the foot of Christ. It had never quite caught her attention as it had just then. A chill ran through her body, and she quickly hurried back to the gala on the East Terrance.

Thank God she'd survived the evening without any contact with Senator Mays, not even a casual glance. Her last interaction with him hadn't ended well, contentious to say the least. She didn't know how he'd be tonight or, for that matter, how she'd be. For the time being, she didn't have to worry.

At 9:15 pm, he approached her table. A pit formed in her stomach. Liza stood listening to New Age ramblings from Delphia Himes, a peculiar but gifted young sculptor and painter with shoulder-length, neon-pink hair, a few too many facial piercings, and an aversion to men in suits.

"Mrs. Carlotti," Mays said as he neared. More than a foot taller than Liza and sporting a charcoal Armani blazer and a red and gold paisley necktie, he carried himself as if he were the guest of honor. Not a strand of his perfectly sculpted salt and pepper hair was out of place.

"Senator Mays," Liza said, then turned toward Delphia.

"This is Delphia Himes. You might have seen her work at the Rittenhouse Square Art Festival in September."

"Regretfully, I didn't, but it's a pleasure, Miss Himes," he said, extending his well-manicured hand.

Delphia glanced at the ground, fidgeted with her hands, then peeked up under her bangs at Liza. Liza gave her a reassuring nod.

Delphia reached out as Mays' hand returned to his side. Mays moved to give it a second go, but Delphia dropped her hand and shoved it into the front pocket of her baggy jeans.

Mays shrugged with a hint of a frown deepening between his eyebrows. He turned back to Liza. "Great turnout."

"Yes, I'm quite pleased," she said.

"That's you, Ali," Mays said. "Go big or go home."

Liza stiffened. She shot Mays an irritated glance. Delphia ran her teeth over her lower lip. "Right on. Gotta run," she said, and then promptly headed to the open bar.

Mays' gaze followed Delphia's ungainly shuffle. He shook his head. "Interesting young lady."

"She's special," Liza said.

Mays nodded. "I'm sure she is. I heard you're writing a novel."

"From whom?" A smug smile formed on Mays' face. "I have my sources."

"It's a work in progress," she said, thinking hard for an out.

"A murder mystery or a thriller?"

"Neither. It's a romantic comedy, a little love and laughter. We need more of that, don't you think, Senator?" she said, her tongue sticking to the roof of her mouth.

"Senator? Come on, Liza, you can drop the formalities."

"I'd just as soon keep it that way."

"Your choice, Mrs. Carlotti. So, the novel— a spoonful of sugar helps the medicine go down, huh?"

"And how does Mary Poppins apply here?"

Mays paused and took a sip of his beer. "You pen romance and comedy, the sugar, while you live in a world of deceit and corruption, the foul-tasting medicine. Maybe your fictional fantasy allows you to escape the truth of your real life."

"You know I'm not a part of that world. Tony's business is his business."

"You're his wife, Liza. No offense, but you're in bed with it. You could have walked away whenever you wanted." He smirked. "But I get it. Hear no evil, see no evil."

"Look, Lloyd, if you have issues with Tony, take them up with him." Liza picked up her wine glass and her purse and turned to walk away.

Mays stepped to his left, blocking her path. "You invited me here tonight. I thought maybe you had a change of heart." Mays took another swig from his glass.

Liza stood tall but still had to tip her head back to look up into his eyes. "I really don't know what you're talking about," she said, her forehead wrinkling. She glared at him. "I didn't invite you. You invited yourself."

Mays inched closer. "I'm interested in Rodin's Gates of Hell. Maybe you could show me the way?"

Liza reached into her purse and pulled out a museum map. "I need to head back to the board members table. Enjoy the exhibit. It's extraordinary." She pushed her way past him. "Second floor, European Art, 1500–1850. I'm not much of a tour guide."

Liza arranged a ride home for Delphia, then left the gala at 9:35 pm, telling her fellow board members she felt sick to her stomach and needed to slip out early.

A steady wind howled as Liza exited the parking lot stairwell. Sideways curtains of rain sprayed though the lot's slotted walls. Liza shielded her face with her hand as she quickened her pace toward her car. She pulled in a shaky breath. Her throat felt like it was closing in. She tried to convince herself that she'd be okay. It was just a coincidence, Mays seizing an opportunity for a little philanthropy and a tax write-off.

"Liza, please!" His imposing baritone voice echoed from the lot's concrete columns. Liza stopped dead in her tracks. For a split second, she didn't know whether to be afraid or just angry. Why would he be pursuing her? Why now? She spun around. "What do you want from me, Lloyd?"

Mays stopped ten feet away, the garage lights casting his shadow at Liza's feet. His shoulders slumped. "Nothing, I guess. I just had this delusion you wanted me here tonight."

"I told you I didn't invite you."

Mays sighed. "I assure you, my assistant said we received an invitation from your board."

"We didn't send it. I'm sorry for the confusion," she said.

Mays took a step forward.

Liza put up her hand. "Lloyd, don't."

For an instant time stood still and her anxious thoughts melted as if she had control over him.

He stopped and stared into her eyes for just a moment then turned away.

Liza hurried to her car as the sound of his footsteps faded. When she pulled onto the Sckuylkill Expressway, the sky opened up.

1

LIZA NEVER REGAINED consciousness after the crash. She survived just shy of thirty-six agonizing hours on life support before Nick's father opted to pull the plug, early Monday morning. Nick hoped that when the ventilator's bellows ceased to fill his mother's lungs with life-giving oxygen, the end would come quickly. It didn't.

Moments before the nurse disconnected the ventilator, Father Anthony Taglione administered the Sacrament of Last Rites. As he concluded the ritual, he anointed Liza's head with oil. "Through this holy unction may the Lord pardon thee whatever sins or faults thou hast committed."

Nick scowled. His mother wasn't perfect, but still the priest's words pissed him off. Sins and faults? If the Lord couldn't pardon his mother, whom Nick couldn't remember having committed any transgression beyond letting an occasional 'damn it' slip from her lips, then he didn't stand a chance.

Liza's chest continued to rise and fall without the assistance of the ventilator. Irregular, strained, and drowning in mucus, her breaths marched on. She refused to quit.

Nick wasn't surprised. His jaws clenched in anger toward his father and God. His mother had tried so hard to nurture his faith, but Nick had never quite reconciled human suffering and a supposed God of love.

How could God sit idle as his daughter died a slow death, her once radiant face burned beyond recognition, most of her once flowing hair now singed to the raw and blistered scalp? Nick's stomach contracted, and a foul taste of bile caught the back of his tongue. He pulled in a deep breath, swallowed hard, and squeezed his eyes shut. Perhaps God was impotent, unable to intercede. Maybe he didn't exist, or maybe he just didn't give a shit.

He recalled a scene he'd rehashed over and over for twenty-nine years. The quiet drive home from church took an unpleasant turn when a monarch butterfly splattered against their car's windshield. Immediately transformed into an unrecognizable blur of orange, black, and green death, it spread across the driver's side glass. Even at the tender age of seven, Nick couldn't understand why God would create such a stunning creature then let it succumb to such a random case of bad timing.

Seeing the horror in Nick's eyes, Liza had done her best to explain God's attributes: his being all-knowing, all-powerful, and having the ability to see how even tragedy fits into his perfect eternal plan. Her efforts fell woefully short, nullified as Nick's father turned on the wipers and smeared butterfly parts across the windshield. He'd shouted profanities with each failed swipe of the wiper blades.

Unfortunately, Liza's theology lesson vanished in the fray. It foreshadowed Nick's spiritual decline, and over time, Nick slipped into a deep valley somewhere between apathy and atheism.

Growing up with a mafia boss as a father didn't help. Nick just couldn't see past the blatant hypocrisy. His father donned a three-piece suit, dipped his hand in holy water, genuflected, and recited the Lord's Prayer, then, on the car ride home, talked about the "damn niggers" taking over Philly.

Nick's mother sat without responding, her gaze turned downward. Nick knew she was praying by the way she moved her lips. Some would have considered her feeble, but Nick knew her faithful restraint took more grit than reacting badly. He regretted his mother dying without the comfort of knowing her son's faith was at least as big as a mustard seed. This day's events snuffed out any lasting remnants.

A horrible gurgling from his mother's breathing tube shook Nick back into the present. It tortured him to see and hear his mother's life slipping away. Mom, please let go! He bit his cheek and turned to his father.

Rock, a stern-looking, solidly built man, slouched in the corner chair, his head leaning against the wall. A gray eye-patch covering his right eye matched the color of his seasoned side-burns. He gazed straight ahead with a blank stare from his functioning eye, no redness or tears. Nick wondered why his father wore the patch that day. He usually left it at home, not afraid to reveal the sightless hazy-white orb in its socket.

In contrast, Nick's older brother Eddie stood next to his father wiping his sleeve across his wet face, a face hardened on the inside by hate and pockmarked on the outside by an unrelenting case of teenage acne.

Nick glared at his father, waiting for the inevitable meeting of the eyes, but it didn't happen. He wanted to speak, but no words came, as if his mother had gently covered his mouth. "This isn't the time or place for that." She was right. No good would come of it, but how the hell could the man be so damn cold! He signed the consent to discontinue care and sat in the chair with less emotion than he'd shown when they'd put their dog down twenty years ago.

Rock made a career out of being steely and unshakable, but this wasn't mob business, importing emeralds, or smuggling cocaine out of Colombia. This was his wife, a woman who gave up her dreams for a trail of broken promises. Nick stormed from the room.

A large window down the hall overlooked an indoor Japanese "healing" garden designed to help patients and family members find a peaceful space to think, meditate, or step outside of their situation for a brief moment. Nick peered out and noticed an elderly man pushing his wife in a wheelchair along the path that weaved its way among bonsai trees and fountains. An IV pole hung from the chair, and the woman's pale skin-and-bones, legs extended from beneath a drab, pale-blue hospital gown. Every so often, the man stopped, reached down, and took his wife's hand in his own. They paused in front of a small koi pond. He bent over, kissed her forehead, and continued on.

Nick leaned his head against the glass. "You deserved a man like that, Mom. I'm sorry you never found him."

He knew how his mother would respond. "Nick, God had me right where he wanted me. If he hadn't, I would never have had you." She would have said it with a confident and comforting smile. Nick returned to his mother's bedside, knowing in a matter of minutes or hours she'd be gone. He wanted to be there to say goodbye.

~

THE NURSES TURNED off the EKG monitor's sound and disabled the alarms to prevent the disturbing tone they would emit when his mother's heart stopped. But Liza wasn't a quitter, never had been, and Nick didn't expect anything different in her last moments. For two hours and twelve minutes more, she battled as her family looked on. At 8:57 am, she gave up the battle. The only evidence of her passing was the silent flat line that raced across the dark green monitor.

Nick's dad sat in his corner chair, his long face set like flint and his breathing deep and steady. Still not a tear.

Grandma Camilla wasn't so stoic. Her four foot, ten-inch frame seemed so frail as she slumped over her daughter's lifeless body, stroking what was left of her hair. She mumbled in Italian. Every so often, with a trembling in her voice, the name "Jesus" broke through her sobs.

Nick never knew his grandfather Joseph or his uncle Joey, both of whom died when Liza was a young girl. His grandmother's life was replete with pain and loss, and her daughter's death was more than she could handle.

With tear-filled eyes, Nick's older brother Eddie hugged his grandmother, laid his hand on his mother's forehead, and walked out.

Voices wafted in. "We're sorry, Eddie," Peter Coroneos, Rock's best friend and business partner said, "Your mother was a fine woman. I can't believe she's gone."

Nick left the room to join them. Eddie made an abrupt exit the instant they made eye contact. God forbid he let his younger brother see him in a moment of weakness.

"Peter, Sarah, thank you for coming," Nick said. Coroneos' wife threw her arms around Nick and bawled. Nick gave Sarah a minute to settle herself. She pulled away. "It's surreal," Nick said. "I'm glad you both could be here."

Coroneos clutched Nick's shoulder but didn't say a word. He was a handsome man with a warm olive complexion, a sloping Greek nose, and jet-black hair parted just left of center. As far as Nick could remember, he'd looked the same, time somehow not taking its inevitable toll. At sixty years of age, the man could have passed for ten years his junior.

A low-pitched chuckle broke the somber mood. Nick spread his legs as a garnet-red, classic corvette matchbox car raced between his feet. He couldn't help but crack a smile when he made eye contact with the full-faced young man whose odd-looking ears stuck out from his head like a set of curved wings. The man's already narrowed eyes squeezed tight as he belly laughed.

"Hi Sam," Nick said, picking up the car. He knelt down and rolled it back.

"Sam, you can't race your cars in here," Sarah said.

"He's fine," Coroneos barked.

Sam let out a huff and frowned. A four-year-old mind trapped in a twenty-three-year-old's body, Sam had inherited one too many twenty-first chromosomes. Given his unintelligible speech and constant need for parental care, the doctors had classified Sam's Down syndrome as "low functioning." What Sam lacked in IQ, he more than made up for with his loving nature. Nick coveted Sam's simple outlook and gentle naivety. Seemed like a wonderful way to be.

Nick knew Sam was a bone of contention between Rock and Coroneos. Rock was pragmatic, invariably making his decisions based on how they might affect the bottom line. It didn't matter whether it destroyed relationships or even life itself. If it hindered his ability to make a profit, it had to go, and when Sam's expensive care began to take a toll on Coroneos' finances, he wasn't afraid to voice his opinion.

When Coroneos paid $136,000 cash for Sam's heart valve replacement, Rock said it was a waste of hard-earned money when the "kid wasn't gonna live past twenty anyway." It was the only time Nick saw Coroneos come close to a physical altercation with his father. Despite his position in the mob and his lucrative business ventures, Coroneos poured much of his income into keeping his son alive. For the most part, he didn't live high on the hog.

Nick thanked Coroneos and Sarah for their love and support, then found the nearest empty room. He wept. Maybe his mother's stories about heaven were real, that she now strolled streets of gold with Moses, asking what it was like to part the Red Sea. Or maybe she ran into her father and told him about her screwed-up family. Then again, she might just be gone, burned out like a used light bulb.

After he regained his composure, Nick spent the next half hour comforting his grandmother, his emotions put on hold. Maybe it was a defense mechanism or just denial, but either way the tears stopped flowing.

He watched as his father's countenance changed. For the first time, Rock appeared broken. Slumped in his chair, his right hand over his face, and with the exception of two sons he'd alienated, he was alone, a widower, an only child, both parents long since deceased.

They held the funeral at St. Cecilia's Catholic Church three days later. Nick grieved to his core but found comfort in knowing that so many people loved his mother. Nick and his brother joined the other four pallbearers carrying Liza's snow-white casket to the front of the sanctuary. Slow and arduous, each step bore not merely the casket's weight but the heaviness of Nick's own heart. He wanted it to end, but he knew that when it did, he'd be that much closer to putting her into the ground.

A sea of flowers surrounded the altar, extending down the aisles on either side. The six men set the casket on its brass stand. To the left of the front row, a stunning arrangement of at least five dozen fully bloomed white roses stood out from the rest. As Nick took his seat, he leaned over and glanced at the card . . . With deepest condolences, Lloyd Mays. Albeit peculiar, death occasionally brought civility to conflict, even if only temporarily.

The ushers struggled to find seats in the packed pews for the last few guests. Nick scanned the sanctuary in awe at the diversity of mourners and understood the impact his mother had made in the city. The words of adoration spoken by friends and loved ones were not the obligatory, trite words muttered at a memorial to make up for the lack of something meaningful to say. Liza's life extended into every facet of the community. It stood as a testament to her independence and the backbone it took to step outside her husband's dark shadow.

Inside the church's back door, Nick glimpsed a young woman

standing in a tight black dress that extended below her knees. Tufts of pink hair peeked out from beneath a deep, red beret, tipped to one side. She seemed to be weeping privately behind her oversized dark sunglasses. Slipping in after everyone else had been seated, she disappeared before the Mass ended.

Liza's maid, gardener, and best friend, Maria Hernandez, sat in the second row behind Rock. A dark lace veil hid her face, but the rhythmic movement of her head gave away her grief. She'd lost a surrogate daughter and a spiritual sister.

The funeral concluded with the priest sharing a letter Liza had written to God when she was eight years old. Liza's mother had given it to Father Taglione to use at the viewing as part of a collage of photos and clips from Liza's writings.

He held the letter up in his right hand. "We all know Liza was a talented writer, but few of us have had the opportunity to read her earliest works. This one is circa 1944."

Dear God,

Thank you for my fast feet. Today Randy Dillon tried to run away with my Cracker Jacks, and I caught him before he made it to the swings. I'm sorry for punching him in the nose, but I was really mad.

Love Liza

A FEW QUIET chuckles sounded from the pews, Nick included. The priest offered a moment of silence before the pallbearers took their positions around the casket. Nick squeezed the cold metal handle. He couldn't believe she was dead.

As the men carried the casket back down the aisle, the

congregation sang, "No sweeter love than His love." Nick shook his head. No sweeter love? Really?

After the service, immediate family and a few close friends attended a private graveside burial. When the solemn ceremony had ended, Maria approached Nick, her eyes bloodshot. "Thank you for sharing your mother with me," she said, her voice cracking. "She was good to me."

"And you were good to her, good to all of us," Nick said.

Maria opened her mouth, but no sound came from her trembling lips. She gave Nick a long embrace, turned, and walked away.

Nick moved to the row of chairs closest to the casket and sat with his arm around his grandmother. She felt so small and brittle, a woman ready to go home. This world had dealt her enough pain.

The few remaining mourners exchanged tears and hugs as dark clouds moved overhead, A slow steady rain began to fall. Nick helped Camilla into the black limousine but chose to stay back to be alone with his mother.

His stomach turned as he rested his hand on the casket. He ran to the base of an old oak tree, knelt, and dry heaved, his eyes and mouth watering. After three more attempts to empty a stomach that hadn't seen food for days, he turned and sat, resting his back against the tree.

Why was she driving so damn fast? He couldn't shake it. Under those conditions she should have been going half that speed. Was it the weather? Did an animal run in front of her car? Perhaps the estimate of her speed was wrong, or she was just trying to get home in a hurry. Friends at the fundraiser did say she wasn't feeling well. Nick's stomach flip-flopped again, but after a few deep breaths, the feeling passed.

It certainly wasn't the best time for rational, deductive reasoning. He ruminated for a while over God's apparent lack of concern for Liza, a woman who so openly professed his love. The more Nick tried to reconcile the glaring disparity between his mother's devotion to God and his letting her suffer, the angrier he became.

He just needed to give himself time to deal with the acute trauma of her death. If questions still lingered, he would pursue answers, but for the time being all he could muster was resentment and grief. His mother's final words, "Lord, no!" were forever etched in his mind. Although thankful he was 'with his mother' in her last waking seconds, he couldn't bear to have those cries ringing in his head forever.

2

BUREAUCRATIC RED TAPE made obtaining a copy of his mother's accident report more involved than just a simple phone call. Three and a half weeks had passed, and as much as he tried, he couldn't quell the restlessness. He hadn't slept more than four hours a night since the day she'd died. Things just didn't add up.

The Inquirer stated that "Liza Carlotti, wife of reputed mob boss Tony 'Rock' Carlotti, died in a weather-related car accident on the Schuylkill Expressway." Police reported she'd hit the median at approximately ninety miles per hour. The article went on to say that one potential witness noted a black Cadillac Escalade driving at an excessive rate of speed at the approximate location and time of the accident, but authorities had no further information.

Nick questioned the police's account and wanted to see it in writing. First, he had to get past the secretary of Philadelphia's fifth-district police headquarters, a pedantic woman with a drab, robotic voice.

"You'll need to fill out a form eighty-two dash twenty-three. Were you personally involved in the accident?" the woman asked.

"No, it was my mother— she was killed."

"I'm sorry for your loss, but only individuals involved in the accident, an agent for the insuring company, or an attorney representing the insured may apply for a copy of the incident report."

Nick took a slow, deep breath. "Ma'am, my mother is dead and obviously can't apply for a copy herself, nor can she retain a lawyer. Her insurance company won't communicate with me."

"Unfortunately, you won't be able to —"

"I want the damn report!" He pulled the phone from his ear and grit his teeth to restrain the profanities.

After a brief pause, the woman continued, her tone more sympathetic. "I suggest you leave a message with one of our investigators. I'll forward you to his voicemail."

"Forgive me, I'm just frustrated," Nick said.

"I understand. Again, I'm sorry for your loss."

Nick left a message, detailing his doubts regarding their findings.

Next, he called a well-known private investigator who made it perfectly clear that neither he nor any other investigator within a hundred-mile radius would take a case potentially involving Tony Carlotti.

Finding an attorney proved equally impossible. Nick's divorce lawyer gave him a shortlist of names, but again, none were willing to travel down a road that could get them killed. For now, he'd go it alone.

The thought of trying to talk to his father initiated a cold sweat. Maybe start with his brother. Eddie would have to agree that the circumstances of the crash were at least not as neat and tidy as the authorities reported. Still, remaining civil would be no small task.

Nick and Eddie had never clicked. Nick fancied sports and pretty girls while Eddie hung with a rougher crowd. While Nick shot hoops in the driveway, his brother sat in his bedroom wearing oversized headphones, listening to Ozzy Osbourne and

Judas Priest albums his mother didn't know he owned. He hid them within two towering stacks of records, both strategically padded with more palatable artists like Jim Croce, ABBA, and Cat Stevens.

Eddie had moved to Boston for a short stint in an effort to distance himself from his father while Nick pursued his medical career - a decision that didn't sit well with either Eddie or his father. The final blow came when Eddie returned home to work for the mob. Nick became the defector, the pretty boy too good for the family business.

A shroud of darkness hung over Eddie like a malignant spirit that followed him wherever he went. His eyes never seemed to radiate any light, any life. So, his return to Philadelphia and to his father's side came as no surprise to Nick.

The two hadn't talked since the funeral. Nick called to request they meet to discuss their mother's death.

"What is it you have to say that you can't say on the phone?" Eddie snapped.

"That's about the response I expected."

"I'm a busy man."

Nick tightened his grip on the phone. "I'm your brother. I'm asking for half an hour of your time."

"It's 10:36. Go— tick-tock."

"Look, we both lost a mother here! The least we could do, out of respect for her, is to be civil. What the hell have I ever done to you?"

"Tick tock."

"Has it ever crossed your mind that Mom's accident wasn't really an accident?" "No."

"When was the last time Mom drove more than sixty miles an hour? And in a storm at night, for god's sake?"

"I take it you have another theory?"

"No, not yet, but if there's another possibility, wouldn't you want to know?"

Eddie huffed. "It was dark and raining. She felt like shit. She could have passed out, and her foot pressed into the gas. Who the hell knows?"

"I want to see the police report."

"I think you need more sleep. Apparently, the long hours have clouded your judgment. Trust me, if Pops thought someone caused the accident, he'd have put a bounty out and taken care of the situation. Go back to the hospital and stick to boob jobs or whatever it is you're doing these days."

Nick didn't reciprocate the dig. It never served him well, only playing into his brother's narcissism. He'd heard, what he hoped to be just a rumor, that his father was dating some bimbo from a high-end strip club.

"Is it true, Dad's seeing someone?"

"You have a problem with that?" Eddie asked.

"Seriously? Hell, Mom hasn't even been dead a month."

"He's grieving. What can I say?"

"How about that hooking up with an ex-Penthouse centerfold turned lap dancer isn't just shallow, but incredibly callous."

"How about you mind your fucking business?"

Nick pulled the phone from his ear and reared back. His arm froze in the cocked position. Maybe it was the thought of having to go through the hassle of replacing a smashed cell phone or a sudden, rare burst of self-control but the phone returned safely to his ear. "You're such a dick! Thanks for nothing, Bro." He hung up. He wasn't at all surprised that his father would fawn over a stripper. After all, Peter Coroneos owned two 'gentlemen's' clubs outside of Camden. But the timing seemed heartless, even for a Carlotti.

Nick paced the living room floor, giving his heart a chance to slow. When the inexorable urge to put a hole in the wall subsided, he sat down, took a few deep breaths, and recomposed himself. Why couldn't he just have a healthy relationship with his brother? It had been contentious almost from the start.

After his First Communion, Nick's mother had given him a Bible storybook. It pictured Cain lifting a jagged rock as his brother, Abel, cowered on the ground beneath him. Abel held his arm over his head in what turned out to be a failed effort to protect himself.

"Momma, do ya think Eddie would hit my head with a rock like that?" young Nick had asked.

"Of course not," his mother had said. "Eddie loves you."

Nick had serious doubts back then, and doubted he'd fare any better now if the situation arose. Eddie had an advantage over Cain in that he carried a .38 Special and not a lousy chunk of granite.

Two days after his unproductive talk with Eddie, Nick received a call from the officer assigned to oversee the accident investigation. The officer reiterated his inability to release the accident report, and in no uncertain terms, let Nick know they'd closed the case. Nick shared his concerns regarding his mother's estimated speed and inquired about the suspicious Cadillac Escalade.

"I can't tell you why your mother was driving at unsafe speeds for the road conditions, and there's no indication anyone tampered with the car. As for the Escalade, an SUV speeding down the Schuylkill isn't exactly noteworthy," the officer said. "But regardless, as I said, I can't provide any additional information."

"I believe it's all noteworthy, and with all due respect, my mother never drove that fast on dry roads at midday."

"I understand the pain of your loss, but we've finished our investigation. Your father has durable power of attorney, and we've provided him with a copy of the final accident report. If you want to see it, you'll have to take that up with him."

"Thanks for your time," Nick said, slamming the cordless phone on the table, sending shards of plastic and batteries flying. He buried his face in his hands.

Multiple calls to his father over the course of the next week went without a reply. Hopefully, Eddie hadn't shared with him their confrontational discussion. When Nick reached Rock on the fifth try, the conversation started cordially. Maybe he hadn't.

"Pops."

Rock cleared his throat. It was more of a habit than anything but years of cigar smoking and yelling had left his already imposing voice deep and coarse. "Nick," he said.

"How are you doing, Pops?" Nick asked without expectation of an honest answer.

"Gettn' by. And to what do I owe the pleasure of your call?"

"I was wondering if I could get a copy of the accident report."

"What the hell do you want with that?" Maybe Eddie had spoken to his father.

Nick hadn't anticipated an amiable "Sure, Son," but the terse response caught him off guard. "I need closure."

His father's tone mellowed. "How's that gonna help?"

"I don't know. Maybe just to put it all together. I'm still reeling, Pops."

Rock cleared his throat again. "There's nothin in that report that's gonna make you feel better. I assure you." "Maybe, but I'd still like to see it."

"You wanna be a masochist, have at it. But then I don't wanna hear another word about it. Got it?" "Yeah. Thanks." Nick hung up before Rock had the opportunity to renege. The report came three days later.

THIRD BOX DOWN, right side of page one: *Body Region with most Severe Injury*–circled in red, choice number one: *Head*

Below, in a box labeled *Ejected/Trapped*, choice number five: *Trapped - Equipment used in extrication.*

Nick fought back tears as he pored over the accident report. His mother's last waking moments cataloged in a cold and indifferent nine-page collection of check boxes, circled choices, and short fill-in-the-blanks. He downed a large swig from his glass. Crown Royal, no ice. He'd need more than one drink to make it to page nine.

He pressed on.

Weather conditions: rainy

Lighting: dark

Contributing Factors (Driver): exceeded authorized speed limit, driving too fast for conditions.

He bit his lower lip and shook his head in doubt.

Driver's Condition: possible illness

Sequence of Events: loss of control of vehicle, collision with median barrier.

The middle pages contained more mundane information:

license content, medical transport records, description of vehicle damage, and other material that seemed of little value.

He flipped to page seven. Before he could turn his head or squeeze shut his eyes, the grim image had already registered. It lingered behind his lids like the haunting blood on Lady Macbeth's hands. Rubbing his eyes didn't blot out the snapshot of mangled steel and the blood on the dash. He reached across the coffee table and downed the half-full glass of whiskey, refilled his glass, and sunk back into the sofa.

It had to be wrong. "*Exceeded authorized speed limit*" wasn't possible, at least not without a darn good reason, and an upset stomach wasn't one of them. His mother had more common sense than the rest of his family combined. She wouldn't have risked death to avoid an embarrassing situation with her gut. Something had to be missing. But what?

With Crown Royal coursing through his veins, he fired up the Porsche and cruised back and forth past the accident site. Besides the obvious danger to life and career, his emotional state magnified the pain of each pass down the Schuylkill. He slowed as he neared the spot where the withered flowers had hung for so long. Long streaks of silver paint remained, permanent scars on the concrete median like some cruel joke. His mother's final haunting plea to God echoed from its hidden place in Nick's brain. It sounded so real, so present, drowning out the highway's noise but it wasn't real. It was just a memory, right? Nick moved on down the road. He'd had enough.

Why that particular stretch of road, straight and well lit? Why not a half-mile prior where the road curved and the lights had burned out?

He pulled off the next exit and turned toward the city's southwest side. From the top of the Passyunk Bridge, a sea of spent cars and trucks appeared in the salvage yard below. Finding his mother's BMW among a couple thousand rusted, crushed, and otherwise barely recognizable cars seemed daunting if not impossible.

Nick pulled up to the attendant's hut at the entrance to the lot. The dilapidated building looked as downtrodden as the grave-yard of vehicles it guarded, its yellowed-white paint peeling off in strips. The tin roof was littered with pigeon crap.

The gorilla-like figure inside didn't budge when Nick rolled down his window. Surly with tufts of gray back hair pouring out of a grease-stained wife-beater, the man kept his gaze focused on an eight-inch square, black-and-white TV. Nick beeped the horn.

The man swiveled on his metal stool toward the window. With an apathetic look, he slid open the glass. A thick cloud of white smoke rolled out. "What can I do ya for?" he asked. The stench of stale cigars drifted into Nick's car.

"I'm looking for a silver BMW 325i. It came in eight days ago."

"Huh, good luck," the man said with a mocking huff. He pointed his stubby index finger out the window. "Newest ones are that way, but ya never know. Cars come in and outta here like drunk cowboys from a whore house."

Nick rolled his eyes. "Uh . . . Yeah, I'm sure. Thanks." He turned down the muddy, pothole-ridden road.

There didn't seem to be any rhyme or reason to the place-ment of vehicles in the lot. Wrecked cars, rusted-out trucks and vans, rows of transmissions, and stacks of old tires lined both sides of the drive. At least they hadn't piled the cars two or three high. The only reasonable chance of finding the BMW would require starting at the far end and working down each row.

Nick parked his Porsche to the side of the drive. The brilliant sun shone in the azure sky, but the mid-March air had barely reached fifty degrees. After the first couple steps, he paused to zip his black leather jacket. He continued on.

It seemed befitting, the metaphor for this here-one-day-gone-the-next life. Cars, once shiny and new, odometers set to zero, ready for a hundred and fifty thousand miles of adventure, now relegated to scrap metal. Each must have harbored its own sad story from the dealer to the dump. Like that god-awful, mustard-yellow LeSabre to his left, the front end smashed in and both front doors missing. It likely didn't die a slow, natural death of attrition but succumbed to a more tragic event. Maybe someone's mother died in there. Nick picked up his pace.

After three arduous rows and at least two hundred cars, the only thing resembling his mother's BMW was a cut-in-half, deep green 318i. He leaned against the car, its dusty hood radiating heat from the midday sun. Warm air moved around him, and his chill subsided. He took a deep breath and scanned the lot. One more row. It had to be there.

His gaze shifted side to side as he eased down the middle of the road. This row seemed indistinguishable from the previous until he neared the end. Something caught his eye. Through the missing driver's side window, they appeared, dangling from the rearview mirror. He froze. A lump formed in his throat as he inched toward his mother's crumpled car. His feet grew heavier with each step. The rosary beads blurred before him as his eyes welled with tears.

The photograph in the report nearly wrecked him, but laying his trembling hands on the car, seeing the destruction, the steering wheel jammed up against the driver's seat, the shattered windshield was more than he could stand. "Lord, no!" The car seemed to cry out her last words. Nick slumped over the hood and wept.

When no more tears would come, he stood himself up. Nick squeezed his upper body through the bent and narrowed window opening. His reach fell an inch short of the rosary. He strained and extended his fingers but to no avail. He twisted and turned his head and shoulders to the side. In this position, he couldn't see them, his gaze forced instead toward the driver's side dash. But, with one more stretch, he was able to lift the beads from the mirror. He squeezed them in his hand.

But his victory was short-lived. "No . . . Please . . . No . . . Oh, Mom. I'm so sorry." The stains, although nearly black, were unmistakable. A smear on the dash, a small trail, and a large stain on the floor's carpet. He ran a fingertip slowly over the blood on the dash. His eyes fell shut.

One by one, he passed the rosary beads between his index finger and thumb, gently squeezing each before moving to the next. Ten small beads . . . One large . . . Ten more small . . . One large. In his mind, his mother's voice whispered, "Hail Mary, full of grace, the Lord is with thee . . . " Nick clenched his jaw. The Lord surely hadn't been with his mother. Why no grace for her?

With his eyes still closed, he continued the ritual that Sister Mary Catherine had taught him in parochial school, a practice that now seemed all the more futile. This time, only three beads after the large, then another large. Expecting the crucifix to follow, he reached with his opposite hand and felt not just the smooth ivory cross, but something else, cool and metallic. He opened his eyes, and through tears, strained to bring it into focus. After a couple purposeful blinks, the object took shape. It was a small brass key tied to the same metal loop as the crucifix. Funny. Why would his mother have attached a key to her rosary? He reached back and shoved the fistful of beads into his jacket pocket.

Glancing one last time at his mother's blood on the carpet, he knew he'd had as much as he could take.

4

It wasn't that he didn't have a choice. He clearly did. But, from the moment he stepped into the restaurant on the evening of June 14, four months after Liza's death, Senator Lloyd Mays traveled the road prepared for him.

Though a savvy politician, Mays had a weakness for younger women. He'd cared little to hide the character trait while he was a senior partner in his Center City law firm, but he'd managed to keep it in check during his brief tenure as the Philadelphia DA.

As DA, Mays had proved to be an ardent crusader, set on taking down organized crime in Pennsylvania. At the time, he honestly believed it was good versus evil, Mays against the mob— a battle he could and would win. Now that he was a newly elected state senator, his fight had waned, and any appearance of passion continued merely for show, for a check mark on his growing resume. He wanted to move up the political ladder but ending up like Hoffa or Bobby Kennedy wasn't on the agenda. Still, his previous ventures put him directly in the mob's crosshairs, especially in Philadelphia, a town owned by the very men he'd once tried to destroy.

Given that he'd just left a law-enforcement convention, Mays strode along the Center City sidewalk without a worry in the world that sultry summer evening. Surrounded by twelve hundred local, state, and federal officers, he couldn't have been safer.

A small group, including Mays and his staff assistant, left the Philadelphia Convention Center to attend a reception and dinner at Sergio's on the thirty-seventh floor of Two Liberty Place, a chic restaurant with rich walnut molding and floor-to-ceiling windows sporting burgundy velvet drapes swagged with gold ropes and tassels.

Mays scanned the room as was his habit of late in venues where he had a reasonable chance of hobnobbing with people of power, those who might further his future political aspirations. His attention turned to a waiter carrying a plate of pasta Bolognese. Its aroma of nutmeg and white wine reminded him that he hadn't eaten since breakfast.

Maurice Rawls, a veteran detective with the Philadelphia Police Department, sat to Mays' right. Rawls had joined the force nearly a century after the city had hired its first black police officer. He'd earned the department's "Officer of the Year" award two consecutive years and in 1994 received the President's Medal of Valor for disarming a crazed man who'd held three children at gunpoint in a North Philly daycare center.

Mays turned in his chair. "Detective, I'd like your perspective on our broadened efforts to enforce RICO. What's the word from the streets?" he asked.

Rawls set down his water glass but didn't immediately make eye contact. "We've been on the losing side of the battle for a long time, Senator."

"And I'd like to see that change," Mays said.

Rawls slid back his seat and looked up. His smooth bald head and thick charcoal goatee intensified his gaze. "We're underfunded, undermanned, and the Feds are much better at demanding information than sharing it. I'm carrying a slingshot into a gun battle."

"We have to start somewhere," Mays said, taking a sip of his Cabernet. "It isn't just the money, it's logistics, and the ability to collect the information. We need to prosecute more than the middlemen and street-level thugs. We have to bring down the Capos and the money launderers."

"Like I said, we're outgunned," Rawls said. He sliced a piece from his steak. "You know as well as I do, they have payrolls inside the local precincts. I'm sure some of my own men are on the take. This is complicated business, Senator."

Mays put on his best 'I'm passionate about this thing' expression. "Tony Carlotti has been running this town for the past fifteen years, and he thinks he's untouchable. He's going to make a mistake. If you can put a case together, I promise I'll make sure he doesn't see the light of day."

"The Feds are — "

"The Feds are incompetent. If they had their act together, he'd have been behind bars years ago," Mays said.

Rawls turned back to his plate and lifted the fork to his lips without looking up. He took his time chewing his filet. "Senator, no offense, but the DA's office didn't do any better when you were there."

"Ouch, that hurts," Mays said, half smiling.

"Not a dig, just a statement of fact. The tentacles of organized crime reach deep, and unless our efforts come together, local, state, and federal, the beast will continue to survive. We'll do our part, but in the meantime, I'm doing my best to keep young boys on the streets from dying in this war."

Mays backed off. He knew Rawls' story, growing up in the East Liberty housing projects of Pittsburgh. How two days after his seventh birthday, he'd witnessed his older brother Lester's brutal murder on the front porch of their apartment. But it was that heinous tragedy that had given birth to Rawls' zeal for justice. "Fair enough," Mays said.

As the waiters served dessert, the lights dimmed, and she

stepped to the piano. Stunning, tall and exotic, maybe a mix of Spanish and Asian? Her short, straight, ebony hair framed a face like none he'd ever seen. From the first note, she captured his attention. Her sleek eyes remained closed for most of the song, but each time they opened, her gaze locked onto his. It was mesmerizing. She sang Mazzy Star's "Fade Into You." Was she really looking at him, or was he wishing her to be?

"Senator, it was a pleasure," Rawls said, extending his hand as he stood to leave. "We're on your side, really."

With all of his senses engrossed in the angel on the stage, Mays didn't respond. His assistant nudged him. Mays turned to see Rawls' hand returning to his side.

"Forgive me, Detective," Mays said, standing briefly to return the handshake. "Thank you for your service to the City of Philadelphia."

As soon as Mays sat back down, he turned his focus back to the girl.

"It's an honor," Rawls answered. He walked out with two of his men.

She sang the last note just before midnight. The few remaining patrons gave her a scattered, last-call sort of applause as she stepped off the stage and wound her way through the room. As she approached Mays' table, she paused long enough to place a lavender business card next to his empty wine glass. She didn't make eye contact, but her slender body brushed against him as she passed. Mays felt that head-to-toe sensation that causes you to lose self-control, lose yourself.

The scent of her perfume lingered in the air long after she'd left the room. It provided a third dimension to his infatuation, hardly necessary given her looks, her sultry voice, and the way she moved. Turning the card over, Mays smiled and slipped it into his shirt pocket.

He called her from his silver Mercedes, and she suggested

meeting at Pier 33, a nightclub near the marina close to where he docked his seventy-two-foot motor yacht, the Gypsy Rose.

Inside the club, the bright lights and the music's pounding bass reminded Mays of his earlier days, when his evenings started at midnight and ended at 4am — nights he rarely came home alone. Maybe he had his mojo back.

He detoured to the restroom as the woman took a seat at the bar. On his return, he noticed the bartender lean over the bar and give the girl a kiss on the cheek. She smiled, took two drinks in her hand, and turned as Mays approached.

"I hope you don't mind my ordering for you. Martini, dirty," she said with a playful smirk.

"What gave me away?" he asked.

"It's in your eyes," she said, handing Mays his drink. She reached out and introduced herself. "Anya."

"Lloyd," he said, taking her hand in his. He drew it to his lips. "It's a pleasure. For the record, you're gorgeous and gifted."

"Thank you — it pays the rent."

At a table looking over the dance floor, they laughed, made small talk, and finished their first drinks.

When the song changed, Anya caught Mays by surprise when she took hold of his wrist and pulled him to the dance floor. Graceful, sensual, and clearly a trained dancer, she moved around him, close to him, and teasingly away from him. For once, Mays was out of his league. She pulled him in, slid her body down his. They embraced. She kissed him hard as the music slowed.

Mays' hand drifted down her back but stopped as he wobbled. The floor moved beneath his feet, and he strained his eyes to prevent seeing his impromptu date in stereo. He hadn't had that much to drink. But it seemed to be catching up with him.

After another dance, Anya brought two more martinis to the table and suggested they move the party back to his place. Mays set his untouched drink on the table and stood to leave, steadying himself with the chair's back. "We can take them with us," she said.

"The drinks?"

"I'm a VIP," she answered, "It's a perk."

They walked past the bouncer at the exit, drinks in hand. Anya stopped, turned around, and lifted to her toes, giving the muscle-bound man a one-armed hug and a peck on the cheek. Mays staggered when Anya moved from his side. The bouncer grabbed him by the shoulder and propped him up.

"Steady there, dude," the bouncer said.

Mays shook his head to clear the cobwebs and wrapped his arm around Anya's waist.

She smiled and slid her hand into his back pants pocket. "I've got you, baby."

Lloyd remembered their stroll to the Gypsy Rose and vaguely recalled entering the bedroom. When his eyes opened, his life changed forever. He awoke to the blood, the missing girl, the panic, and an ominous phone call.

The deep voice on the line thanked him for being such an easy target. He gave Mays the figure he needed to pony up if he wanted to stay out of prison. With the girl likely dead, he'd most certainly be the prime suspect unless he complied. He had no intention of going to jail, so for now, he did just that.

5

A PHILADELPHIA POLICE patrol boat met the shaken fisherman just upstream from Governor Prinz Park, the woman's body still tangled up in his anchor rope. The police transported the corpse to the dock at the Wellington boat club where Rawls and Taylor waited. A rickety aluminum fishing dinghy puttered in the distance.

A small crowd gathered behind the yellow barrier tape. The usually quiet Sunday club had become a bustling crime scene. Members pointed and whispered and jostled for a better view. The police boat came to a stop at the end of the dock.

Two officers lifted the gurney and extended the wheeled legs onto the weathered wooden dock. The body lay covered with two braided yellow nylon ropes extending from beneath the blue plastic sheet. Each rope ran to a separate mud-covered cinderblock resting at the foot of the body.

Rawls and Taylor met the officers on the dock.

"Hard to swim with all that extra weight," Rawls said glancing at the cinderblocks. He ran his fingers down his sharp, black goatee.

One of the officers nodded. "Someone wanted her down there for good."

Rawls lifted the tarp's edge. The woman's bloated body bore only a thin pink bra and lace panties that cut deeply into her bluish, mottled skin. Her abdomen, distended with air, made her appear eight months pregnant and the wrinkled skin of her fingers had peeled away from the underlying tissues, exposing whitish-pink muscle below.

The material of Rawls' shirtsleeve only partially reduced the stench as he buried his nose in the bend of his arm and leaned in. Something caught his eye, a green plastic card poking from the left cup of her bra. He slipped it out and wiped the mud away with his gloved finger. "She doesn't look like a William A. Santini." He handed the credit card to Taylor.

Taylor scanned the card. "I'm sure there's more than one dude named William wearing a bra and panties in this city, but those breasts look real."

"Track down info on Mr. Santini. I want to take a closer look at the body before the fisherman gets here."

"On it," Taylor said, turning back to their car.

Rawls held his breath. He knelt down next to the woman's body and lifted one of the ropes encircling the her neck. The other twisted like a tourniquet above her right knee. Her turgid tongue, approximately the size and color of a ripe plum, protruded from her gaping mouth and her shoulder-length ginger hair lay spread out in clumps, wet and covered in debris.

The fisherman's engine slowed to an idle as it reached the dock. Officers helped the old man secure the boat and led him to Rawls.

Still trembling, the man's face fell flat. Rawls had seen that look many times. It showed in the eyes of people who'd seen things they wished they hadn't — an almost zombie-like expression.

Rawls peeled off his gloves and placed his hand on the man's shoulder. He escorted him to a bronze metal bench at the edge of the dock. "Here, have a seat."

Peeking up at Rawls from under the bill of his weathered Phillies baseball hat, the man seemed to awaken slightly from his stupor. "Thanks," he said, his knees wobbling as he sat down. The added weight of the situation seemed more than his feeble old legs were willing to carry.

Standing above the man, Rawls pulled out a notepad and pen. "I'm sure this isn't how you planned to spend the day."

A strained smile came to the man's leathery and wrinkled face. "Uh, no. Not really." His head slumped.

"Just do your best and tell me what happened."

The man lifted his head. "Mind if I have a cigarette?"

Rawls nodded.

With a calloused hand, the man pulled a pack of Marlboros from his breast pocket and took one from it. He slipped the cigarette between his lips and struggled as the flame of the lighter bounced around with the shaking of his hand. Rawls reached down and steadied the man's hand. "Thanks," the man said. He pulled the first drag deep into his lungs and let it stream from both nostrils. His shoulders relaxed.

"Tell me what happened," Rawls said.

After a brief pause, the man looked Rawls in the eye. "I was fishin above the park. Hadn't caught nothin all mornin, so I decided to quit. Went to pull up the anchor and was like, what the hell! Thought for a sec I got stuck on some concrete, or rebar, or somethin. But it started to budge, so I kept on pullin. Usually, it's a big ol' clump of mud and weeds but, holy crap, it was a frickin body. Looked like a fish that's been dead for a few days, all puffed up and nasty. I just let it be and called nine-one-one."

Rawls took the man's contact information, made sure he felt okay to drive his boat back to the launch, and thanked him for his time.

The crime scene investigators arrived to do their preliminary examination. Rawls approached the female investigator.

"How long do you think she was in the drink?" Rawls asked.

"Given the minimal amount of tissue loss, I'd say three, maybe four days. Water's pretty warm so the sloughing on her fingers started earlier than it would have had she been in cold water." The investigator lifted her camera and snapped a picture of the woman's head and neck. She turned the woman's head to the side. "Can see that depressed skull fracture even under all that swelling."

Rawls nodded and turned to see Taylor returning from the car. "Whatcha got?"

Taylor grinned. "Jackpot. Santini's a known enforcer for Rock Carlotti. He used the credit card three nights ago at the Econo-Lodge near the airport."

"That's why I love this job," Rawls said. "It's like Christmas. Never know what's going to be under the tree. We need the surveillance video from the motel."

"Already sent the request."

6

A THIN, pulsing jet of blood shot from a tiny arteriole at the cut edge of the peeled down scalp. It painted a fine, bright red, serpentine line across Nick's blue surgical gown. Nick squeezed the skin tightly between his thumb and index finger, temporarily halting the flow of blood. He held out his opposite hand. "Raney clip."

The scrub nurse slapped a metal-handled instrument with a blue plastic clip on the end, into Nick's hand. He aligned the clip over the bloody scalp edge. As he loosened his grip, the clip snapped onto the scalp. He pulled his fingers away, and the bleeding stopped.

"Okay, now you've seen one." Nick took a step back from the table.

The intern's eyes grew wide as he peered above his surgical mask. Nick recognized the young man's expression, a paradoxical union of excitement and terror. He'd been there himself, but it seemed like a lifetime ago. His first case, a hernia repair, had felt like walking on the moon, the culmination of years of study, test-taking, and lost sleep. Finally, he wore the gown, mask, and gloves. At last, he held the scalpel in his hand. Not that moments of tension and exhilaration didn't still arise, but that kind of nervous thrill had long since passed.

The intern's hand trembled. "Raney clip," he said, his voice tentative and hushed. As he advanced the clip toward the wound edge, he prematurely loosened his grip and the clip fell from the instrument. It slid down the surgical drapes and hit the floor. The young man's shoulders slumped. He let out a disheartened sigh and glanced back as Nick stood shaking his head.

Across the table, a tall, slender surgical resident with deep blue eyes shot Nick a disapproving look, her delicate blonde eyebrows furrowed. She turned to the intern who looked like a running back who'd just fumbled the football on the two-yard line. "It's cool. I dropped a guy's rib on the floor once." She nodded toward the scrub nurse. "Hand him another clip, please."

A glimmer of light returned to the intern's eyes.

Nick drew a deep, impatient breath. "Gotta get moving. I'd like to minimize blood loss."

When his chief resident looked his way the second time, Nick rolled his eyes, nonverbal surgical code for "You're too damn soft." What happened to the rite of passage? The demanding road to surgeon-hood came with emotional battle scars. No pain, no gain. But now it seemed surgeons-in-the-making needed coddling. Everyone was a winner. Everyone got a participation trophy and an encouraging pat on the back. Wouldn't want the delicate new doctors getting their feelings hurt.

Nick knew, as he opened the door to the physicians' lounge two hours later, he'd get an ear full. Although residents and fellows rarely second-guessed their attending surgeons, Danielle didn't hesitate to speak her mind with Nick. They'd first met six years prior during Nick's general surgery residency. Danielle was a third-year medical student. The hierarchal respect lines blurred more at that stage of the game. It set the tone for their professional relationship, and since then, Nick had given her license to cross the line. Within reason.

Danielle reclined on the well-used paisley sofa, her feet resting on the coffee table. She sipped from her mug, and when she had his attention, raised her right eyebrow. He'd seen that trick before. Sometimes she did it with a hint of playfulness but not this time. She meant business.

Nick chuckled. "All right, let it out. I wouldn't want you to explode."

Danielle took another sip. "You couldn't just let it slide?"

"What?"

"Did you have to make the poor kid feel like an idiot?"

"This is surgery, not youth soccer. I think he'll be okay." Nick poured himself a cup of four-hour-old coffee. "You're his senior resident, not his mother."

"And you're his mentor, not his probation officer."

Nick lifted the coffee cup to his lips, grimaced, and immediately set it on the counter. "Jesus, I might as well chew on the grounds."

"Why are you telling him?" Danielle said, her tone still on the riled side.

Nick shrugged. "Telling who?"

"Jesus."

"You're hysterical," Nick said, walking toward Danielle. "Can we call a truce? And, do you think maybe you could, once in a while, pretend that I'm your attending?"

A half-smile formed on Danielle's face. "Be nice. I promise it won't hurt."

Damn, if she weren't so gorgeous. Nick couldn't force himself to treat her like the average resident, but her unabashed Christianity held any possible romantic inclination at bay. Regardless, Dr. Danielle Sorenson had gotten under his skin.

Hopefully, good news would be waiting for him when he got

home, and he'd be leaving Philadelphia soon. Not a good time to start something, to cross a line he'd have to uncross later. Maybe his brain made a subliminal but deliberate attempt to shoo away absurd feelings, a built-in safety mechanism. It worked for the time being. Johns Hopkins would be a good change of scenery.

7

WILLIE "SQUIRREL" Santini turned his gaze straight into the surveillance camera. His long face, slicked-back black hair, and droopy eyes filled the screen, the image as unmistakable as the picture on his driver's license. As he turned to his left, she appeared for a split second. Rawls grew tall in his seat. "Run it back again, slow-mo."

As Taylor replayed the video, Rawls leaned closer to the screen. "Freeze it," he said. "Is it her?"

"That's our girl. Macey Beckham, twenty-three-year-old hooker from Voorhees."

"Positive ID?" Rawls asked.

"Through dental records but still waiting on DNA." Taylor turned off the video. "The two entered the motel at 2:34 am and never came out."

Rawls nodded. "Well, not out the front door anyway."

"Yeah, out the first-floor window." Taylor showed Rawls the picture of the opened window leading to the back parking lot.

Rawls slipped a thin file from a manila folder and tossed it on the table. "Rap sheet not all that remarkable. Long stints in juvie for possession of weed, petty larceny, simple assault. Spent a night in Camden County for solicitation in December of '90. Since then, clean as a whistle except for a DUI last September."

Taylor picked up the paper. "Word is his aunt begged Carlotti's bodyguard Mickey Scalise to give Willie a job six years ago. She didn't want him ending up dead or incarcerated."

Rawls peered over the thin gold rims of his reading glasses. "So, she gets him a gig with the mob?"

Taylor chuckled. "Not the best choice, huh?"

Rawls took the file from Taylor and slid it back into the envelope. "I'll put together an affidavit for Judge Egan. In the meantime, check in with the medical examiner."

"Doubt we'll have Santini's DNA. Even if he was stupid enough not to use a condom, the water likely degraded the evidence," Taylor said.

"As long as both of their DNA is found in the hotel, especially her blood, it'll be enough." Rawls drummed his fingers on the desk, his deep brown eyes drifted upward.

Taylor smiled. "I know that look. The gears are turning."

"You do know the Feds are going to come in like the cavalry."

"And?"

"And— we need to grab Santini sooner rather than later. Maybe we can seek an indictment before they totally blow the case. You know they're going to want to use him to get to Carlotti."

"Seems reasonable to me, no?"

Rawls smirked. "Let me tell you how this plays out. They let him off easy and get nothing in return. We lose a second-degree murder conviction, and Carlotti brushes it off like a gnat from his shoulder."

"You're probably right," Taylor said. "I want the rest of his credit card records. Find his friends if he had any and talk to the girl's pimp."

Taylor scribbled a few notes in a hand-sized spiral notebook as his gaze turned toward the corner of the room. He rose from his seat and snatched up a paper airplane from the floor next to the wastebasket. "Now that one's cool!"

"F-15 Strike Eagle— looks sweet but flies like shit," Rawls said. He stood to leave then straightened his navy-blue tie, leaving the knot an inch from the unfastened top button of his white shirt. "I'll order surveillance of Santini's apartment on Fitzwater. Hopefully, Egan will turn this warrant around in a hurry."

The judge came through, and twenty-two hours later, the police arrested Willie as he left his apartment.

His jet-black hair stuck up on one side as though he'd just gotten out of bed. Armpit stains on his wrinkled t-shirt evidenced the stress he'd been under since the murder. Words slipped from Willie's mouth with a drunken slur. "I didn't d — do nothin'. You got the wrong dude."

Rawls pursed his lips and nodded. "I want to remind you that you have the right to call an attorney or have one provided by the court."

"I don't need a damn lawyer. I don't even know what the hell you're talking about." Willie slouched back in his chair, his gaze turned toward the floor.

Rawls placed a brown leather briefcase on the table. "I want to be clear. You're declining legal counsel?"

Willie lifted his head and glared at Rawls. "I said I don't need a fuckin' lawyer."

Rawls flipped open the briefcase and pulled out Willie's credit card. He slapped it on the table. "Any idea how your credit card ended up in the girl's bra?"

Willie crossed his boney arms in defiance and turned away from Rawls.

Rawls reached back into the briefcase, pulled two still images taken from the surveillance video, and set them next to the credit card. He read from the hardware store receipt. "One ten by twelve-foot medium-duty, blue painter's tarp, two eight by eight by sixteen-inch cinderblocks, and fifty feet of yellow nylon rope charged to your credit card at Burns Hardware. Hmmm? Whatcha building, Willie?"

The metal feet of Willie's chair screeched on the hardwood floor as he squirmed. Rawls waited for Willie to request a lawyer. Maybe he was too ignorant or too proud to do so. Either way, Willie remained closed-lipped, and Rawls continued to press. He glanced down at the receipt and back at Willie. "Crazy, just so happened to be the morning after you bashed in the girl's head. Seems like you've gotten yourself into a pickle, Willie."

Tiny beads of sweat glistened on Willie's pasty white forehead. He gnawed the inside of his cheek but remained silent.

Rawls stepped behind Willie's chair and spoke in a matter-of-fact tone. "I get it. She pissed you off and you didn't mean to kill her. Maybe she just needed to learn a lesson. Sound about right?"

Willie's jaw muscles bulged and his eyes looked like they might spring from his head. He slammed his fist on the table, the sound reverberating in the room. "The bitch was trying to steal my cash!"

Ten minutes later, Rawls held a signed confession in his hand. He returned to his office to find two federal agents waiting for him.

The taller man reached out his hand. "Detective Rawls, I'm Special Agent Collins, FBI. We'd like to talk to you about Willie Santini."

Rawls reciprocated the handshake. "Right on cue."

"Pardon me?" Rawls smirked. "Nothing, go on."

"We'd like to put him in play. It might be our best shot at Carlotti."

"I'll need more than that."

"You and I both know the son-of-a-bitch is an enforcer. If we can catch Carlotti ordering a move on tape we may have enough for an indictment. He's in deep. Extortion, murder, money laundering, and we believe he's moving narcotics into Philadelphia through Mexico."

Rawls shook his head. "If Carlotti knows Santini has been in and out of here, he'll avoid him like the plague. Besides, I don't think Carlotti would trust this weasel with much more than buying his cigarettes and beer."

Collins pulled out a small tape recorder. "Funny you should mention cigarettes and beer." He hit the play button. The voices on the recording cut through the background static.

"Mr. Lawson, good to see you."

"You're not supposed to be here until Tuesday." The second man's voice sounded shaky.

"Well, I'm early."

"I don't have the money. Please give me two more days. I promise . . . "

A sharp slap interrupted the man's plea.

"Please, Mr. Santini. I have a wife and two kids."

Another loud slap followed, then scuffling and the muffled sound of a man crying.

"Lawson, it's your lucky day. I'm in a good mood. You have twenty-four hours."

Collins flipped off the recorder.

Rawls raised his eyebrows. "Good stuff but explain the cigarettes and beer thing."

"Jack Lawson owns a mom-and-pop corner store at South Seventh and West Oregon — cigarettes, booze, and lottery tickets. Santini's been shaking the poor guy down for years. Carlotti has been extorting the small shop owners, but we can't pin it on him without Santini's help."

"Why not just get him to admit that Carlotti gave him the marching orders?"

"Then it's a he-said-she-said. I want Carlotti to hang himself."

Rawls opened the file and glanced at the picture of the dead woman's body. "And you'd offer him?"

"As it stands, he's looking at second-degree murder, life

without the possibility of parole. If he cooperates, voluntary manslaughter, fifteen years, out in ten with good behavior. Witness Protection Program after that."

As much as Rawls knew he had to give up Santini, he also knew he'd be setting aside a slam dunk for a slim maybe. Seeing Carlotti behind bars would be worth the plea, but he cringed at the thought of handing the reins to the FBI. "Don't blow it."

Collins smiled and shook Rawls' hand. "We'll keep you in the loop."

"I'm sure."

8

NICK'S HEART raced when he eyed the envelope from Johns Hopkins Hospital sitting atop the pile of mail. He peeled it open before he got through the door, then took a seat on the couch as he read. Hopefully, he'd soon be packing his bags and heading to Baltimore, away from the dark shadow of his family name, ascending the surgical and academic ladders of success.

His four-year-old Jack Russell Terrier, "Rhino," short for rhinoplasty, curled expectantly at his feet.

Dear Dr. Carlotti, I want to thank you for applying for the Chairmanship of the Plastic Surgery Department and also for your recent visit to Johns Hopkins Medical Center. We had a small pool of highly qualified applicants, and you were among our top prospects. After careful consideration, I regret to say, we have filled the position. The decision was a difficult one, and we would like to thank you for taking the time to submit your resume and application for consideration. We wish you the best of luck in your career and have great confidence that you will chair a department in the future.

Sincerely, Dr. Erwin J. Grossmann MD
Chairman, Department of Surgery Johns Hopkins Hospital

NICK CRUMPLED THE LETTER. So, why should they choose a thirty-four-year-old surgeon, three years out of a fellowship, for the chairmanship of a surgical department at Hopkins? "Maybe because I'm the best damn craniofacial surgeon on the East Coast, that's why!" He threw the letter across the room.

Rhino leaped from the couch, caught the balled-up paper before it hit the ground, and ran back, tail wagging. He dropped the soggy wad of paper at Nick's feet. "Throw it again, man!" Instead, Nick picked it up and tossed it in the garbage. Rhino lay down, put his head between his front paws, and let out a long, pathetic sigh.

Nick had never been rejected for anything in his whole life, not once. He'd graduated as valedictorian of his high school class and summa cum laude from Yale, where he'd captained the football team. He hadn't ever been turned down by a woman. Now he knew why he'd avoided rejection for so long. It really felt like crap.

From the corner of his eye, it caught his attention. Why now? It wasn't like it hadn't been sitting up there for the last twelve years, a reminder of happier times, a worn leather memorial of his final game as a Bulldog. He reached up, wiped away a cobweb, and lifted the football from atop the armoire. A thick cloud of dust fell.

"Son-of-a-bitch!" he said, blinking hard and rubbing his eyes. When the burning ceased, and his vision cleared, he gazed upon his teammates' fading signatures. So, this was what it looked like when you realized your glory days were over.

His coach and teammates had awarded him the ball after they'd defeated Harvard in the final game of his college career —

three hundred seventy-two yards passing, four touchdowns through the air, and one more on the ground. A fitting finish under Saturday night lights way too many years ago.

The small collection of pictures, trophies, and framed news articles, including one naming him as runner-up for the Asa S. Bushnell Award for the top player in the Ivy League, seemed no more valuable than a cabinet full of cheap china. Trinkets collected a whole lifetime ago, now just a playground for spiders.

Slouched on the couch, his head hung low, he pondered his downward spiral— a rejection letter, a dusty old football, and a dead mother. The football slipped from his hands and fell to the floor. Before Nick traveled too far down the road of despondency, Rhino stepped between his legs and swiped his tongue across Nick's face. Nick chuckled. "Thanks, I needed that."

He gathered himself, wiped the football clean, and placed it back on the armoire.

Twenty minutes later, he received an email from a good friend in the anesthesia department at Hopkins:

Nick,

I'm sorry you didn't get the position here. I'm sure you're disappointed, as am I. It's a little crazy that the guy they hired is also from Penn., a Dr. David Siegel. Must be a colleague of yours. Hang in there. Your time will come. I'll let you know when I'm in Philly.

Aasim

OF ALL PEOPLE TO undermine his opportunity to chair a department, it had to be David Siegel. What a charlatan and a hack! Siegel's leaving Penn seemed the only silver lining to this ugly cloud. It couldn't be soon enough. Since medical school, Nick had watched David Siegel make up for his lack of surgical skills with slick talk and butt kissing.

Nick slammed his laptop shut and headed straight for the kitchen, his focus fixed on a bottle of Jack Daniels on top of the refrigerator.

Before his hand reached the bottle, his on-call pager beeped with a muffled tone from beneath a heap of clothes on his bedroom floor. It interrupted his short-lived post-rejection pity party. He tossed aside a couple wrinkled shirts and socks and found the beeper clipped to the belt of his navy-blue pleated pants.

"Dr. Carlotti, please call the ER, UPENN."

He didn't need to scroll down to the number. He'd dialed it at least twelve hundred times during his fellowship and a few more during his latest role as attending surgeon.

The phone rang three times before a female receptionist with a harsh South Philly accent answered.

"ER, please hold."

Before Nick had a chance to voice his objection, Neil Sedaka's "Calendar Girl" replaced the background sounds of the hectic ER.

Next to the screech of a fork on a ceramic dish, the music of Neil Sedaka and Barry Manilow was enough to make him rip his hair out. The hospital hadn't changed its on-hold music rotation since Nick had been a first-year medical student. He should have grabbed the shot of Jack while he'd had the chance. He hung up and redialed the number, hoping to stop the woman before she could put him on hold.

Like clockwork. Three rings and, "ER, please. . . "

"This is Dr. — "

".... hold, thank you."

"Calendar Girl" marched on.

A couple minutes later she returned to the line. "ER, may I help you?"

"This is Dr. Carlotti. I would appreciate you not putting me on hold. . . twice, after interrupting my day with a page."

"Please hold for Dr. Randall."

Here it came, "Copacabana." Barry Manilow continued to piss him off for a couple more minutes until Dr. Randall picked up.

"Dr. Randall here."

"Hey John, it's Nick. What's up?"

"Got a good one for ya. Twenty-nine-year-old male with gunshot wounds to the abdomen and face. The first bullet blew through his right lower jaw, took out most of his back teeth, and then exited through his left eye. The second and third went through his liver and colon. The trauma team has him in the OR now. If he survives, they'll control any bleeds from the facial wound but will defer definitive treatment to your team. Your chief resident, Dr. Sorenson, took a look at him in the OR and didn't want to do anything until she reviewed a CT scan and talked with you."

"Has ophthalmology seen him yet?" Nick asked.

"Yeah, they've already been here but seriously, there wasn't anything left for them to examine. They said they'd be glad to clean up the remnants of the eye when you do your thing."

"Get the CT when he leaves the OR if he's stable enough," Nick said.

"That's a big if. By the way, the guy is a heroin dealer probably caught in a drug deal gone bad. The police want to question him as soon as he's able. I told them it will be a while, if ever."

"Uh . . . ya think?"

Dr. Randall chuckled. "I hope the cop brought a good long book and a bag of donuts. He's already outside the ICU waiting for the guy to get out of surgery."

"Our tax dollars at work, huh. Meanwhile, while the cop is

sitting on his butt waiting for a guy in a coma, there's a fifty-fifty chance your Lexus gets jacked up on cinderblocks in the parking garage, all four tires gone," Nick said.

"No joke, it's getting dangerous down there. By the way, I forgot to tell you, the patient's name. It's Danny Torello."

"Thanks for the heads-up. I'll be there as soon as I can."

9

"Santini's dead."

Those were the last words he wanted to hear. Rawls let out a huff. "That's gotta be a new record. What's it been? Three hours?"

Agent Collins shot back. "Look, the guy OD'd in his apartment. It was out of our control."

"Let me see if I've got this straight. A junkie who's been feeding his habit without incident for years, a guy holding down a steady job for the East Coast's most notorious mafia capo, happens to accidentally overdose the same day he's sent out wearing a wire."

"He left a note," Collins said.

"You're telling me he committed suicide?" Rawls grit his teeth. "What the hell was he doing alone in his apartment? I thought the meeting was at Carmine's?"

"He walked into the restaurant at 9:32 in the morning. We had eyes on both exits. The bastard never came out."

"And the audio?"

"Superficial banter for fifteen minutes then just crowd noise.

The wire ended up in a dumpster down the alley forty minutes later."

"I won't ask how he made it to his apartment."

"Good, because I have no idea."

At least Collins was honest. His candor put the kibosh on a snide comeback. Instead, Rawls took the high road. "Saved the taxpayers a couple hundred grand but not necessarily the justice I'd hoped for."

Collins broke the momentary silence. "Shit happens. You know we can't control all the variables."

"Yeah, I get it. Is the scene secured?"

"Yes. 3155 Hartwick, Apartment 3c."

$$\sim$$

"He's on the floor in the bathroom," Collins said as Rawls and Taylor passed through the main door of the apartment building. "Third floor, last door on the left. Follow the smell of cat piss and weed."

Collins wasn't kidding. The tiny one-bedroom apartment reeked of ammonia and the musky, sweet scent of cannabis. Rawls stepped into the cluttered living room and noted remnants of a candle, an empty glass vial, and a small silver spoon on the smoked glass coffee table. Next to the drug paraphernalia, a wrinkled sheet of paper lay stuck to the glass by a small pool of wax. The candle had burned down, fixing the paper to the tabletop.

"What's it say?" Rawls asked. Taylor knelt on the floor to read the note.

Aunt Rose,

Thanks for supporting me but I can't spend the rest of my life in the joint.

Squirrel

TAYLOR SNICKERED. "Or bear the thought of having all of his teeth knocked out before Carlotti fed him feet-first into a wood chipper."

"Or that," Rawls said, moving into a narrow hallway.

Santini's brown leather wingtips appeared in the bathroom's open doorway on the left. Taylor followed one step behind.

As they rounded the corner and peered into the bathroom, Rawls startled. Santini's head appeared to move as an emaciated gray cat crept out from behind the toilet and rubbed back and forth against the dead man's blue-faced head.

"Go on! Get outta here!" Rawls said, shooing away the cat.

Rawls stepped over Santini's legs and positioned himself in the tight space between the bathtub and toilet. The body, stiff with rigor mortis, lay stretched out on the floor.

"Must have been some potent stuff," Rawls said, gazing at the needle still stuck in Santini's left arm. The tourniquet rested in a heap a few inches away.

"Why do you think he shot up in the bathroom?" Taylor asked.

"Beats the hell out of me," Rawls said.

Collins poked his head into the room. "Tough break."

Rawls smirked. "You could say that." He paused and surveyed the cramped room with its mauve walls and cigarette burned linoleum. "So, why do you think he shot up on the bathroom floor? Don't you think it's strange he prepared his fix in the living room and didn't stay on the comfy couch?"

"Maybe he had to take a shit."

Something caught Rawls' attention. He reached down and took a closer look. A small amount of dried blood had collected in Santini's left ear. "Might want to have forensics look in there."

Rawls kept the remainder of his thoughts to himself and refrained from a tirade of I-told-you-so's as he passed Collins in the living room on the way out.

10

THE GYPSY ROSE had always been a place of escape, a little piece of heaven on earth. Mays' luxury yacht had instead become a floating hell. Every corner reminded him that his days were numbered: the bed, the bamboo floor, the eight steps from the bedroom to the deck, and the bow's chrome railing. Somewhere along that trail one strand of DNA had to remain, a microscopic witness with a perfect memory. Maybe he could sink her, orchestrate an explosion, a Mayday call, and a fortuitous escape to the dinghy. Just one thought among many came and went as he scrubbed.

His knees hurt. The wealthy grandson of a Pittsburgh steel baron had no business crawling along the deck of a boat with a bucket of Lysol and a scrub brush. Mays pulled his hand from the soapy water and continued scrubbing. He'd done it twice before, but something in his mind wouldn't let it go, like he had missed a drop, a single red blood cell. It was driving him mad.

He hadn't been this tormented, this confused since his parents' plane had crashed into a mountainside on the way to their vacation home in Aspen. He'd just returned to boarding school in Boston after his fourteenth birthday and, being the only child, the entire hundred and fifty-million-dollar estate had been transferred to a trust in his name, waiting for him when he turned eighteen.

He spent the next three years living with a great aunt who had the personality of Almira Gulch. Despite her permanent scowl and gravely, two-pack a day smoker's voice, she at least knew how to cook. Four years later, he took control of his fortune. On the sidewalk outside of Mary Lyon dorm at Swarthmore College, he gave his grumpy aunt a kiss and, with his Louis Vuitton luggage stuffed with more than any eighteen-year-old boy could need, became the master of his own destiny.

Now, more than four decades later and half a billion dollars richer, he'd give it all away if it could save him, if he could set the clocks back. But not even his riches could undo what he'd done. If only he'd walked out of that damn restaurant with Detective Rawls and not fixed his gaze on the girl.

He slipped his hand back into the bucket. A voice boomed from the adjacent slip. "You're welcome to come over and do mine when you're finished!"

Mays' heart skipped a beat, and he dropped his brush. "Shit, Neil, you scared the crap out of me."

"A little on edge, Lloyd?" the stocky man said as he leaned over the stern of his decked-out fishing boat, his naked pot belly overhanging the waistband of rainbow-striped Bermuda shorts.

"No, you just caught me off guard." Mays stood up and took hold of the rail.

The man smirked. "You're going to need a new coat of deck paint if you keep scrubbing that hard."

Mays laughed and shot the man a quick wave. He opted to put the bucket and brush away before people started talking. He didn't need his marina neighbors telling the authorities that Senator Mays was 'acting suspicious,' like he seemed to be trying to 'hide evidence.'

Exhausted both mentally and physically, he sprawled out on

his bed. New Egyptian cotton sheets covered an equally new mattress. He dozed off. Startled, he ripped his arms from under the covers and held them before his eyes. They felt cold and wet, still covered in old blood, blood that had lost the warmth of the living body from which it had been drained. Seeing the pale skin of his hands dry and without a hint of red, he relaxed. Get it together, Lloyd!

He rolled over and picked up a newspaper from the night-stand. Liza stared at him from the grainy black and white image on the page. He couldn't believe she was gone. He recalled their clash years before, the hurtful words she'd spoken to him. "I'm sorry, Lloyd. Goodbye," as Rock Carlotti had led her into his black Lincoln with his hand in the small of her back. The dejection had long faded but seeing her the night of the fundraiser had stirred the feelings again. They lingered still, the pit in his stomach, rage toward the piece of scum who'd stolen the love of his life, the weeks of restless nights and the despair. Now, with two girls dead, he somehow had to carry on like nothing had happened.

The rest of the morning he spent leaning over his desk with a draft of the appropriation bill spread out before him. He'd read it three times and it might as well have been written in Mandarin Chinese. Something had to change. He drew a long, deep, purposeful breath. Maybe this was what it felt like to lose one's mind.

11

THE ER BUSTLED AS USUAL, the waiting room filled with nameless faces, mostly the down-and-out. A distinctive odor permeated the halls, an unpleasant combination of blood, alcohol, and sweat. The overlying scent of disinfectant never entirely masked it.

A despondent place, it reeked of pain and brokenness, most of it emanating not from the patients' ailments or trauma, but from lives shaped by abuse, poverty, and addictions.

They watched Nick as he walked through the waiting room. He expected that some looked at him with envy, some with respect, and still others with resentment. He was the rich kid, with the red Porsche Boxster parked in the "Doctors Only" spot.

As a wide-eyed medical student, ready to change the world, he'd felt more sympathetic. But, somewhere along the line, a portion of his compassion had turned to indifference. He wasn't unsympathetic to their disease or injury but had become somewhat numb to their social plight.

He'd worked hard to make something of himself. How easy it would have been to go down the road of least resistance, to take the dirty cash, to be a chip off the old Rock. So, if they chose to drop out of school, join gangs, or smoke crack, then they could reap the consequences.

Not long before his mother's death, he'd shared with her those feelings. She'd smiled and replied, "But for the grace of God, go I." Maybe she was right, but allowing himself to go there seemed to suck him dry. He resolved to be the healer of the body and let someone else deal with the rest. Whether rationalization or realization, it allowed him to keep his emotional distance. Deep down he knew it was just a case of self-preservation.

Nick climbed three flights to the ICU. As he opened the door from the stairwell, Dr. Danielle Sorenson stood on the opposite side with her hand on the knob.

She jerked back. "Wow, you caught me by surprise."

"Sorry, bad timing," Nick said, although the timing was actually just right.

He held the door as she passed by, her shoulder brushing against his chest. His heart pounded. He let the door close behind her.

Danielle smiled, her electric blonde hair braided and pulled into a sleek ponytail. "I examined Danny Torello in the OR. The guy's a mess. Comminuted right mandible fracture, a left maxillary fracture, orbital blowout, and a ruptured left globe. Half of his tongue is missing. I'm just waiting on the CT."

"I got the low down from John in the ER. We'll have our work cut out for us," Nick said, his visceral reaction catching him by surprise.

Danielle nodded. "Yeah, it's not pretty."

"I'll go check him out and touch base after his scan," Nick said, quite sure she noticed his face flushing. He stared at her and quickly turned away his gaze before it became awkward. Not that he hadn't recognized her beauty before, he wasn't blind, but today he must have let his guard down. She'd always come off as coy, not shy but purposefully choosy about her words. People knew she was a Christian. She wasn't preachy or a Bible thumper, but Nick knew his rough edges grated on her. She never seemed to be an option.

Danielle glanced at her inpatient list. "Chikelu is running around his room like the Energizer Bunny. He's ready to be discharged today," she said, speaking of a three-year-old Kenyan boy with a severe congenital facial defect Nick had repaired the week prior. The story made the national news with a five-minute humanitarian piece on CNN. They showed the boy before the surgery and more footage of him with Nick afterward. Both Nick and the hospital provided the boy's care pro-bono.

"That's good news," Nick said.

Danielle's sparkling blue eyes lit up. "I asked his father today what Chikelu meant, and he said, created by God."

Nick grinned. "It's a shame God couldn't get the face right."

A deep vertical line formed between her downturned golden eyebrows. "Really?"

He'd seen her get feisty before, but she looked like she wanted to take it outside. "What?"

"You're such a cynic."

"And you don't see the irony in it?"

"I see an opportunity for him and his family to grow in their faith and provide thousands of others a ray of hope. You, on the other hand . . . "

"Me, on the other hand, what? Am a jackass?"

"If the saddle fits." Danielle smoothed the patient list she'd unconsciously crumpled in her fist.

Nick wasn't ready for a religious debate in the hallway. "I didn't mean to offend you. I'm sorry. And thanks for the update."

Danielle shook her head. "My pleasure." She disappeared into the stairwell.

There you go. What was he thinking? As a likely indication of what a potential relationship would look like, the conversation quelled the unexpected flame that had just ignited. Thank God. He certainly didn't need any more distractions. He brushed it off and left to examine Danny Torello.

When Nick arrived in Torello's room, two nurses hustled around reconnecting monitors.

"Hey, ladies, mind if I do a quick exam?" Nick asked.

"Sure, we're nearly finished. He just came from the OR," Lauren said.

Nick read through Torello's chart as the nurses completed their work.

Danny Torello was an on-and-off-again construction worker from South Philly. The police said a lone masked gunman put three bullets into him as he walked out of a deli on South Street.

Nick glanced at the toxicology report. Heroin, amphetamines, and alcohol. Big surprise.

"He's all yours, Dr. Carlotti," Lauren said.

"Thanks, Lauren," Nick said, passing the armed officer sitting by the door. Odd, the police stationing an officer outside the room of a common street junkie.

Torello was a heavyset man, his head grossly swollen and covered with blood-soaked bandages. He looked to be resting comfortably, the combination of morphine and Versed doing its job.

Nick donned exam gloves and removed Danny's bandages to examine the carnage. As expected, just below the right jaw, a small entrance wound, a little bigger than the 9mm bullet that created it. Not so neat on the opposite side of the head. The energy of the mushroomed hollow point left a massive exit wound. The cavernous defect encompassed his left cheek, eye socket, and ear, with a large gauze-packing in the place where an eye should have been. Sharp fragments of his shattered lower jaw bone nearly ripped through Nick's glove. Barely a third of his tongue remained. It looked like a handful of raw hamburger.

John was right, Torello wouldn't be talking to the police any time soon.

He jotted a quick note in the chart and left to review films in the first-floor radiology department. Passing the elevator, he opted instead to take the stairs down the three flights. His friends and colleagues thought his stair preference was a fitness choice, and Nick was okay with their misconception. Some phobias were hard to kick. Last summer he'd flown six hours from San Francisco to Honolulu with a full bladder because he'd rather have wet his pants than spend three minutes in the cramped airplane restroom. He endured recurring images of being in a casket as shovelfuls of dirt slowly buried him alive, a terrifying sound magnified by the utter darkness. Since he believed life ended at death, it seemed like a long, painful trip to nowhere.

As he left the radiology department Nick heard a commotion in the direction of the ER. A middle-aged black woman lamented in the hall, her wailing a combination of despair and drowning.

Two young men, one at each arm, held her up, her legs refusing to carry her. As Nick neared, the woman ripped away from the two men and fell to the floor, where the wailing faded to muffled sobs. Nick let the ER doors close behind him.

The first two of three trauma bays stood in disarray, empty packaging from IV catheters, fluid bags, and blood-stained towels strewn about the floor. A single body draped by a thin white sheet lay on each of the two rooms' tables. Dr. Randall exited Bay #3 shaking his head as Nick peeked in. Nurses were cleaning up around the dead girl.

"Damn it, Nick. We couldn't do a thing. Father, son, and daughter. MVA," Dr. Randall said without stopping.

Nick stood and stared at the girl, her once vibrant face now dulled and spiritless, probably just a couple hours ago smiling as she listened to the car's radio. Her mother broken to pieces in the hallway outside those doors, would likely grieve until her own life came to an end.

In medicine, death is the enemy. It represents the losing side of the battle, and frankly, Nick wasn't fond of dealing with the aftermath. Part of the appeal plastic surgery held for Nick was that only rarely did he need to have the 'I'm sorry, but your child didn't make it' discussions. Painful discourses were unavoidable, but thank God, he hadn't chosen oncology.

Doubts about heaven and the afterlife made his conversations concerning death or impending death feel trite. He found it hard to provide much hope or comfort in hopeless situations since, in his mind, dead was . . . Well, dead, nothing more and nothing less. He wanted a silver lining to death, but he couldn't buy it. It surely showed in his eyes. Maybe, though, the tone of his voice or the choice of his words masked his skepticism. Someone once gave him sound advice: "Fake it 'til you make it."

It had been a rough year, a rough day, and the weekend wasn't looking much better. Nick hated weddings, and this one was bound to rank among the worst. At 2:00 pm, on Saturday, he would have to endure an emotional kick in the gut as his father tied the knot with a lap dancer. He had forty-eight hours to find a plausible excuse to stay home.

Nick made a quick call to his next-door neighbor Helen, asking if she'd mind taking Rhino for a walk. She gave him the usual "Of course, I love him like my own" response. Helen had a key to the house for such occasions. Nick and Dr. Sorenson spent the next four hours in the OR reconstructing Torello's face.

The drive home seemed a blur, Nick's eyes half-closed most of the way. The note on the dining-room table from Helen let him know Rhino had dinner and did his duty, but Rhino's tipped head and pleading upturned eyes did the trick to earn dessert. Nick tossed him a cold meatball from his leftover sub.

"Your vet would have my hide if she knew I fed you like this."

Rhino devoured the meatball and licked his chops. He leaped to Nick's lap.

Nick let his head fall back against the sofa and he closed his eyes as he stroked Rhino's back.

In less than two days, Rock and his stripper would transform St. Cecilia's Church into a proverbial den of thieves. Thankfully Nick could sleep for most of Friday and forgo having to think about it.

12

———————

RAWLS LISTENED and bit his tongue as Agent Collins defended the Bureau's handling of Willie Santini. "This is a give and take, Detective. We have information that Danny Torello and Santini had a history of shooting up together, friends since high school. We expect you to keep us in the loop if you hear anything," Agent Collins said.

Rawls couldn't help himself. "Let me get this straight. We make a clean bust on Santini for offing the hooker. We have surveillance video, Santini's credit card, prints and blood from the hotel, and eyewitness testimony. You make him a deal, and within three days he's dead and now his needle partner is lying in the ICU with half his face missing."

Taylor sat across from Rawls' desk and whispered, "That's about the size of it."

"Get over it!" Collins shot back. "Santini's dead, and I don't appreciate your condescending tone. The bastard killed himself, and there wasn't a damn thing we could have done about it. Now Danny Torello may have crucial information, so we'd appreciate your cooperation."

"Sounds like the guy's probably not going to make it. At a

minimum, he won't be making any statements this week." Rawls said. "Maybe he tried to kill himself too."

"I'm hoping we're on the same side, Detective."

Rawls flattened the last crease on a glossy silver paper airplane that looked like a wing with Batman ears. He flung it past Taylor's head. Taylor spun around and watched as the plane hit the wall behind the basket. It dropped straight in. "We both want to see Tony Carlotti behind bars. I'll let you know if anything pertinent comes up."

Taylor squirmed in his seat.

Rawls hung up the phone and rolled his eyes. "Go ahead, Sean. Let it out."

"Want to hear the craziest thing?"

"Do I have a choice?"

Taylor shrugged. "Rock Carlotti's youngest son, Nick, is Torello's facial surgeon."

Rawls raised his eyebrows. "What are the chances?"

"Apparently a hundred percent," Taylor said.

"Sean, that was rhetorical."

"I knew that."

Rawls stood and opened the door. As Taylor paused in the doorway, Rawls gave him one last request: "Find out as much as you can about Torello's association with Rock Carlotti and Willie Santini. Maybe he was an innocent bystander, but if not, I'd like to know."

Taylor gave a thumbs-up. "Will do."

"Oh, and Sean, get me the forensics on Santini ASAP."

13

THE WEDDING CAME off as predicted, ostentatious, suitable for royalty but rather exorbitant for an ex-stripper and a crook. Nick closed his eyes, trying to enjoy the drone of the Celtic bagpipes, relishing them out of context. He couldn't quite picture the Scottish Highlands, so he surrendered to the present painful reality.

The thought of his father remarrying so soon after his mother's death, not even five months for god's sake, turned his stomach. But Rock wasn't the kind of guy who could be alone. He ruled a small dynasty but couldn't or wouldn't boil pasta or fold a pair of boxer shorts. Then again, Jennifer didn't necessarily seem the domestic type. Surely, she'd fill other voids.

As Father Anthony performed the Catholic Mass, Nick couldn't help but see the irony in the priest's presiding over both his mother's last breath and this wedding circus. Father Anthony, a close family friend, was well aware that the man whose marriage he would soon bless had many dark and unconfessed sins. It must have been easier for the priest to turn a blind eye after tallying the weekly offering. Apparently, St. Cecilia's still practiced the medieval system of indulgences.

Nick zoned out during the brief ceremony, the priest's words turning to white noise. Then, a phrase from the priest's mouth caught his attention. "That is why a man leaves his father and mother and is united to his wife, and they become one flesh."

What a bizarre statement. One flesh? He'd heard the words at weddings before, including his own, but this time they hit him as peculiar. In his brief, ill-fated marriage, he certainly hadn't considered him and his wife 'one flesh.' As far as he was concerned, they remained separated, each with their own plans and agendas, occasionally in synch, but mostly going their own directions. Nick unconsciously resisted the merging as one flesh, maybe out of fear of losing himself, perhaps out of selfishness, but either way the two never became one.

As he gazed upon the newlyweds at the front of the church, he doubted they would ever be one flesh. Rock wouldn't allow such an affront to his power.

The wedding ended grandly with the couple parading down the aisle as the pipe organ, accompanied by bagpipes, played Mendelssohn's Wedding March. He took a few, slow breaths to prevent himself from vomiting on his great aunt seated in front of him. If Nick hadn't been immediate family, he'd have exited the church and headed straight to the bar. Sadly, the festivities had only just begun.

14

THE ORNATE LOBSTER DISH, a thing of beauty but sliced thinner than cellophane, left Nick woefully insatiate. He regretted not stopping for a cheeseburger on the way. He'd never been a fan of French food, so Rock's choice of La Rose Blanche only added to Nick's distaste.

What kind of mafia boss forwent lasagna and meatballs for crepes and bagpipes?

On cue, Rock worked the crowd. He fluffed his feathers like a peacock. He drove fast cars and called Atlantic City's Trump Taj Mahal his second home. Having center stage with a captive audience fed his colossal ego.

Jennifer's thick, flowing, mahogany hair reached to the small of her back. Her Hollywood smile took a close second place to her perfect breasts, which she did her best to showcase in a low-cut, snow-white Versace wedding dress. Nick would have been proud to say he'd performed her implant surgery but couldn't take the credit. He found it difficult to keep his gaze off her. Given that Jennifer was now his stepmother, his wandering thoughts bordered on incest.

Nick had the dubious honor of sitting at the head table. The newlyweds sat front and center with Peter Coroneos and his wife to their right, and Mickey Scalise, Rock's long-time bodyguard, to their left. Nick and his brother took the end seats opposite each other, which, whether purposeful or not, prevented salt in Nick's already painful wound.

Peter's wife Sarah leaned forward and turned to Nick. "I watched your interview on the news last week— the little boy from Kenya with that facial deformity. It was fascinating. We're so proud of you."

"Thank you, Sarah. I'm sure it made Mom smile."

"I have no doubt."

Nick turned in his chair and rested his hand on hers. "How's Sam?"

Sarah's eyes glassed over.

"Forgive me, "Nick said. "You don't have to talk about it now."

She lifted her napkin to her eyes. "No, it's okay. We saw the cardiologist on Wednesday. His heart is failing, and there isn't anything else they can do."

"Transplant?"

"They said they didn't think he'd qualify because of other medical problems. I just hate to see him suffer. Sometimes he can hardly brea . . . " her voice cracked.

"I'm so sorry, Sarah. He looked so happy when I saw him last."

"He has good days and bad days, but it's getting harder and harder. He's so strong though. You know, Sam is just— well, just —Sam, almost always happy."

A high-pitched clanking of a knife on a wine glass interrupted their conversation.

Rock grabbed the microphone and cleared his throat. "I want to give you folks an update. My boy Nick here is still getting screwed by those doctors at Penn. I told him a year ago that they'd run his Guinea ass out of there. Should have gone into business with his old man like his big brother."

Eddie smirked and raised his glass. Nick glared down the long table at his older brother. The little bastard didn't even know he was a puppet on a string, still operating out of fear and insecurity, flavored with a big dose of ignorance. Eddie didn't make eye contact.

Rock reached behind Jennifer and slapped Nick on the back. "You know I'm just playin with you."

Nick suppressed his indignation as he had each time his father had gone on some asinine tirade. He smiled politely, nodded, and took a gulp of his Merlot. His third glass hadn't yet provided the desired effect.

Jennifer spoke up. "Tony, quite frankly, I'm glad Nick went his own way. Who'd take care of all the nips and tucks I'm going to need to keep me aging gracefully?" she said. "I will receive some sort of family discount?"

"By the time you start aging, Jen, I hope to be retired," Nick said. Her plastic surgery bases seemed well covered and Rock would no doubt keep her looking good for his sake as much as hers. "Besides, I'm shying away from cosmetic surgery these days. Adults are too hard to satisfy."

"Oh, I'm sure you don't have a problem satisfying women," Jennifer said with a cute smile.

"Except for his ex-wife, that is," his father added.

There was an awkward pause, but when Nick grinned and raised his glass, the wedding party joined in restrained laughter. No one wanted to be singled out for not acknowledging Rock's attempt at humor.

"Yo, Doc. Think you could fix this?" Scalise grabbed the bridge of his broad and misaligned nose with his thumb and index finger. He ground the bones side to side with an unpleasant crunching sound.

Sarah threw her hands over her ears. "Mickey, stop that."

Jennifer's eyebrows furrowed. "That's disgusting."

Nick shrugged. "I think it makes a great party trick. I wouldn't change a thing."

Scalise shot him a wink and a nod. "You should see what the other guy looks like."

A mountain of a man, six-foot-six and well over two hundred and fifty pounds, his lower jaw protruded beyond his upper. Mickey Scalise had served as head bouncer at Cameo's in the early '80s before Nick's father had offered him a job as a body-guard. Two years later, Rock promoted him to head of security.

"Rock, did you hear that the FARC released its hostages a couple weeks ago?" Coroneos asked.

Rock shook his head. "Same ol', same ol'. The Marxist sons of bitches won't give up and as far as I'm concerned, the crazier it is down there, the better."

"Six of one, half-dozen of another," Coroneos said. "Peace makes getting in and out of Colombia easier, but it also increases the value of Colombian Peso, which cuts into our profits. Since Escobar died like a rat in '93 and the Medellín and Cali cartels collapsed, the whole economy has changed for the better. Smaller factions, less-concentrated power."

Rock motioned to the maître d. "We've seen four Colombian presidents come and go since '86 and the only thing that changes is the date. The longer the guerrillas keep the government busy, the fewer hassles we have."

The maître d returned, placed an ebony humidor on the table in front of Rock, and opened the top. Rock put his face close to the box and wafted the air to his nose. He drew in a slow breath as the Cohiba Esplendido Cuban's aroma drifted from the black box. He slid his hand into his tuxedo jacket pocket and removed a double guillotine, twenty-four-carat gold cigar cutter given to him in 1995 by Colombian President, César Gaviria. Gaviria had honored Rock for his "outstanding business relationship" with the country of Colombia. A photo of the two men shaking hands had graced the front page of El Espectador, Bogota's oldest newspaper. Aside from his favorite handgun, a .40 S&W, the cutter was the only thing Rock never left behind.

"I'd just as soon go in when it's the most chaotic. Most buyers won't take the risk, and it gives us more leverage," Rock said, sliding the humidor toward Mickey. "Besides, I know that Mickey would take a bullet for me if it ever got really hairy. Ain't that right?"

Mickey lifted a cigar from the humidor. "Already did," he said, referring to a failed hit by the Soriano crime family nine years prior.

"Come on. It barely broke the skin," Rock said with more than a hint of sarcasm.

Scalise didn't smile.

Nick chuckled quietly, having been in the hospital the night of the shooting. The supposed "scratch" was actually a .38 caliber bullet lodged in Scalise's left shoulder. Nick took a sip of wine and leaned back, trying to enjoy the show like some prime-time TV drama, thankful not to be the target of his father's bullshit.

Jennifer leaned over and pulled out a cigar. "Tony, you're not going to share these with the ladies?"

"Well, where are my manners?" Rock said, glancing over his right shoulder. "Mrs. Coroneos, would you like one of Castro's finest?"

"Thank you, no, gave them up for Lent. Quite tempting, though," she answered.

Rock leaned back, picked out a cigar, and sniffed it under his nose. He cut the tip, held the lighter to the end, and took a few puffs. He passed the box down the opposite side of the table along with his cigar cutter. "Let's stop talking business. I want to make a toast to the beautiful woman who was loco enough to marry this old man."

He raised his wine glass. "I've spent most of my life looking for precious stones, and when I first set my eyes on Jennifer, I knew I was in the presence of a rare, flawless gem. Had I known that there were jewels of this beauty in Philly, I'd have spent less time in South America. To Jennifer, my new bride."

Jennifer's bare breasts and seductive lap dance on the day they met undoubtedly biased his assessment, but who was Nick to judge? The guests' glasses chimed as they ritualistically tapped together. Nick gladly finished off the last of his Merlot. Thankfully, the numbness was beginning to kick in.

After the toast, Nick eased up to the bar to refill his glass. Someone laid a hand on his left shoulder.

Nick turned around. "Peter," he said, extending his hand. Coroneos gripped Nick's hand and held it tightly, his deep-set brown eyes unblinking. "I know this is difficult for you, your mother's death so recent. It's been hard on us all. You know how much we loved her," he said, still holding onto Nick's hand. A gaudy gold ring on Coroneos' hand dug into Nick's finger.

"Thanks, Peter. It's still a little raw, I have to say," Nick said, taking his hand back.

Coroneos' eyes narrowed. "It crushed him, Nick, your mom's death. I think he just desired companionship. Don't be too hard on him."

"It's cool. I get it. Thanks again for the words, Peter."

A portly, sixty-something woman with thinning white hair approached Coroneos. Bloodshot eyes and downturned corners of her mouth unveiled her grief. "He should have been here." Her lower lip quivered as the words slipped from her mouth.

Coroneos put his arm around her. "I know, Rose. Willie was family."

Rose sobbed in his arms, then pulled away. She turned toward Nick. "I'm sorry, I didn't mean to interrupt."

"Not a problem," Nick said.

Coroneos gently squeezed the woman's shoulder. He turned to Nick. "You might have heard, Rose's nephew Willie worked for us for several years, but unfortunately he passed away on Wednesday."

"I'm so sorry," Nick said.

Rose nodded as she wiped the tears from her cheeks.

"We'll keep your family in our prayers, Rose," Coroneos said as the woman moved past them and back to her table. "Willie got himself into a real mess. He took his own life," Coroneos continued.

"That's a shame," Nick replied, hoping the subject was over. The less he knew of his father's business, the better.

Coroneos ordered two glasses of Chardonnay, then smirked, "Your father's wedding today, Willie's funeral tomorrow. I can't be caught wearing the same suit."

Nick set his now empty wine glass down on the bar. "Good to see you, Peter." He grabbed a Heineken and forced himself back to the head table. Big band music played while some people danced, others gossiped, and most everyone drank.

By seven o'clock, Rock had graduated from Merlot to Dewar's, straight up, and his deep, imposing voice had jumped twenty decibels. Nick avoided him most of the evening but felt obliged to offer his departing congratulations. He wasn't sure why, but he actually felt sorry for his new stepmother. After all, her only wrongdoing was falling for his father's persuasive line of bullshit at Sophie's Den.

"Congratulations, old man," Nick said as he smiled at Jennifer.

"Nick, you better get a move on yourself lest our family name ends with you or your brother."

Eddie slipped his arm around his girlfriend of two months and puffed on his cigar. "Don't worry, Pops, we've got it covered." His date's face turned red.

"Jennifer, you must want to have children," Nick said. He turned back to his father. "If Eddie can't rise to the occasion, maybe you and Jennifer will get lucky and have a boy, Rock

Carlotti the Second. If you need a script for Viagra, let me know."

Rock lifted his fists in a pose reminiscent of a heavyweight prizefighter and bobbed his head side to side. "Wanna go at it?"

"You know, Pops, that I'm a lover, not a fighter."

"Okay, boys, enough, kiss and make up," Jennifer said.

Rock dropped his hands briefly, then shot Nick a fake right cross, tapping his fist lightly on Nick's chin.

Nick threw his hands up in mock surrender. "You win. You're too quick for me."

They shook hands and gave each other an obligatory man-hug.

"Congratulations, Jen, or should I say, Stepmom," Nick joked, as he gave her an embrace and a kiss on the cheek.

"Jen would be fine," she responded.

He wanted to shout, "Run! Run away as far as you can!" But she chose this road. Her marriage was going to commence with a prelude of things to come. Instead of dashing off to an oceanside resort, sipping piña coladas on her grand honeymoon, she would spend a couple nights in Vegas followed by a week sitting alone at home while Rock and the boys flew to Colombia. Business always came first.

15

_____

A FEW SCATTERED raindrops fell as Nick escaped the reception and handed the valet his parking receipt. Minutes later, the smooth purr of the Boxster's engine sounded, and the drops turned to buckets. Nick sprinted to the driver's side door, handed the valet a ten-dollar bill, and took shelter.

A bolt of lightning lit up the sky and the ensuing crack of thunder rattled the car. Nick leaned his head back and shook the water from his hair. Time to forget the whole damn mess, at least for a while. With a twist of the stereo's dial, the music overcame the rain's musical drumming on the Porsche's ragtop. Song thirteen played as Tom Waits' raspy voice told the story of "Georgia Lee."

A few days after his mother's accident, someone had placed a rose-covered cross over the guardrail near the spot where his mother's car had come to rest. It had hung there four or five weeks before the road service removed it, the rose's petals long since withered and lifeless. As much as Nick appreciated the memorial, he welcomed the end to the constant reminder.

As the song finished, Nick decided to drown his sorrows but

didn't want to do it alone. He pressed speed-dial. "Want to join me for a Guinness or three?" Nick asked.

"I take it the wedding didn't go so well," his best friend Steve said. "Where would you like to meet?"

"O'Sheas, I'm two blocks away. I'll probably have one down by the time you get there."

"Keep your eyes on the road, buddy. Give me twenty."

O'Shea's Irish pub was obscure enough that Nick rarely ran into hospital staff — a feature he found most appealing. The aroma of shepherd's pie, fish and chips, and cabbage hit your nose the moment you passed through the door, and if you closed your eyes, you'd think you'd stumbled into the O'Malley family reunion. And the stout! Based on the way it settled in your glass, you'd swear they'd pumped it direct from Dublin, via transatlantic pipeline.

Nick had frequented the place since medical school. He'd met his ex-wife there seven years ago and mourned his divorce with one too many shots of Jameson Irish whiskey five years later.

MJ's Southern accent, cobalt blue eyes, and tight Crimson Tide t-shirt had captivated him from the first drink she'd served him at the bar the night after his physiology final. They married that same fall.

But they came from different worlds. MJ grew up in the country, kind, sensitive, and more naive than she appeared. She thought a year in the city would "broaden her horizons" and didn't plan to stay until she met Nick. Sadly, medical school took the majority of what Nick had to give, and he knew, too late, that she needed more. She grew resentful and shut down.

During the last couple months of their marriage, he and MJ passed in the halls like strangers. Sure, every couple had their ups and downs. But, theirs started like a summer picnic: Sunny, cool breeze coming off the pristine lake as they sipped wine and snacked on smoked salmon and fresh strawberries. It was sublime until twenty minutes later when the fire ants came. The picnic was heaven. The ants— hell.

After they separated, MJ moved back to Folsom, Alabama and eventually married an old high school sweetheart. Although Nick believed he and MJ weren't meant to be together, he felt guilty for the pain he caused her. Of course, Rock never embraced MJ. She wasn't Italian, Catholic, or from Philadelphia. How ironic that Rock's new bride was a Polish agnostic from Piscataway, New Jersey.

"Nick, my friend, don't tell me that you forgot your umbrella," the bartender joked as Nick walked in, his hair dripping and his shirt and tie soaked through.

Nick approached the bar close enough to flick his fingertips, landing a row of water droplets across the bartender's cheek. "No, Pat, stopped by the Y for a quick dip but forgot my bathing suit," Nick said over his shoulder as he walked to the men's room. "Pour me a black and tan."

The man laughed and wiped his ruddy face with his sleeve. "No problem, Doc."

Nick gazed at the man staring back at him in the bathroom mirror. He looked older, more tired. The dark circles under his eyes seemed new. Maybe just a bit more sleep. He dried his face, shed his tie, ran his fingers through his rain-drenched, raven-black hair, and returned to the bar.

"What's new, Doc?" Pat asked as he scrubbed glasses in the sink below the bar.

"Hmm, my father just married a lap dancer who's six years younger than I am."

"Good for him! Did you ask him how he did it?"

"I imagine he shoved a Benjamin Franklin in her G-string, took her for a ride in his Jag, then gave her a tour of the estate. And me, I'm still sitting on a hundred grand in student loans."

"He didn't offer to help with school?"

"That's a joke," Nick huffed. "He wanted to make me pay for

leaving the family business. Said I was on my own. Actually, I think he said, 'fucking own.'"

"And you answered?"

"That I was glad not to owe him a damn thing. That I didn't want his filthy money."

Pat raised his eyebrows. "I'm sure that went over well."

"Not so much."

"Okay, but why's it eatin at you so much?" Pat asked.

Nick knew that Pat considered himself a freelance therapist and a pharmacist of sorts, a master at mixing the right beverage to quell any personal crisis.

"Probably because I haven't gotten lucky in over six months and I just spent the last few hours doing all I could to keep my eyes off my stepmother's breasts," Nick said, taking a swig of his beer. "It's been a rough week."

Pat looked up at the TV mounted above the liquor shelves. "Hey, isn't that the guy who made so much trouble for your father back when?"

A campaign ad flashed across the screen with State Senator Mays wearing a hardhat and touring a foundry with two steel-workers. Lloyd Mays: Fighting for the middle-class. Tough on taxes. Tough on crime. Your next voice in Washington, the ad said as the image of Mays faded in the background. Along the screen's bottom scrolled the words: "This ad paid for by Lloyd Mays for United States Senate."

Nick nodded with a half-smile. "Yeah, he apparently gave up trying to break the Rock in exchange for spending quality time with his good friends Bill and Hillary. The guy sent an arrangement of roses to my mother's funeral that looked like a float at the Rose Bowl Parade."

Pat chuckled, his gaze moving past Nick toward the door. "Sloot, hope you brought a box of tissues, Nick's cryin me a river here," he said. "I see you were smart enough to bring an umbrella."

Steve shook the water from his red umbrella, folded it, and set it next to the door. He fit right in at O'Sheas with his tousled red hair and freckles, a gift from his Irish mother. His six-foot-two stature came from his father, a second-generation Dutchman from West Michigan. Steve could pass for a college kid with his baby face and hoped it would serve him well three decades from then.

Nick considered Steve VanSlooten to be his closest friend. They'd met the first day of medical school and spent a semester hovering over a cadaver in Gross Anatomy. Nick did most of the dissecting while Steve rattled off the names of the bones, muscles, and nerves, his words hampered by an occasional, annoying stutter. It emerged only in times of stress, such as the oral exam at the end of Anatomy and Physiology. The two had little in common except their love of medicine, good food, and a good laugh but soon bonded like brothers.

"What can I get you, Sloot?" Pat asked.

"Diet Coke please." Steve took a seat next to Nick at the bar.

"Careful, Sloot, you don't have a designated driver," Pat joked.

"I'm on call. No one wants to have their neurologist looking more like he had a stroke than they did. Light on the ice, please."

Pat set down the glass.

"Okay, Nick, let it out," Steve said.

Pat jumped in. "Nick was just telling me about his new Oedipus complex."

Steve turned to Nick. "So, this is the big crisis. You've got eyes for your father's bride?"

"Have you seen her?" Nick said, extending his cupped hands a foot out from his chest.

Steve rolled his ocean blue eyes and shook his head. "Seriously, what's up?"

"I'm sick of watching con artists make it to the top. It pisses me off!"

"And your dad marrying the centerfold broke the camel's back."

Nick took two big swallows of his beer. "I've busted my butt for the past sixteen years. You know what it takes, the sacrifices we've made, the sleepless nights, and the mental abuse. No one gave me a free pass, and I didn't cheat anyone along the way."

"Your father must have sacrificed something to make it to the top. They don't just hand you the job."

"Sure, he sacrificed any meaningful relationship with his wife and kids. And I'm sure countless others sacrificed in more direct ways. In his line of work, others sacrifice for your gain. Whether they want to or not!"

"I get that. But I mean in his legitimate business, before the mob."

"He worked hard in the old days. He built his uncle's rinky-dink pawn shop on South Street into one of the elite stores on Jewelry Row. He did it with blood, sweat, and tears. But now he gets what he wants through fear and intimidation."

Steve finished the last of his Diet Coke. "So, when did it change?

"He got into financial trouble because of accounting mistakes and had to crawl back to my grandfather, who worked for Sal Paccione, the previous mob boss. My father needed a loan and I guess you could say that's when he sold his soul to the Devil."

Steve nodded. "From what I've heard, the Devil didn't fare so well after your father took him out."

Nick didn't lift his head as he peeked up beneath his furrowed eyebrows. "Uh, you think. The pathetic guy ended up a quadripalegic in diapers. Didn't live a year. His sons moved to New York and joined the Soriano crime family."

"Sounds like a scene from Goodfellas."

Nick huffed. "Yep, that's my life, a god damned . . . I'm sorry . . . a damn real-life Scorsese movie."

"No, it's not your life."

"Oh yeah, I tried to do things right and see where it's gotten me? My dad is a crook and the dough rolls in and a centerfold sleeps with him at night. That's the Carlotti legacy. Nice, huh?"

Steve turned in his chair, his pale, freckled face losing its usual happy-go-lucky expression. Nick knew that look. Here came the lecture.

"Come on, Nick, the guy's sixty years old, self-centered, materialistic, and without God. With that worldview he had three choices: spend the rest of his days alone, find someone his own age, or use his wealth and power to catch a bombshell. So, is he smart? Probably not. He's just following his hormones like most men. And you, you're one of the most respected craniofacial surgeons in the country. That counts for something, no?"

"I used to think so." Nick finished off his glass. "And while we're on the subject of con artists, David Siegel, the new chair at Hopkins? Are you kidding me? David Siegel couldn't operate his way out of a wet paper bag." He turned to Pat. "How about a shot of Patrón?" he asked, as he put the empty beer mug down.

"Sure, but I'm cutting you off after this. I don't want to read your name in the paper tomorrow morning."

Steve nodded. "Nick, Siegel is a master at manipulating people. Hell, he managed to persuade Harriet Danbury to donate two million dollars to the Children's Cancer Center. She hadn't given more than two grand to charity in the past ten years. How much do you think that helped his cause? Siegel has the uncanny ability to tell people what they want to hear and at the same time not make himself appear self-serving."

"Bullshit. You'd have to be in a coma not to see right through that guy. How can it be so blatantly obvious to me and not to everyone else?"

"People are easily duped," Steve said. "Turn on the TV Sunday morning and watch the masses digging deep into their pockets, giving their hard-earned money to some big-haired evangelistic clown slapping believers on the forehead, supposedly curing their arthritis and gout. There are charlatans, and there are saints. There are preachers and thieves, and not everyone can tell the difference."

"I'm sure that'll be his next gig," Nick said. He raised his shot glass. "To strippers and shysters."

Nick downed his tequila and placed the shot glass upside down as Pat moved out from behind the bar to clear some tables in the back.

"There's something else," Nick said, turning to look Steve in the eye, "I've been thinking about my mother's accident. I have this weird sense there's more to it."

"What do you mean?"

"She wouldn't be driving ninety miles an hour. My mother drove like an old lady in a Studebaker. We laughed when she bought the Beamer. I told her, 'You don't buy a thoroughbred to pull a donkey cart.' Besides, the weather sucked."

Steve gnawed on what little was left of the fingernail of his right index finger. "So, what are you thinking?"

Nick shot a quick glance toward Pat, who continued his work at the back of the bar. "I'm telling you I think that maybe someone had her killed."

"Seriously, for what reason?"

Pat stepped back behind the bar. Nick let the question go unanswered.

Pat picked up Steve's empty glass. "Ready for another?"

"No thanks. I'm good," Steve said. "I have to hit the road."

"I'll see you at grand rounds Monday morning," Nick said.

"Wouldn't miss it. Danielle is doing the honors," Steve said.

Nick's stomach did a flip-flop. He hoped it didn't show in his eyes.

Steve turned his gaze downward, then peeked up between rusty strands of his wavy hair. "I've been praying for you. I know your mother's death has been hard on you."

"Yeah, it's been getting in my head for sure."

"Maybe you should let God in there."

"I appreciate the sentiment," Nick replied. "But I don't like other people in my head."

"Not enough room in there for the two of you, huh?"

"Something like that." Nick stood and patted his friend on the back. "Thanks, pal. See you Monday."

~

A LARGE CARDBOARD box sat next to the door from the garage to the kitchen. It had been collecting dust in his office since the day he and MJ had signed the papers. The big block letters "DIVORCE" that he'd penned after sealing the box of legal papers, bills, and other records, seemed brusque and cold. He'd recently decided to move it to storage but managed to get it only as far as the garage.

He shook his head, wondering why he felt compelled to keep that stuff around. It bordered on masochism, but then again, so did the marriage that its contents dissolved. Amazing that such intense feelings of love, sexual infatuation, and mutual admiration could turn to resentment and mistrust in four short years, and then be so neatly packed away in a box like so many pairs of old socks.

Seeing the box seemed a fitting culmination of a lousy day. Nick sighed. He thought he'd reached the summit of his private mountain of self-pity until he unlocked the door, stepped into the dark foyer, and slid his hand up the wall, flipping on the lights. That unmistakable smell!

"Damn it, Rhino!" Nick said, looking down at his right foot, which stood firmly planted in a large pile of dog crap. Instead of spending the next half hour cleaning his shoe, he carried it at arm's length back into the garage, slipped off the other, and tossed them both in the trash.

The note on the table from Helen confirming they'd gone on

their evening walk gave Rhino no good excuse for the steaming gift but when the dog sprang from the bed and ran to greet him, Nick melted. After all, Rhino had been a faithful roommate for the past four years.

Nick's legs felt like cast-iron. He learned a valuable lesson as a surgical resident: "Eat when you can. Sleep when you can."

Exhausted and in a foul mood, he rationalized that getting an extra thirty minutes of sleep justified trashing a two hundred-twenty-dollar pair of Cole Haans. On Sunday morning at 4:30 am when he couldn't find his shoes, it didn't seem quite worth it.

16

GRAND ROUNDS, an academic ritual that, on the surface, serves to educate the surgical hierarchy — attendings, fellows, residents, interns, and lastly, lowly medical students. Below the surface, it's a stage for flexing surgical muscles, an opportunity to present textbook cases complete with fancy play-by-play slide presentations intended not just to convey knowledge but to impress one's colleagues with medical knowledge and wit.

An unspoken rule dictates where in the auditorium people sit. Medical students congregate in the back, interns closer to the front, followed by residents, chief residents, and fellows. Attending surgeons earned the coveted front-row seats.

Invariably, the three seats, front-row center, had belonged to the same figures for the past two years. In the left-most chair was the current Chairman of the Department of Surgery Dr. Ken McCabe. To his right, a spry eighty-three-year-old retired professor emeritus perched in his chair like the concrete Lincoln in his memorial. He still woke each morning at 5:00 am, donned a dark gray three-piece-suit, and dazzled the audience with his surgical knowledge. He had the uncanny ability to cite journal articles like he'd pulled them from a flash drive in his head, complete with the date of publication and the page number.

Dr. David Siegel enthroned himself in the third seat. He'd soon be off to Johns Hopkins to chair his own department but not fast enough. Nick quelled his ire by reminding himself that while Siegel sat in that seat he wasn't actually operating on a human being.

Presenting at grand rounds isn't all pomp and circumstance. At times, it's akin to a circus clown in a dunk tank, doctors lined up, each paying a buck for the opportunity to get you wet. If you're lucky, at some point during your medical career, you reach unsinkable status and the relentless grilling ceases, the questions or comments taking on a respectful sharing of wisdom. Unfortunately, Dr. Danielle Sorenson hadn't quite reached that level of distinction.

Danielle possessed qualities Nick couldn't quite wrap his mind around. Strong but humble, kind but not a pushover, and her wit kept him on his toes. She exuded a sensuality that stopped short of sexual. He'd never met a woman like her. But still, she seemed just a little too virtuous for a guy like him.

Danielle walked to the podium, her hair swaying with every step like a hypnotist's pocket watch. Mesmerized, Nick followed her with his gaze until Steve cleared his throat. Nick turned. Steve wore an I-caught-you grin on his face.

"What?" Nick asked.

Steve just smiled all the wider.

Like a soldier, Danielle stood tall, lips taut, her radiant eyes scanning the audience with poise. She hit the first slide. "Good morning . . . "

After presenting her case on the surgical treatment of high, mandibular subcondylar fractures, the barrage began. Dr. Siegel's hand shot up the moment Danielle opened the floor to questions.

"Dr. Siegel," Danielle acknowledged. She rubbed the side of her nose with her right index finger.

Nick knew her subconscious nervous twitch. Okay, girl, be strong.

Siegel let out a warning shot with a low, "Ahem." Peering over thin tortoise-shell, half-rim reading glasses perched at the tip of a narrow, eagle-like nose, he readied himself to drop the hammer. "Dr. Sorenson, you do realize that your decision to surgically treat this patient unnecessarily placed him at greater risk? Not only are the functional results of open treatment of this type of fracture often unsatisfactory, but, in my opinion, the risks of malocclusion and significant facial nerve injury far outweigh any possible benefits."

Danielle shuffled her papers and rubbed her nose again. "In my experience, Dr. Siegel, our treatment modality for these fractures has been quite successful. And, at the same time, has allowed patients to regain function immediately, avoiding the muscle wasting caused by more conservative nonsurgical treatments."

Nick whispered to Steve, "I love the way she holds her own with him. It's a shame that in this case she's wrong."

Danielle's gaze turned toward Nick. "Dr. Carlotti, do you have an opinion?"

It was too damn early. His head pounded. Looking down at his three-year-old, badly worn penny-loafers, he shook his head then made eye contact. He'd just been thrown into a lose-lose situation: Put aside his surgical reputation and support her regardless of the evidence to the contrary or support Siegel, which was akin to sleeping with the enemy. Self-preservation won over valor.

"The literature does show that conservative treatment with a short course of intermaxillary fixation is generally preferable to open surgical treatment. Patients heal well without the risks of surgical treatment. That's not to say you can't obtain a good result with surgical treatment but is it worth the risk? I would have to say that in many cases that answer is no."

"Thank you for your input, Dr. Carlotti," Danielle said, looking right through him with a furrowed brow.

Steve jabbed Nick in the side with his elbow. "If looks could kill," he said.

"She'll get over it. Besides, I need to distance myself a bit."

"I think you'd make a fine couple. You could use a woman like that," Steve said.

"So could you."

"Not sure I'd want to date a doctor. Besides, I think she's out of my league," Steve said, as Dr. Siegel turned in his chair and looked their way.

"Excuse me, Dr. VanSlooten. Were you offering your thoughts on the subject? I couldn't quite hear what you said," Siegel said. "Would you mind sharing with the rest of us?"

Nick wanted to rush down the aisle and drop-kick the condescending bastard, but trusted Steve could hold his own.

"Yes, I just told Dr. Carlotti that Dr. Sorenson's presentation was superb, and although I'm not a surgeon, avoiding muscle wasting seems like a reasonable indication for open surgical treatment. So, in summary, I agree wholeheartedly with my colleague, Dr. Sorenson," Steve responded, drawing a grateful smile from Danielle.

She shot a second stern look in Nick's direction.

"What a suck up you are. You're a neurologist, for god's sake," Nick whispered. "What the hell do you know about facial trauma?"

Steve smirked. "Apparently enough to stay out of Danielle's cross-hairs."

"If you want to ask her out, I'd let you borrow my Cole Haans but I'll have to fish them from the trash. By the way, I despise that guy."

"I wouldn't have known," Steve said.

"He's a parasite burrowed deep in my skin. It's causing a festering boil."

"Nick, I think it might behoove you not to burn too many bridges," Steve said.

Nick's pedigree ensured he'd start his career with one strike against him. Dr. Nick Carlotti was an outsider, a South Philly Italian and the son of Rock Carlotti to boot. That alone spurred trepidation. They put up with him partly out of fear of reprisal but mostly because many considered him the best craniofacial plastic surgeon on staff, if not the Eastern Seaboard.

Aside from one stodgy ER receptionist, the hospital employees loved him, his patients adored him, and he had gifted hands. He knew it. At times, he wore his ego on the outside like a fine suit. Even with the chip on his shoulder, he connected with the orderlies, clerical staff, and nurses much better than he did with his colleagues.

As he exited the lecture hall, Nick's gut tightened at having thrown Danielle under the bus. He tried to ignore it as he kept walking, but something forced an about-face. He fought his way against the flow of the crowd. "Steve, I'll catch up with you a bit later. I'm going to build a bridge."

17

DANIELLE LINGERED AT THE PODIUM, stacking her notes as Nick reached the stage. She lifted her head, rolled her eyes, and continued stacking.

"Okay, so I'm a loser. I'm sorry for bailing on you like that."

"Sorry? Not sure I've ever heard that from your lips. So, to what do I owe the privilege?"

"I feel bad that . . . "

"I don't need your sympathy."

"Danielle, I'm . . . "

"It's okay, Nick, I'm a big girl. Oh, and for the record, you taught me open reduction of high subcondylar fractures. I spared you the embarrassment of sharing that fact with the audience."

"Danielle, I was just making the point that, all things considered, nonsurgical treatment . . . "

"Spare me your thoughts, Nick."

"All right, I should have had your back. I dropped the ball."

"No, you didn't just drop the ball, you kicked it in my face."

"So, apology not accepted, I take it?"

Danielle shoved her papers into her briefcase and grabbed the handle tight. The knuckles of her already milky-white hands went pale. She hesitated before looking up. "Nick, you're a great surgeon, and I admire your gift, but sometimes you're so self-focused. I know how you feel about Siegel and rightly so but you're starting to act a lot like him, minus that heinous bow tie."

"Really, you're comparing me to Siegel?"

"Yes, unless you'd rather me compare you to my narcissistic father who walked out on my mom and me when I was seven."

Nick sighed. "You're being a bit melodramatic don't you think?"

"I recognize the pattern," she said, starting down the steps.

Nick followed. "Danielle, stop."

She ignored him, instead quickening her long-legged strides down the aisle.

"Please stop."

She hesitated before turning around, her eyebrows bumped together in a scowl. "What?"

"I said I'm sorry. You haven't heard Seigel say that, or maybe your father either?"

"Nick, I haven't seen my father in over twenty years. He packed his bags and never looked back."

How, after knowing her this long, had he not known that? He stepped toward her. "Danielle, you've never shared that before."

She loosened her grip on her briefcase. "Maybe you never seemed to care enough for me to share it."

"I said I was sorry, and I meant it. I do care."

"Nick, I raised my little sister because my mother worked six nights a week cleaning office buildings. You have no idea what it's like having to claw your way up like I have. It's no picnic training as a female surgeon in this old boys' club. So, either be my advocate or get out of my way."

Nick smiled and extended his hand. "Truce?"

It took a few seconds, but a hesitant grin formed on her face as she reached out and shook his hand. "Apology accepted." Her tone softened. "I've been taught to love my enemies."

"Did they also teach you, in your 'loving your enemies class,' that it's customary to dine with your enemies as a tangible confirmation of forgiveness?" Why did he just say that?

"Are you really asking me out?"

No turning back now. "Well, that depends on what the answer might be."

"What? Like scratching off the instant lottery ticket before you buy it? I think I'm busy."

"I didn't even ask you out yet."

"I know."

"Ouch!"

"Let's keep this professional. But I'd like your help with a patient on twelve if you have time. It's a thirty-five-year-old with a deep neck infection. We can't seem to get a handle on it."

Two solid rejections in three days, awesome! "Fair enough, I'll meet you on twelve in a few minutes."

Danielle started back down the aisle. "Let's go together and I'll fill you in on his history. It's complicated."

Nick thought twice about taking the elevator but didn't want to do any more damage to his now-slim chances with Danielle.

They entered the empty elevator on the third floor. She shared a quick patient history before they stopped on seven, where a rounding medical team of four climbed aboard. Nick had no choice but to step back against the far wall. His breaths became more rapid and labored. He reached up to loosen his tie, which felt like a noose tightening around his neck. Thank God they didn't press another button! Danielle focused her attention on the patient's CT report. She didn't seem to notice his impending panic attack.

The numbers ascended. Eight – nine – ten – eleven. The elevator came to a stop. The doors opened on the eleventh floor and a rather rotund family of three stood looking in. "Go on, boy!" the mother said to her young son. "There's plenty of room in there."

The boy weaved his way through the group as the woman dragged her second child by the hand. Like someone had taken all the air and sucked it from the now shrinking elevator with a massive vacuum, it hit. Not until Nick forced his way through the crowd, thrust his hand between the closing doors, jumped out, and gasped for what felt like his last dying breath did the humiliation replace his fear.

"Momma, what's wrong with that man?" the young boy asked.

"Keshon, mind yo business," the mom said, putting her arm in front of him in a protective posture.

They all stared like visitors gazing at the crazy gorilla behind a thick glass wall at the zoo. Danielle's jaw dropped. All Nick managed was a shrug and an expression of shame. The look reflected only a fraction of his disgrace.

The doors closed. It seemed to take forever. Nick regained his composure, found the nearest restroom, and splashed a handful of cold water on his face. How could a guy who peeled back scalps of sleeping patients, drilled holes in their skulls, and placed titanium screws millimeters from the brain without blinking an eye, decompensate when riding in a damn elevator? What the hell was wrong with him?

Walking up the one remaining flight of stairs, Nick stopped just inside the door. Through its long vertical window, he glimpsed her slender figure standing outside the patient's room. Somehow in the past few days, something had changed. Maybe he'd locked it out before, ignored the subtle quickening of his heart, the need to swallow once before he spoke, the involuntary change in his posture. He couldn't ignore it now. But between the door and the fifty feet to where she stood, he needed to negate the mortifying elevator incident.

She turned as he reached the room. "Are you okay?"

"Yeah, sorry about that. I had oysters last night. I knew one didn't taste quite right. Haven't felt well all morning."

She smirked. "Be still my beating heart. Did my ears betray me or did you actually say 'I'm sorry again'?"

"Remember today's date because it could be years before it happens again," Nick said. Okay, back to work. Clear your head. He took the chart from her hand. "So, tell me about our patient."

"Guy came in yesterday with cellulitis and a large abscess in his left neck. We did an extra-oral I&D, sent cultures, and started him on Clindamycin but this morning looks like he's developing necrotizing fasciitis . . . "

After the patient exam, Nick contemplated canceling his appointment with his shrink, Dr. Makos, but given the events of the last fifteen minutes, he nixed the thought from his head. She practiced in the adjacent building and, yes, on the tenth floor.

18

As HE ENTERED the psychology department, Nick hoped his white lab coat with his embroidered name followed by MD would distinguish him from the real patients, the ones who had a screw or two loose. Everyone else in the room was nuts, while he, on the other hand, just had a small hang up. He scanned the waiting room. Thankfully, no familiar faces. He approached the front desk.

"Dr. Carlotti, you're here for your 4:30 appointment with Dr. Makos," the receptionist said.

Nick nodded and took a chair in the far corner of the waiting room, one of two unoccupied seats. All the crazies who couldn't see the shrink on the weekend rushed in bright and early Monday morning to get their heads on straight.

He hid behind an issue of Sports Illustrated. He much preferred being a doctor than a patient and did his best to consider this a meeting of the minds, two colleagues having a mutual consultation of sorts. But, in reality, Dr. Makos had access to his personal thoughts and feelings while hers remained veiled. She asked the questions, and he answered. In addition, he dished out a hundred and fifty dollars an hour for the privilege. He requested that she not bill his insurance company because he didn't want the counseling to come back and bite him. No matter how he painted the picture, this was indeed . . . therapy.

Subtle earth tones, not too bright but not bland decorated the space, all intended to put patients at ease. She'd arranged the furniture sparsely, giving the room an open, unrestricted feel. Just what Nick needed, space. Two plush, brown leather chairs angled toward each other with a contemporary, smoked-glass coffee table in between. A large window behind them let in the amber morning sunlight.

"How are you, Nick?" Dr. Makos asked with a distinctive Mediterranean accent. She motioned for him to have a seat, then sat across from him. Greek, in her early sixties, and quite good-looking for her age, Dr. Makos repositioned a pair of glasses hanging from her neck by a thin gold chain.

"Fairly well until I made an ass of myself in an elevator this morning," Nick said.

"Would you like to elaborate?"

"Not much to say, really. The usual apprehension, followed by panic, ending with humiliation. This time, I came unglued in front of a female colleague."

"Elevators were off-limits, no?" Dr. Makos said.

"She went in, and I followed."

"Like a lemming?"

"The elevator was empty, and it seemed like a good time to give it a shot. It unraveled from there."

"Where do you think it comes from?" Nick shrugged. "I thought it was your job to figure that out."

"My job is to help you clear the way to discover it yourself."

"I've told you I have no idea."

"I'm not buying it. Not that you don't think you know. That part I get, but I believe it's in there, and we need to find it."

"Oh yeah, this is the part where you tell me I have repressed memories of some horrific childhood trauma. Well, I don't."

"Okay," Dr. Makos said with a grin.

"That's it? Okay. Just like that. Aren't you supposed to suggest hypnotism or something?"

"When you're ready to go there, I'll go with you. Until then . . . yes, it's okay."

Nick looked her in the eye. "You think I'm a chicken-shit."

Dr. Makos didn't blink. "I think that whatever happened elicited enough pain that your subconscious pushed it to a corner of your mind you haven't been able to access. But you have to be willing to dig a little if you want to be free of it." She tapped her pencil on her pad.

Nick lowered his head and rubbed his stubbly cheek. His eyes watered but he refused to let a full tear form. "Seriously, I don't know."

"Maybe you don't want to know."

Nick chuckled. "You sound like Jack Nicholson."

Dr. Makos squinted at him. "Huh?"

"Never mind. Just a joke." Apparently, she had never seen the movie.

Dr. Makos smiled. "That's fine, but I want you to face your demons."

"You've told me before to face my demons. I took your advice today, and the little bastards kicked my ass."

"Who is she?"

"The demon?"

"Uh, no. The young lady who twisted your arm."

"I know, I was avoiding the question. Her name is Danielle, or should I say, Dr. Sorenson. She's a surgeon in our department. I'm not seriously interested, and we're as opposite as two could be. But, she's damn good looking."

"She got you into an elevator. That tells me you're fooling yourself— about not being serious, I mean."

"Okay, let's move on, Barb," Nick said, squirming in his chair.

Dr. Makos slipped on her glasses and jotted a quick note.

"Nick, I've said this before, but I think it's worth repeating. You are strong, confident, intelligent, and successful. We all have something, some weakness or flaw, so don't let this define you. You will move past this phobia but you . . . we will have to find a path to that destination."

"We've been at this for over a year, and every time I think I'm getting somewhere I crash and burn."

"What else is going on that might have set you back or at least decreased your threshold?"

Nick hesitated not sure he wanted to share his suspicions, but it came out of his mouth of its own volition. "I believe my mother's death wasn't an accident. I've been trying to find answers, and it's killing me."

Dr. Makos' eyes grew wide behind her glasses. "That's quite a revelation. What makes you think so?"

Nick leaned forward. "The circumstances around the accident, her speed, the driving conditions . . . It's like a song that keeps playing in my head."

"And the motive?"

"I'm not sure. Mom didn't have any enemies, but my father has enough for both of them."

Dr. Makos paused, allowing Nick to continue his thoughts, but none came. "Have you talked to your father?"

"I wouldn't call it much of a conversation. He pretty much stuck to the findings of the police report and let me know he wasn't interested in rehashing things. As you might imagine, my father isn't one you can push too hard."

"He scares you, no?"

"Uh— yeah. He scares everyone, but if you mean scared for my life, no. Maybe I should be," Nick answered.

He got up with his empty glass and walked over to a small table holding a round marble tray and a stainless-steel pitcher of water. He glanced briefly at the latest issue of Philadelphia Magazine lying next to the pitcher. The cover featured Lloyd Mays with his arm around the shoulders of a miner as they stood at the entrance of a coal mine in Armstrong County, Pennsylvania. The caption read: Lloyd Mays, Pennsylvania's best hope for the US Senate?

Twice in two days, this man's face in the news. How had a man the Rock detested made it so far in the state of Pennsylvania? He was either really sly or on the take, but then again, who in the government wasn't? Nick poured a glass of water, took a sip, and walked back to his chair.

Dr. Makos removed her readers, letting them dangle from the chain. "I know your father was a heavy-handed disciplinarian and the physical and mental abuse was real, but is there some part of you that can forgive him, if not for him, then for your own healing?"

"I know his own childhood was no picnic, that his father treated him like shit. I understand the psychology. But, forgiveness — no."

"You might want to explore that a little more. I think it would be freeing."

"Maybe," Nick said, with a dubious tone.

"Nick, other than closed spaces, you aren't afraid of much. I haven't heard you say anything irrational and you certainly aren't delusional. If something doesn't feel right, I think you should pursue it. God knows that your family isn't unfamiliar with crime, no offense."

"No offense taken. It's no secret."

They spent the remainder of the appointment on what Nick considered standard psychobabble, but he did his best to play the compliant patient. He thanked her for her time and told her that he would make another appointment, but only if he felt the need. They both knew that would be likely.

Despite the busy day ahead, he resolved to confront his father before Rock left for Colombia the following day. The time constraint didn't give him room to procrastinate. He wasn't a procrastinator by nature anyway, but no one would have faulted him for side-stepping a confrontation with Rock Carlotti. Corporal punishment, bordering on abuse, wasn't foreign to the Carlotti boys, but Nick wasn't a child anymore. Intimidation and the threat of physical pain weren't going to prevent this show-down. His mother deserved that much.

19

ON AN AVERAGE DAY, the elderly couple creeping along side-by-side, taking up the whole sidewalk, would have annoyed him. He'd have sighed as he stepped into the road to pass them and doubled his pace as he made his way back onto the walkway. Today, however, Nick appreciated the extra time on his trip down Sansom Street toward his father's jewelry store.

His pace slowed, the closer he got to the storefront. He readied himself for a showdown. Rock didn't appreciate challenges to his authority, and being Rock's son provided no protection from his wrath. Despite his father's violent past, Nick was more than motivated to push his luck. His mother would have done the same for him.

He walked in the front door and without hesitation, moved past the salesman straight toward the back office.

"You should probably knock first," the salesman said, the last word leaving his mouth as Nick burst through Rock's door unannounced. Rock kept the phone to his ear and shot Nick a fiery look, his teeth clenched as the muscles of his jaws bulged. He stared at Nick with a cold, unblinking eye. That expression usually preceded a good ass-kicking. Nick shut the door behind him.

"I'll have to call you back. In the meantime, I want information on this Danny character." Rock slammed down the phone. "I assume you lost your mind for a second or just forgot your manners because I didn't hear a knock."

Nick swallowed hard. "I want the truth."

"Excuse me?"

"You know damn well it was no accident. Mom wouldn't be driving ninety miles an hour unless she feared for her life." The conversation escalated sooner than he'd hoped.

"You have the audacity to waltz in here and accuse me of having something to do with the death of my wife? How dare you!"

"Then tell me you didn't."

"You best change your tone in a hurry, son, because you're way out of line." Rock stepped out from behind his desk.

"Or what? You're going to shake me down?"

Rock exploded from his desk and took a fistful of Nick's shirt in his fist. He thrust Nick up against the wall. "My wife is dead, you little shit! Who do you think you are?"

Nick kept his eyes locked straight ahead. "It didn't take long to move on though, did it?"

Rock's hand flew from his side, landing across Nick's cheek. A white flash filled Nick's eyes as the sting peaked and quickly subsided. Before Nick's eyes regained their focus, Rock let go of his grip on Nick's shirt and turned away. Nick straightened himself and stood tall.

"Get the hell out of here," Rock said as he walked back toward his desk.

Nick didn't budge. "That's how you treat your own son?"

"Don't be a pussy. My drunken father blinded me with a socket wrench when I was eleven for tipping over a bucket of motor oil. I just wanted to watch him change the oil in the car.

And your spineless grandmother told the doctor I fell off my bike. So, consider yourself damn lucky to have me."

Nick took a couple steps toward his father. "Look, I'm not accusing you of anything. I just want an answer that makes sense. I'd expect you'd want the same."

Rock didn't turn around. He reached up with his right hand and pushed his lower jaw to one side. The bones of his neck cracking broke the silence. "It rained like hell that night. Your mother wasn't feeling well, and she lost control of her car. Why isn't that enough for you?"

"Ninety miles per hour. Really? Mom?"

Rock looked back toward Nick. "Okay, so who would want to kill your mother? Everyone loved her."

Nick bit his tongue wanting to say, everyone but you. "I don't know, but if there's a possibility this wasn't an accident, I'd like to know."

"I own this town, and if someone wanted her dead, I'd know. Drop this ridiculous wild goose chase and don't forget I'm still your father. Have a little respect!" Rock sat back behind his desk.

Nick turned the door handle and hesitated. "For the record, I'm not satisfied with the official version of the story and I'm going to keep digging until I am."

"Have at it but stay the hell out of my business. I know you're my son, but there is a limit to my patience."

Nick glared at his father; his eyes narrow, rigid, cold. "Yeah, I know." He wasn't going to win a stare-down, and he wasn't willing to waste a minute more of his life in a worthless ego battle. As Nick passed the counter, the salesman tried to look busy, undoubtedly having heard much of the conversation.

"Have a good day," Nick said.

"You as well, Dr. Carlotti." Emotionally drained, he still had to round on his patients before he headed home. However, a brief but encouraging page from one of the ICU nurses brought a bit of needed energy. *Dr. Carlotti, Mr. Torello is responsive.*

20

FOUR DAYS AFTER THE SHOOTING, Danny Torello opened his one remaining eye. Although he was still in critical condition and a long way from talking, the change marked a substantial turn for the better. The police officer stationed outside the room heard the chatter and asked to talk to Danny, but the nurses denied his request. Nick walked past the frustrated officer and shut the sliding glass door behind him.

"Danny, I'm Dr. Carlotti," Nick said as he laid his hand on the man's shoulder.

Danny recoiled from Nick's hands. His heart rate jumped from 80 to 130.

"Whoa, I'm just changing your dressing," Nick said. "I'm the one who operated on your face. You've had serious gunshot wounds, but you're going to be okay," Nick added, doubting the truth of what he'd just said. Persistent fevers continued, triggered by the feces that had spilled into Torello's abdomen when the bullet ripped through his colon.

Danny's muscles relaxed slightly, but his fearful eye remained fixed squarely on Nick.

The cop hurried into the room. "Is he talking?" he asked, approaching the bed.

Nick took a step to his left, blocking the man's path. "You're kidding, right?" he said.

"Let me rephrase that, Doctor. Is he responding?" The cop leaned around Nick and made eye contact with Danny. "Can you hear me?"

"Excuse me, Officer. Please step away from my patient. We'll let you know when and if he's well enough to answer questions."

"No problem, Doc, I'm not going anywhere," the cop said, glaring at Danny. He walked from the room.

Nick slid shut the large glass door. He finished his exam and re-dressed Danny's wounds. "Are you having pain?"

Danny shook his head. A wet gurgle preceded a coughing fit as phlegm shot up from his tracheostomy. He moved his lips, unable to produce a sound.

"You won't be able to speak until we change your trach," Nick said. "I'll have the nurse suction you when I leave." He raised the head of Danny's bed.

Danny tried to move his arms, but cloth restraints held them tight to the bed-rails. He became combative, rocking his body back and forth. The metal railings clanged loudly enough to turn the police officer's head.

Nick grabbed Danny's hands. "Danny, you're restrained because the nurses don't want you to pull out your IV or disconnect your monitors. We can take them off as soon as you're more alert."

Nick released his grip, and for a moment the man remained calm, but soon began shaking his right hand back and forth.

"If you want the restraints off, you'll have to chill out," Nick said.

Danny's eye widened as he moved his head side to side. He shook his right hand again, this time noticeably holding his fingers as if gripping a pen.

"Be careful. If you start communicating the cops will want a piece of you," Nick said quietly. He picked up a pen and pad of paper from the bedside table, then placed the pen in Danny's hand and held the pad of paper for him to write.

In shaky, barely legible printing Danny wrote the name *Carlotti* followed by a large question mark.

"Yes. Dr. Carlotti," Nick replied.

Danny signaled again for the paper. *Rock* he scribbled.

"He's my father. Do you know him? I mean, do you know him personally?"

Danny shook his head. *You close?* he wrote.

"My father and I?"

Danny nodded. "Not so much, if that gives you comfort," Nick said, noticing Danny's right eye starting to close.

Apparently, it did. Danny fell back asleep, and Nick finished his work.

"How's he looking?" the officer asked as Nick left the room.

"Like a man shot three times at close range," Nick said without initially slowing his gait. Then he turned back around. "It's tenuous. He sustained a significant injury, and it'll be touch and go for a while."

The officer smiled. "Thanks, Doc. Luckily, they pay me by the hour."

21

THE MORNING HEADLINE READ: Mob hit suspected in July 3 shooting. The article in Tuesday's Inquirer stated the police suspected the Carlotti crime family's involvement in the attempted murder of Danny Torello, a small-time heroin dealer with ties to a recently deceased mob hitman turned informant named Willie Santini. Santini apparently committed suicide after his arrest for the murder of a high-end call girl. The article went on to say that Torello was a friend who probably knew too much and later that, in a strange twist of fate, Dr. Nick Carlotti, the son of mob boss Rock Carlotti, operated on Torello's facial injuries.

It didn't take long for the news to blaze its way through the hospital and nearly as little time for the call to come from the chairman of the department of surgery. Dr. McCabe stood briefly, acknowledging Nick's presence, then took a seat behind his desk. "I'm sorry, Nick, I'm taking you off Torello's case. David Siegel will be taking over."

"You're what?"

Dr. McCabe looked Nick in the eye. "You heard me."

"What the hell for?" Nick leaned over the desk. "I put the son-of-a-bitch back together, and you're taking me off the case?"

"It's more than a minor conflict of interest, given recent revelations. God knows this hospital doesn't need the negative publicity. It's like the damn cover of the National Enquirer."

"Ken, that's crap, and you know it! What do they think, that somehow I spent thirteen years in medical training to position myself for this one moment in time, to finish off a failed mob hit?"

McCabe remained calm, his voice low but firm. "I'm sorry, Nick, but you can understand my position and the stance of the hospital administrators. This stuff is fodder for the news outlets, and we just can't have that now."

Nick let out a sarcastic chuckle. "You mean, you can't. Wouldn't want to risk losing your cozy corner office to stand up for a friend."

"Don't make this personal."

"Too late!" Nick stormed from McCabe's office, slamming the door behind him, rattling the waiting room windows. The secretary shuffled papers, keeping her eyes down as Nick passed.

Danielle stepped through the reception room door as the shaking of the glass waned. Nick nearly ran her over. "Where are you going in such a hurry?" she asked.

"Ask Ken," Nick said but continued walking.

She grabbed his arm. "No, I asked you. What's going on?"

Nick turned, nostrils flared. "Did you read today's paper?"

"No, but I did hear about the Torello thing from Steve. I wondered how you were going to handle that."

"I don't have to. Ken handled it for me."

"How?"

"He took me off his case."

Danielle let go of Nick's arm. "Can he do that?"

"Apparently, yes, I . . . I mean we put the guy back together, and Siegel does the follow-up. Maybe it's what the junkie deserves. Payback is hell. I'm going to the ICU to sign Torello over to Dr. Frankenstein." Nick walked briskly with Danielle in tow.

"I'm going with you. You could use a little diplomacy or at least a buffer," she said, catching up to his side.

Nick wasn't the least bit surprised to see David Siegel already in Torello's room examining the wounds. As Nick and Danielle approached, Siegel came out to meet them.

"I've reviewed the chart and examined my patient. He'll require significantly more surgery if he survives the abdominal trauma. In the meantime, I need you to jot a note in the chart confirming that you've delegated further surgical care to me."

"You're enjoying this, aren't you?"

Siegel peered above his glasses. "I'm doing what Ken asked me to do."

"You might want to keep your head down when you're in his room and stay away from the windows. You never know when they'll want to finish what they started."

The five-foot four-inch, thin-faced man straightened himself up and pulled his half-rimmed readers from his face. He glared at Nick. "That's exactly why they removed you from this case. You're too close to this, and they know the apple doesn't fall far from the tree."

The Carlotti half of Nick wanted to strangle the man with the chain of his glasses, but his mother's genes gave him enough pause to channel his rage from physical to verbal. "At least it's going to be difficult for you to make Torello look any worse."

Danielle stepped between them. "This isn't helpful. David, how about an ounce of sensitivity? And, Nick, you know the decision came from above, so leave it at that."

Siegel spoke first. "If Mr. Torello doesn't continue to improve, it won't matter which of us is on this case." He reached into his lab coat, pulled out a small folded piece of paper, and handed it to Nick. "When I told the charge nurse I'd taken over his care, she handed this to me and asked me to give it to you. It's from Torello."

Nick took the paper and shoved it into his pocket. He walked away while he had the chance. Any longer and he might have succumbed to the paternal voice in his head urging him to knock the man's teeth out.

Thankfully, his mind wasn't entirely consumed with the situation at hand, for he couldn't help but wonder why Danielle was there. She had no stake in this, and as far as he knew, she wasn't all that fond of him. For some crazy reason, she, by her own volition, stood there by his side. Her presence provided enough distraction to prevent a scene, to keep him in check. He didn't want to admit it, but it felt good.

"Do you have time for a cup of coffee?" Nick asked as they left the unit.

Danielle hesitated. "Sure, I have half an hour before I start clinic."

In between the breakfast and lunch crowds, the two sat across from each other in a quiet booth. "Aren't you curious?" she asked, cupping a warm cup of coffee in her hands.

"About what?"

"The note."

"The note?"

"The one Siegel gave you . . . from Torello."

"I forgot about it actually," he said, reaching into his right front pocket. The scribbled words took his breath away. He froze.

"What does it say?" Danielle asked.

Nick stared at the barely legible note in his hand. *Your mother. No accident.*

"Nick, are you okay?"

He laid down the paper and slid it across the table. Danielle spun it around, and her eyes sprung open. "He knows this *how?*"

"I'm not sure," Nick said, jumping up. "But I'm going to find out."

Danielle didn't move as her gaze remained locked on the note.

Nick grabbed the note as Danielle's eyes peeked up from behind her golden hair. "You coming?" he asked, hoping that her recent concern wasn't a one-time event.

Danielle stayed at the nurses' station as Nick turned the corner toward the door of Danny's room. He blew past the police officer.

Nick still gripped the note as he reached the bedside. Danny's eye remained closed, his breathing slow and steady.

"Danny!" Nick tapped the man on the right shoulder.

Danny awakened abruptly as Nick unfolded the note and held it to the man's now wide-open right eye.

"How do you know this?" Nick demanded.

Danny motioned for a pen. With a shaky hand, Danny scribbled the name *Willie*.

"Who's Willie?" Nick asked, his gaze focused intently on Danny's hand and the pad of paper.

Willie Santini ~ Squirrel. Worked for your father.

Nick recalled his interaction with Willie's aunt Rose at his father's wedding reception. He turned his head, looking back toward the door as the officer glared at them from his chair in the hall. Nick moved his body to shield Danny from the officer's view.

"What did he tell you?" Nick asked.

'It wasn't an accident. That's ALL. Smiled like he knew it for sure.'

"When did he tell you that?"

A commotion came from outside the room. Through the glass walls, Nick spotted two nurses dash past, one carrying a fire extinguisher. He tore off the top page and shoved it into his lab-coat pocket, then tossed the pad back onto the bedside table, and sprinted from the room.

A thick cloud of black smoke billowed from the break room door. With the left side of his lab coat pulled over his nose and mouth, Nick scanned the unit for Danielle. The hospital staff ran room to room, closing patient doors to contain the smoke. He didn't see her in the crowd.

Amidst the fumes and chaos, Nick watched the police officer step away from Torello's door long enough to pull the fire alarm, then hurry back to his spot. As a nurse approached Danny's door, the officer waved her off. "I'll get this one, you can get the next." The nurse nodded. She rushed past him to the adjacent room.

As the smoke dissipated, Nick caught a glimpse of Danielle's slender silhouette. His muscles relaxed. He sighed in relief. "Danielle!"

She turned and ran to him as the fire alarm's ringing stopped.

A young fireman slowed as he passed, shaking his head. "Plastic in the damn toaster oven!"

Nick grabbed Danielle's hand. "Let's get out of here until this stuff clears."

He took one last glance toward Torello's room and locked gazes with the police officer. The officer turned and spoke something into the radio attached to the upper left of his jacket. He took his seat next to the door. Nick placed his hand on Danielle's back and led her from the unit.

They weren't thirty feet down the hall when the PA rang out: 'Code Blue Four West ICU.'

Nick stopped in his tracks. His stomach sank. "Shit!"

"It's probably not him," Danielle said, her soft blue eyes narrowing as she bit her lower lip.

They sprinted down the hallway just in time to see the code team filing into Torello's room. The cop moved away from the door. A resident leaned over Torello, compressing his chest, as someone else gave him breaths with a bag.

A doctor placed the paddles on Torello's chest. "Clear!" he said.

The team members stepped away from the bed. Torello convulsed as electricity surged through his body, but his heart refused to respond. Nick could only watch as they tried to save the man's life. The team spent twenty-two minutes and gave three defibrillator shocks before they called the code. Torello was dead.

Standing frozen in the doorway, Nick stared at the lifeless body, the body of the man who may have held the key to his mother's death. Danielle rested her hand on Nick's shoulder. Any further information Nick might uncover about his mother's death wasn't going to be coming from Danny Torello.

Nick watched in consternation as the medical team disconnected monitors and performed the usual post-code procedures. He'd just taken a sucker punch to the solar plexus. Someone had murdered his mother, and his only source of answers lay dead fifteen feet away.

Nick's blood boiled. He clenched his teeth behind tightly closed lips and barreled past Danielle, directly toward the officer standing off to the side.

"How was Torello connected to my father?" Nick snapped.

"You tell me. You're his son," the officer answered. "For that matter, it's a little disturbing that you were Torello's doctor, had access to him, and now he's dead."

"Are you insinuating that I killed him?" Nick asked, taking a step closer, now toe to toe with the officer.

The cop placed his right hand over his sidearm and extended his left hand into Nick's chest. "Step away, Doctor."

Danielle's voice cut in. "Nick, please . . . "

Crazy! The words, the tone of her voice, they stopped him in his tracks. His muscles relaxed. He took a couple steps back. "So, was that your implication?"

"You were alone in his room just before the fire. Coincidence?" the officer answered.

"I'm his doctor, you moron!"

"Maybe you should ask your father how he knew Mr. Torello. We'll be doing the same. And, as far as your connection, we'll be in touch if the autopsy shows anything out of the norm."

A hefty black orderly wheeled Torello's covered body from the room on a gurney. Nick followed for a few steps as Torello headed to the morgue.

Danielle eased up to Nick's side. "What are you going to do?"

"I'm going to find out who killed my mother and rip their heart out through their chest. And if my father had something to do with it, I'll kill him or die trying."

"Nick, I don't know what's going on here, but this isn't a game. Why don't you talk to the authorities and give them Danny's note?"

"You don't understand. Who do you suppose I can trust? The cops? My father or brother?" Nick walked toward the stairwell. "And Siegel, who knows if he read the note or if the nurses read it last night."

"I don't know any of that, but I'm worried about you," she said as Nick stepped through the door.

"I'm worried about me too. I appreciate the concern, really. Please keep this to yourself, okay?"

"I will."

The door closed behind him, the sharp clang echoing through the concrete void of the stairwell.

22

LIZA HAD ONCE SAID in an interview that most authors have a creative space, a setting where words seem to come easier. At her quaint, antique oak desk overlooking scenic Lake Naomi, inspiration had flowed like wine as she put pen to paper. In that place, she'd found her zone, her sweet spot.

She'd considered it her sanctuary, her place to escape the spotlight that followed her nonstop. If she'd left behind something, anything that might have provided a clue as to who wanted her dead, it would be there.

With his father in Colombia for the week, it seemed like a good time to call Jennifer and borrow the keys to the lake house.

"So, who's the lucky lady?" Jennifer chided.

"I'm flying solo," Nick responded. "I'm in the midst of a deep dating drought these days."

"I find that hard to believe with those chocolate brown eyes, but if you say so."

Jen's playfully flirtatious style got his heart going, and for a second some pretty crazy notions went through his head. He didn't let them linger too long. "Mind if I stop by when I finish up at the hospital Friday evening . . . around 7?"

"Anytime. You're more than welcome to join me for dinner if you'd like. This big old house is kind of lonely with Rock and the boys gone."

"Thanks, Jen, but it's already been a long week, and I'll want to get out of Dodge."

"Well, the offer's open-ended."

Nick got to the house at 7:45 pm. Jen opened the front door wearing a ruby-red bikini top with a white silk wraparound. Beads of water dripped from her long brown hair in a steady march as they hit the stone tile floor. Her wet bikini top accentuated parts that needed little accentuating. Barefoot with her toes painted the same shade of red as her top, she carried two Mojitos. The scent of fresh mint mixed with her perfume. "You will join me for one drink and a swim before you head out, won't you?"

"I don't have a bathing suit, but I will take you up on the drink."

"Who said anything about suits?" Winking, she handed Nick the drink. He followed her through the kitchen slider to a large indoor pool enclosed by glass walls on three sides. Tropical flowering plants and potted palm trees lined the colorful mosaic tile walkway around the pool's edge. Although towering oaks and maples dotted the estate's lawn, the pool house looked more like Key Largo.

"I'm not sure the Rock would appreciate his son skinny dipping with his new bride."

"I'm just playing with you, Nick," she said, fluttering her feet back and forth in the water. "So, how are things?"

Nick slipped off his sandals and sat down next to her. "Fine— a little tired of hospital politics and I'm working out some old hang-ups, but all in all, I'm doing all right. How's married life?"

"Mostly it's good but . . . " She looked down at the water. "No, it's fine." She took more than a small sip of her drink.

"That was an it's not-so-fine, fine. You don't have to talk if you don't want to, but remember, I've known the man a lot longer than you have."

"Nick, honestly, I love him, but there is so much secrecy. It's like I'm married to half a man. The other half is a stranger, a mystery. When we're alone, he treats me good, but when we're out, I think I'm just arm candy. I'm sorry, Nick, I'm being insensitive, I know this is hard for you."

"It's not your fault, Jen. I have no hard feelings toward you. My old man, that's another issue."

"Well, I'm still sorry." Jen reached over and turned Nick's head toward her. "Don't think I don't feel bad. I know how fresh your mother's death is for you." She let go of his chin and looked into the pool, the reflection of her centerfold face distorted by the ripples on the water. "I wanted to put off the wedding until next spring, but your father wouldn't have it. You know he's a hard man to argue with."

"You've been in this town most of your life, Jen. You know the Carlotti name. You must have had a hint of what you were getting into."

"I guess so, but do you ever really know, until you're in it?"

Nick reflected on his own failed marriage and nodded. "No, I suppose not. Keep your head on straight and don't let him in too far. Be careful, that's all."

"Like I said, it's fine. Life is good. I'm a lucky girl."

Nick smiled. Time to change the subject. "What are you going to do here alone all week?"

"I think I'm going to Cherry Hill to stay with my sister. It's silly for the cook to come in to make me dinners so I can sit at the dining-room table and eat alone. Miss Daisy with a Jersey accent."

"I don't see the resemblance," Nick said with a smile. "When are you leaving?"

"I'm going to stay here tonight and leave in the morning. You have a key so feel free to use the pool this week if you want."

"Thanks, Jen. I'm not on call so I might just take you up on that."

They finished their drinks over another fifteen minutes of small talk. He thanked Jen for her hospitality, put the lake house keys in his front pants pocket, and headed out.

He looked forward to the hour and a half drive, just enough time to clear his mind. But the cottage held decades of memories and he readied himself for an emotional ride.

23

In a real-life version of Rock, Paper, Scissors the two men would soon sit face to face, both cold-blooded killers leery of each other but willing to make a deal. The Rock and El Cuchillo, The Knife, were to exchange the down payment, $550,000 at a recently abandoned farmhouse thirty-five miles northeast of Bogota. The final payment, equal to the first, would be made when Coroneos took possession of the cocaine at an obscure location in central Kentucky two weeks later.

Rock, Coroneos, and Scalise landed at the El Dorado International Airport on Tuesday night and settled into the Cattleya, a posh boutique-style hotel in the historic section of Bogota. As they had done for years, they traveled to Muzo the following day, where Rock purchased a small number of select raw emeralds directly from the mine's owner. The ritual served as cover for the less legitimate purpose of the trip while providing a business write-off for travel expenses.

Back in Bogota by Thursday, they spent the next two evenings at the Rockefeller Casino drinking top-shelf Colombian rum at the blackjack table. On their last night in the city's Zona Rosa, they discussed the next day's affairs while lady-watching at the nightclub Playa Coral.

"I don't think it's a good idea for you to go," Coroneos said above the pounding dance music.

Rock leaned back and rolled his cigar in his lips. "It'll be fine."

"The guy's a nut case, Tony," Coroneos said. "I don't trust him."

"And he don't trust me. That's the point."

Coroneos stood up, and pulled a picture from his jacket pocket and set it on the table in front of Rock. "Whacking someone on occasion is part of our business but lining twenty-six heads up on sticks is a whole 'nother thing. He's unstable."

Rock slid the picture away. "I've seen it."

Scalise picked it up and glanced at the rows of bloody, ghost-white heads impaled on wooden stakes. "No wonder they call him 'El Cuchillo.'"

Rock grabbed the picture from Scalise's hand and tore it to pieces. "Who gives a shit? Castillo wants to deal with me mano y mano. I'm going."

Coroneos shot him a hollow you're-the-boss, smile and downed his tequila shot. He'd done his due diligence. If Andres Castillo lopped off Rock's ugly one-eyed head, then Coroneos could fly home with a little more leg-room on the plane.

Saturday morning, as the sun peeked above the horizon, the three men headed up I-50 toward Lake Guatavita.

Coroneos scanned the steep tree-covered mountain peaks surrounding the emerald-green, crater-shaped lake fifty-seven kilometers northeast of Bogota. The black Lincoln Town Car bounced side to side as the dirt road dwindled to a rough, dusty two-track.

From the back seat, Coroneos banged on the driver's head-rest. "Pull over!"

"What?" Rock asked, looking out the window.

Peter reached out his hand. "Mickey, give me the binoculars."

Rock turned from his front passenger seat. "What is it, Peter?"

"I saw a flash of light up there." Coroneos lowered the window and raised the binoculars. He focused on a rocky ledge twenty feet down from the tallest peak and caught sight of a man with a pocket-sized mirror reflecting a bright beam of light from the rising sun toward two armed guards a few hundred feet below.

"It's our welcoming committee," Coroneos said, handing the binoculars to Scalise.

"We don't have time to dick around," Rock said, spinning back around. "Get back on the road."

Coroneos shook his head as the car pulled back onto the two-track.

A quarter-mile from the farmhouse, beyond the first sharp bend, the two men dressed in drab green military fatigues stood blocking the way. One older, his face weathered like tawny shoe leather, stepped out first. The second, barely old enough to shave, followed, aiming his weapon at the windshield. The older man approached the car and tapped on the tinted driver's side window with the barrel of his rifle. Rock's driver showed the guard his empty hands.

"¿Cuál es su negocio aquí," the guard said: What is your business here?

"Estamos aquí para ver el señor Castillo," the driver answered: We're here to see Mr. Castillo.

The gunman motioned with his rifle. "Salir del coche," he demanded: Get out of the car.

The driver exited the car and opened the remaining three doors. Rock, Coroneos, and Scalise stepped out, and the two men patted them down for weapons. The men searched the car. The older man instructed the driver to open the trunk.

"No tengo las llaves," the driver said: I don't have the keys.

Rock turned to walk around the car.

"¡pare!" the man shouted, aiming his rifle at Rock's head.

Rock shot the man a nasty look. "I have the key to the trunk, so if you want it opened put down the damn gun," he said.

The man narrowed his eyes, but lowered his weapon and motioned Rock toward the car's trunk. Rock took the key from his pocket and popped open the trunk. It appeared empty, except for a car jack, a tire iron, and a case of Negra Modelos.

"Where is the money?" the man asked.

Rock slid the case of beer to the side and lifted the floor mat.

"Lentemente," the man said: Slowly.

Rock raised the mat revealing a locked, aluminum briefcase.

"Abrelo." Open it.'

Turning the tumbler and dialing in the combination, Rock paused before pressing the button. The lock snapped open and Rock lifted the case's cover, revealing neatly stacked bundles of fifty-dollar bills. He shut the case and pushed the lock closed without reengaging the tumbler. He slid the case back into the trunk.

The younger gunman radioed ahead to inform Castillo that Carlotti was on his way. The men allowed them back in the car and to proceed down the road toward the farmhouse.

The dilapidated house sat in disrepair, its cracked wood peeking out from beneath peeling, old paint. A thick layer of brownish-green moss covered the sagging roof, making the new, white Ford Expedition look out of place parked a few yards from the doorway. An imposing Colombian national stood outside the door with an M4 carbine in his hands, his feet spread apart, eyes hidden behind mirrored sunglasses.

The inside of the house resembled the outside, dusty and weathered with splintered and separated floorboards. Located six miles from the nearest town, the house had only one way in and one way out. Its isolation, along with its proximity to the natural lookout carved in the mountain ridge, rendered it the ideal place to make the exchange.

Two armed men were poised in opposite corners as Coroneos entered the room first. His gut felt like he'd eaten a handful of nails. He'd been careful to drink bottled water, but his intestines hadn't been quite right for the past few days. Not good timing.

The floorboards creaked under his feet as Coroneos stepped into the room. Andres Castillo took a slow draw on his cigar. A smug smile formed as he exhaled a thick cloud of smoke. Rock followed. "Welcome to Guatavita, Mr. Carlotti. Forgive me for the mess, the owners have been away for a while, such a shame."

"No apology needed," Rock replied.

Castillo reclined with his thin legs crossed and resting on a rickety, wooden table. His Lucchese alligator-skin cowboy boots clearly hadn't spent any time on a working ranch, and his slate gray suit and Stetson hat were the only things in the room not covered with dust. He looked younger than Coroneos expected, thirty-five at best, but his lack of years hadn't slowed his ruthless rise to power.

Castillo had taken control of the Moreno drug cartel when rival cartel members assassinated Carlos Moreno one year ago outside a nightclub in Solidad. Rock and Moreno had done business the previous two years, and as long as Rock delivered the cash, the drugs made their way to the States as per their agreement. A working relationship, however, didn't preclude the mutual understanding that things could turn ugly fast. Each man came with a healthy distrust of the other.

Rock and his men were sailing untested waters with Andres Castillo. The drug cartels were, by nature, nefarious. However, Castillo had earned a far more shameless and brutal reputation than his predecessor. As the now destroyed picture revealed, Castillo wasn't afraid to leave behind bodies or parts of bodies as reminders for those who might get in his way.

Coroneos glanced toward Scalise, standing near the door, his fingers rolling nervously. If the deal went south, his big friend wouldn't be much help without his Glock. Castillo motioned for Rock and Coroneos to take seats across the table. Scalise remained near the door. Rock placed the briefcase on the table, and the two took their positions.

"It's all there. You can count it if you'd like," Rock said.

Castillo pulled the briefcase closer, pressed the lock button, and opened the top. He lifted one bundle, flipped through the bills with his thumb, and placed them back in the case. "No need, Mr. Carlotti, we'll do the accounting later. The exchange will take place at the time and place we discussed and, if all goes as we planned, I'm confident this will be a mutually beneficial relationship."

Scalise took a step from the doorway. "How can we guarantee the quality of the product?"

Rock turned his head toward Scalise, his eyebrows furrowed. The muscles of his jaw quivered as he clenched his teeth.

Castillo remained silent and still, his eyes unblinking. A moment later, he stepped from the desk and eased toward Scalise. "Is this man saying he doesn't trust me?" He took another puff of his Cohiba, blowing a steady stream of smoke into Scalise's face. Scalise didn't budge. Castillo glanced at one of the armed men, who returned a slight nod.

Coroneos waited for Rock to speak out, but he didn't. Instead, he sat drumming his fingers on the dusty table.

"Estaban, this man doesn't trust me," Castillo said, looking toward his armed guard. "Maybe he should play the trust game."

The guard aimed the gun at Scalise and motioned for him to take a seat at the table.

"Mr. Carlotti, it's apparent that you don't have control over your men. They should speak only when spoken to. As you can see, my men treat me with honor." Castillos motioned with his right hand for the guard to continue moving Scalise to the table.

Rock raised his hands. "What is this, Castillo? We followed through on our part of the deal."

"I told you, Sir, this is about respect. No one questions my integrity, so when your friend dishonors me in front of my men, it demands a little re-education."

Scalise dug in his heels, refusing to move from the doorway. Crack! The guard fired a single round through the ceiling and rammed the gun's butt into Scalise's stomach. Scalise shuffled, bent at the waist, and took a seat next to Coroneos. Castillo grabbed Scalise by his left wrist and pushed his hand flat with his fingers splayed apart. He pulled the famed knife from its sheath and rested the blade on Scalise's middle finger, just above the last joint. Rock continued to hold a poker face. Scalise's usually narrow eyes shot wide open, and his barreled chest rose and fell with each panicked breath. Glistening drops of sweat formed on his forehead. He attempted to pull his hand away.

Castillo glared at him. "If you pull away again, you'll lose more than a finger, my friend."

"He gets the point," Coroneos said. "Can we move on?" He raged inside, as much toward Rock for his gutless lack of action as toward Castillo for his insanity.

Castillo turned back to his guard. "Esteban, what do you think? Should we move on?"

The burly guard shrugged. Castillo lifted the blade a couple millimeters from the skin. Scalise relaxed. In a flash, Castillo forced the razor-shaped edge through the finger. A sharp knock sounded as the blade severed the joint and hit the wooden table beneath.

Scalise screamed. He pulled his hand to his chest as a pulsating crimson flow saturated his shirt. His scream dwindled to a deep groan. The dusky, ashen fingertip lay on the table in a small pool of blood. It twitched twice then fell still.

"I trust we will not question each other's honor again," Castillo said as he put his knife back into its sheath, picked up the briefcase, and walked toward Rock. He extended his hand and Rock stood to return the handshake. Castillo and his men exited the house, climbed into their Expedition, and drove off disappearing in a cloud of dust.

Rock shot Scalise a scowl. "Who the hell told you to speak, you jackass? The man just walked with half a million dollars of my money, and if this deal doesn't happen, I'm holding you responsible."

Scalise, pale as a corpse, squeezed what remained of his finger. He didn't look up or say a word.

Coroneos shot Rock a scowl. "Tony, what the fuck? Mickey lost his damn finger!"

Already halfway to the door, Rock didn't respond. Coroneos lifted Scalise to his feet.

"My finger," Scalise said, staring at the lifeless piece of flesh lying in a pool of blood.

"Mickey, it's too damn hot. It wouldn't last the ride. Let it go."

Scalise's legs buckled slightly before he drew in a deep breath and seemed to regain his stability. He shook his head. "Get me the hell out of here!"

24

THAT SUMMER'S heatwave broke a thirty-year record, so the cool evening wind blowing through Nick's hair came as a welcome change. As he drove north on Route 33, with the top down from Buckingham toward the Poconos, he set the CD player to shuffle and cranked up the volume. The music of Led Zeppelin competed with the roar of the wind.

North of Saylorsburg, the road twisted and turned as it snaked its way through the mountains. Nick rounded a bend and it seemed he'd driven into a watercolor. A weathered Amish barn sat nestled in an ochre-colored wheat field, the farmland framed by a forest of green oaks, maples, and white pines. Mom would have loved this.

The pleasure of the drive soured as the lyrics of "In my time of dying" brought the thought of his mother's last moments roaring back.

Nick slammed his hand against the dash, shot a bitter look toward the sky, and yelled, "Where the hell were you? If you exist, where the hell were you?" He ripped the CD from the dash and threw it like a Frisbee. It caught the stream of air flowing over the windshield and disappeared from sight.

Sometimes it seemed so pointless; the waking up and going to bed, eating just to be hungry again, the good days, the bad days, and the so-so in-between days. All the while, creeping toward that inevitable end. Maybe it didn't really matter. Mom died at sixty, but ten thousand years from now would it matter if she'd had twenty more birthdays? Well, to him it did, for his remaining years, to have her in his life.

His head hurt, probably too much ruminating about things he couldn't change, or just as likely, the excess Scotch he'd downed since the accident. Thankfully, the white noise of the rushing wind, the tire's steady hum, and the occasional semi he left in his wake created a reasonable distraction. An hour and a half later, he pulled up to the security gate and punched in the code. The large iron gate swung open.

The house, like everything his father owned, reeked of vanity, gaudy and excessive. Roman statues and a massive marble fountain decorated the front lawn, not a blade of grass out of place. Liza would have been content with a simple log home but, to her, those battles were superficial and not worth the time. Rock gave her space to make her own, and that seemed enough.

As Nick passed through the doorway, the sweet, aromatic scent of lavender set him at ease. His mother and Maria had made potpourri from scratch. Surprisingly, the fragrance hadn't faded.

He climbed the stairs to the third-story loft and straight past the cedar chest positioned at the foot of a spare bed. That war would have to wait.

A wrought-iron spiral staircase led to a small octagonal observatory overlooking Lake Naomi. The observatory housed an old mariner's telescope made of cherry and brass. They'd relegated the once vital piece of equipment from a ship long since retired to maritime decor and amusement, receiving an occasional curious peek from visitors and guests.

Nick put his eye to the lens. The view across the lake could just as well have been of Lake Tahoe. The houses expansive, landscaping immaculate, and top-of-the-line boats tied at each dock. Through one giant bay window, Nick caught a glimpse of the flat-screen TV. Curt Schilling delivered a fastball to the Marlins Bobby Bonilla, but as Nick strained harder to see, he remembered why he'd made the trip.

Back down the spiral staircase he went. His foot hit the last step. He froze. The wooden beast seemed alive, not merely existing but gawking at him, laughing; a sinister snicker, reeking of evil. Somehow, the antique chest made of narrow strips of dry cedar bound together with tarnished bronze metal straps, had power over him. It always had. He hated that damn box. He could never put his hand on why, but he felt it.

After Nick's mother died, Rock had moved the cedar chest along with most of Liza's possessions from the house in Bucks County. There were a few things he wanted to keep for sentimental reasons, but the cedar chest certainly wasn't one of them. Rock said he didn't want the persistent reminder at the house but he couldn't stand to part with it either. Off it went to the Poconos while her clothes went to charity.

Despite the bottomless pit in his stomach, Nick knelt before the chest and lifted the top. The pungent odor of mothballs caught him by surprise and he backed away to let the fumes dissipate for a minute. He peeked inside.

Once brilliant white, now yellowed with age, his mother's wedding dress lay folded neatly at the top. He recalled his mother's desire to pass the dress down to a daughter, but after two boys, Rock didn't want any more children. So, there it remained without a future bride, banished to the box. Nick empathized with its plight, especially given the added misery of the mothballs, so he lifted it out and momentarily set it free.

Under the dress lay a small Italian music box crafted of burl elm with a rosewood top, inlaid with a flying dove made from green abalone shell. Nick tried the lid, but it didn't budge. He flipped over the box, looking for the key he thought he remembered being taped to the bottom, but only residue from tape remained.

He set aside the music box and pulled out a small hardcover book and an old leather Bible that once commanded a permanent spot on his mother's nightstand. She'd received the Bible as a gift from Maria, who'd tirelessly served as their maid and gardener since Nick had started the first grade. Nick had picked it up a couple times as a teenager. Gibberish. What in the world did his mother glean from this ancient book?

Many years prior, Maria had befriended a young Protestant missionary who came yearly to her hometown of Nuevo Laredo, Mexico. In return, Maria visited the woman's church in Laredo, Texas each time she crossed the border on her way to Pennsylvania. The woman gave Maria the Bible and she, in turn, passed it on to Liza.

After Liza died, Maria couldn't stand being around the house. Even though she could do the work of a forty-year-old, she retired and moved back to Nuevo Laredo to live with her daughter and son-in-law. The only thing she took with her, aside from her clothes, was a silver locket with an ichthus symbol Liza had given her for her seventy-seventh birthday. Nick hadn't heard from her since.

Nick opened the Bible's front cover and found a note from Maria:

A mi amiga íntima Liza Ann,
Vive devote a Cristo y Él será tu protección.
Con amor, Maria.

To my dear friend Liza Ann,
Live devoted to Christ, and He will be your shield.
With love, Maria

APPARENTLY, Maria was mistaken. His mother had devoted her life to him, but Jesus wasn't her shield, at least not at the moment her car slammed into the concrete median. Yet, during her life, religion had provided his mother with comfort, so he let it go at that.

Nick set the Bible on the floor along with the music box and the book. He turned back to the cedar chest. A brown leather journal he hadn't recalled seeing before caught his attention.

"I'm sorry, Mom. I hope you don't mind," he said, flipping to a random page. As he read, he tightened his grip. His mother's pain seemed to pour from the page. In an entry dated March 14, 1996, he felt her pain.

They say ignorance is bliss, and how I wish I were ignorant of this; the disgusting noises coming from the bedroom upstairs, my bedroom. The image of her face, the way they stared at me. They ripped the heart from my chest today. I didn't expect to find them there in our bed! Lord, you command me to love my enemies, yet I despise them both. Once again, power and pride have trumped love.
I believe it's right what the Apostle Paul said in his letter to the church at Ephesus. My battle isn't against flesh and blood but against evil in the heavenly realms. But, it often plays out right here on earth. Even right here in this house.

SEVERAL PAGES later she'd penned an entry dated April 23, 1996. It contained only a reference to a Bible passage: Psalm 140:5.

Nick set the journal next to the Bible and eyed the empty cedar chest. He placed the wedding dress and hardcover book back into the chest. Grabbing the Bible, the journal, and the music box, he headed downstairs. Psalm 140:5. He brushed it aside and continued down the steps, but before he reached the bottom, it rang so loudly, he had to know. The verse read:

> *"Proud men have hidden a snare for me; they have spread out the cords of their net and have set a trap for me along my path."*

ALONGSIDE IT, she'd penciled a notation.

> *Psalm 22:11 "Do not be far from me, for trouble is near and there is no one to help."*

IN THE MARGIN to the right of the verse was the date, *12/21/96*, just two months before his mother's death.

An image flashed in his head of her mangled car, the blood, and the contents of her purse strewn across the expressway. The Bible slipped from his hand and tumbled to the landing. He stood there, frozen until his mind cleared.

When he reached the landing, he paused for a moment before picking up the open Bible.

Exhausted, he collapsed on the couch and slipped into a coma-like sleep. His eyes sprung open. The darkness of night still remained except for the clock's faint red glow. 2:47 am. He pulled a wool blanket over himself, closed his eyes, and surrendered again to the fatigue.

Sunlight shone through the window at 6:55 am and Nick peeled himself off the couch. Why would someone kill his mother? It didn't make sense. Clearly, she'd feared for her life and didn't know where to turn for help, except this to God of hers, who, if he existed, was unable or unwilling to come to her rescue.

The ride back to Philly was a blur.

When Nick entered his townhouse, Rhino danced around him in tight circles, his tail wagging like a metronome on speed. Nick reached for the leash, hanging on a hook inside the foyer. He set the music box, the Bible, and the journal on the coffee table. Then Rhino pulled him out the door. The walk lasted long enough for Rhino to do his business but not long enough to investigate the local telephone poles and fire hydrants. Not tonight, Pal.

He could have stood there all day, the hot water soothing his exhausted body, the monotoned drone of the shower's rain quieting his mind. Unfortunately, rounds started in forty minutes.

Nick wrapped a towel around his waist and walked into the living room. He glanced up at the football on the armoire, and this time it seemed okay. It was a different season then, a good season, but eventually you had to part with fading glory. He lifted the ball from the armoire and replaced it with the music box. The football found a new, more humble home on the shelf inside his closet.

After a quick trip to the hospital to make rounds, he spent the afternoon at home poring through the journal. Liza wrote with passion and transparency, her aching heart filleted before Nick's eyes. Her poetic words revealed loneliness and heartbreak but also joy and pride in her boys. She seemed to be sailing her ship in a sea of spiraling emotions.

Nick smiled when he read her entry from the day he graduated from medical school.

Dr. Nicholas Joseph Carlotti, MD. I love the sound of that. He earned it. What a proud mother I am today!

BUT MANY ENTRIES confirmed her desperation. The words bled from the soul of a woman who yearned for love, but found it only in her God and an elderly Mexican woman.

THE NEXT TWO entries from September read:

> *8th: Isaiah 21:2 A dire vision has been shown to me: The traitor betrays, the looter takes loots.   9th: Matthew 26 Spent time with Rebecca today.*

NICK RAN his fingers through his hair, stopping at the top of his head. He let out a sigh. The first entry seemed both cryptic and unnerving and the second utterly mundane. Admittedly, he didn't have a great handle on the Bible, but dire visions, betrayals, and looting didn't sound good. Nick hadn't heard his mother mention a Rebecca, but then again, he hadn't spent much time with his mother the past couple of of years. She'd called him not three weeks before her death, asking him to come for a home-cooked dinner, and he'd made some lame excuse to avoid seeing his father.

"Damnit!" Nick shouted. "I'm sorry your son was such a selfish shit." His mother gave so much, and he returned so little.

Nick wanted a fresh set of eyes to see the big picture, maybe someone who could view it from a different angle, someone whom he could trust to be discrete. A little Bible knowledge wouldn't hurt. Thankfully, Steve fit the bill.

Besides being loyal and steadfast, Steve was both a Christian and a brainiac. A quick phone call secured a meeting the next morning at The Grind, an eclectic coffee shop close to the hospital. Nick said he needed a little unbiased perspective about something odd. If he'd lost his mind, Steve would let him know. He had a way of calling Nick out without pissing him off. It was a unique gift.

He took one last look at the music box atop the armoire before heading to bed. It wasn't the most masculine of centerpieces, but Liza had left part of herself there in its red velvet-lined compartments and its timeless melody. It seemed well worth giving up a little testosterone. He recalled the song it played as his mother lifted the top and how the ballerina spun, her ceramic hands held gracefully over her head.

He loved the bedtime game he played with his mother. He'd put on his pajamas, run into her room, and open the music box. As the music played, his mother would sing: You are my sunshine, my only sunshine, you make me happy when skies are gray. You'll never know how much I love you. Please don't take my sunshine away.

The idiom, 'You never know how much you'll miss someone until they're gone' seemed spot on.

He'd draped her rosary beads from the mirror of his dresser, keeping her the last thought on his mind before closing his eyes each night. Maybe he was a glutton for punishment or perhaps just consumed with finding her killer. Either way, he just plain missed his mother.

25

A STEADY DRIZZLE of rain fell over the city, one of those gray days, a wishing-you-were-in-bed-with-a-good-book day. Nick's light sweater provided little resistance to the brisk breeze. He held the books close to his chest, protecting them from the rain as he hurried from the car to the café.

An embracing warmth from the fieldstone fireplace met him as he stepped through the door. The faded barn-wood walls and plush, cozy sofas and chairs made it feel mountainesque. It served as Nick's go-to place when he needed an hour to escape without the aid of alcohol.

The barista had his skim latte ready by the time he reached the counter. "Thanks, Char," he said.

She answered him with a warm smile.

He chose a secluded space away from the crowd and set the Bible and journal on the table. Halfway finished with his latte, it hit him. Run! Forget the whole damn thing and for god's sake, do not share this nonsense with anyone else. As he reached for the books, the café door opened and Steve's entrance subverted any plans of escape.

They made eye contact as Steve motioned toward the

counter, raising his hand in a faux sip of coffee. Nick nodded, glad for the extra couple minutes he had to think of what he wanted to say.

Steve took a seat across the table and set down his coffee mug. "Unbiased perspective on something odd. You have my attention," Steve said.

"I'll cut to the chase. My mother was murdered."

Steve froze. His eyes were fixed open and his jaw dropped. "I thought you said something odd. That isn't odd. It's horrendous."

Nick slid the note across the table. "Before Danny Torello died, he gave me this. I don't know how he knew my mother, but it makes my father suspect."

Steve glanced at the note, then back at Nick. "Are you saying that your father had your mother killed?"

"I don't know what to think, but if Torello had information about my mother's death, and, if my father ordered the hit on Torello, then one plus one equals two. Doesn't it?"

"Well, the math is correct, but why?"

"Not sure, but there's more. Friday night I went to the lake house and looked through my mother's old cedar chest. I found her Bible and her journal. There were a few disturbing entries in the journal, references to Bible verses." Nick opened the journal and handed the Bible to Steve. "Psalm 140:5."

Steve turned to the verse and read it aloud: "Proud men have hidden a snare for me; they have spread out the cords of their net and have set a trap for me along my path. Not a verse I'd expect as a journal entry, but certainly not proof of murder."

"She was afraid of someone, my father, I think. From what I could tell from her words, he cheated on her."

"Okay, even if that were true, wouldn't divorce have been a more rational move? But, then again, it wouldn't be the first time that a love triangle ended in murder."

"My father's estate is worth millions and divorce can be a

costly gig for a man with much to lose," Nick said. "Read the next verse. Psalm 22:11."

Steve read the verse and asked to see the journal. He flipped through the pages, his eyes zipping back and forth as he read. "Who is Rebecca?"

"I'm not sure. Mom never spoke of her."

Steve continued skimming. "I'm not noticing any other mention of Rebecca or any such trite entries. No 'lunch with Betty' or 'went to the gym with Karen.' Know what I mean? Her entries were emotionally deep and never insignificant. I find it a little unusual that she'd find it essential to journal that she'd spent time with this Rebecca."

"The verses from the Psalms caught me off guard. I didn't think about that, but I agree."

Steve closed the journal and lifted the coffee cup to his mouth. His face scrunched as if he'd eaten a bug. "Blah, not a fan of lukewarm. Ever notice they sell hot coffee and iced coffee but never lukewarm . . . "

"Focus," Nick said, reaching across and tapping his finger on the table in front of Steve.

Steve set down his mug. "Sorry. Have you read Matthew 26?"

"No, I hoped you knew it by heart and could save me some time."

"Sorry to disappoint you but I can't quote it exactly. It's mostly about betrayal. First, Judas betrayed Jesus for thirty pieces of silver and did so with a kiss on the cheek. Second was Peter's betrayal or, should I say, his denial of Jesus."

"I'm impressed," Nick said.

"Don't be. It's sort of an obsession," Steve said. "Do you think she was alluding to your father's apparent unfaithfulness?"

Nick opened the Bible to Matthew 26 and read to himself for a few minutes. "I don't think it's the same thing. I mean, these aren't romantic betrayals." Nick took a sip of his now room temperature latte and immediately set his cup to the side. "What do you think she meant?"

"I'm not sure."

"Not the answer I'd hoped for."

Steve picked up the journal and flipped back and forth between the last two entries, pausing at each one. "You need to find Rebecca. Maybe she knows something."

Nick frowned. "I wouldn't know where to begin to find her. I certainly don't want to ask my father questions. A last name would be helpful."

"Where did you say you found the Bible and the journal?"

"In her cedar chest. Why?" Steve tipped his head. "Hmm."

"Where are you going with this?"

"What else did you find in there?"

"Her wedding dress, a music box, the Bible, her journal, and some random novel."

Steve peeked over the top of his glasses. "Some random novel? Everything in that box seemed important or deeply senti-mental. I doubt it was random." He slid the journal back toward Nick and leaned back, clasped his hands behind his head, and puffed up his chest with a deep audible breath through his nose.

"Great, now I have to go back for the book."

"Uh, yeah— but."

"But what?"

Steve shrugged. "I know you're Rock Carlotti's son and all, but please be careful. If you're right and he is somehow involved, he isn't afraid to kill a member of his own family. And now that I said that, I'm getting a little freaked out myself."

"I shouldn't have gotten you mixed up in this, even this much, especially if my father is the one who did this, but you're my best friend, and I had to know if I was crazy." Nick picked up the books and put them under his arm.

"I don't think you're crazy. A little passionate at times but definitely not crazy. As for me, I guess I'm already vested, but if you don't mind, we'll keep my involvement covert."

"Deal. Thanks for the help. I knew your inner nerd would come through."

"Nice, I love you too," Steve said. "I'll be praying for you, seriously, I mean that."

"I know you do. Not sure it'll help, but it can't hurt."

As Nick stood to leave, Steve stopped him. "Hey, I didn't ask what you found in the music box."

"It was locked and I couldn't find the key. I considered prying it open, but I'd hate to ruin it."

"Just curious," Steve said. "I would do the same if it were my mother's."

Nick nodded. "I'll see what I can find out about Rebecca and catch up with you later." He left, not all that excited about another trip to the Poconos, but patience wasn't one of his stronger suits. With the keys in his pocket and the day still young, he'd already made his decision.

26

THE MONOTONOUS RUMBLE of the tires down the rough dirt road broke up the excruciating silence. Rock stirred in the front seat, his face beet-red and the flexed muscles of his jaw twitching. He looked like he would explode.

Slouched against the car door, Scalise clenched his tip-less finger in the bloodied end of his shirttail. Streams of sweat poured down his face. Mickey was one of the toughest men Coroneos knew, but this seemed to have brought him to his knees.

Envisioning reaching over the seat and slipping a piano wire around his old friend's neck, Coroneos fought to keep his breathing slow, deep, and rhythmic. Karma, he said to himself. Karma.

With the city skyline in view, Coroneos instructed the driver to drop Scalise and him off at the University Hospital of San Ignacio. A baby-faced male doctor looking way too young to be a physician stepped into the cramped ER cubical.

"¿Que´paso'?"

"Doesn't anyone in this fucking country speak English?" Scalise snapped.

The doctor smiled. "I won't take that personally since you're probably in pain. For the record, I trained at UC Davis, and I think my English is actually quite good." He paused and lifted Scalise's hand. "So, what happened to your finger?"

Scalise looked at the ground and didn't answer.

"Cooking accident," Coroneos said. "Cutting meat."

After a quick exam, the doctor cleaned up the wound, trimmed back the bone of Scalise's finger with an instrument that looked like needle-nosed pliers, and stitched the skin closed. Scalise handled it well thanks to an injection of local anesthetic and the half-pint of sixty-proof Aguardiente he'd downed during the trip.

Coroneos left Scalise at the hotel and took a fifteen-minute cab-ride to La Ladera, a quaint and romantic cottage perched atop a steep hillside on the outskirts of the city. From the stone terrace, he gazed over the valley below and the fertile, green hills beyond. He'd tried to ignore his excited anticipation for this part of the week, but aside from the drama at Lake Guatavita, it was all he could think about.

He missed her, the way she wrapped her slender body around his the second he walked into the room, the sparkle of her piercing coffee-brown eyes, the softness of her delicate lips on his. He remembered the first time they met in a swank club in the Zona Rosa and how he didn't want to leave the cottage the next morning. It was the first time he'd cheated on his wife.

Coroneos owned strip clubs. Beautiful women surrounded him, but he'd never strayed. He loved Sarah, but they hadn't been close for years. He knew she wasn't to blame. She gave him her attention as best she could, but given Sam's constant needs, at the end of the day, she didn't have much left. Three and a half decades of marriage and the inevitable backlash that the brutal coldness his career choice demanded had put the final nails in the coffin.

With the traffic noise and the congestion of the city replaced by a gentle evening breeze, Coroneos ran his fingers through his thick black hair and straightened his shirt collar. He looked up toward the second-floor room. Soft amber light illuminated the shades. She'd gotten there first, flown to Colombia just to relive their first encounter three years prior. She loved him, and he knew it, but his was an obsession, an unrelenting desire to steal her away to someplace where his past would be unable to pull them apart.

How could a man so in control of every aspect of his life, a man with the chilling ability to inflict pain on others and then sit for dinner without a second thought, feel his heart wanting to jump out of his chest? He'd moved her to the States more than a year ago. They spoke by phone every day, and he snuck away as often as possible to be with her. Yet, this planned rendezvous, at the same place where he'd left her crying on the same veranda the morning after they met, felt like the first time.

She aroused in him feelings no one had ever evoked before. Her beauty caught his eye, but her fiery passion won his heart; physical attraction, yes, but something so much deeper, more soulful.

He took his time climbing the brick steps, forcing himself to maintain some semblance of composure. He paused at the door. The faint rich fragrance of cacay wood burning in the fireplace spawned an instant and arousing déjà vu. They'd made love on the sheepskin rug in front of the fireplace, and each time he dreamt of that moment, the enchanting scent of the fire seemed to surround him.

He knocked twice. The door opened and she flew into his arms, her lips locked onto his, and he melted. Three nights wouldn't be enough.

~

"MR. CORONEOS," the manager of the Orchid said, as Coroneos stepped through the hotel door on Tuesday morning.

"Yes?" Coroneos said.

The man reached out with a yellow postcard in his hand. "Sir, your wife called last night at 2 am. We rang your room, but you didn't answer."

Coroneos took the card.

Urgent: Please call asap, Sarah.

SARAH KNEW BETTER than to bother him when he was on business. Coroneos hurried to his room. He hesitated before he dialed. He wasn't sure he wanted to know. He'd dreaded the day he'd receive the call. Aside from his brewing romance, the only person he really loved couldn't even understand the word. An anxious wave swept over him. Maybe it wasn't that at all. Relax. The phone rang.

"Oh, Peter . . . " Her voice cracked.

"Is it Sam?" He knew the answer by the despair in her voice. "Sarah?"

"He woke me up in the middle of the night. He looked so afraid, Peter. He. . . " Her voice fell silent for a moment. "He couldn't catch his breath."

"Where are you?" Coroneos asked.

"In the ICU. They had to put in a breathing tube." She sobbed.

God, why now? "He's going to be okay, right?"

"The doctor said Sam's heart is failing, and he has fluid in his lungs. They're trying to get the fluid out, but his kidneys aren't doing well."

The image of his boy with tubes and wires sticking out of his body turned Coroneos' stomach. Sam wouldn't understand. He couldn't. Sam was as pure a human being as Coroneos knew. "Damn it, Sarah! You tell them to do whatever they can."

Sarah coughed to clear her throat. "When will you be home?"

"We're supposed to leave first thing tomorrow morning, but I'll fly stand-by today. I'll get there as soon as I can. Tell Sam I love him."

27

HE COULDN'T SHAKE IT, sort of an eerie chill. What the hell was it? It didn't matter really because as far as he was concerned, this was the last time he'd have to look upon the hideous box.

Lying on the wedding dress, just as he'd left it, the cover facing up, its title stared him in the face — Rebecca's Box, a novella written by a woman named Laura Carson. Nick shook his head and sighed. Rebecca wasn't a real person, just a character in a novel. It better be a damn good book.

He thumbed through the pages. Not wanting to make a third trip to the Poconos, he'd take the book home. Maybe she found some deeper meaning in it, or it gave her inspiration. If it had been influential to her, the book might have something for him too. If not, a couple shots of tequila would.

"Well, I killed two birds with one stone," Nick told Steve over the phone. "Got the book and found Rebecca at the same time."

"You contacted her?"

"You could say that. She's coming home with me."

"What are you talking about?"

Nick laughed. "She's a book. The book's title, it's Rebecca's Box. My mother had lunch with a novel."

"So, you think your mother kicked back reading this book and found it so inspiring she needed to journal the moment? I could see maybe if she'd referenced it earlier or, like the Bible verses, recorded a quote, but this seemed out of the blue. She also didn't say that she spent the day with Rebecca's Box, just Rebecca."

"Okay, Sherlock, you can look at it yourself. I'll drop it off when I'm back in town."

"Why don't you bring it to the hospital in the morning?"

"I don't read mysteries because I don't have the patience. I skip to the end to see who done it. If there's something in this, I'd like to know."

"Fair enough," Steve said. "See you in a bit. Oh, and bring me the Bible and journal as well. I don't want to pry into your mother's personal life, but they might be useful."

"I'll swing by the house and grab them. Keep this stuff to yourself, okay?"

"Trust me, I'm already peering around corners. Don't take this the wrong way, but I wish you were a third-generation Fitzpatrick from Iowa."

"Me too, "Nick said. "Me too."

28

Nick stood in Steve's doorway, books in hand. "Just a little light reading for your Sunday night."

"You don't want to come in?"

"No, I have to get back to the hospital to do a case they bumped for a dissecting aortic aneurysm." Steve took the books. "What's the case?"

"Twelve-year-old kid with osteosarcoma of his tibia. Ortho asked me to do a free flap to repair their resection."

"That's unfortunate," Steve said.

"It's probably not the time for a philosophical or theological debate, but for the record, I think that if God exists, you're right, it's quite unfortunate, putting a kid and his family through this crap."

Steve bit his cheek and nodded. "Maybe right now's not the time but it's also not a discussion that I'm going to pass on indefinitely. Remember, you're the one who opened the door."

"Don't suppose I can close it again?"

Steve smiled. "Nope."

"Didn't think so. Thanks again for looking through this stuff. I'm too emotionally tied to it to be objective," Nick said.

"No worries, I'm glad to help. Besides, everyone knows I'm smarter than you."

"And they'd be right. They're the same ones who know I'm better looking."

"Touché. I'll let you know if I find anything."

∼

STEVE CALLED Nick Monday morning and gave him an abbreviated version of the novella and his conclusions.

"I have to say that the story's a little eerie, especially given that it ends in Rebecca's murder. Rebecca finds this mysterious box about the size of a Rubik's cube in her grandmother's attic. The dark, lacquer box is completely closed without any seams, like someone carved it from a single piece of wood. A small hole in one side is covered by a thin gold button that can be swung aside, revealing a hole emanating a dim light. Looking into the hole, she sees events play like movie clips and the first one reveals a murder that actually transpires days later. She knows the identity of the murderer, having seen his face in the box. She's eventually killed because of her knowledge."

"I'd say, a little more than eerie," Nick said.

"Is it possible that your mother had information she didn't necessarily want, information that would be dangerous for her to have?"

"Not that I know of, but she may have stumbled upon something."

"The maid — Maria? Right?" Steve asked.

"Yeah." "Do you think your mother would have confided in her?"

"Maybe, but she might not have wanted to involve Maria if she thought it would endanger her life."

"Where is she now?" "Mexico, I think. She had no reason to stay after my mom died."

"If they were as close as I think they were, she might know something. Even if it seems insignificant, it's more than we have now."

Nick hadn't seen Maria since the funeral. She hadn't left contact information nor kept in touch. It surprised him, given she helped raise him. Maria shut down when Liza died, then just disappeared. He needed to find her.

Steve asked to keep the journal and Rebecca's Box. "I also want to do a little more research into Laura Carson."

Nick sat up in the booth. "How is that important?"

"Maybe not at all, but if your mother sought to find spiritual meaning in a book, I'd expect Thoreau or C.S. Lewis. Oh, yeah, I'll give you back her Bible tomorrow. You could use it."

"What the hell is that supposed to mean?"

"What?"

"That I could use my mother's Bible."

"It's just that I think you could use a little rest for your soul, and the Bible might help."

"I could use a little rest, period."

"By the way, how did your case go?" Steve asked.

"Tedious. The damn tumor wrapped itself around the boy's anterior tibial artery. I had a hell of a time finding an adequate feeder. The flap is a little dusky looking, but I think it'll survive."

"Sorry, brother. Let's catch up tomorrow."

Exhausted, Nick's body wrestled with his mind for control, for the right to sleep versus the demand for truth. His weary body proved no match for his brain as the latter raced from one thought to the next, from the crash to the funeral, from Torello's note to verses of scripture.

He forced him off the couch and into the shower, turning the hot water handle counterclockwise until ice-cold water rained down, jolting him out of his stupor. He stayed there for half a minute. When his body cried 'Uncle,' he shut off the flow, took a deep breath, and readied himself for a trip to his father's house.

29

THE EXISTENCE of records was one thing, but getting his hands on them was another. Maria had worked for the family for many years and Nick was certain his mother had maintained files of her employment: payroll, contact information, and maybe phone bills with calls Maria made to her family in Nuevo Laredo.

Coroneos handled the finances for Rock's Colombian emerald-importing business and all other connected streams of revenue. He also made sure Liza's financial activities lent legitimacy to the home's banking records. Liza wrote checks for all the standard household bills out of her personal account— phone, utilities, dry cleaning, and any domestic help including Maria. Coroneos intentionally wanted the household bills open and obtainable because they were licit. Nick banked on it.

With Coroneos, Rock, and Scalise in Colombia until Wednesday night and Jen in Jersey at her sister's, Nick decided to "take a little swim" at the house. He had, after all, been given an open invite for the week. If someone were at the house, Nick would just use the pool and hit the road. No harm no foul.

His mind drifted to the accident scene and weighed the possibility that his father was somehow responsible. Rock was a brazen criminal and, based on Liza's journal, a cheater. But, none of those things made him culpable in the murder of his wife. What could motivate him to take action so drastic and irreversible? Was he afraid of losing half of everything in a divorce? Maybe, but it seemed crazy. Liza wasn't the type who would have retained lawyers and investigators to track down his hidden wealth anyway. She couldn't have cared less about his money, and Rock knew that. And, from all Nick had seen growing up, Rock loved his wife in his own shallow way.

Nick drove around the circular drive to the house. From the roof, security cameras at each corner kept watch. Undoubtedly, his vehicle would catch the attention of security, but Jennifer could corroborate the invitation. It wasn't like he hadn't lived there before or that he wasn't Rock's son, but he didn't make a habit of coming to the house outside of holidays and special occasions. Today's visit was out of character.

With the likelihood of company, Nick had prepared his lines in advance. He wanted to take a swim, do a little reminiscing. After all, he'd grown up running through these hallways and making bed-sheet tents in his bedroom on the third floor. At least for the time being, his monolog wouldn't be necessary.

With a small navy-blue duffel bag in hand, Nick stepped into the expansive foyer. Empty. His father rarely left it unguarded, but so far, so good.

First stop— his mother's sitting room, as she called it. The smallest of fourteen rooms in the expansive house, it provided her only truly private space. Rock respected that fact, and as far as Liza knew he never set foot inside. When the boys were little, Liza allowed them in, more out of convenience. At least she knew where they were. When they were old enough to be a distraction, out they went for Maria to handle for a couple hours.

A comfortable wooden rocking chair, a modest desk, and a set of drawers were all that decorated the space. Aside from Lake

Naomi, she did her best writing at that desk, but it was also where Nick remembered her making out checks.

Surprisingly, the room looked just as it had before she died. The furniture, the lamps, and even an Amish quilt Liza bought in Lancaster remained as she had left them. Rock hadn't purged the room after the funeral. It seemed the opposite, more like a memorial. Maybe Rock grieved after all.

Nick searched and found the drawers empty. But, given the mob's need for a guise of legitimacy, Nick didn't think that Rock would have destroyed financial records. Nick decided to investigate his father's personal office, a gamble he wouldn't have taken if the stakes weren't so high.

Rock left the door unlocked. Despite his being a powerful mob boss, a man with a laundry list of potential criminal offenses, he rarely locked his office. It was like the piece of cheese on a rat trap, out in the open, begging to be taken, but woe to him who did.

No one violated Rock's personal space. Liza, and now Jennifer, knew and respected the unspoken rule, more out of fear than respect. As children, Nick and Eddie wandered into the office a couple times but learned unequivocally that it wasn't a wise endeavor.

Rock treated the office as much as a museum as a place of business, at least on the surface. He showed off his keepsakes from time to time, but otherwise, it was off-limits.

Nick gazed at the far wall adorned with photos of his father hobnobbing with celebrities, heads of state, and wealthy businessmen from around the country. He paused at the picture of Rock in a boxing pose with Sylvester Stallone, taken at the top of the art museum steps. It hung next to one of him shaking hands with Bill Clinton at a Democratic fundraiser.

In one corner, a glass case housed a Swarovski crystal eagle with inset emerald eyes and a blue sapphire head. Rock had received the eagle from the ICA (International Colored

Gemstone Association) for his work in facilitating emerald exports from Colombia and for his contributions to the prestigious organization. The crystal eagle's gaze seemed to follow Nick as he stepped toward one of two black metal filing cabinets that sandwiched an oversized walnut desk at the center of the room.

The center drawer below the desktop held a small-caliber handgun, a Nazi marked Browning high-power 9mm pistol that Rock's father had peeled from the hand of a dead German officer in Duisburg at the end of the Second World War. It symbolized Rock's resentment of the Jews who owned the majority of the jewelry and precious-stone business in Philadelphia and New York. It had been in that drawer for as long as Nick could remember.

Nick turned to the left set of drawers. He pulled on the first of the three and found it locked, as were the next two in line. He tried again with the right-side cabinet drawers, and the top two opened easily.

Shuffling through the few files in the top drawer, he found nothing of interest. In the second drawer, he noticed two unmarked folders, one with a few un-cashed checks, the other with various news clippings. The remainder of the files contained old household bills. Nick lifted out a folder labeled ATT. The date of the first bill was August 1996. He looked through the long-distance calls. Two calls had been made to Rome and London, likely his mother contacting artists or museum curators, but nothing to Mexico. He moved onto the next. Like the first, there were no calls to Mexico.

As he scanned the pages of the third bill, the front door of the house closed with a thud, and a familiar male voice echoed from the entryway. "Hello! Jennifer . . . you here?"

Nick grabbed the next few phone bills and the two unmarked folders. He slid the drawer shut and snuck down the hallway into the bathroom, easing shut the door.

"Jennifer!" the voice rang out, louder this time.

Nick turned on the shower, wet his hair, and opened the door a bit. "Eddie, it's me! Just getting dressed up here."

"Well, well . . . if it ain't my little brother, Nico."

"I took a quick swim and wanted to rinse off. I'll be down in a sec," Nick said as he leaned with both hands on the counter. He took a couple deep breaths and looked in the mirror. His breathing slowed.

"Glad you answered because I was ready to take you out! Get your butt down here when you're finished."

He messed up his hair, unfastened the top four buttons of his shirt, and took off his shoes. He pulled a black towel from the closet and shoved the folded bills and folders into his duffel. One more slow, deep breath and he headed down the stairs.

Eddie stood at the landing with a cocky smirk plastered on his face, gun in hand. "I thought that was your Boxster, but I haven't seen you in a while, so I wasn't sure. Have to say, you were ten seconds from a world of hurt," he said, slipping his handgun back in the holster in the small of his back.

"I think I'm always seconds from a world of hurt, so thanks for the confirmation," Nick said as he hit the last step. "The water felt great. Jen told me to help myself since she was heading to Jersey to see her sister."

"Not like you to pop by the house like this. A rich doctor like you can't afford a pool?"

"Not much room for a pool a block off of South Street."

Eddie's face hardened. "Not room in this house for a brother who leaves the family. You can't just come and go as you please."

"What's your problem? This is as much my home as yours." It wasn't a good time for a confrontation, but he couldn't let it go.

"Uh . . . Think again. You chose your own path, and the family wasn't it. You want a fucking swim, go to the Y!"

Before Nick had a chance to jump down his brother's throat, a second man walked into the room. Young, late twenties maybe, muscles well defined under his one-size-too-small white t-shirt.

"We got a problem here?" he asked, moving toward Nick.

"Stand down, Tommy. It's my kid brother, Doctor Nick Carlotti."

The man smirked. "Didn't know you had a brother," he said, extending his hand. "Just jokin'."

Nick shot Eddie a quick glare, ignored the man's handshake, and took a step toward the door. Eddie slid to his right, blocking Nick's path, grabbed the neatly folded black towel from under Nick's arm, and squeezed it a couple times. "Don't forget this, Bro," he said as he opened it and draped it over Nick's shoulder.

Clutching the towel in his hand, Nick side-stepped his brother and slipped past Tommy. He didn't look back as he hurried to the car.

Nice move, ace! He pulled the obviously unused towel from his shoulder and threw it on the passenger seat of the car. The engine roared as Nick pulled around his brother's cherry-red Hummer and out through the gate.

He glanced again at the dry towel and shook his head. Maybe Eddie hadn't connected the dots, but their previous conversation wasn't helpful to the situation. Eddie already knew Nick was playing detective.

But where were the two men earlier? Rock's entourage wasn't in the habit of letting their guard down. Maybe they were sitting in the control room watching the whole time. Couldn't undo it. Had to hope he hadn't raised any red flags, or in this case a black towel.

He spent about as much time looking in the review mirror as he did out the windshield. The whole thing was getting in his head. Dr. Makos might have to add paranoia to claustrophobia in his patient record. As far as he could tell, no one had followed him home.

With Rhino's bodily functions satisfied, Nick scoured the bills he'd managed to sneak out of the house. Nothing, not one single call to Mexico. "Shit!" he yelled, crumbling the final page. He shook his head and did his best to smooth out the paper, sticking it back in the folder on the kitchen table.

After wolfing down a cold slice of three-day-old pizza and a bottle of beer, he opened the remaining folders. One of the two contained a record of Maria's hours along with returned, cashed payroll checks. The other folder held receipts for payments Liza had received for published works, correspondence from publishers, and two letters from her literary agent, Harman Drake, a man Nick had met once during Liza's first book signing at a quaint but well-recognized bookstore in Heritage Hill.

He'd run out of ideas. Hopefully, Steve would have some revelation after reviewing *Rebecca's Box* and the journal.

Nick's nerves were shot, and good sleep had been eluding him for the past three nights. He settled at the kitchen table catatonic, staring into space. Rhino dropped a shaggy, saliva-saturated tennis ball on his lap. Nick picked up the wet ball with the tips of his thumb and index finger and threw it down the hall into the bedroom.

Rhino darted after it and flew back in six seconds flat. Two more round trips and Nick called it quits even though his roommate wasn't ready to do the same. Rhino dropped the ball first at his feet, then on his lap. When Nick let the ball fall to the floor, he gave up, carried the ball to the side of the couch, and sulked.

This precarious path he'd started down was no game, and if he made another stupid-ass mistake, he might end up with a bullet to the head. He buried his face in the palms of his hands. Rhino hopped onto Nick's lap and nuzzled his moist nose in Nick's left ear. Nick fought it for a moment, but he couldn't stop the smile. Dogs loved you no matter what.

30

WHEN THE REPORT of the missing girl reached Rawls' desk, he instantly recognized the striking lounge singer from Sergio's. It just happened to be the last night anyone had seen the girl alive.

Rawls ran his fingernail over the last fold of the mint-green paper airplane, the Raptor, one of his favorite designs. He spread it into its final form and gave it a gentle toss toward the square, wire-mesh wastebasket in the farthest corner of the room. It sailed halfway with an upward arc, tilted down, and glided straight in. Rawls grinned. An array of missed attempts lay scattered on the floor.

It seemed to many a strange hobby for a grown man of Rawls' stature, and in an office setting to boot. He'd brought the basket and a stack of special paper on his first day at the job. When asked why he couldn't use the paper from his printer, Rawls replied, "It's all about aerodynamics! Short wings-regular paper, longer wings-card stock."

He'd become a connoisseur of paper, and a student of flight since his older brother had Lester taught him how to make his first airplane the morning before his murder. Rawls would never forget climbing the back of the sofa, lifting open the window, and tossing out the plane just as the shot rang out. He wanted so badly to make his brother proud but instead watched him tumble down the porch steps with a bloody hole ripped through the back of his white t-shirt. The plane landed at the same time Lester hit the ground.

The morning ritual, one plane per day, wasn't superstition. Part of his brother came to life as the plane took flight. Whether they hit their target or not, it reminded him that even if his life wasn't perfect, if he failed in some way, he at least had taken the leap and caught a little air.

He brought the club's manager in for questioning later that afternoon.

The stocky, pale-faced man with spiked bleach-blond hair, thin black eyeliner, and small hoop earrings in both ears spoke in a high-pitched voice. "She sang at least once a week over the past few months. People loved her."

Rawls nodded. "And you had her scheduled to sing later in the month?"

"Actually, no, said she'd found another gig — wouldn't be back. She picked up her last paycheck before she left that night."

"Better pay?"

"Beats me," the manager said, flipping back a thin lock of hair that had fallen in front of his eyes.

"Anything else seem odd to you? Her behavior, her actions, anything?"

The manager placed his index finger to his cheek. "Hmm— she wasn't supposed to play that night. She had planned to play the Friday prior but switched with the band slated to play the evening you're talking about."

"Did she say why?"

"No." The manager leaned forward. "Not to be disrespectful, but I find it a bit disconcerting that she vanished in the middle of a venue full of cops and politicians."

"Your point?"

"It was the night of that big law-enforcement convention. This place had more guns and badges than a John Wayne festival."

Rawls didn't smile. "Thanks for your time. Just a heads up, you might have to testify in court."

"That would be radical!"

"Yeah, that's one way to put it," Rawls said, handing the man a business card. He gathered his things and left to meet Taylor at Anya's apartment.

The landlord had opened the girl's apartment door earlier that morning and found it wreaking of decomposing flesh. Without entering the apartment, he called the police, fearing she might be dead.

Rawls and Taylor approached the apartment as the landlord unlocked the door.

"There ya go," the man said, stepping away shaking his head. "Such a beautiful young lady."

Taylor knocked. No answer. He knocked again a little louder. Still no response.

"Police! Is anyone home?" he yelled, then turned the door-knob and eased open the door. The rancid odor hit them almost immediately. Taylor covered his nose and mouth with his bent arm. "Holy crap!" He did an immediate about-face.

The air conditioner had been off, and a recent stretch of days in the high nineties had made a bad situation worse. The men followed the scent of death to the kitchen. When Taylor opened the garbage, Rawls heaved a sigh of relief. An expired package of slimy, green chicken breast sat at the top of the nearly full bag of trash.

"Do something with that. Please!" Rawls said.

The landlord put the bag inside another, gave it a twist, and carried it out to the dumpster.

Rawls and Taylor searched the apartment. Rawls entered the bedroom first and noticed the bedsheets in complete disarray. "She's either a restless sleeper, a total slob, or she had company."

Women's clothing lay spread out next to the bed, and a burgundy and gold striped men's tie stuck out from under a multi-color sequin skirt. Taylor picked up the tie, and rubbed the silk between his thumb and fingers. "Not a tie you'd want to leave on the floor."

"Why's that?"

"It's a Charvet, French silk, probably a couple hundred bucks."

"How would you know? You haven't spent more than twenty-five dollars on a tie in your life."

"I had a salesman try to sell me one last year. Told him I had a closet full of Charvets and was just browsing," Taylor said. He placed the tie in an evidence bag. A glimmer caught his eye. The morning sunlight streaming through the bedroom window reflected off one of two empty wine glasses sitting on the dresser.

Slipping on a glove, Taylor picked up the glass by its stem and twirled it around.

Rawls stepped toward Taylor. "Well?"

"Perfect imprint of a lower lip. . . bright red lipstick. Looks like partial fingerprints on both glasses."

"Pack'em up for DNA and prints." Rawls drummed his fingers on the dresser. "Funny, no jewelry box. Clothes and shoes, but no jewelry."

Taylor squinted and shrugged. "What are you getting at?"

"Either someone lifted them, or she took them with her."

"No sign of a break-in or that anyone rifled through her stuff. I'm leaning toward the latter," Taylor said. "I'd really like to know who belongs to that tie."

After they completed their investigation, they questioned three of Anya's neighbors. All agreed that Anya was a pleasant girl who kept to herself, but an elderly woman in the adjacent apartment had a somewhat different perspective.

"I never noticed anyone else coming or going, but I'm pretty sure she had a lover," she said.

"What makes you think so?" Rawls asked.

"More than a few times, they woke me up in the middle of the night. She was into that loud sex. . . her telling him what she wanted and such. I assume it was a him, but you never know these days."

"You never know," Rawls said.

They stopped back at the rental office to ask the landlord a few more questions. Did he ever see her with anyone, male in particular? Why did he think she paid her rent in cash?

He had no idea why she paid her rent in cash and as to the company she kept, he made it clear that he had better things to do than keep tabs on the personal habits of his tenants. However, he did provide one more piece of information. Anya had paid extra for a covered parking space for her "hot" cherry red Audi Cabriolet convertible that fit her like a glove. Unfortunately, the landlord didn't require license-plate numbers from his tenants, so the information wasn't immediately helpful.

Rawls rehashed the night of the convention. One thing hit him as curious. Lloyd Mays stayed after he had left and seemed quite preoccupied with the woman. Rawls jotted a note to contact Senator Mays to see what he recalled from that night.

31

MAYS' head pounded. He strained his eyes to bring the blurry room into focus. Rolling to his left, he reached across his body, expecting to feel her body but instead, his hand found only empty sheets, wet, empty sheets. He blinked hard and rubbed his eyes, initially seeing a thick red haze, but soon the scene became clearer. Half-dried blood covered his hands and chest. His bedding was stained crimson red.

"Oh my god!" he cried, jumping naked from the bed. His clothes lay in a heap with hers on the floor next to the bed. A grisly trail of blood led up the stairs to the deck. "No! No! God, no!"

He grabbed his robe as he ran up the steps. The splatters of blood led to the harbor side of the deck. The last drop ended in a large pool at the railing, just to the bow's port side. Scanning the water, back and forth, up and down. Nothing. He glanced at his watch. 5:36 am, the scarlet sun just peeking above the horizon. Aside from the lonely cry of a seagull, the marina was quiet, the early morning's stillness leaving the water's surface like a mirror. It reflected Mays' ashen face back to him. He gazed into his own terror-stricken eyes, then dashed back to the bedroom.

He thought about calling the police but came to the realization that, although "you're innocent until proven guilty," he'd be the main suspect. In a frenzy, he threw the sheets, the clothes, and his blood-stained robe into garbage

bags. The blood had soaked through to the mattress. He racked his brain,
trying to figure out what to do next when his cell phone rang out.

The nightmares never varied, not just bad dreams conjured
up by an overactive imagination, but each an accurate replay of
the events that had occurred that night. He tried meditating,
drinking a glass of wine or three, and even downing ten
milligrams of Valium before bed, but the nightmares continued.

Tuesday morning, July 15, a month and a day after the girl
disappeared, Mays sat, slouched at the foot of his bed, not eager
to put on his game face yet one more time. He had no choice but
to carry on, to sit at his desk and put the final touches on his
portion of the bill. He planned to introduce legislation on the
Senate floor that afternoon. Mays wished his life were as dull and
mundane as the document he had prepared. It was going to be a
bumpy ride.

Later, Mays froze at his office desk, his eyes fixed on the
article in the Inquirer's Local Section, page two. His stomach
sank. It wasn't yet headline news, but it wasn't supposed to be
news at all, the missing lounge singer with only the first name
Anya.

Mays had done his best to make sure the story didn't leak.
This wasn't part of their agreement. Keeping it quiet came at a
high cost, sixty-thousand dollars per month cash. The first install-
ment apparently not well spent.

The article said the girl's landlord reported Anya had been a
model tenant and was religious about paying the rent precisely
one week before the first of each month. He'd tried to contact her
by phone for a week after she failed to pay July's rent, but she
didn't answer or respond to voicemails. A certified letter also went
unclaimed. He decided to call the authorities after a neighbor
noted a rancid odor coming from the girl's apartment. A search
for the girl had come up empty. The authorities urged anyone
with information about the girl to call the Philadelphia Police.

Mays crushed the newspaper and threw it across his office.

With a swipe of his arm, papers, the phone, and his half-full coffee mug flew across the room. "Damn it!" he yelled as his secretary knocked on the door. "Hold on a second," he said, setting the phone back on his desk and putting the jagged mug pieces in the trash. "Come in, Joan."

She opened the door tentatively and peeked her graying head into the room. She eyed the streams of coffee running down the wall and the papers strewn over the floor. "Senator Mays, Senator Stevens is waiting for you in his office. He said you were going to meet before you introduced your bill on the floor today."

"Tell him I'm on my way."

"Uh, may I pour you a new cup of coffee. . . to go?"

"No, thank you, Joan, I'm all set. I need just a few minutes, so if you don't mind, I don't want any interruptions."

"Of course," she said, closing the door.

Mays' cell phone rang. The voice on the other end was all too familiar. "The story broke today," the man said.

"I'm well aware the damn story broke!" Mays quieted his voice. "What the hell am I paying you for?"

"It was bound to happen. People don't up and disappear without being noticed," the man said.

"I've dropped sixty grand to make sure it wasn't."

"As far as the cops know, she skipped town. Remember, Senator, this could get a lot uglier if pieces of the girl start washing up along the Delaware, or if an anonymous tip puts you with her at the marina that night. So, as for our arrangement, it's business as usual."

He didn't have a choice but to continue paying. It was apparent, however, that even this was no guarantee of immunity. He had undoubtedly been with the girl at the nightclub and probably been caught on surveillance video but, as of yet, none of that had come forth. "Business as usual," he said. "For now."

He picked up his briefcase, straightened his tie, and headed to his meeting with Senator Stevens. The bill passed with cheers, forty-seven yeas / two nays / and one no-vote. Mays managed a fake smile and made his compulsory rounds to shake hands, all the while knowing that unless something changed, he'd soon trade in his Armani for an orange prison jumpsuit with black stenciled numbers.

32

SOMEONE at the museum had to have noticed something. Nick left a message for the only board member he knew personally, Helen Granger, a former Broadway actress and playwright known for her rare ability to pull off poignant and awe-inspiring soliloquies. She informed Nick that Liza came to her table around 9:30 pm, said she wasn't feeling well, and needed to leave.

Liza looked forward to the museum's fundraiser every year and invested both her time and emotions into its success. It would have taken a ruptured appendix to drag her away.

Helen described Liza as "looking a little anxious" but not pale or otherwise sick. She had seen his mother talking with Delphia Himes for an extended amount of time early in the evening before Senator Mays joined the two. Liza and Mays were together for only a few minutes before Liza left the museum.

"Senator Lloyd Mays, really?" Nick asked.

"Yes, we added him late to the guest list." Nick's eyes widened. "Why was he invited?"

"Well." She hesitated. "He wasn't. His staff called and asked that he be sent an invitation. He gave a substantial gift in appreciation. Is there a problem?"

"No, not at all. I just want to have a clear picture of my mother's last hours."

It seemed that Mays had gone out of his way to attend the fundraiser to spend time with Liza. But why? Nick didn't want to raise any flags with the board member, so he backed off and thanked her for her time.

As much as Nick wanted to confront Mays, getting information from a well-protected state senator would be a challenge. He called and left a message requesting a meeting but didn't expect a response any time soon.

Delphia Himes didn't list her phone number, but Helen reluctantly provided Nick with the address. "Tread gently. Delphia has Asperger's syndrome, a form of autism. And don't wear a suit, wingtips, or a tie. You won't get one foot in the door."

"I've heard my mother talk about her. What's up with her disdain for fashion?"

"Beats me. She's a bit odd, but she's a savant. Her mind's like a black hole. Things get sucked in and never come out."

"Really?"

"I never believed in photographic memories, but she's the real deal. Oh, and your mom gave her a ride to the fundraiser because her Volkswagen Beetle died a couple days prior."

Thankful for the heads-up, he searched his closet for artsy, nonthreatening apparel, a look he could pull off without much work. He hadn't shaved since Sunday morning and opted to keep the stubble. He pulled a white, short-sleeved t-shirt over his head and put on faded jeans with a large, frayed hole over his right thigh. His tan cowboy boots were well worn, souvenirs of a weekend romance with a medical school classmate from Austin.

Just past noon, he reached Delphia's door at Eighty-nine Shackamaxon Street, a quaint, brick townhouse in the Fishtown neighborhood of Philadelphia, an area known for eclectic galleries and trendy bars. A bright yellow Beetle sat parked across the street.

"Who is it?" Delphia asked from behind the closed door, her voice curt, paranoid in tone.

"Miss Himes, it's Nick Carlotti, Liza's son."

"How do I know you're you?"

Nick pulled his wallet from his back pocket and removed his driver's license. "If you open the door a crack, I'll show you my ID."

Delphia unlocked the deadbolt and opened the door two inches, but left the door's security guard engaged. "Let me see," she said.

Nick passed the license through the small crack. The door shut and reopened a few moments later. "Come in," she said, still sounding quite nervous.

Delphia's black painted toenails peeked out from beneath the cuffs of her torn, paisley pajama pants. Crossed arms partially hid the faded image of Che Guevara on the front of her t-shirt. Nick stepped into the foyer. Delphia uncrossed her arms and fidgeted with a long lock of her messy pink hair. Her gaze moved slowly from the floor to Nick and back again.

"Miss Himes, my mother spoke very highly of you and your artwork. She considered herself one of your most loyal fans."

Delphia smiled sheepishly, and her posture relaxed. She let go the lock of hair that now poked up, twisted into a rigid spike.

Nick continued, "I'm sorry I didn't call ahead, but I'd like to talk to you about the night my mother died."

Delphia's head dropped.

"I know you drove together. I'm trying to wrap my head around what happened between the fundraiser and the car accident. She trusted you, and if she could trust you, I can as well."

Without looking up, Delphia nodded and turned toward a spacious room to their left. At least a dozen empty cardboard boxes and tall stacks of books littered the hardwood floor. A red velvet sofa, an old wooden rocking chair, and an oversized round ottoman surrounded a weathered red barn door set on three columns of cinderblocks. A dim glow shone from a candelabra hanging over the makeshift coffee table.

Nick followed Delphia, and after she sat cross-legged on the ottoman, he took a seat on the sofa. Before he opened his mouth to talk, Delphia buried her face in her hands. Nick remained quiet while Delphia cried quietly.

A couple minutes later, she lifted her head, her eyes welled up with tears and her black-lipstick-coated lower lip quivering. "Liza was my friend," she said, her voice cracking.

"She felt the same about you. She considered you a good friend."

"You can call me Del. That's what your mother called me. She said she was name-lazy and didn't like three syllables."

"Thank you, Del. You were talking to her right before she left. Is that right?"

"Yeah."

"Did she look sick or tell you she wasn't feeling well?"

"No. She seemed okay to me."

"If you don't mind my asking, what were you discussing?"

Delphia's face lit up. Her eyes opened wide, and she straightened up on the ottoman. "I told her about a book I'd been reading on the coming enlightenment of this age. It's going to unite all the sources of divine energy that exists in all things; you know like the air, the trees, the animals, and even rocks . . . everything actually. It will bring peace, love, and harmony to the universe when it happens. And Liza just told me more about Jesus. She always talked about him, you know."

"Yes, I know. Did she act nervous or scared?"

"Not so much. . . well." She paused. "Not until he came over."

"Who?"

"The senator with the stiff gray suit. He gave me the creeps, so I booked. She didn't seem scared or anything, but I don't think she wanted to talk to him. I probably should have stayed but I just couldn't," Delphia said. She got up from the ottoman and paced the room with her thin, pale arms folded again in front of her chest, her head hung low.

"Did she talk to him long?" Nick asked.

"Five and a half minutes. She probably didn't like his suit either, not a single wrinkle. Gag me."

Nick glanced at the holes in his jeans, thankful he'd followed Helen's advice. "Suits like that look good only when you're lying in a casket," he said, scoring a sheepish grin from Del. "Did you notice anything else unusual?"

Delphia stopped pacing and for the first time, looked Nick in the eye. "He called her 'Ali' and I don't think she liked it much."

Nick had heard only one other person call his mother 'Ali,' her college roommate Susan, whom he'd met at one of his mother's book signings a couple years ago. Susan had greeted Liza that day with an enthusiastic, "Ali!" and a tight hug before Liza introduced her to Nick.

"Ali?" Nick whispered in his mother's ear as Susan walked away. Liza shrugged.

"She used to call me by my last name, but after a week she cut it in half. Said four syllables took too much effort. You know I'm the same way."

Nick looked up at Delphia and raised his eyebrows. "In what context did he call her 'Ali'?"

"The senator said, 'Great turn out,' and Liza said, 'Yes, I'm quite pleased.' Then he said, 'That's you, Ali, go big or go home.'"

Nick shook his head. "You remember the exact conversation from April?"

Delphia shrugged and tipped her head to the side. Her voice shook. "I miss her."

Nick stood, wanting to give her an embrace, but he wasn't sure how she'd react, so he just nodded. He thanked her for her time. Before the door closed behind him, he paused. "Delphia, one more thing. Did you notice what time the senator left the museum?"

"Ten-sixteen."

"That's remarkable," Nick said.

"Yeah, stuff sort of sticks in my head like that. I can't help it, really."

Nick smiled. "It's a gift. If anything else comes to mind, please let me know." He handed Delphia a business card and turned down the steps. The lock turned and the security guard engaged with a metallic clank. Despite Delphia's quirky persona, Nick understood why his mother had taken a liking to her. He sensed a kinship with her, like they were somehow family, related by their mutual love for Liza.

Nick hadn't taken more than a dozen steps down Shackamaxon Street toward his car when his cell phone rang. He didn't recognize the number. "Hello."

"Is this Dr. Carlotti?" asked a woman in a pleasant but business-like tone.

"It is."

"I'm calling from the office of Senator Lloyd Mays. He's responding to your call and would like to meet with you this Thursday evening, at seven o'clock in his office at the Capitol. Does that work, Doctor?"

"I'll make it work," Nick said as he reached his car.

"His office is room 325 in the Main Capitol Rotunda at Third and State Streets. I'll inform security of your pending arrival, and please be sure to have a photo ID. Senator Mays looks forward to your meeting."

Nick wanted to say, 'I'm sure he does,' but instead took the high road. "Tell him I appreciate his promptness and willingness to meet with me."

"I'll pass it along. Have a pleasant day."

33

Sarah flew across the waiting room and threw her arms around him. She sobbed. Coroneos held her briefly then let his arms fall to his side. Sarah squeezed him all the harder as if she would drown if she let go. He patted her back and pulled away.

"I need to go in alone," he said.

Sarah looked up and nodded with glassy, bloodshot eyes. She'd seemed to have aged five years in the week he'd been gone. He owned some of it, some of her heaviness, her disappointment. He wished she didn't hurt.

It hit him like a bulldozer before he stepped past the pale blue curtain, the mechanical swooshing sound of the ventilator. Twenty-two years ago, Sam lay in a tiny bed in the NICU a block away at the Children's Hospital. Surgeons had just repaired a hole in his heart and fixed a narrowed artery to his lungs. Coroneos' then eleven-month-old Down syndrome son had looked like a China doll overrun with tubes, wires, and bandages. The sight of it nearly crushed him. He turned the corner and peered past the curtain.

Nothing could have prepared him for this moment. A lump formed in his throat as he gazed upon his grown son in that bed.

He would have traded places with him if he could. At least he would have deserved the suffering. Sam had only enriched the lives of everyone with whom he came into contact.

A much bigger version of the China doll now lay restrained with soft blue fabric wrist bands loosely tied to the bed rails. The breathing tube extended from Sam's mouth as his chest rose and fell in sync with the ventilator.

Coroneos fought to keep his lower lip from quivering as he took hold of Sam's limp hand. "Hey, Pal, I missed you. Did you take good care of Momma while I was gone?" He wanted to say the right thing. Could Sam hear him? Might these be the last words he'd be able to share with his boy?

Sam's precious round face blurred as Coroneos' eyes welled with tears. He didn't want Sam to see him cry, but maybe that had been one of his biggest failures, not showing his boy what it meant to be real. But then again, Sam didn't need the lesson. His emotions flowed freely, undefiled by self-consciousness or ego. Sam just lived. Coroneos wiped his eyes.

"I'm sorry Samuel, sorry for all the days I missed watching you grow into a man, sorry for the choices I've made but sometimes you just can't go back, you know?" Coroneos laid his hand on Sam's forehead. "You need to get yourself better because I bought two tickets for the NASCAR race in Dover next month." He reached in and pulled something from his pants pocket. He placed it in Sam's right hand.

As he turned to leave, he took one more look at the only part of his life that was pure. He hoped he'd have more time. Sam would have been over the top with the miniature red Ferrari in his hand. "I love you, Son."

34

NOT SURE HE could wait two days to confront the senator, Nick left Delphia's apartment and contemplated driving straight to Harrisburg. Mays just happened to be one of the last people to have seen Liza alive, and his adversarial relationship with the Carlotti family made his interaction with her suspicious. However, Mays' mere presence at the fundraiser didn't constitute guilt. But why was he there? Why did he call her Ali?

Nick wasn't halfway home when he received a troubling call from Danielle. Zach, the twelve-year-old boy he'd operated on a couple days ago, had spiked a fever of 102, and his leg had grown increasingly red and swollen.

"How bad's it look?" Nick asked.

"Not good. The flap isn't necrotic, but the entire lower extremity is erythematous, and the distal wound margin has some purulent exudate."

"Shit! Why the hell didn't someone call me earlier?"

"He looked fine when we rounded last night. I spent all morning in the OR closing lacerations on some poor guy after a psycho filleted his face with a razor blade. We just rounded on Zach twenty minutes ago."

"The fu . . . the poor kid can't catch a break," Nick said, biting his lip. "Send wound and blood cultures. He's on Ancef already. Go ahead and add Flagyl 500 milligrams Q twelve hours to cover for anaerobes until we know what bug we're dealing with."

Nick called the child's parents and explained the situation, telling them that post-operative infections weren't uncommon and that the antibiotics would likely turn things around. He, however, wasn't so sure and rushed straight to the hospital.

By 6:00 the boy's fever had risen to 103. Aside from the expected spike in his white count, the boy's most recent lab results showed both his kidneys and liver were shutting down. Nick had just hung up the phone after discussing the case with the infectious disease specialist when Danielle snuck up behind him. "What do you think?"

His heart skipped a beat at the tenderness of her voice. Nick spun around in his chair. He didn't want to admit it, but he was glad to see her. "Like you said. Not good."

Danielle frowned. "The cultures are pending but we d/c'd the Ancef and Flagyl and started Cephtriaxone based on the gram stain. Gram-negative rods."

"Bacteroides?"

Danielle nodded. "Possibly."

Nick sighed and shook his head. "His parents are bringing their pastor and a group of people to pray over him soon. I'm sure that'll fix him all up."

Danielle's fair-skinned face turned red. "What do you mean by that?"

"Come on, his parents have been praying since they got here two days ago, and I'm certain— a long time before that. Despite their celestial petitions, Zach's cancer doubled in size. Now he's lost a good portion of his leg, and he's septic, possibly dying. So, yeah, I think it's bunk." Nick shoved the boy's chart against the wall.

"Nick, I understand your anger. God — "

"Don't tell me about God. My mother had more faith than anyone I've ever known. She spent hours on her knees praying to a God who sat back and watched her Beamer roll down the Schuylkill, her spine severed and her skull crushed. So, sorry, Danielle, your God is impotent. But that's just my opinion."

Danielle pulled her lower lip between her teeth. Her blue eyes softened as she just nodded gently. "Nick, I'm here if you need me." As she stood to walk away, she laid her hand on Nick's shoulder.

His muscles relaxed. He regretted upsetting her, but not for speaking his heart. Even after his harsh words, she didn't snap back. She commanded a self-control he certainly didn't.

Nick slid the chart back toward him. As he wrote his note, the patient's parents, the pastor, and three others approached.

"How is he doing?" Zach's father asked.

"Not much better, Rich. I'm hoping the antibiotics kick in soon. We're doing all we can."

"Is it all right if we go in and pray over him?" his mother asked.

"Of course, but you'll have to put on gowns and masks. They're on the cart outside the room."

Nick watched the six enter the room and encircle Zach's bed. The pastor opened his Bible. The remaining five laid their hands on Zach's body, one at each arm, one at each leg, and one at his head. The pastor read loudly enough for Nick to hear: *"At sunset, the people brought to Jesus all who had various kinds of sickness, and laying his hands on each one, he healed them."* When he'd finished, they sang softly.

Nick's emotions cycled between feelings of skepticism, anger, and yearning. As indignant as he was with God, something in him hungered for that kind of courage, that kind of faith.

Later that evening, Nick took the boy back to the operating room to open and clean the leg wound. The infection had spread, so much so that the swelling prevented Nick from closing the incision. He left the wound open, packed it with surgical gauze, and transferred Zach back to the floor. The prayers for healing weren't working, but to this point, neither were the antibiotics.

Nick sat on the cold, wooden bench, took off his surgical mask, and let his head fall back against the metal door of his locker. So far, his career and life in general had fallen well short of what he'd dreamt as a younger, more naive medical student.

His pager beeped. He dialed the hospital extension. "Dr. Carlotti here."

"Just checking in. Any luck finding Maria?" Steve asked.

"Not so much," Nick said. "Where are you?"

"On twelve."

"Sit tight. I'll be up in ten." He had little energy to climb eight flights of stairs but wasn't in the mood for an elevator ride, either, so he opted for better of the two evils.

When Nick reached the twelfth floor, huffing and puffing, he found Steve at the desk looking through a patient chart.

Nick shared his concerns regarding his young patient's status and his frustration with his lack of progress in finding contact information for Maria.

"I found old phone bills from the house but no calls to Mexico. I'm not sure where else to look. What are we missing?" Nick asked.

"I'm glad you asked," Steve said as he reached into his right front pants pocket. "It came to me this morning as I flipped through the Bible. I noticed a stamped church label inside the back cover, maybe Maria's church?" Steve handed Nick a folded piece of paper.

Laredo First Baptist Church
2733 E Del Mar Blvd.
Laredo, TX 78041

NICK RAN his fingers over the dark two-day stubble of his chin. "From what I remember, Maria received the Bible from a missionary in Mexico, then gave it to my mother. Maria spent a couple days with this woman every time she crossed the border into Laredo. I don't know her name, but I'm sure this is the church Maria used to visit. It's a start."

"Well, let me know," Steve said. "Keep me up to date on the boy."

"Will do."

35

"Define odd." Coroneos cast Eddie a skeptical look, doubtful that a little R and R was the impetus for Nick's visit. All the heads in the room turned in Eddie's direction.

"Unusual, you know, Nick being at the house on Monday. Said he went for a swim, but his towel was dry and folded up like the maid does 'em. I think it was one of Dad's black ones."

Coroneos followed up. "Where'd you find him?"

"The bathroom, upstairs, not the one in the pool house." Eddie glanced toward Scalise's bandaged hand. "What the hell happened to you?"

"What's it to you?" Scalise shot back.

"Sorry man, I was just asking."

"How about the security cameras?" Coroneos asked. "And why didn't you have eyes on him the whole time?"

"I ran out for a little grub. Tommy stayed there."

Everyone's attention turned to Tommy. His face flushed. "I was on the can. Damn gut hurt the whole day. When I got back to the control room, I noticed the Porsche in the driveway. Eddie walked in the door before I could get there."

Rock straightened up. "So, what are you saying, Nick's

stealing from me or something?" He snapped. "Come on!"

Eddie shook his shaved head. "I'm not accusing him or anything, Pops, just seemed weird."

Coroneos stood and rested his hand on the corner of Rock's desk. He cocked his head to one side and turned his gaze toward Eddie. "I'm not sure what he was doing, but Nick hasn't been here since Liza died." He looked down at the lapel of his smoke gray suit jacket and brushed off a piece of lint. "Quite frankly, he doesn't come here except for family functions. Was he carrying anything?"

"A duffle bag," Eddie said.

"And he had the same bag on the way out?" Coroneos asked.

"Yeah."

"You're sure the towel was one from the house?"

Eddie hesitated and looked down at the floor. His posture didn't change as he answered, "Yeah, black with the gold 'C' in the corner."

"Seems like overkill to bring a duffel bag for just a swimsuit, especially if he didn't bring his own towel," Coroneos said. "I know he's your boy, Rock, but I think we need to keep an eye on him."

"What the hell would he be looking for? He's got no interest in our affairs, and he knows the rules," Rock said.

Eddie stood, leaning against the wall. "I'm not so sure, Pops. He called me last month and went on this ridiculous rant about mom's accident. He thinks she was murdered."

Rock shook his head but didn't respond.

"There's one more thing," Eddie said. "I reviewed the surveillance from both the house and the lake house over the weekend. Nick showed up here last Friday and at the lake house that evening. He left the lake at 7 am, Saturday morning then went back again on Sunday. He stayed less than half an hour. It looked like he had books in his hands when he left both times, but the video isn't clear."

Rock walked to the door and leaned his head out. "Babe, come up here a second." He turned back into the room. "Jennifer didn't leave for her sister's until Saturday."

Jennifer peeked into the room but didn't broach the doorway.

Every head turned her way as Rock spoke. "What was Nick doing here last Friday?"

Her lips quivered. "He came by for the keys to the lake house. He said he needed to get away. He's your son, I didn't think you'd mind."

"Why would he come back on Monday?" Coroneos asked.

"I don't know. I said he could use the pool while I visited my sister. Maybe he just wanted to swim."

"Okay," Rock said. He motioned for her to leave as if she were his hired help. "See, it all checks out. Jen invited him to take a swim, so he's fine."

"It doesn't explain his being upstairs, the dry towel, or the second trip to the lake house," Coroneos said, not willing to let it go.

"I said it's fine!" Rock shot back. "Everyone but Peter hit the road."

Eddie, Scalise, and Tommy exited the room, leaving Rock and Coroneos alone. Rock moved his chair and took two steps toward Coroneos. "Peter, remember who the hell you're talking to. Nick may or may not be up to something, but don't you dare second guess me in front of the men. And don't interrogate my wife like that again."

"Tony, I'm sorry. We have a lot on the line, and Nick has never been part of the family in that way. He's been on some sort of mission lately. I'm not sure what he's up to." He wasn't really sorry at all. Nick's meddling in the family business caused a distraction they didn't need and Rock's paternal instinct, warped as it was, clouded his perspective. Coroneos doubted Rock could be objective. Rock's response proved him right.

"Back off of my son! He's my problem, not yours." Rock

opened the top drawer of his desk and pulled out articles from the Inquirer, the one from Thursday implicating the Carlotti crime family in Danny Torello's shooting and the follow-up piece on Friday stating that Torello had died while under the care of Carlotti's son, Dr. Nick Carlotti. He spread them out on the desk and pressed his index finger on Torello's name. "I don't like attention where there should be none! Who the hell is this guy?"

Coroneos raised his bushy eyebrows and shrugged. "I have no idea. This wasn't our job."

"No shit!" Rock said as he ripped the paper from Peter's hand and slammed it back on the desk. Coroneos threw up his hands.

"Someone whacked the guy on the Thursday before your wedding, and he died last Tuesday. We were on our way to Bogota!"

"I can read the damn paper, Peter! Why's this bozo's name next to mine?"

"Yours isn't the only name associated with him. Nick's name is right there too. I'm telling you, he's up to something."

Rock crumpled the articles in his hand. "I'll deal with Nick, but I want to know who took this dirtbag out."

"I'll look into it," Coroneos said. "But I can assure you it has nothing to do with us."

"Well, get it straightened out. And what's up with your eyes?"

"What are you talking about?"

"They look like you haven't slept in two weeks,"

"I've been up with Sam. He's not doing well."

Rock slapped Coroneos on the back. "Take a couple shots of Jack and get some sleep. You'll need it."

Right on cue. The asshole couldn't give two shits about the kid, only about how it might affect the deal. "Don't worry Tony, I'm good to go." Coroneos bit the inside of his cheek and left to return to his son's side.

36

By Wednesday evening, little had evolved in Zach's condition. Nick had hoped that twenty-four hours would bring some improvement. In this case, he considered no change a modest win given the possible alternatives. He decided to rest in the doctor's lounge and wait it out.

A nagging desire to call Danielle kept him from drifting off, but what would he say when she answered? "Uh, this is Nick. You don't want to go out with me, right?" Or, maybe just fabricate some reason why he needed her opinion on a pending case. At least he could hear her voice. Hard to admit but he wanted her around. Nick gave in and called.

"Are you still in the hospital?" he asked.

"Just walking out the door. Why?"

"I know it's late, but I thought you might have time for a quick bite. Don't worry, I'm not asking you out."

Danielle chuckled. "Good, because I'm out of your league."

"I'm well aware of that. How about I buy you a gyro in exchange for twenty minutes of your time?"

"That comes out to about twelve bucks an hour. Throw in a Diet Coke, and it's a deal. I haven't eaten since noon anyway."

They met at the Greek food truck parked outside the hospital's main entrance. Nick grabbed the bag, and they headed toward a small square across the street. Neither spoke as they walked. He'd never been at a loss for words or nervous around a woman— until now. They took a seat on a park bench overlooking a stone fountain in the square.

"I'm sorry," he said.

"For what?"

"Jumping down your throat about the prayer thing. I appreciate your faith, but I just haven't had much luck with God the past few years."

"It's fine, Nick. We're all in different places on the journey," she said, her voice tender and empathetic.

Nick set the bag of food at his feet. "The kid's only twelve years old, and I'm not sure he's going to survive this infection. Seriously, Danielle, what did he do to deserve this?"

She didn't answer. Maybe he'd stumped her, threw a wrench in her theology. She lifted her head and looked into his eyes. "Nothing. He didn't do anything to deserve it."

That was it? 'Nothing.' No trite Christian platitudes regurgitated like some holy reflex. No 'God's ways aren't our ways' or 'everything happens for a reason.' What a breath of fresh air.

The corners of her lips turned downward. "I'm sorry about your mother's accident and that you feel God let her down."

"You could say that."

"I understand. I lost my uncle to a heart attack when I was in the seventh grade. He was thirty-four, worked out every day, and never smoked a day in his life. When my father walked out on us, Uncle Jack became my rock. He didn't have any boys, so he taught me how to fly fish and shoot a bow. It shakes you."

Nick nodded. "One night you're talking to someone you love and the next, you're watching them die." He hesitated before continuing. "My mom had a special way with people. She could connect with them without words, speak to them with her eyes. Know what I mean?"

Danielle rested her hand on his knee, her eyes glassed over. Nick handed her a napkin, surprised by her reaction. "I didn't mean to upset you."

"You didn't," she said, wiping the tears from her eyes.

Nick hadn't seen this side of Danielle before, soft, vulnerable — adorable. "Can I tell you something in confidence?" He wasn't sure why he needed to tell her.

"Of course," she said.

"Steve and I have found some things that back up Torello's claims."

Danielle straightened up. "Such as?"

"Some things she wrote; Bible verses she recorded in her journal. She feared someone. My father, I think, but I'm not sure."

"Why would someone want to kill your mother?"

"I don't know, but she left clues. It's complicated, and I can't go into it now. You and Steve are the only ones who know, and I need it to stay that way."

"I won't say a thing. Nick, I'm in shock."

They sat quietly for a few minutes. The bag of food lay untouched on the cobblestone walk. The fountain's cascading water drowned out the conversations of the scattered people milling around the square.

Nick took a couple breaths. Ah, what the hell. "I know it's probably not the best time to ask, and I know you're not all that fond of me, but I'd love to see you again. And I don't mean in the hospital. For some crazy reason, I can't get you out of my head."

Danielle bit her lip and avoided his gaze. "Nick — "

The consolatory tone in her voice left a pit in his stomach. You're such an idiot! "Okay, forget I asked," he said.

"It's just that we're in different—"

"Seriously, I'd rather you leave it unanswered."

She peeked up with a rueful I-don't-want-to-hurt-you look. Even in the dim glow of the vintage street lights, her eyes reminded Nick of the clear blue skies over Telluride in December.

"Danielle, it's cool. Strike two is close enough to an out that I'm going to lay down my bat." Nick smiled but was dying inside. For god's sake, why did he go there? Regardless, it was a blessing in disguise. He already had enough on his plate to keep him busy, and a relationship would only be a distraction. He knew he'd fashioned his own version of Aesop's sour grapes, but went with it anyway.

"I'm sorry," Danielle said but didn't sound confident in her stance — just enough to give Nick a wisp of hope.

"I need to head back and check on my patient," Nick said as he stood.

Danielle nodded and gave him a half-smile.

When Nick returned to the floor, the nurses informed him that the boy's fevers hadn't improved, and his blood pressure remained low. Still, it could have been worse. Not a reason for celebration but Nick wasn't throwing in the towel.

In any comparable situation, Nick would have gone home and asked the nurses to call with any changes, but something stopped him. He felt a deeper connection to the boy, like somehow he wasn't just another patient, but a spiritual kin. Strange. He stayed at the nurses' station outside the room.

Ever since Zach returned from the OR, alternating groups of church members had positioned themselves around his bed. They laid hands on Zach and prayed. At 10 pm, visiting hours had ended, and the last group left, leaving Zach's parents alone at his bedside. At 2 am, Zach's mother tapped Nick on the shoulder, waking him from a brief catnap. Nick lifted his head from the desk.

"Dr. Carlotti, we're thankful for you and know you're doing all you can," she said, her eyes red and puffy but resilient. "Zach looked forward to playing football this fall. He loves . . . " She broke down.

Nick stood and put his hand on her shoulder. He didn't say a word.

When her crying ceased, she rested her hand on top of his. "Go home and rest. You need some sleep. Zach's in good hands."

Funny, Zach's mom telling him to go home and rest after she'd spent sleepless nights on her knees. Nick had to admit, they seemed to have an unshakable peace amid a parent's worst nightmare. If he'd have asked how, he imagined they would have said something along the lines of '*God never gives us more than we can handle.*' Having seen more than his share of failed and successful suicide victims, he doubted that line of reasoning. Regardless, he admired their strength. His own strength wasn't a virtue waxing at the moment. Failure and loss seemed to be lurking around every corner, and he needed a change, any change.

37

As the garage door closed behind him, Nick's tension eased. Thankfully he didn't have to walk two or three blocks from a parking space on the street, especially late at night. A couple years ago, three teens had shot a young man in the head outside Nick's previous townhouse, robbed for a lousy five bucks and left for dead. A .22 caliber hole in his left temple oozed blood and brain matter on the sidewalk three feet from Nick's steps. The boy died in Nick's arms.

Crime in Philadelphia had become more frequent and more random over the past ten years. He considered a house with a garage a definite plus.

Nick turned the key, expecting to hear the scratching of Rhino's claws on the slate foyer. Most evenings a hyperactive terrier waited expectantly for the hum of the overhead door and the key's clink in the lock, but this time something seemed different. No claws, no barking, nothing from within, only the background street noise from nearby South Street.

Nick eased open the door and flipped on the light. Rhino cowered in the corner, shaking with his tail between his legs, his head hung low. As Nick stepped toward him, Rhino inched closer with a noticeable limp, his left hind leg unable to bear weight.

Turning the corner toward the dark living room Nick slid his hand up the wall until he came into contact with the switch. Light filled the room. "Jesus!" Nick jumped back, slamming his elbow against the wall. He shook his numb hand, trying to shake away the pins and needles. "How the hell did you get in here?"

"Nice pad," Rock said, his legs crossed, feet resting on the coffee table. "Sú cosa es mí cosa. Tit for tat."

Nick's face grew red, his heart still racing. "What's that supposed to mean?" He threw his briefcase on the chair. "And what did you do to my dog?"

"The stupid mutt slobbered on my suit pants. A little negative reinforcement works wonders. Might want to try it."

"Did your father teach you that?

Rock smirked. "What were you doing at the mansion while I was gone?"

"Swimming."

"How was the water?"

"Refreshing."

Rock stood and made his way toward the bar, took out a glass, and poured himself a shot of bourbon. "Cut the bullshit, Nick. Maybe you didn't hear me at our last meeting. What part of 'stay out of my business' didn't you get?"

Nick approached and stood opposite him at the bar. "Who killed Danny Torello?"

"Funny, I was going to ask you the same thing," Rock said. "Seems he was in your care when he died."

"And the papers said the mob made the hit. Last time I checked, you were the boss."

"Not that I owe you an answer, but it wasn't our job."

"The papers said differently."

"The papers were wrong." Rock poured himself a second shot. "Now, I'll ask you again. What were you doing at the house?

And while you're at it, you can explain why you went to the lake house."

"I want to know who killed Mom. Danny Torello believed she was murdered. He could have gotten that information only from Willie Santini, and Santini was your man. Either you know what's going on or you're losing control."

In an instant, Rock closed the distance between them. With their faces just inches apart, Rock's hot, cigar-laden breath blew into Nick's face. Refusing to blink or even twitch, Nick straightened up, his muscles stiffening. Rhino moved behind Nick and let out a slow, deep growl.

"I'll tell you one more time because I'm feeling gracious. Your mother, and my wife, by the way, died in a car accident and that's all there is to it. I'm starting to lose my patience." He lunged toward the dog. "Boo!" he yelled, stomping his foot. The dog ran three-legged into the bedroom. Rock tipped his head back and poured down the last of his bourbon. Nick stood his ground as Rock put the upside-down shot glass on the counter. Rock took a few steps into the kitchen and opened the refrigerator.

"When was the last time you bought groceries?" Rock said. He pulled out a white cardboard box of Chinese fried rice, opened it, and took a quick sniff.

Nick's face reddened. How could he be this man's son? "I wasn't planning on guests."

Rock moved to his right to open a drawer as Nick caught sight of the folders he'd taken from the house sitting on the kitchen table. His stomach tightened and he took a deep breath. Maybe his father didn't notice. He didn't seem to have. Nick diverted his gaze from the folders and moved to the front door.

"Visit's over," Nick said, opening the door.

Rock smiled and took a fork-full of the fried rice in his mouth. He tossed the box into the trash. "A little ripe. You might want to put a date on these things."

As much as Nick wanted to land a right cross to his father's jaw, it wouldn't be worth it. Despite his age, Rock still had biceps like steel girders. Rock whistled as he walked out the door. Rhino let out another growl from the bedroom. Nick pushed shut the door just as Rock jammed his foot between the door and the casing.

"Last warning, son," Rock said, his voice quiet but stern.

Rock pulled back his foot and Nick slammed shut the door.

38

AT 7:30 AM THURSDAY, Nick found his young patient's room empty. Nick rushed to the nurses' station. As he approached, the two nurses turned their heads and made themselves look busy.

Nick's heart sank. He didn't want to ask. "Where is Zach?"

The nurses glanced at one another, neither appearing excited to answer. The older one turned to Nick. "I just paged you, Dr. Carlotti. They transferred him to the ICU. He went into respiratory failure and needed to be intubated."

Nick raced to ICU and hadn't yet stepped foot into the boy's room when his pager beeped. He recognized the extension, Dr. McCabe, the department chair. Whatever it was could wait. He entered the room to see the young boy with the breathing tube in place, his parents by his side.

He wanted to speak, but for the life of him, Nick couldn't think of anything appropriate.

The boy's father turned, his face wearing the burden of a man on the verge of losing everything, but still his voice was strong. "We're still resting on God's perfect plan. No matter what the outcome." He put his arm around his wife and stepped back to their son.

Nick tightened his lips and nodded. As he walked from the room, his pager rang out a second time. Two pages in less than three minutes couldn't be good. Despite not wanting to deal with hospital politics, he made the call.

"Nick, it's Ken. I need to see you in my office."

Nick kicked into defense mode. "I've got a couple things to do here, and then I'll be down."

"No, I think you need to come down now."

"Ken, if you're having chest pain you should hang up and dial 911."

Ken's silence confirmed Nick's suspicion. "I'm not laughing, Nick. And neither are the two police officers standing in my office."

"Ken, what the hell is going on?"

"They want to ask you some questions."

The policemen met Nick as soon as he opened the door to McCabe's lobby. "Dr. McCabe wants to talk to you before we take you in," one cop said.

"Take me in?"

"We'd like to ask you a few questions about Danny Torello's death, but we'll be doing it down at the station."

"Do I need a lawyer?"

"That's up to you."

"This is a farce. You know damn well I didn't have anything to do with Torello's death."

"Then I'm sure you won't mind answering some questions."

Nick stormed into McCabe's office and slammed the door behind him. "Well, what exactly are they saying, Ken? That I murdered Torello?"

"You were in his room before he coded. I'd taken you off his case, so what were you doing in there?"

"Tying up loose ends."

"Loose ends?" McCabe asked. "Such as?"

"Such as someone killed my mother, and Danny Torello knew it."

McCabe raised his eyebrows, the wrinkles of his forehead deepening. He lowered his voice. "Look, Nick, you've been under tremendous pressure since your mother's accident. The Torello thing doesn't look good for you, and I heard your young sarcoma patient is doing poorly. You're not at the top of your game, and you need a little time to recharge your batteries."

"So, you're saying you don't believe me?"

"I've known you a long time, and I trust you. But you should lay low for a while, and I'm helping with that."

"Are you telling me I'm out of a job?"

"No, not out of a job. I'm giving you some time off to get your life in order."

"I'm not asking for time off. I'm fine."

"It wasn't a suggestion. It's an order. Take the week off, or you will be looking for a new job. This isn't punitive, just prudent."

Nick agreed to drive to the police station, but the officers followed close behind.

As he contemplated what they could possibly have to implicate him in Torello's death, the door of the interrogation room opened.

"Dr. Carlotti, I'm Detective Rawls and this is my partner Detective Taylor." Rawls slipped off his midnight-blue suit jacket and draped it over the back of his chair. His rookie partner stood to the side, leaning against the wall. He didn't look old enough to be a detective, and the sparse chestnut stubble above his upper lip looked like a fading chocolate milk stain.

Rawls got right to the point. "Doctor, what can you tell me about succinylcholine?"

"Why are you asking?"

"Just answer the question," Rawls said, standing across the table.

Nick sat up straight in a dark-green, metal, cushion-less chair. "It's a polarizing neuromuscular blocker."

"How about in English?"

"We use it to paralyze patients when we put in a breathing tube."

Rawls rounded the table, nodding with pursed lips. He stepped closer. "Given that Mr. Torello already had a tracheostomy, is there any reason he would have received succinylcholine the day he died?"

Nick's eyes opened wide in surprise. "No. Are you telling me that he did?"

"It would be a pretty good drug to off someone with, wouldn't it, Doctor? Something that breaks down in the body — hard to find."

"Sure, if you wanted to kill someone."

Rawls sat on the table's edge and slid next to Nick. "You'd think someone smart enough to pull off a murder like that would be smart enough not to leave the syringe in the patient's room. And how about this little factoid — the medical examiner's toxicologist found a large amount of succinic acid in your patient's brain tissue. I assume you know what succinic acid is, Doctor."

"I do, and I assume you've done your homework as well."

Rawls continued, "It's a breakdown product of succinylcholine, but also a chemical produced in the human body. The medical examiner assures me that the amount he found in Torello's brain far exceeded normal. So, let me be blunt. Did you kill Danny Torello?"

Nick shot up from his chair.

Rawls recoiled. "Sit your ass back down!"

"I'd rather stand."

"This isn't a democracy, Dr. Carlotti. Sit down, or you can finish this discussion with cuffs on."

Nick glared at Rawls and turned to Taylor. He dropped back

into the chair. "I'd been doing my best to save his life. Why would I want him dead?"

"You tell us," Taylor asked.

Nick wasn't sure whom he could trust and chose not to mention Torello's note. "Someone shot the guy point-blank twice, and I did everything I could to put his face back together. I have no idea who'd want him dead, but I assure you it wasn't me."

Rawls looked over the top of his glasses and scratched the beard on his chin. "From what we can tell, Torello was an addict connected with one of your father's men. Does the name Willie Santini mean anything to you?"

"Sounds familiar," Nick said.

Taylor reached into Rawls' leather briefcase and pulled out a blank pad of paper. He tossed it in on the table. "Recognize this?"

Nick ignored the cell phone vibrating in his pocket. He glanced at the paper with the red, white, and blue Penn shield logo. "Hospital stationery. This test is getting easier by the minute."

"Maybe this one will be a little more challenging. What did Danny write on the page you tore out right before you killed him?"

"I didn't kill him, and the note is physician-patient privilege."

"Let me refresh your memory," the officer said. "No accident? What did he mean by that?"

"Look, if you already knew what the note said, you'd know I would have every reason to want Danny alive. You'd also know that someone murdered my mother like I said when I called you in May. Somehow, Danny Torello knew it and so did Santini. Either book me or let me go."

Rawls stood and opened the door. "Since you were one of the last ones to see Torello alive and you have access to succinyl-choline, not to mention your last name is Carlotti, you can understand our concern."

"If you're so concerned, you might want to investigate my father and — while you're at it, Senator Mays, who talked with my mother the night she died. Coincidence? I doubt it."

Rawls furrowed his brow and turned his head in Taylor's direction.

Taylor shrugged.

"You're free to go for the time being, Doctor, but you'll need to stick around town. We'll be in touch," Rawls said.

As Nick walked out the door, he gave a parting shot. "I hope so because if you two can't do your job, someone else has to."

39

THE LIST of people Nick trusted had dwindled to two: his best friend and the woman who had just shot him down — twice.

Steve answered on the first ring. "Danielle already told me. I'm sorry man."

"So, you heard I'm taking a little forced vacation," Nick said.

"Yeah, and in the meantime there's a firestorm of speculation around here surrounding Torello's death."

"Apparently someone shot him up with Sux, and for now I'm the prime suspect."

"Well . . . "

"Well, what? You don't think I killed him?"

"Of course not. I can just see why you're on their shortlist. Your name, access, and the fact you were there before he died."

"Sounds like you have doubts."

"Nick, I know you didn't do it. But we're going to need to find out who did. Otherwise, you're going to be the fall guy. You're an easy out."

Nick pulled in a deep breath. "I know the connection."

"What connection?" Steve asked.

"Willie Santini!"

"And?"

"Torello told me that Willie knew my mother's death wasn't an accident." "I thought we already knew that."

"We did, but Danny did too, and now he's dead. The newspaper said Willie committed suicide, but a suicide letter doesn't prove he offed himself. If Danny died because he had information he received from Willie, it's likely Willie died because he had the information to begin with."

"Okay, but how would we find out if someone killed Willie, and even if that were true, what does that prove?"

"I don't know."

"Well, I feel better, I thought I might be missing something."

Rock had to be embroiled in this mess, but how? He was as heartless as they came, but still, Nick just couldn't fathom him taking his wife's life.

In the brief pause, a very unsettling thought hit him. What if Steve ended up dead, like Torello and Willie? Nick wouldn't be able to live with himself, but who else could he turn to? Steve was his best friend, and Nick needed his help. He vowed to cut Steve loose at the slightest hint of danger. "Anything else from the journal or the book?" he asked.

"No, but I am still curious about the author of Rebecca's Box. I have a strange feeling your mother knew her, as if they were somehow connected."

"Why?"

"The book is so obscure yet seems too similar to your mother's last months. I mean, what are the chances she'd randomly come upon a book like that? It isn't like she picked it up from the bestsellers table at Barnes & Noble."

"She knew nearly every aspiring author and artist in Philly. Who knows? Maybe there's something to it."

"I'm going to check out the publishing company in Scranton,

Blue Heron Press," Steve said. He told Nick he had to run but would let him know if he found anything.

Nick dialed Danielle. After pressing "Send," he thought, why did I call? He didn't want to rehash the day, and now that he had earned an involuntary sabbatical, he had no patient business to discuss. He never contemplated making the call. It just happened, like an involuntary reflex.

Three rings, no answer, straight to voicemail. When the tone sounded, Nick stammered, "Uh . . . it's me." Pause. "Hope you're having a good day."

Nick hit 'End.' What in the world was that? 'Uh, it's me.' Really? He groaned. For a split second, he thought about calling back but decided to cut his losses. He chose instead to concentrate on finding Willie's aunt Rose. He glanced at his watch, 12:30 pm. He now had lots of time on his hands.

The drive to Harrisburg for his meeting with Lloyd Mays would take a little less than two hours. Nick wanted to be on the road by 5, so he drove home to change his clothes and search the phone book and Internet for Willie's aunt. There were thirty-seven Santini's in Philadelphia, and none bore the first name Rose. Was she married? And for that matter, was her last name Santini?

An online search of obituaries revealed that Willie was survived only by an older sister, Theresa, living in Portland, Maine, and his aunt Rose Martinelli. Back to the phonebook he went. Bingo! One Rose A. Martinelli on South Beulah Street in South Philadelphia, a few blocks from Veterans Stadium. He tore the page from the phonebook, took a fast shower, and hit the road by 4:50 pm.

The call from the car lasted only a few minutes. Initially, Rose seemed guarded, but when Nick made it clear that he believed Willie and Liza had both been murdered, the walls came down.

"He didn't write that note," she said, pleading for someone to hear.

"What note?"

"The suicide note. The police gave me a copy and said Willie wrote it to me, but I know he didn't write it. Or at least not the way they said."

"Why do you say that?"

"He wrote it to 'Aunt Rose.' Willie never called me Aunt Rose. All my nieces and nephews call me Zizzi." Her voice cracked. "He called me Zizzi Rose."

"I'm sorry, Mrs. Martinelli. I didn't mean to open old wounds."

"I raised Willie from the time he was nine years old," Rose said, sounding more resolute. "That's not all, he signed the letter 'Love, Squirrel.' He was Willie to me, never Squirrel. He knew I hated that name."

It had to be either an inside job, or a rival mob hit. Clearly, Willie and Danny Torello met the same fate at the hands of someone tied to Nick's mother's death.

He readied to end the conversation when Rose spoke. "Nick, I want you to know that I prayed for Willie and loved him like a son, but he lived for momentary pleasures. He turned his back on God," she said. "Someone may have taken his life, but the Devil had already taken his soul."

Diavalo! Nick's grandmother's voice rang out in a flashback to her near exorcism of Eddie after she caught him listening to "Hells Bells." Maybe the similarity of Rose's inflection, the forceful intonation of her words, or the ridiculous notion that some clown with a red tail and a pitch-fork stood ready to cast you into a fiery pit caught his attention, but he'd had enough. "I'm sorry for your loss," Nick said. "Thank you for your — "

"I met your mother a few times," Rose interrupted. "You have her eyes, and I sense you're a lot like her, a soft heart. God's heart."

"Thank you, Mrs. Martinelli. I appreciate your kind words."

This constant God-talk was getting under his skin.

The road sign read Exit 43 Capital / 2nd St. 1 Mile. Nick's grip on the steering wheel tightened, and the muscles of his forearms bulged as the leather beneath his palms became the skin around Mays' neck. Maybe Satan wore a three-piece suit.

40

ABSURD, Capital Security attempting to keep bad guys out as a possible murderer nestled safely in his swank office three floors up. Nick stepped through the metal detector and took a temporary security pass from a straight-faced guard.

He marched across the Capitol Rotunda's mosaic tile floor, peering up toward the ceiling's dome as it rose 250 feet above him. Twilight's amber sunlight streamed through its windows. The Rotunda's pearl-white walls and gold-leaf crown molding gave the room a regal appearance. Three Roman columns flanked each side of the three exiting hallways.

Nick climbed the grand Carrera marble staircase to the third floor and stopped short of the door marked 325. Leaning out over the balcony, he glanced toward the expansive murals adorning the dome's base. They depicted the "Four Forces of Civilization," art, justice, science, and religion. The tiled words below the murals read:

"There may be room there for such a holy experiment. For the nations want a precedent. And my God will make it the seed of the

nation. That an example may be set up to the nations. That we may do the thing that is truly wise and just."

WHOSE GOD? Even here, in Pennsylvania's seat of government, the walls proclaimed God. *Enough!* Had the men who founded this state and those who'd built this nation really laid their hopes and dreams at the foot of an invisible deity? Nick shook his head and peeked at his watch: 6:57.

"Dr. Carlotti," said a deep voice from behind him.

Nick turned to see Mays approaching. Three-piece, charcoal gray Brioni suit. Check.

Mays stopped and rested his arms on the railing, his hands clasped together. There he stood, just like Nick imagined, as if he'd just popped out of the salon chair, hair flawless and cuticles perfectly manicured. "'That we may do the thing that is truly wise and just.' William Penn wrote those words three hundred years ago. It's a good reminder, don't you think?" Mays said, looking up toward the dome.

"And do you, Senator?"

"Do I what?"

"Do you do what is wise and just or do you just do what you want because you can?"

Mays turned and glared, his narrow, deep-set eyes a good four inches above Nick's. He spoke with a low tone and volume but not at the sacrifice of authority. "I find your question a bit sanctimonious coming from a Carlotti, but I'll answer it anyway. I'd like to think I try, but let's say I'm human." The last word echoed in the open space of the domed roof.

Nick straightened up tall and didn't bat an eye. "You were with my mother minutes before she died, and I know it wasn't random chance."

"I'm sorry you lost your mother, but if you're insinuating that I had something to do with her accident you're mistaken."

"Prove me wrong."

Mays nodded. "Ah, guilty until proven innocent."

"From my perspective, yes."

"Okay, then. Well, your mother introduced me to a strange young sculptor, told me about a novel she was writing, then gave me directions to Rodin's unfinished Gates of Hell. She excused herself to return to the board members' table. It shocked and saddened me to hear about her accident."

Nick struggled to keep his voice down. "You were an uninvited guest, and I find it hard to believe that you and my mother being in the same room, let alone standing at the same table wasn't premeditated. You've been trying to break my father for years, and maybe you finally found a way to do that."

"I'd love nothing more than to see that piece of human waste behind bars until he rots like a dead rat in a trap, but that's not my job anymore. Your mother was the only thing about Rock Carlotti that wasn't corrupt, and the insinuation that I had anything to do with her death is ludicrous," Mays said, his long, aristocratic face flushed red. "And, for the record, my office received an invite from the board of directors."

"The board says otherwise." Nick moved in close to Mays. "How did you know my mother went by Ali?"

Mays dropped his shoulders and he looked away. "I'm not sure what you're talking about."

"I think you're full of shit. You called her 'Ali' and I want to know why."

"Doctor Carlotti, I'll tell you that I'm not the adversary and never have been. Your mother and I were friends. I'm warning you to be careful where you dig because you're playing with fire."

"Is that a threat?"

"No, Nick, it's a favor."

Nick put his right index finger into Mays' chest. "I'm

pursuing this to the end, Senator, and if I find your hands are dirty, I promise I will take you down." Nick turned to walk away.

"Your mother was a good woman, Nick. I'm truly sorry."

Nick stopped in his tracks. "The flowers at the funeral. . . nice touch."

Descending the marble staircase, Nick wasn't sure what to think of Mays' interaction with his mother that night, but still, it wasn't fortuitous. Mays wanted or needed to confront Liza, but Nick couldn't grasp why. If Mays was telling the truth about his invite, something even more convoluted had to be in play.

He had a sense that he and Mays would see each other again in the not too distant future.

As he exited the parking lot, his phone vibrated once on the dash. The missed call came from Danielle. He felt the tug, but probably just a patient question. He put the phone to his ear.

"Nick, it's Danielle. I'm sorry I missed your call. Please be safe. I'm worried about you."

Danielle was worried about him. Probably not a satisfactory consolation prize, but it was better than nothing. He wanted to call her but remained content to leave her words lingering as the one peaceful thought in his weary mind as he headed back to Philadelphia.

41

VISITING hours ended at 10 pm, but the nurses didn't bat an eye when Nick walked past them in street clothes just past midnight. Not that he expected a confrontation but still he felt a sense of relief when their loyalty proved itself. After all, Nick could justify his visit because he came as a family friend. And peeking at the chart, well, he couldn't resist.

"Dr. Carlotti, I hope you know we're on your side," Yumi, one of the nurses, said as she stepped into the room.

Nick nodded. "Thanks, Yumi. I can use all the help I can get."

"I think you'll be pleased with what you see," she said.

He couldn't believe it. Zach's fever had broken and his labs, although not yet normalized, were better. His kidney function had improved, and although still intubated, he initiated his own breaths. "He's turned around."

Yumi's narrow Korean eyes widened as she slapped Nick on the front of his shoulder. "Right! Crazy, huh?"

Nick stepped back to prevent falling over.

Yumi grabbed his arm, her jaw dropped. "Oh my god, I'm so sorry."

"No worries," he said with a chuckle. "So, what's the scoop?"

"This afternoon he continued breathing above the ventilator, and we've been able to wean him down. He hasn't spiked a fever in twelve hours, and his leg looks a ton better. Zack's parents believe it was a miracle and I have a hard time disagreeing," Yumi said.

Nick stepped into the room, relieved to see Zach's face, the pale dusky look of impending death now replaced by a slight pink hue. He appeared comfortable, his breathing slow, steady, and unlabored. Nick rested his hand on the boy's head. "Thank God."

The phrase just slipped out. Nick couldn't take it back and wasn't sure he wanted to. He didn't care where the help came from as long as Zach lived. 'Thank God' certainly didn't have to hold any serious religious connotations. What difference did it make anyway? Zach's condition had improved and Nick could leave with one less worry on his mind.

He grabbed the boy's hand. "You had me scared, Buddy. It looks like your parents have favor with the man upstairs." He gave Zach's hand a squeeze and patted his forehead.

The 'Doctors Only' spots right outside the ER exit were hard to come by, and on this night, he'd parked his car up one level. The parking garage was generally well lit, and a security guard patrolled the main level.

As Nick reached the second floor, section B12, he noticed several ceiling lights were out, and he could barely make out his car in the darkness. He scanned the garage, as was his routine when he left late at night. He pressed his key fob. The dull mechanical clunk of the door's lock echoed off the concrete walls. The dome light of his car shed a small amount of illumination around him.

He reached out for the door's handle. A large, calloused hand grabbed him from behind, covering his nose and mouth. The rigid barrel of a handgun pressed into his ribs. The instinct to fight back was short-lived, as the thought of a bullet ripping through his lungs gave him pause.

A dark sedan raced around the corner and screeched to a stop. The man with the gun pushed Nick hard against the car and forced a burlap bag over his head.

"We're taking a little ride, Doctor," the man said. The car's door opened, and the man shoved Nick into the back seat, then slid in next to him. Nick felt another person to his right. The tires squealed as the car's acceleration jolted Nick's head backward. The occupants of the car remained silent.

The coarse bag stunk like old coffee grounds tainted with kerosene and each breath seemed harder to pull into his lungs. Oh God, was this it? What a hypocrite for crying out to God, but if God were indeed listening, Nick needed his help.

"Dr. Carlotti, you've been doing a little investigative work as of late," said the person sitting to his right, his electronically altered voice an octave lower than normal and robotic in tone. "Might I remind you that you're a surgeon, not a cop, a lawyer, or Magnum PI, so it might behoove you to put an end to your snooping. You know how this will play out. You are a Carlotti, for god's sake."

Nick forced his feet to the floor and lunged at the man. "You're the son-of-a-bitch who killed my mother? Who the hell are you?" A firm blow landed on the side of Nick's head. The gun barrel rammed deeper into his side.

"Your mother died in an unfortunate, tragic car accident. It's all in the police report. You can leave it there, or you can join her. If I wanted you dead, you would be, so consider this a gift but take this as your only warning," the man said. They drove for about ten minutes before the car came to a halt.

"This isn't over!" Nick said.

A second crushing blow landed on the left side of his skull. His head spun for a moment, then came the searing pain.

"On the contrary. If you stay on the present course, you'll

wish I'd have killed you today. Now get the hell out of my car," the man said as the door flew open.

Someone grabbed Nick by the shirt collar and yanked him from the car. He landed flat on his back, his head slamming against the concrete. Everything went dark.

Dazed, he lay there for a few seconds as the roar of the car's engine faded. He pulled the bag from his head and opened his eyes in time to see the black sedan turn a corner a couple blocks away.

His heart pounded like a drum in his head as he sucked in a deep breath and stood to his feet. His briefcase lay a few feet away. A quick scan suggested he wasn't in an ideal place, at least not for an Italian with a $750 Barney's briefcase at 12:45 am.

The signs on the corner read Kensington and E. Somerset. North Philly — perfect! The rusty steel beams of the elevated tracks shook as the El train thundered above him. When the last train car rolled out of sight, the corner turned eerily quiet.

Nick spun his head around. A pawnshop to his right had its entrance protected by a secondary barred security door, and graffiti decorated its sign. Directly across the street stood a buxom black woman in a red leather mini-skirt, a lacy black halter top, and stilettos. The sign above the bar behind her read Double Barrel. She cocked her head to the side and stared at Nick like maybe she'd spotted an alien from another planet. When their eyes met, she smiled and ran her tongue along her upper lip. The night just kept getting better. Nick looked away and reached into his pocket for his phone.

Cabs didn't cruise this part of town looking for fares, so he'd have to call for a ride. It could be a long wait. He thought about calling Steve but didn't want to involve him any more than he already had. Instead, he called the cab company. As expected, the dispatcher said the taxi wouldn't be there for at least thirty minutes, and Nick wasn't enthusiastic about standing on this particular corner. For now, he had no alternative.

As he leaned against the steel beam of the train track, his right hand ached. He'd been gripping the handle of his briefcase like it contained gold bars. He relaxed his hand and dropped his shoulders.

A car door slammed shut across the street. Opposite the hooker, three young black men stepped out of a pimped-out silver Suburban. They marched through the intersection like they were on a mission. The largest man in the lead, his shoulders pulled back, moved with a slow, cocky swagger.

'Bro, you must be lost, crazy, or stoned, because this is my corner, and you're standing on it!" the big man shouted as they approached.

Nick turned and walked in the opposite direction.

"You deaf?" the man yelled as the other two ran to surround Nick.

Trying to flee wasn't a viable option. Instead, Nick turned to the gang's apparent leader. "I'm on my way home. I'm not looking for trouble."

"Well, seems trouble found you," a second man said, ripping the briefcase from Nick's hand.

"Shut up, fool. I'm doing the talking," the leader said. "You looking to score some blow or just sightseeing?" he said as the second shrugged.

"Neither. I was dumped down here. I just want to get back home.

"You have my rent money in that fancy case?" The leader lifted his shirt, revealing a compact, black semiautomatic pistol tucked in his jeans. His pants rode way too low on his hips, showing the top third of his blue and white striped boxers. "If you're on my corner, you need to pay me rent. Give me your wallet and show me what's in that case of yours!"

Nick reached into his pocket to get his wallet. The man drew his pistol and backed Nick toward the building. "Don't be doing nothin' stupid!" he said. He waved his gun toward the smaller man. "Get his wallet."

The man took the wallet from Nick's pocket, opened it up, and smiled. He took out the four hundred and twenty dollars that it held.

The leader tapped on the briefcase. "Open it up."

Nick complied, showing the men two patient charts and a few loose papers. Business cards in the front cover emboldened with the name Dr. Nick Carlotti showed through a clear plastic cover.

The leader's eyes shot open, and his jaw dropped, his swagger replaced by a tremor. The pistol nearly slipped from his hand, but he regained control before it fell to the ground. "Stefon, give the doctor back his stuff," the man said, garnering bewildered looks from the other two. "You heard me. Give the man his damn wallet!"

The smaller man stuffed the cash back in the wallet and handed it to Nick.

"Sorry, we didn't know who you were," the leader said. "You need a lift?"

"Yeah, I think I might take you up on that. The ER parking garage at Penn would be fine. I won't tell the old man about this. We all make mistakes," Nick said, patting the man on the shoulder.

When the men dropped Nick off at his car, Nick took out two fifties and a business card, and handed them to the leader. "Thanks for the ride," he said. "My mother died not far from here and I'd like to find the scumbag responsible. If you happen to hear anything that might be helpful, call me."

The man took the money and business card and nodded. They drove away, leaving Nick standing right where the night's drama had begun.

Nick reached for the door handle, this time without worry. The chances of being accosted three times in one night were slim to none. He left the lot thankful that for the first time in a very long time, the Carlotti name had served to his advantage.

42

FEAR WAS AN INTERESTING EMOTION. Elevators and a rancid burlap bag triggered near-death experiences but a gun to the ribs didn't. Regardless, pissed-off seemed to be gaining traction over fear, and Nick sensed it was a good thing.

He'd been in the presence of his mother's killer. The asshole knew Nick wanted him dead yet let him go. Why? If they'd murdered his mother for her knowledge, wouldn't his meddling warrant the same?

The lump in his throat didn't come from fear but self-condemnation; guilt for being spared, shame for not having done something to avenge his mother's death. Damn it! He'd sat three inches from the son-of-a-bitch! *I'm sorry, Mom. I would have torn him apart. I tried.*

He'd bought a 9mm Beretta three years ago, two days after the young man died outside his front door. The gun hadn't been out of his bedside safe since he'd brought it home. He had a concealed weapon permit but didn't carry because he refused to portray even a hint of resemblance to his father and brother. But he contemplated revising his policy based on recent events.

Sliding the small safe from under his bed, Nick hesitated as he stared at the keypad. The 'easy to remember' three-digit combination that he'd chosen for the sole purpose of avoiding this circumstance fled to some dusty corner of his brain.

"Seriously, Nick!" He tried the usual combinations: his birthday 3-1-6, the first three digits of his Social Security Number 1-5-9. Nothing. He closed his eyes tight, resisting the urge to throw the safe across the room. "No shit, Einstein!" Nick punched in '9-1-1 Enter.' The safe sprung open, and the matte black Beretta appeared with an extra full magazine by its side.

Not sure it was even loaded, Nick ejected the gun's magazine and examined the ammunition. He clicked the magazine back into place with the palm of his left hand and chambered a round. From here forward the pistol would remain on his nightstand with the extra magazine in the top drawer. He shoved the empty safe back under the bed and felt better knowing that he wouldn't be asking a would-be intruder to hold on a second while he tried to remember the combination.

At 2:37 am, he turned off the light and pulled the covers over his shoulders. Physically and emotionally drained, he felt exhausted, but nonetheless, sleep eluded him for another hour and a half. His brain refused to shut down.

The phone rang just before noon, waking Nick from a near coma. With his eyelids still pasted shut he reached for the phone on his nightstand, knocking it to the floor. By the fourth ring, his vision had cleared enough to grab the receiver.

"Hello," he said with a gravely morning voice.

"Nick?" She was the last person he'd expected on the other end. He pulled the phone away from his mouth. "Ahem! Good morning, Danielle."

"Is this a good time?" Nick couldn't think of a bad time for Danielle to call. "Of course."

"I thought that maybe we need to talk. You've been through a lot, and I haven't given you a fair shake."

He shook his head, trying to dislodge the cobwebs. He felt

pretty sure he wasn't dreaming, but the possibility of Danielle consenting to a date on her own accord seemed remote at best. "Are you saying you'll go out with me?"

She paused. "I'm sure it's against my better judgment, but I think so."

"You think so?"

"You know what I mean. Don't press your luck."

Nick didn't want to take the chance she'd change her mind. "No pressure. Just a bite to eat and if I haven't completely turned you off, maybe a show?"

Danielle chuckled. "What if you only partially turn me off?"

"We can flip a coin."

"I'm in."

"I'll pick you up at 7. What's your address?"

When he hung up, he lay there repeating the address over and over in his head. He felt like a fifteen-year-old who'd just asked out his first girlfriend. Either he was getting soft, getting destitute, or this woman totally overwhelmed him. He couldn't quite put his finger on it, but he hadn't felt this way in years.

43

"Senator Mays, there's a Detective Maurice Rawls on the phone for you," Joan said over the intercom.

Although the two knew each other well and their careers occasionally put them on mutual ground, Rawls had never called Mays.

Mays swallowed hard. "Put him through."

"Detective Rawls, what can I do for you?"

"Good afternoon, Senator. I'll cut to the chase. Does the name 'Anya' mean anything to you?"

The air rushed from Mays' lungs in a single beat of his heart. He pulled the phone from his lips. Inhale. Calm yourself. "No, should it?"

"The singer from the restaurant the night of the convention. She's been missing for over a month."

"The singer?"

"From Sergio's, Asian-Hispanic mix. Hard to miss."

"Yeah, I vaguely remember her, but what does that have to do with me?" Mays wiped the sweat from the palm of his free hand on his thigh.

"Not sure, but as I recall, you were quite fixated on her."

"And?"

"And, I thought you might have noticed something. You stuck around after we left, no?"

"I left a few minutes after you did, so no." Rawls cleared his throat.

"And you went right home?"

"To my boat, yes."

"I'd like you to come down to answer some questions," Rawls said.

"I just did. I'm not sure where you're going with this."

"Oh, I think maybe you do, Senator."

Mays felt like a caged animal. "I have a meeting this morning but — "

"There's a patrol car waiting for you in front of the Capitol building. I thought it would make less of a scene. I'm doing you a favor."

Mays squeezed his eyes shut and shook his head. "I'll be down. Give me a minute to gather my things."

~

MAYS SHORED up his version of the story as he waited alone in the interrogation room. He'd seen Rawls break men down. But not him. Not today. Dark blue stains grew in the armpits of his hand-made British shirt. Where'd he say they went? What time did he leave her? Why was there blood all over his fucking boat? He needed a cigarette.

The stark, cold space seemed much smaller from the detainee's foldout metal chair than it had when he'd stood over prisoners in his position of power. He rested his long arms on the dented army-green metal table. Each dent on the table's top recorded, in perpetuity, the angry fist of either the interrogator or the interrogated. One or two seemed just about the average size of the male forehead.

The linoleum floor had yellowed and was peeling in spots from years of industrial-strength disinfectant. A television monitor hung on the wall, and a video camera, a recent upgrade from the obligatory two-way mirror, peered down from one of the corners.

Rawls hit play. The surveillance footage rolled with the time stamp in the lower right-hand corner. Mays watched the screen; his story was about to unravel. He and the girl entered the bar at 12:22 am. They exited precisely an hour and thirteen minutes later, Mays' left arm wrapped around Anya's waist. He held a martini glass in his right hand and appeared to be wobbly on his feet.

"Would you like to change your story, Senator?" Rawls asked, stopping the video.

"Okay, we were together."

"And you lied because?"

Mays shifted in the chair. "Because I knew it wouldn't look good, but I haven't done anything wrong."

Rawls opened a manila envelope, took out the burgundy and gold tie, and laid it on the table. "Your Charvet?"

Mays took the tie in his hand. "It could be. Where did you find it?"

"In the girl's bedroom along with your martini glass and I'm sure enough DNA to prove both belong to you."

Mays shot up from his chair and pointed his finger in Rawls' face. "I was never in her place! I don't even know where the hell she lives. This is a setup!"

"Setup? By whom?"

"I don't know."

"You don't know?"

Mays turned away from Rawls. "Look, it's complicated."

"I'd say so," Rawls said. "Any chance that Liza Carlotti's accident is part of 'complicated'?"

"What the hell are you talking about?"

"Do you know her?"

It seemed to touch a nerve as Mays let out a short huff and smirked but didn't say a word.

Rawls stepped around to face Mays. "If you don't want to spend the rest of your life behind bars, you might want to uncomplicate this for me in a hurry."

"Conversation over, Detective," Mays said moving toward the door.

Rawls slipped a single sheet of paper from his folder and handed it to Mays. "Before you leave, here's a warrant to search your boat. In the meantime, you might want to find yourself a good attorney."

"Corpus delicti, Detective. She might be missing, but that's not proof of a crime," Mays said, brushing by Rawls as he passed through the door.

"Body of evidence, Senator, not the body of the victim. You should know better. We may not have the latter, but if she's dead, we'll build the former. Oh, by the way, my men should be getting to your boat anytime now, so you'll need to stay away until they're finished with their work. I also have teams at your townhouse in Philly and apartment in Harrisburg."

The forensic team was bound to find something on his boat. As DA, Mays had known them well. They were top-notch professionals. If one strand of her hair, or a single drop of blood, remained in his bedroom, they'd likely find it. Mays wanted to run, but it would only imply his guilt. Sitting idle didn't seem a whole lot better. If his luck didn't change, he might as well forget his political career, skip the trial, and head directly to prison. One thing was clear— the payments to the men who'd set him up would cease. He now had to be the master of his own fate.

He called Joan on his excruciating cab ride back to Harrisburg and informed her that he'd be out of the office for at least the first part of the following week. It was Friday, and she reminded him that he had a senate appropriations committee meeting on Wednesday afternoon and two appointments prior. He assured her he'd be there, although he had serious doubts it would turn out that way.

As he sat looking out the window of the cab, he thought about Nick. Nick's distress about his mother's death seemed genuine, and he didn't seem to have any knowledge of the missing girl. If Nick wasn't in any way involved with his father's business, and indeed sought the truth, maybe they should be allies, not adversaries. It would undoubtedly be an unlikely alliance, but Mays needed to make Nick believe his innocence and begin to share information. Just maybe they'd been caught in the same web.

The authorities had to be watching him, and every phone call would be suspect. He couldn't drive to his condo, apartment, or boat, so he opted to make the drive back to Harrisburg and attempt to look as natural as possible. He would make the call to Nick from a phone within the Capitol.

Joan's head popped up and she closed her *Better Homes and Gardens* magazine when Mays walked through the door. "Senator Mays, I didn't expect you back. I'm just about ready to leave for the weekend. Is there anything I can do for you before I head out?"

"No, Joan, I just wanted to grab a few things, including the Department of Transportation funding recommendations and minutes from the last appropriations committee meeting," he said with a smile. "Have a nice weekend. I'll see you on Wednesday."

After Joan left, Mays picked up the phone at her desk and dialed Nick's number. On the fourth ring, the call went to voicemail.

"Damn it!" He left a brief message and hung up. Not having a place to go for the night, he considered sleeping in his office but opted instead to make the half-hour drive to the Hotel Hershey, the only five-star hotel near Harrisburg. He booked the 2100 square foot Milton Hershey suite. If he had to spend the rest of his life behind bars, sleeping on a musty prison cot, his last days of freedom might as well be spent in luxury.

44

To be late or not to be late, that was the question. If he showed up on time, he might look desperate. Show up late, a bit cocky. Danielle already thought Nick was full of himself, so he decided to err on the side of desperate.

He knocked on the door of her apartment at 6:45 pm. No answer. Peeking beyond the edge of the shade covering the front window, he saw only a dim, warm glow. Music played in the background. A few moments later, he raised his hand to strike the door again when it opened, leaving his fist hanging in the air.

A ravishing barefoot woman in tight, faded jeans and a fitted, cherry-red blouse welcomed him with a bright smile. Her sun-kissed hair, still damp, draped over her shoulder. She wasn't wearing a hint of makeup. Danielle's natural beauty was a rare and refreshing sight.

"I have to dry my hair. Help yourself to a drink in the fridge, then check out the leather book on the third shelf," she said.

She pointed to a four-shelved bookcase against the far wall. "It's by Emily Post. Check out chapter three, '*Being Fashionably Late.*'"

Nice start! Nick smiled. "For the record, I'm on time because desperate won out over cocky."

"I'll give you points for thinking that much about it. I'll be out in a few minutes."

Danielle turned back down the short hallway to her room, her wet feet leaving short-lived prints on the hardwood floor. He'd rarely seen Danielle without a white lab coat or surgical scrubs. He'd always found her attractive, but the MD and her professionalism veiled her raw beauty. She disappeared around the corner.

Nick opened the refrigerator and found a lone bottle of Bud Light tucked behind the Diet Coke, orange juice, and skim milk. He took the first swig from the bottle and browsed the book titles on each shelf.

The first two shelves held classics, including Shakespeare's *A Midsummer Night's Dream*, works by Thoreau and J.R.R. Tolkien, and a section of mysteries by Elizabeth George and John Grisham. The second shelf contained mostly medical and surgical books. The whole third shelf held books bearing religious titles: *Mere Christianity* by C.S. Lewis, a couple Bibles, and *The Way of Deliverance* by Watchman Nee.

The brown leather book on that same shelf stood out among the glossy hardcover and paperback books on either side. Danielle had planted a blatant bait and switch. No Emily Post jacket on the leather book whose pages were darkened, dried, and brittle, but otherwise were well preserved. The title: *Pilgrim's Progress* by John Bunyan, published in 1678 and printed in 1849.

The muffled sound of Danielle's hair-drier droned below the jazz music coming from her stereo. Nick opened to a random page and read:

> *"Now I saw in my dream, that the highway up which Christian was to go, was fenced on either side with a wall, and that wall was called Salvation. Up this way, therefore, did burdened Christian run, but*

*not without great difficulty, because of the load on his back. He ran
thus till he came at a place somewhat ascending; and upon that place
stood a cross, and a little below, in the bottom, a sepulchre. So I saw
in my dream, that just as Christian came up with the cross, his
burden loosed from off his shoulders, and fell from off his back, and
began to tumble, and so continued to do till it came to the mouth
of the
sepulchre, where it fell in, and I saw it no more."*

NICK SMILED as he pushed the book back into its spot. His mother's funeral invaded his thought and brought a sudden jolt of grief. What would she have felt about Danielle's book collection? For that matter, what would she think about Danielle? She would have been over the moon.

She certainly would have approved of her faith. Nick's mother had dragged him to St. Luke's church every Sunday and holy day from birth until he graduated from high school. It had always sounded like a bunch of repetitious, meaningless chatter. As he got older, he just didn't need the guilt trip.

Once in college, away from his mother's influence, he ended the facade and spent his Sundays sleeping in and watching football like the rest of the people living in reality. He believed in God or at least a higher power most days, questioned it on many others, but the whole church thing never fit. And God's unwillingness to save his mother may have been the last shovel of dirt on the casket of his faith.

He'd just settled on the couch when Danielle stepped into the room, her hair like honey, flowing over her shoulders. Maybe she really was out of his league. She was a magnet. He tried hard to not make his locked gaze visible, but he just couldn't look away.

"Did you enjoy Emily Post?" she asked.

"I think Emily must have been writing under an alias, John Bunyan. A little proselytizing before dinner?"

Danielle lifted her shoulders and looked at him with innocent puppy dog eyes.

Nick laughed. "Some form of Christian foreplay, I presume?"

"Well, I never quite heard it put that way, but maybe," she said with a grin.

"I like the book collection. Right up my mother's alley."

Danielle's grin faded as she took a seat next to him. "I'm sure we would have hit it off. Do you want to tell me more about your concerns?"

"I don't want to spoil the mood."

"I think you need to let it out. Then we can set it aside and enjoy the rest of the evening."

Nick told her about the journal entries, the Bible verses, and Rebecca's Box.

"I'm speechless," Danielle said.

"I don't want to believe my father's involved. He's certainly capable, but I can't figure out a motive."

"Adultery, insurance, maybe to save his estate?"

"Maybe all of the above, but why risk it? You think I'm crazy."

"Nick, if it were only you seeing it this way I might wonder, but since you have corroboration, I think not— Steve's pretty level headed," she said with a slight grin.

"And I'm not?"

"You're Italian and you're a surgeon. Need I say more?"

Nick smiled.

"I'm afraid for you," Danielle said.

"I'm afraid too, but more angry."

"I'll be praying, Nick. Like it or not."

"Thanks, I appreciate it. Any requests for dinner?" Nick asked.

"Casual. Other than that, it's your choice. Surprise me."

"Got it." He stood and opened the door. As she passed, he gently led her out, his hand resting on the small of her back. He wished he could reside in this moment, on this date, forever. No fear, no death, no family history, just joy and excitement. He hadn't experienced those feelings in longer than he could remember.

He knew just the place. She wanted casual, and casual she was going to get.

45

THEY PARKED a couple blocks away and strolled down South 9th Street, neither sure what to do with their hands or how close together they should walk. Was this a real date or just two colleagues making peace over a good meal? From a distance, a bright blue and red neon sign in the shape of a cheesesteak stood atop the iconic corner building. A long line stretched out the door. A middle-aged couple in business attire waited in stark contrast next to a lanky young man with powder-white skin, both arms veiled by tattoos and more piercings than available facial parts.

Before they reached Giovani's, Nick's phone vibrated in his pocket. The number wasn't familiar, the area code 717. He felt, for the first time in months, light-hearted and didn't want to spoil the moment. He let it go to voicemail.

The man at the counter took orders and barked them to his two line-cooks, with a rough Italian voice — a cross between an auctioneer and Rocky Balboa. The diner ran like General Motors' best assembly line. The cook diced the meat and sautéed peppers and onions with metal spatulas moving at light speed. It wasn't just a meal but a cultural adventure.

They picked up their orders and grabbed an upstairs booth.

"I hope this isn't too low-key, but you did say 'casual.'" Nick said.

"It's the perfect end to this ridiculous diet I've been on. Nothing sounds better right now than a greasy, onion-smothered cheesesteak. Nothing except for these gooey cheese fries." She put one in her mouth, a small bit of orange Cheese Whiz sticking to her chin. They both laughed.

Reaching across the table with a napkin in his hand, Nick wiped the cheese from her chin. "Unless you were planning to save it for later?"

"If you aren't going to treat me to dessert, you might better have left it there." Danielle's smile waned, and her soft blue eyes narrowed. "I'm sorry it didn't pan out at Hopkins."

"I wasn't aware you knew."

"Steve told me. He knew you didn't want it to be common knowledge, but he thought you might need to vent."

"I held it close, you know, like a woman who doesn't let people know she's pregnant until she's a few months along. I didn't want to have to share bad news if something didn't go well. In this case, it appears I had a miscarriage."

Danielle peeked at Nick through a long lock of hair in front of her eyes. She swept it back with her fingers. "I think it's more like a post-term pregnancy. The dream is very much alive. You just need to be patient until the delivery."

Nick smiled. "Nice metaphor, Doctor Sorenson. I'll add quick wit to your long resume of admirable character traits."

"I have my moments," Danielle said. "And, if I remember my fifth grade English class, I think it was a simile but who's keeping track?"

"Apparently you are."

Danielle smiled then looked more serious. "You deserved the position."

"I'm over it."

"Right! One thing you don't do well is hide your emotions. Oh yeah, you're level-headed, I forgot."

"It's in my genes, and speaking of jeans, I want to say that it's refreshing to see you in them, a welcome change from scrubs and a surgical gown."

"Nice segue."

"No, it's just that there's nothing I can do about Hopkins so I'm not going to mull over it."

Nick noticed Danielle's empty tray. Remarkable, eating like that and still looking so damn good. She said she'd been on a diet, but as far as he remembered, she always looked like she'd just stepped out of a yoga class. Some people were blessed that way.

"Have I earned date part two?" Nick asked.

"Oh! So, this is officially a date, huh?"

"Boy shaves and puts on cologne. Girl puts on jeans and does her hair. Boy picks up girl. Boy wipes Cheese Whiz from girl's chin. I think it's a date."

"Fair enough. So, what's part two, before I give my consent?"

"I have two tickets to the Wilma Theater, Ariel Dorfman's *The Other Side*. I've heard rave reviews. But if you want to do something else, I'm open to suggestions."

"I'm in. You probably didn't know this about me, but I played Maria in West Side Story my senior year at the University of Montana. I love the theater," she said as their gazes locked.

Nick melted inside. Her beauty was hypnotic, and seemingly, she had talents she'd kept to herself.

"I didn't know you sang, and for that matter, I didn't know you went to the University of Montana. Interesting they chose a tall, blonde Swede for the part of a short Hispanic woman."

"We had an excellent makeup department."

They laughed as Nick gathered their wrappers and napkins when someone yelled, "Yo, Doc!"

Mickey Scalise lumbered toward them, both hands tucked in

the pockets of his coffee-colored leather jacket. "Who's the lovely lady?"

"Danielle, this is Mickey Scalise, an associate of my father's." Turning to Danielle, he added, "Mickey, this is Danielle, a colleague of mine." Nick purposefully didn't say her last name. The less his father knew of his friends, the better.

"Colleague, huh? Is that what they call it these days?" Mickey said with a smirk. "Mind if I have a seat?" he asked, sliding into the booth next to Danielle before Nick had a chance to respond.

"Are you eating, Mickey, or just happened to stop by?"

"Came by for takeout. You can't get a good cheesesteak in Colombia."

"I bet not," Nick said. "But I hear the empanadas are to die for."

Mickey smiled. "Eddie said he ran into you at the house while we were gone. Glad to know someone is using the pool."

"Jennifer offered it up, and I needed the break," Nick answered.

"I guess so. Two trips to the cottage and a swim at the house. They must be working you too hard," Mickey said, reaching over and taking a sip of Nick's drink. "Diet, I should have known."

Nick didn't blink. "Tell the old man thanks for letting me use the pool and the cottage. I needed the R and R."

Mickey stood and slapped his hand on the back of Nick's neck, then squeezed hard. "Careful wandering around though, we wouldn't want to mistake you for an intruder."

"I'll keep that in mind."

Scalise turned to Danielle, extending his hand. "Do you have a last name, Doctor?"

Before Nick could kick her under the table, Danielle took hold of his hand and answered, "Sorenson."

Scalise put his bandaged hand over his chest, feigning a heart attack. "I think I need a mouth-to-mouth," he said, tightening his grip on Danielle's hand.

"I'll call EMS," Nick said, staring into Mickey's eyes.

Scalise loosened his grip, and Danielle pulled back her hand.

"Enjoy your date," Scalise said. He turned his back and headed out the door.

"He didn't order anything," Danielle said.

"He's a little ADD. Your beauty probably distracted him."

"Smooth," she said, rolling her eyes.

"Not smooth, just observant," he said.

Nick wished she hadn't divulged her last name but didn't want to alarm her.

They finished their drinks and took a short eight-minute drive to the Wilma Theater. From center stage, fourth-row seats, Nick and Danielle witnessed the comic portrayal of a husband, a wife, a house, and even the couple's bed split apart, falling on opposite sides of two bordering, war-torn countries. It seemed a good representation of his parents' relationship and was, metaphorically, the sad reality for the majority of marriages he'd witnessed, including his own. The wars of words, selfish ambitions, and uncontrolled lusts falling like an executioner's sword, dividing parents, children, homes, and possessions. He had wielded that sword himself and caused at least as much pain as he'd endured. He was no saint.

As he walked Danielle to the steps of her apartment, Nick couldn't for the life of him comprehend how such an amazing woman remained veiled under a surgeon's cap and lab coat. How could he have not known? Maybe he wasn't ready or was just too proud to notice. Regardless, it had all changed now, and he knew there was no going back.

"Thank you, Nick, for a wonderful night. I had a great time."

"I hope this makes up for my crash and burn at Grand Rounds."

"It's a start, Dr. Carlotti. You're off the hook, for now."

Nick offered a handshake to seal their pact, and she reciprocated. He remembered having done the same when she turned him down and relished the second chance. They shook hands for longer than necessary. Nick pulled her gently toward him, gazed into her azure eyes, and kissed her. Her soft lips melted into his, and her delicate hand squeezed his a little tighter as they embraced. His body responded with an increasing urge to carry her inside and make love to her but he found himself doing something entirely out of character. He stopped, hugged her tightly, kissed her cheek, and said, "Thank you, Danielle. I hope we can do this again."

"I think there's a reasonable chance." She gave his hand another squeeze as he turned toward his car.

He didn't know if he'd retreated out of fear of being rejected or because he knew Danielle deserved his respect. Probably both, but she had him tied up in knots. Maybe he'd lost his mind. A couple extra sessions with his shrink would clear up the confusion. He vowed to call Dr. Makos on Monday to set up the next appointment.

His mind grew restless, flying back and forth all night between thoughts of Danielle, images of his mother's mangled car, and his backseat car ride to the hood, all the while carrying on a contorted monologue with God. He wished that he and Danielle were still together, not just because he didn't end up in her bed, but because he felt at peace around her. And peace had become a rare commodity.

46

Rawls was sitting at his desk Saturday morning, trudging through a monstrous pile of departmental paperwork when an annoying metallic tapping on the window caught his attention. Taylor stood outside, waving a manila folder, with an excited grin plastered on his face.

Rawls motioned for him to come in, then raised his hand, causing Taylor to pause in the doorway. The flying fox zipped past Taylor and crashed into the wall. It dropped nose first to the floor.

"At least it had speed," Taylor said.

"Too much caffeine," Rawls said. He took two more sips of black coffee. 8:15 am and he'd already started his third cup. He hadn't taken a Saturday off in three months and had already been there an hour and a half. Whatever Taylor had in his hand would hopefully provide a momentary diversion from his administrative duties.

Rawls wasn't a control freak, although one might have made that assumption if they'd gazed upon his corner office with its two nearly wall-sized, single-panel windows facing the police station's main room. It wasn't that he wanted to peer out and keep tabs on people. Rather, he wanted to be a part of them. They were a tight-knit family. They respected his leadership, his skill as a detective, and his unwavering loyalty to his people. If you earned his respect, he treated you with respect.

He maintained an equal demeanor with the custodial staff, the mayor, and a district court judge. A week ago, he'd looked up from his desk and taken note of his windows. They were spotless, like they had no glass at all, just open air. Rawls set aside his pile of reports, drove two blocks to Starbucks, and bought a twenty-five-dollar gift card. He jotted a handwritten note and gave the cleaning lady, Miss Hester a little dose of gratitude. In his eyes, respect came from a job well done, not from a title or the thickness of one's wallet.

Detective Taylor strode through the door and dropped the folder on Rawls' desk. "We have a match," he said. "Actually, two matches. The DNA from both Anya's lipstick and toothbrush match the hair and blood we found on Mays' boat. The DNA from the second martini glass belongs to Mays. We matched it to DNA from cigarette butts Mays left in an ashtray on the bridge of his boat. The prints were only partials, but they're spot on."

Rawls opened the folder and scanned the data. "I'm not one of the Senator's biggest fans, but I didn't make him out to be capable of murder. What a waste," he said, shaking his head. "Prepare an affidavit for Judge Egan. When the warrant's on my desk, we'll bring him in."

"I have one more bombshell for you," Taylor said.

"Drop it."

"Just received an anonymous call from a guy who said he saw Mays and Liza Carlotti arguing in the art museum parking garage the night of her accident. He said Mays' black Escalade spun its tires as it pulled out of the garage right after Mrs. Carlotti left in her BMW."

"The black SUV sited near the crash site." Taylor raised his eyebrows.

"I'm thinkin'."

Rawls handed Taylor the folder. "We may just kill two birds with one stone. Any word from forensics on Santini?"

"Yeah, definitely died from a narcotics overdose. Super strong stuff apparently. And the blood in his ear, an acutely perforated eardrum."

"How do they suppose that happened?"

"They aren't sure but said it had to have happened just before he died because of the blood. Looked more like a small laceration and not a rupture."

"From?" Taylor shrugged. "Beats me."

"Make sure we keep our eyes on Mays. I don't want him taking so much as a leak without us knowing about it. Twenty-four-seven," Rawls said.

Rawls had put Mays under tight surveillance since he'd left the station the day prior. As expected, he made no mistakes. Mays placed only two calls from his cell phone— one to his office and one to a ranking member of the Senate appropriations committee.

Mays' Bentley hadn't left the Hershey Hotel lot since he'd parked it there the previous night. Six different vehicles were registered to Mays including the black Escalade. Rawls hoped they'd find it at the marina parking lot or either of his other residences in Philly and Harrisburg.

Officers stood positioned near the hotel's exits as they waited for the go-ahead to take him in.

∾

MAYS PACKED his things and penned a quick note on hotel stationery. He removed a large hardcover book from his briefcase, flipped through its pages, and came to a stop. It seemed like yesterday, not forty-plus years ago — a light-hearted, simpler time. The picture blurred as he carefully tore out the page.

Folding it in thirds small enough to fit in a business envelope, he set it on the desk.

He slipped his wallet from the left inside pocket of his suit jacket and pulled out a photo from behind his credit cards. Transfixed, gazing at the image, he bit his lower lip, then placed the picture, the folded page from the book, and the note into an envelope and headed to the hotel's lobby.

A young woman at the checkout desk greeted him with a warm smile. "Senator Mays, I hope you had a restful stay with us. Will you be checking out?"

"I did and yes." He did his best to return a smile as he set the envelope on the desk. "I have a big favor to ask. I'd like to mail this but don't have the address. Would you be so kind as to track down the address for me and stick it in today's mail?" He placed a fifty-dollar bill next to the envelope.

The woman slid the cash back to Mays. "I'd be glad to, Senator. The money isn't necessary." She glanced at the name. "Dr. Nick Carlotti. I saw a news piece about him recently, about treating a little kid from Africa. That poor boy."

Mays nodded. "He lives in Philly, somewhere near South Street. Sorry, that's all I can give you, but I'd like it sent today. Overnight if possible."

"He might not receive it until Monday. I don't think they deliver on Sunday."

"That'll be fine. Thanks again."

The woman picked up the envelope. "My pleasure. I hope you come back to see us again soon."

Mays shot her a wink, but behind the facade, he was coming apart. A return visit would be doubtful unless his luck changed in a hurry.

As he walked to his Bentley, a wave of anxiety coursed through him. He stopped, pulled a pack of Newports from his breast pocket, and lifted a cigarette to his lips. It felt like marching to his own funeral as he took a drag and continued on.

He surveyed the parking lot, doubting he was alone. The moment his hand reached for the door handle, two unmarked cars raced in from his right and left, tires squealing. Four men flew from the vehicles, handguns drawn.

"Put your hands on the car!" one officer yelled. Another rushed directly at Mays while the remaining two stayed positioned at each side.

Mays dropped his bag and put both hands on the hood. The officer grabbed Mays' left wrist and pulled it behind his back, slapped on a cuff, and repeated the move with Mays' right wrist. "You have the right to remain silent. Anything — "

"Save yourself the trouble. I know my rights," Mays said, letting the cigarette fall from his lips. He bent down and backed into the car.

The officer continued. " . . . you say can and will be used against you in a court of law."

Mays sank into the seat and contemplated how one night of weakness could have created such a mess. How could he possibly defend himself if he didn't even know what the hell he did? One thing was certain. As an ex-DA, if he landed in prison, his days were numbered.

47

The scrolling headline read: *Pennsylvania State Senator Lloyd Mays, previous Philadelphia DA, son of a wealthy steel family, arrested for the murder of a Brazilian lounge singer.*

Nick sat in his boxer shorts on Sunday morning as he stared wide-eyed at the screen.

Mays' mug shot flashed on the screen, juxtaposed with an image of Anya from one of her CD covers. The only thing missing was a "GUILTY" sign across Mays' chest. His shoulders were slumped, his face long and pale. The deep, dark circles below his eyes painted a portrait of a man defeated, a man resigned to life behind bars or a quick death by lethal injection.

The news anchor stated that the woman was last seen leaving a downtown club with Mays on June 14. Her body had not yet been found. They'd scheduled his arraignment for the next morning, and it crossed Nick's mind to be in the courtroom, front row, eye to eye with the scum who'd probably killed his mother.

Nick's thoughts raced as the image of him and Mays in a stare down almost felt real. His blood boiled. A loud knock shook him back to reality. Rhino jumped from his curled-up place at Nick's feet and barked as he ran to the door. Sprinting to the bedroom, he threw on a t-shirt and a pair of gray sweat pants. He slid open the drawer to his nightstand and pulled out his Beretta.

As he crept toward the door, three more rapid taps interrupted his steps. Rhino let out a coarse growl as he stood on his hind legs with his front paws reaching up the door. Nick peered through the peephole. A figure wearing a blue hooded sweatshirt paced nervously on the porch. As the man turned, Nick caught a glimpse of bushy red hair. He lowered the gun to his side and opened the door.

Steve eyed the gun in Nick's hand and took a half step back. "Wu-whoa there, c-cowboy! You expecting s-someone?" he asked, fixated on the gun. "I told you I'd stop by on my way to church."

"I'm sorry. I forgot. I'm a little on edge," Nick replied, scanning the street. "Come in."

Nick shared the events of Thursday night, and Steve soon understood the reason for Nick's newfound fondness for his Berretta.

"I'll make this quick," Steve said, stepping away from the street-facing picture window in the living room. He took a slow breath and exhaled with the same cadence. Nick knew the maneuver, Steve's attempt at preventing a stutter fest. Sometimes it worked, sometimes not. Steve continued. "I've been thinking about the clues your mother left, especially Rebecca's Box." Steve set the book on the coffee table.

"I'm listening," Nick said.

"Neither the publisher nor her agent, Harmon Drake, would divulge information about the author. Both offered to pass my information to the person with the current legal rights to her book. I assumed it was your father, so I declined. Point is, I think the story is parallel. Your mother clearly had information she inadvertently stumbled upon. I believe that information led to her murder."

Nick huffed. "Like, maybe, the murder of a lounge singer?"

"That was random," Steve said.

Nick took a seat on the arm of the sofa. "Did you see the news this morning?"

"No, why?"

"They arrested Lloyd Mays yesterday for the murder of some Brazilian singer."

"Mays, the senator?"

"No, Mays the baseball player."

"Funny."

"Sorry, yes, Mays, the senator."

"When?"

"I told you, yesterday."

Steve tipped down his freckle-covered chin and peered up at Nick with an "I'm not an idiot" look. He shook his head. "No, I mean, when was the woman killed?"

"I'm not sure. I just caught a headline. Looks like there's a press conference soon."

Steve's gaze drifted to a random corner of the ceiling as he chewed on the last vestige of his thumbnail.

Nick nudged Steve's shoulder. "I know that look. What are you thinking?"

"Obviously, if he killed her before your mother's crash, it's possible your mother was somehow privy to it, but regardless, if Mays is a murderer and he and your mother were together the night of her accident, it's a bit creepy."

Nick glanced back to the TV as a news conference began. He picked up the remote and turned up the volume. Detective Rawls stood at a podium flanked on either side by flags of the US and the State of Pennsylvania. Rawls gave a brief, less-than-detailed account of the case against Mays. Anya had disappeared after leaving a club with Mays on June 14.

"Okay, so this was four months after the accident. I guess it's not the information that got my mother killed," Nick said.

"No, but if he is guilty of the girl's disappearance, then it still makes him suspect."

Rawls opened the floor to questions. Their voices joined together in a chaotic, unintelligible buzz. Reporters raised a sea of hands as they jockeyed for position. Rawls pointed to an attractive young female reporter to his left, in the front row. "Miss Donnelly."

"Detective Rawls, could you give us the woman's full name?"

"That is her full name. Anya. She has no last name, like Cher."

Before the reporters' voices rose again, Rawls nodded to an NBC reporter from Channel 6.

"If you haven't found a body, how can you be sure she's dead?"

"Suffice it to say we have sufficient evidence, both forensic and otherwise, to have charged the senator with murder."

"Can you elaborate?" the woman said.

"This is an ongoing and active case, and I am not at liberty to share any further details. We'll provide information as it becomes available, so long as it doesn't jeopardize the prosecution of the case."

The reporter shot out again. "Detective, one more question, please."

"Go ahead."

"We have information from an anonymous source that Senator Mays might have been involved in the February 22 accident that took the life of Rock Carlotti's wife, Liza. Can you confirm that for us?"

Rawls appeared caught off guard and didn't immediately answer.

Nick clenched his teeth and tightened the grip on the gun. He aimed it toward Mays' face on the screen. "Bang," he said quietly, his hands rising in pseudo-recoil.

"Maybe you should put that thing away," Steve said.

Rawls answered the reporter, "No, I can't confirm that."

Nick set the gun on the coffee table next to *Rebecca's Box*.

"This doesn't prove he killed your mother. I agree it paints Mays in a pretty dark light, but how does any of this tie in with Torello or Santini?"

Nick's nostrils flared. "I don't know but the bastard's hiding something!"

"Yeah, but there are too many other pieces to this puzzle that don't fit. Torello and Santini bring your father into the mix, and it doesn't make sense that Santini would have been working for Mays, a man who wanted to take down your father."

"Maybe Mays abandoned his efforts to destroy my father through legal means and offered Willie enough cash to do it from the inside."

"Then why not pay him to kill your father instead of your mom?"

"Sometimes watching people suffer provides more satisfaction than seeing them dead," Nick said. He hadn't yet told Steve about his conversation with Willie's aunt Rose. "Willie's aunt is convinced that he didn't commit suicide. And I believe her."

"How did they say he died?" Steve asked.

"A drug overdose. Heroin, I think."

"Why don't you get a copy of the coroner's report?"

Nick let out a sarcastic half chuckle. "Right. I've been down that dead-end road before."

"Willie's aunt should be able to if she was his next of kin."

"Good point. It's worth a shot."

Steve glanced toward the table. "Are those the bills from your father's house?"

"Yeah, nothing really, household bills, receipts, Maria's payroll information. Take a look if you want."

Steve picked up the folder with the receipts from the publisher. He skimmed one and smiled.

"Something funny?" Nick asked.

"Nope, not funny at all, just so stinking obvious! She wrote under an alias."

"My mother?"

"Uh-huh, your mother and Laura Carson were one and the same."

Nick grabbed the receipt from Steve's hand. "You're telling me that my mother wrote *Rebecca's Box*?"

Steve nodded. "It was her story. The check came from Blue Heron Press, the same publisher in Scranton. The first check's dated June 13, 1996, with 'advance' written in the memo line. The second check dated, December 27, 1996, coincided with the book's publishing."

Nick took a seat at the kitchen table, leaned back, and ran the fingers of both hands through his hair. "So, if my mother wrote *Rebecca's Box*, she had to know that no one, aside from Inspector Clouseau or a redheaded nerd from Michigan, would make that connection. What was the point of her writing the book?"

"I don't think she wrote it as a clue. Maybe just needed an outlet for her fears. I'm sure she felt scared and alone and had to tell her story, even if it remained veiled. But it does point to the likelihood that she did know someone's secret, and that person felt threatened enough to want her dead."

Nick walked toward the coffee table and took the book in his hand. This was his mother's creation, her heart, her desperate cries to be heard. He fought back the tears.

"Don't imagine I can talk you into joining me at church this morning?" Steve asked.

Nick smiled. "I don't think I'm quite ready for that. Besides, I'm not dressed for church. I'm going to try to find Maria. She's my best hope for finding out what my mother might have known."

"It's a good next move. Don't forget the coroner's report. And, for the record, you can wear sweats and a t-shirt at my church. It's sort of 'come as you are.' Maybe next week?"

"Yeah, maybe. Unless of course, they don't let Catholics in because of the whole Martin Luther thing."

"You're hilarious." Steve looked at the door and hesitated. "Any ch-chance I could use the back door?"

"Probably a good idea," Nick said, motioning with his head toward the hallway leading to the back door.

"Let me know wh-what you find," Steve said as he left.

"Will do," Nick said, bummed his circumstances were stressing out his best friend. He hadn't heard Steve stutter that much since they'd prepared to take their medical boards. It did, however, remain a useful barometer of Steve's level of anxiety.

Nick wanted to go to the jailhouse and rearrange Mays' face but finding Maria came first.

48

LOCATING a nameless woman from a tiny church in Laredo, Texas in order to track down a Mexican woman named Hernandez in Nuevo Laredo, Mexico. Perfect! It would be easier to track down a Chinese man named Wang in Guangdong Province.

Finding the phone number for the church was the easy part. Finding the gift giver — not so much. A call to the church early Sunday morning resulted only in Nick's hearing the church's office hours and worship time on a recorded message. Nick made the second call a little after noon. The church secretary seemed pleasant and immediately connected Nick with the senior pastor.

"This is Pastor Seyfert, how can I help you?"

"Pastor Seyfert, my name is Nick Carlotti, and I'm calling from Philadelphia. This is going to sound like an odd request, but I'm trying to find a close friend, who I believe, lives in Nuevo Laredo, Mexico. A woman from your church, a missionary to Nuevo Laredo maybe thirty years ago befriended her. My friend, Maria, visited your church about once a year. Her last name is Hernandez. Does that ring a bell?"

"Uh, not so much. I've been a bit out of the loop. I just

returned to Texas in December. My father served as senior pastor here for over forty years, and he retired two years ago. I spent the last fifteen years on an Indian reservation in North Dakota."

"You said your father retired two years ago?"

"We had an interim pastor who passed away unexpectedly. It's why I came home."

"It's important that I reach Ms. Hernandez. How can I reach your father?" Nick asked.

"He's in a nursing care facility here in town, but you may or may not be able to get much information from him. My sister and I had to put him in the home because his Alzheimer's had gotten pretty bad. We just couldn't care for him anymore."

"I'm sorry," Nick said, rolling his eyes. Although sorry for the elder pastor and his family, Nick was tired of dead ends.

"He has good days and bad days. You never know, maybe you'll catch him in a lucid moment. He's in the Villa of St. Paul Assisted Living home on Perry Street."

"Your mother . . . "

"She died when I was in seminary. My father never remarried."

"I'm very sorry. Thank you, Pastor. I appreciate your time and hope I didn't come off as insensitive."

"No worries. I hope you find your friend."

"Me too, thanks again," Nick said, hanging up.

He wasn't sure that a trip to Texas to interview a man with dementia would be worth the effort, but he had no other leads. The church staff might be of some help as well, and he was more likely to get useful information if he was there, face to face. By noon he had booked window seats for a one-way flight through Houston the next morning at 11:00.

Nick hated flying — not so much the thought of flight itself, but being trapped in a metal tube at thirty-five thousand feet with no way out, no way down. His destiny rested in the hands of the pilots and mechanics, the weather, and fate. Having a window

seat helped . . . a little. The prescription from Steve, for Xanax —
four one-milligram tablets, one for each of the two outbound and
two inbound flights — would help a whole lot more.

He reflected on his mother's last moments. It stung with such
finality. He'd never ever see her smile, hear her voice, or wrap his
arms around her again. He debated, knowing it would rip him
apart, dragging out that dusty box of old photo albums. He
hadn't mustered the courage to do so since the day she'd died.
But, what the hell, why not? Sometimes you just had to wallow in
the muck.

Nick poured himself a glass of Crown Royal. He glanced at
the clock: 12:38 pm. Good. At least he wasn't drinking before
noon.

With the box at his feet, he lifted out an album and set it on
the coffee table. The first sip of whiskey went down too smoothly,
so he downed another. He flipped open the cover. God, she was
stunning. His mother propped up on her knees in the white sand
of Seven Mile Beach, Stone Harbor, a half-finished sandcastle
rising between her and her five-year-old son. How was it possible
he remembered that day? Maybe he didn't, instead conjuring one
from bits and pieces of old memories. He turned the page and
poured himself another drink.

Five albums and three glasses of Crown later, he'd had his fill.
His face wet with tears and his heart seesawing between grief and
indignation, he lifted the box back onto the shelf. Another knock
came from the door.

HE WASN'T EXPECTING ANYONE, and Steve was probably too scared to come back so soon. Detouring to the coffee table before creeping toward the door, Nick squeezed the Beretta in his hand. He'd dedicated himself to the preservation of life, but knew that on his present course he might well find himself in a position to end one. His legs wobbled as he put his eye to the peephole.

Her cobalt blue eyes sparkled through the distorted lens. He loosened his grip on the gun as he opened the door. If he threw his arms around her, he wouldn't want to let go, so he stopped short and kissed her on the cheek.

"You're a welcome surprise."

Her gaze shifted downward. "Can we talk?"

Here we go, the 'It's not you, it's me' discussion. A pit formed in his stomach. "Sounds serious."

"Are you going to make me stand on the porch or can I come in?" Danielle said, smiling.

"Of course. Sorry, I'm glad you're here," he said, taking her hand in his. He led her in and shut the door. "I'm not sure I want to hear what you have to say."

She looked past him to the charcoal suitcase and matching

carry-on bag sitting by the coffee table in the living room. "Looks like you're going on a trip?"

"I wish I could say it was Maui and you were going with me, but I'm flying to Laredo."

Danielle's eyes narrowed. "For?"

"To see if I can track down Maria, our old maid."

She set her purse on the kitchen table and took a seat on the couch. "Are you okay? You look tired."

Nick paced the room. "Anxious. Not a fearful anxious, just a little unsettled. But I have to see where this leads." He certainly wasn't going to tell her about his lingering neurosis regarding cramped spaces.

"Nick, you and I both know this isn't a game. Whoever killed your mother and Danny Torello already has his sights on you," she said.

"That's why you shouldn't be here."

"I have to tell you something," she said, looking as serious as he'd ever seen her before.

"Okay."

"I haven't shared this with anyone since I moved to Philadelphia." She motioned for Nick to sit by her side. "I met my husband on a mission trip to Guatemala in my junior year of college."

Her husband? What the . . . ?

"We made an instant connection and got married six months later."

Nick looked into her eyes. "How did I not know you were married? It's a past-tense thing, right?"

"Yes. But not in the way you're thinking," she said. "Andrew became a successful partner in a well-known law firm and drifted from his faith, drifted from me. I was no better. I had my head stuck in anatomy and physiology texts and got a bit too comfortable with our improving lifestyle. Our priorities changed. God took a back seat, or, I should say, we shoved him into the back seat."

Nick shifted on the couch. "If you're saying I've turned from God . . . "

"No, Nick, I'm telling you I did," she said, her eyes welling up.

Nick laid his hand on hers. "I'm sorry."

"That summer, Andrew began having severe headaches. Then, at the end of July, he had a massive seizure. The CT showed he had an inoperable astrocytoma. We cried for days. We prayed and begged God for a miracle, but it didn't come. But something crazy happened during his last three months. We remembered what was truly important, our love for each other and our love for God. Those painfully short few weeks were the most precious and intimate of our relationship. Our worst nightmare, our weakest time, became our greatest victory. Andrew died in October."

Nick wiped away the tears rolling down Danielle's face. "Didn't that make you angry with God? I mean, he stole the man you loved and let him suffer."

"Sure, I was mad. I yelled at the top of my lungs. But God reminded me that this life is short, and it's not the end, just the beginning really."

"Do you really believe that?"

"With all my heart. This crisis you're in, your fears, your doubts, and even the possibility of your death allows you the opportunity to trust God and not yourself. He loves you."

"Even if I don't believe he exists?"

"Yes, because he believes in you, Nick, and I think in time he'll help you to believe."

"Danielle, I admire your faith, but I'm just not there. Despite my mother's best efforts, what little I have are the remnants of the nuns' catechism lessons and a few good welts to my backside from a yardstick. If he's a God who looks down on us and keeps score, he'll say, 'Nick, I know you've broken about eight of the Ten Commandments and thought about breaking the other two. You've missed Mass ninety-five times, you drink too much, and I know about the magazines you used to keep under your mattress. Sorry, Pal, you will burn for this. See ya!'"

Danielle's eyes never unlocked their gaze from his. "He's not like that. He's a God of grace. But I don't want to try to convince you of anything you're not ready to believe."

She got up from the floor and walked over to her purse. She pulled out two wrapped presents, one a small box and the other a book. She handed Nick the box. "This is something to remind you every time you look in the mirror that you are loved."

"Are you saying you love me?" Nick asked with a grin.

"Loved by God, Nick. The other is yet to be determined."

He peeled away the wrapping paper and opened the box. He pulled out a small, rough nail hanging from a thin, black leather braided necklace.

"He took the nails for you, Nicholas John Carlotti."

She took it from his hand and placed it around his neck. As she did, her delicate hand brushed lightly against his face. She leaned forward to fasten the clasp and her cheek came close to his. He took in the aroma of her perfume and the feel of her hair on his neck. As she leaned back again, he put his hand on the back of her head and gently pulled her close, pressing his lips to hers. They kissed softly and slowly.

"Thank you, Danielle. I know how much you want me to believe like you believe. Your existence, especially here with me now, is enough to convince me that there is a God, and possibly a loving God at that. I can't quite wrap my mind around the issue of suffering, among a few other hang-ups. I just have to spend some time with it. Fair enough?"

"Fair enough," she said, handing him the second present.

"Ah, Pilgrim's Progress." Nick smirked.

"I thought about giving you Emily Post's book on etiquette,

but you seemed more interested in this one. Honestly, it's a story about the paths we take, the struggles, the burdens, the joys, all of it. It's a story about our journey."

Nick pulled her close. "I'd like the journey to be with you," he said as he ran his fingers through her hair. They kissed, this time longer and more passionately. His hand moved to the front of her body.

She pulled away. "I'm sorry, you probably think I'm a prude or just plain cold. My heart and mind want to make love to you, but I can't. Not yet."

Nick caressed her velvet cheek. "I think I'm falling in love with you."

Danielle leaned in and kissed him gently. When their lips parted, she looked into his eyes. "I want this to be right." She cradled his face between her delicate hands. Her tender touch drew him in as Nick sensed her wanting every ounce of his focus. His whole body relaxed. Like a perfectly choreographed dance, Nick let her lead, and their gazes melted together. "Right before God, blessed by him. If you care about me, are you willing to wait?"

"It's killing me, but yes, I can wait," he said, although he had serious doubts.

Danielle lay her head on his shoulder.

Before she left, Nick lifted the nail from his chest. No one had ever given him a gift of such depth, a gift so seemingly insignificant but so profound. The nails, the crown of thorns, the cross— Nick's mother had talked about them when he was a kid, and the whole idea of Jesus' crucifixion seemed barbaric. Yet today, for some strange reason, the nail had taken on a more profound feeling. Maybe it wasn't the thing itself but the radiance of the giver. But he sensed it was something more. He let the nail fall back to his chest and pulled Danielle to himself one more time before she left.

"Please be careful, Nick," she said as she moved down the steps to the sidewalk.

Nick scanned the street, his gaze moving from car to car and person to person. Everyone looked suspicious. The bearded man in the rusty pick-up truck across the street. Why would he be sitting there? The twenty-something with the black fedora standing on the corner. . . Just cross the street already! Nick didn't consider himself psychic, but a shiver went down his back. "Wait!" he called out.

By the time Danielle had turned around, Nick had reached her side.

"I'm going to walk you to your car," he said, knowing full well that if someone did a drive-by or wanted to pick one of them off from a rooftop, there wasn't a damn thing he could do about it. But he wanted to be her hero, her knight in shining armor, at least in his attempts at chivalry.

"I'm fine. My car's a block away."

Nick put his arm around her. "I insist." His senses were on high alert. While he tuned his eyes and ears to his surroundings, his heart focused on only one thing, the girl in his arm.

When they reached the car, he held open the door, but she didn't slip in. Instead, she turned, threw her arms around him, and kissed him, one of those kisses that seemed to come from nowhere, shutting the whole world down. It stopped everything but that one moment. He didn't know how long their lips touched, but it wasn't long enough.

Her car disappeared down the street, and he was glad he'd followed his gut, that he had stayed in the batter's box and not been afraid to swing the bat with two strikes. He loved her, and it felt good. Really good.

As he finished packing, Nick had a nagging feeling, one of those if *I don't do this, it will drive me crazy, bordering on obsessive-compulsive* things. He stuffed Pilgrim's Progress in his carry-on. The nagging ceased.

50

First thing Monday morning, Rawls received a call from the state police. "Detective Rawls, this is Lieutenant Flaherty from the Skippack station over in Montgomery County. Do you have a few minutes?"

"I do."

"Yesterday afternoon we received a call from the Lower Salford Township Police stating that a farmer outside of Schwenksville found a Cadillac Escalade at the bottom of one of his irrigation ponds. Apparently, he sprayed the pond with algae-cide last week, and yesterday morning when the algae cleared, he spotted the vehicle's roof."

"What's that have to do with me?"

"We pulled the SUV from the pond, and the license plates were missing. The VIN had been scratched away from the door jamb and frame, but we were able to recover it from etchings in the windows. It matches a vehicle stolen from a grocery store parking lot in South Philly on the morning of February 22."

Rawls rolled his eyes. "Lieutenant, we have over ten thousand stolen vehicle reports a year. I appreciate your call but why not just send us the report?"

"Let me finish, and you'll understand the reason for my call."

"I'm all ears," Rawls said, eyeing the large pile of unfinished business on his desk.

"We found a Ziplock bag between the driver's side seat and the center console. The contents were dry— a small amount of weed and a 1980's Zippo lighter with a picture of a busty redhead. We ran the lighter for prints."

"And?"

"And they belong to your dead guy, Willie Santini."

Rawls sat up in his chair. "You've got my attention."

"I thought I might," the lieutenant said. "Your forensics team can pick up the vehicle today. It has some front-end damage, and the fact that they dumped it so far from Philly makes me believe they didn't just take it on a joy ride."

"Great work and thanks for the heads up. Fax me the report as soon as you can."

Until Flaherty's phone call, Mays' Escalade remained the most likely SUV seen speeding away from Liza Carlotti's crash scene. Consistent with the new discovery, when police located it at the marina later that morning, it showed no signs of damage.

Taylor strolled into Rawls' office less than an hour later, report in hand. "The SUV's owner, Philip Gall, an accountant from West Philly, purchased the vehicle new from the dealer in November and had it serviced hours before the theft." He slapped down a yellow legal pad on the desk. "I've done the math."

Numbers, equations, and a couple scribbled notes littered the page. Taylor pointed to the top line with the tip of his pencil. "At the time of the service, the dealer recorded the mileage at 7358. The odometer read 7424 when they pulled it from the pond, a total of sixty-six miles. Gall stated that he'd driven approximately fourteen miles from the time he left the service department to the time the Escalade disappeared from the grocery store lot, leaving a total of fifty-two miles from theft to the pond."

Rawls nodded. "I'm still with you."

Taylor flipped the page. "The detectives ascertained that driving the most direct route from Philly to the farm, up the Schuylkill Expressway to Route 422 then east on Township Line Road, meant the stolen SUV's driver couldn't have made more than a small detour from the time he left the parking lot to the time he reached the farm."

"Like maybe to the art museum?"

"Almost exactly. The lab is analyzing a sample of silver paint taken from the casing around the damaged headlight. They didn't find any other useful items in the vehicle due to its time under water. Santini appeared to be well aware of water's ability to degrade most available evidence, including DNA, body oils, and even metals, but he was apparently too high to remember to take his bag of weed."

"How long do they think the vehicle was there?"

"Hard to say, really. At least a few months based on the plant growth and sediment level."

"And the color?"

"Black," Taylor said. "I think we've found our suspicious SUV."

Rawls walked to the window overlooking the street below. "If Torello knew that Liza's crash was deliberate, then Willie must have been bragging it up to him. Being high has a way of removing inhibitions. After my colonoscopy, I told my wife her sister looked like James Earl Jones."

"Not good," Taylor said.

"Not good at all. I back peddled and said I thought James Earl Jones was damn good looking, but it didn't help."

"He's no Denzel Washington," Taylor said with a smile. "Seems a little loose-lipped gossip got Santini and Torello both killed."

Rawls shook his head. "Torello should have kept better company. How long on the paint analysis?"

"Two weeks, and I'm betting it came from a silver BMW."

"If so, Dr. Carlotti is likely off the hook in Torello's death, and Mays for Liza Carlotti's crash. It also means someone else got to Torello at the hospital," Rawls said. He pounded his finger on his desk. "I want a list of everyone who had access to Torello in the hospital, every doctor, nurse, tech, priest, and janitor. I also want to talk to Dr. Carlotti again. . . sooner rather than later."

Rawls made a call to the lab tech and offered him two tickets behind the Phillies' dugout for their upcoming game against the Dodgers. The lab technician promised to have the results on Rawls' desk by Wednesday morning.

51

ASIDE FROM NICK and his next-door neighbor Helen, Rhino considered Shar, the mail carrier, his best friend. She never showed up empty-handed. As Nick pulled out of his garage Monday morning, Shar smiled through Nick's driver's side window and handed him a small pile of envelopes.

"The one on the top is priority." She reached into her pocket and pulled out a small, green, bone-shaped dog biscuit. "Give Nose-Job a hug for me."

"Thanks, Shar. I'm sure he's already slobbering on the sofa. You've got him conditioned."

"He's my favorite, but for the not-so-nice ones I have this," she said, pointing to a small can of pepper spray on her belt.

"Good plan," Nick said, opening his briefcase and slipping the mail inside. He turned from the driveway and headed toward the Walt Whitman Bridge. A quick glance at his watch: 9:15 am. Perfect. Plenty of time to arrive at the airport early and get the Xanax into his bloodstream.

Passing through security, he beelined straight to a pub adjacent to gate A3. Two preflight vodka tonics later he made the mistake of looking out the window at the gate. There it sat at the end of the jetway, a small regional turboprop. He bet the damn thing didn't hold twenty people. He reached into his pocket and downed one of the oval, blue tablets. Hopefully, the combination of alcohol and Xanax would allow him to make it through the first leg of his flight without trying to open the cabin door at thirty-thousand feet. The second leg might not be as smooth.

After he made his way down the jetway, Nick's heart rate jumped as he ducked his head under the cabin doorway and peered down the narrow aisle. Two seats on one side, a single on the other. Of course, he had to be in the last stinking row. Swallowing another Xanax as they waited on the tarmac, he hoped the previous dose hadn't worn off.

The Beechcraft 1900 raced down the runway, the propellers humming. Shit, you'd think they'd make these things quieter! It sounded like a World War II bomber, for god's sake. Nick arched his back and clamped onto the armrests, his fingertips white and bloodless. An elderly woman sitting in the aisle seat placed her hand on Nick's. A little odd but it helped. His grip loosened. The woman's eyes remained closed as if she were resting. The potential of an imminent crash didn't seem to faze her in the least.

As the plane lifted off, she sang just loud enough to be audible:

Through days of toil when your heart doth fail, God will take care of you; When dangers fierce your path assail, God will take care of you, God will take care of you, through every day, o'er all the way; He will take care of you, God will take care of you.

HE HAD TO ADMIT, he did feel a little calmer after she sang but wished he'd gotten the pills down earlier. His stomach flip-flopped during a five-minute period of turbulence.

The pilot made a smooth landing. As the plane taxied, Nick didn't know what to say to his guardian angel except to share a simple, "Thank you," and a smile. For some reason he didn't feel embarrassed, a grown man acting like that.

She returned the smile and gave him a pat on his hand. "God bless you, Son."

He considered saying, you too, but instead he nodded as he stood from his seat. It was like his mother had come from heaven just to touch his hand and help him through the flight. Or, she'd pulled some strings and persuaded God to send an angel in her place. Nick turned his head and snuck a second look at the woman. She wore a joyful smile as if she were waiting for him to look back. The Xanax must have been messing with his mind.

Nick exited through the cabin door and an instant calm settled over him. Thankfully, he hadn't booked a return trip, otherwise, that flight would already be looming over him. As it was, his mind had already shifted to thoughts about his meeting with the elder Pastor Seyfert. He'd head to the church before visiting the nursing home. He wanted to see if he could garner any information from the secretary or any church members who might have known Maria.

The trip to the church turned out to be a complete waste of time. Nick didn't want to believe that the two women he spoke with in the church office would lie to his face, but they looked at each other oddly when he asked them about Maria, a what-should-we-say? kind of look. Neither one admitted to remembering Maria, but one recalled a frequent Mexican visitor who helped in the kitchen. Nick handed one of them his business card with the name of his hotel written on the back.

"Please let me know if anything comes to mind," he said before he left for his visit with the pastor.

From the outside, the Villa of St. Paul's Assisted Living Center seemed like the kind of place where Nick wouldn't mind living out his final years if his family kicked him to the curb. And since, at the present time, he didn't have a family, he half considered putting his name on the waiting list.

The earthen-toned adobe-style building with its vibrant, rust-colored Spanish-tiled roof sat under the shade of sweet acacia trees. As Nick stepped along the winding, stone walkway, he noticed the lack of obnoxious street noise, a far cry from the filthy white cinderblock nursing home a block from his hospital.

Two decrepit women perched in wheelchairs on the porch inside the arched entranceway. Their eyes didn't move within their emotionless faces as Nick passed between them. They'd entered the late February of their winter years, and their sparse, snow-white hair seemed befitting. At least they had a good view.

The receptionist, a middle-aged Latina woman, greeted Nick with a warm smile and kindly directed him to his right, down the hallway to room fourteen. From the pastor's open door, Nick eyed an old television resting on a table at the opposite end of the room. The elder Seyfert sat glued to a rerun of *The Joy of Painting* with its host sporting an oversized Afro. The artist lifted his brush from the canvas, revealing a mountain wildflower scene.

Nick knocked on the door. "Pastor Seyfert?" he asked, stepping into the room.

The man sitting in a worn, leather recliner shot his right hand into the air. "Not now!" He remained focused on the artist. Nick stopped in his tracks. The show's host finished his brushstroke, set down his brush, and backed away from the painting, admiring his completed masterpiece.

The pastor muted the TV and motioned for Nick to enter the room. "If ya sellin' somethin', I either already have one or don't need one, so don't waste ya time."

Nick approached the old man. "No, sir, I'm not selling anything. I'd like to chat if you have a moment."

"At my age, I'm runin' low on moments, so ya better talk fast."

"It won't take long, just a couple questions if it's all right."

"Depends awe'n the questions, I reckon. You a report'a or a cop?" he asked with a gravelly Texas drawl.

Nick pulled up a chair and faced the pastor's recliner. "Actually, neither, I'm a doctor from Philadelphia and I . . . "

The man shook his head. "Doc Murphy is a darn good man and he don't need help from the likes of you, so hit the road and take ya stethoscope with ya!"

Nick's hopes of obtaining useful information faded. "Pastor Seyfert, I'm not here to replace your doctor. I'm looking for information about a friend of my mother's. She would have been a frequent visitor to your church."

"Why didn't you say so?" the pastor huffed.

"Maria Hernandez, she was a friend of a missionary from your church."

The pastor put his hand to his chin and pursed his lips. "Hmmm . . . Hernandez . . . Not many Mexicans visited our church. Most went to Our Lady of Sorrows, the Catholic Church on 3rd Street. Hernandez . . . Doesn't ring a bell."

Two hours in Laredo and Nick already regretted his trip.

"Uh, there was this woman, a regular visitor but I recall her name was Martinez or Suarez . . . No . . . It was Sanchez . . . Oh, hell, it could have been Alcatraz for all I know. What did you say ya name was again?"

"Nick Carlotti," he said as he stood to leave.

The pastor's eyebrows furrowed. "Do I know you?"

Nick patted him on the shoulder. "You do now. Thanks for your time," he said. He hadn't reached the hall when the painter's voice came from the television.

"Maybe in our world, there lives a happy little tree . . . "

52

Lloyd Mays had been in that very courtroom hundreds of times but never wearing a bright orange jumpsuit and shackles. The prosecutor presented more than sufficient evidence for the judge to move the case forward to trial and Mays waived his right to a preliminary hearing. After signing his waiver, Mays stood at the podium for his arraignment.

The Honorable Harold J. Larson had a reputation as a gruff but fair, straight-faced, no-nonsense kind of judge whom Mays had argued before during his tenure as both DA and assistant DA. After the usual formalities, the judge addressed Mays.

"Senator Mays, you've been charged with murder in the second degree, which carries a penalty of mandatory life in prison. You are also charged with tampering with evidence and obstruction of justice, which carry a penalty of no more than twenty years. Do you understand these charges?"

"Yes, Your Honor."

"How do you plead?"

Mays stood tall and answered, "Not guilty."

"I understand you've waived the right to a preliminary

hearing and have also chosen to represent yourself in this matter?"

"I have."

"Although I think you're making a poor choice, given your legal background and experience I'll grant your request to proceed pro se, but am going to appoint standby counsel to ensure this case runs smoothly."

"Thank you, your Honor."

"Because of your substantial means and the gravity of this case, I'm ordering you to be held without bail. You'll have access to all the materials you need as well as to all discovery necessary to put forth a defense. I'm setting a trial date of September 15."

The bang of the judge's gavel felt like it hit Mays in the chest, like a death sentence. The guard escorted him to the van for his trip back to the prison.

The Curran-Fromhold Correctional Facility was only two years old, so Mays' cell appeared quite new. Still, the cramped cell had a musty, stale smell. Somehow B.O. and the odor of old socks didn't improve Mays' outlook on life.

He could view the common area through a narrow, slit-like window in the door. Thankfully, the dented metal 'mirror' hanging on the stark-white wall returned a hazy and distorted reflection. A more accurate image of his baggy-eyed face would have been too much to handle. For the time being, he didn't have a cell-mate, a definite plus since sharing a steel toilet bolted to the wall with some dude with questionable hygiene wasn't on his bucket list.

That afternoon Mays requested all materials related to discovery and began to put together what little he had. Even though he'd opted to represent himself, he had a low threshold for contacting an old friend in Pittsburgh, a hotshot defense lawyer, if he felt like he was in over his head. As it stood, the water had already reached the bottom of his chin.

The video from both the bar and the pier was indisputable,

and the DNA evidence would confirm he and Anya were on the Gypsy Rose. Mays had to find a way to show that he had never been in her apartment, proof that he'd been framed. But ultimately, the only way to prove he didn't kill the girl would be to find out who did. Harder yet, to convince a jury of the same. If he could persuade Nick to believe him, he might have a chance. At least he'd have an ally not constrained by prison bars. Unfortunately, for now, he had to go it alone.

53

THE HOTEL RIO VISTA was a stone's throw from the Rio Grande and two blocks from the Convent Avenue US Land Port of Entry and the Gateway to the Americas International Bridge. Maria lived somewhere over the bridge in Nuevo Laredo, Mexico. She might just as well have lived on the moon. Without specific information as to Maria's whereabouts, Nick knew he had little chance of finding her in a city of a half-million people.

Nick stood on his balcony, looking toward the river. The sun's bright yellow disc crept toward the horizon, its fading rays painting the clouds like glowing embers. If he could have stopped time, he would have. The sun's exit and the fading light reminded him of his mother, a beautiful light snuffed out. The sun dipped below the horizon, and the cloud's colorful tapestry faded to gray.

The churning of his stomach reminded him that airline peanuts and a vodka tonic weren't considered a meal in most corners of the globe.

After ordering room service, Nick called Willie's aunt Rose and asked if she'd been able to obtain a copy of the coroner's report. She had not and seemed hesitant to do so. When Nick reiterated his belief that Willie had been murdered, and that he wanted to see justice served, she willingly gave her consent. Rose promised to call him when she had it in her hand.

Nick had just closed his eyes when the server knocked on the door. The young man stepped into the room and navigated the bus cart around Nick's suitcase and shoes.

"May I set the tray on the desk?" the server asked.

"That's fine," Nick said, sliding his open briefcase to the side.

When the server left the room, Nick peeled the plastic from the glass and took two large sips of Cabernet. He sorted through the pile of mail Shar had handed him that morning, setting aside two clothing catalogs, a pre-approved credit card mailing, and a postcard guaranteeing he'd won a vacation cruise to Jamaica.

An envelope from the Hershey Hotel nearly made it onto the junk pile when Nick paused. His name and address were hand-written. It didn't appear to be part of a mass mailing, so he slid his finger beneath the flap and peeled it open. It held two folded papers. He spread the first out on the desk— a page from a college yearbook with two black and white pictures. The caption above read: Drama Club's Presentation of Our Town. The image to the left showed a full stage of actors wearing turn-of-the-century costumes. The second was a scene with a young man and woman sitting side-by-side at a stark wooden table.

The smile on his mother's face radiated joy. Her leading man sat tall, head turned toward her, his face not visible. The inscription read:

To Lloyd, my real life "George."
I love you!
Ali

THE CAPTION BELOW CONFIRMED IT: Liza Aliotta, Lloyd Mays. Nick swallowed hard, his gaze jetting back and forth from the picture to the handwritten inscription. His mother's voice rang out in his head: To Lloyd, my real life "George," I love you! It couldn't be, his father's greatest nemesis and his mother's potential murderer. Her college sweetheart?

How had he never known that his mother had been in a relationship with Lloyd Mays? Was it possible that his father never knew? Doubtful. But if he had known, it would undoubtedly have had to come out during one of his father's moments of unfiltered sarcasm or jealous contempt, especially while Mays most intensely investigated the Carlotti family. If Rock knew his wife had been with Mays, it didn't show.

When Nick unfolded the second piece of paper, a small photograph fell face down on the table. The worn picture had lost its luster, but the two faces were clear, their heads tipped together, cheeks touching. Lloyd and Liza smiled as Mays likely snapped the picture with an outstretched arm, the sun rising over the ocean in the background.

Nick read from the letter written on Hershey Hotel stationery:

Nick, I don't have time to elaborate, but you need to believe that I didn't kill your mother. I loved her. I still love her. I've spent years trying to protect her from your father, from a life I knew would someday destroy her. Who do you think hung the wreath on the guardrail? Forty white roses, one for every year since the day we met. Part of me died when she died. I've been set up for Anya's murder, and I believe her death is somehow connected with your mother's. Contact me when you can. Watch your back.

Lloyd

IT BORDERED ON THE PREPOSTEROUS, but somehow the words rang true. If Mays was innocent, Nick's father probably wasn't. It also seemed improbable that Mays' setup had nothing to do with Liza's death. But, why would Mays be framed for a murder? Revenge? Extortion? To make him a more likely suspect in Liza's death? All three? It wouldn't be the first time a man with deep pockets had them emptied by Rock Carlotti. The threat of death or worse proved a strong motivator, but this seemed more contorted.

Steve answered Nick's call on the second ring. "Well?" Steve asked before Nick said a word.

"What if I told you Mays and my mother had a relationship in college?"

"I'd think you'd been smoking something," Steve said, "And you found out how?"

"Mays sent a letter with a clip from the Swarthmore College yearbook, 1957. They were dating, for god's sake."

"Okay, that's big."

"Do ya think! Mays claims he didn't have anything to do with my mother's murder or the missing Brazilian singer. He believes someone set him up. Want to know the craziest thing?"

"What's that?"

"I believe him."

Silence.

Nick continued. "You think I'm nuts, right?"

"No, but he wouldn't be the first murder suspect to claim he was set up. On the other hand, if I were a betting man, I'd put money on his innocence over your father's, no offense."

"None taken."

"Any luck finding Maria?"

"Uh, no. And when I told you I wanted to travel fifteen hundred miles to question a pastor with Alzheimer's, you could have talked me out of it."

"Not sure the Alzheimer's thing came up. On a separate note, I think we should open the music box."

"No key, remember?"

"Yep, and I still think we need to find out what's inside. It wasn't in the cedar chest for no reason," Steve said.

Steve was right.

"My neighbor has a key to the house. I'll call and ask her to put it under the flower pot, next to the doormat."

"And why would she do that?"

"The music box is in Philly, and I'm in Texas. Besides, it was your idea."

"Your dad's always sorta liked me, right? I mean 'Carrot-top' seems like a term of endearment."

Nick's father had taken a liking to Steve. Most people did, but Nick understood. "It's okay. We can wait until I'm back."

Steve paused. "Good answer. It's not that I'm afraid or anything. Just think you should be the one to break it open."

"Uh-huh. I'm sure that's it."

"Okay, maybe I'm a wimp. But, under the circumstances, you'd be a little nervous too, no?"

Nick had to agree. Four people were dead already, and he certainly didn't want Steve to be the fifth. "You're off the hook. I'll call you tomorrow. I'm going to do a little more digging here, but if I don't have any other leads, I'll try to catch a standby flight tomorrow. I'd rather walk home, but it's not terribly practical."

"Not so much," Steve replied. "See you tomorrow."

54

UNLESS SOMETHING credible came to light, he planned to fly standby the next day, hopefully before noon. Nick downed his half-finished glass of Cabernet and fell asleep less than twenty minutes later.

A tentative knock on the door at 5:45 am shot him bolt upright in his bed. Only Steve, Danielle, a couple church members, and a senile pastor knew he was in Laredo. Although Texas allowed concealed weapons, they had no reciprocity with Pennsylvania, and Nick hadn't thought it worth taking the risk to hide his Beretta in his suitcase. Now he wished he had.

"Who is it?" Nick asked through the door.

"Nico, it's Maria."

Nick fell forward, his hands propping him up against the door. He let his weary head sink down until it rested between his hands. Her tender voice settled him as it had when she sang bedtime songs thirty years prior. His heart rate slowed, and he let out a slow breath from his pursed lips. "Hold on."

He threw on a hotel robe and opened the door. For a moment, neither knew what to say, both standing motionless. The wrinkles of Maria's tawny skin had deepened, and the bags under her tear-filled brown eyes evidenced her lack of rest.

Nick wrapped his arms around her and hugged her tightly. She buried her head in his chest and wept, her arms draped by her sides. Nick led her through the door and closed it behind them.

"How did you know I was here?" Nick asked.

Maria cleared her throat. "My friend, the one who gave me the Bible. She said you came to the church today. The women weren't sure if they should talk to you, so they called me and told me where you were."

"I pretty much lost hope of finding you. I planned to fly home today," Nick said.

"It was God's perfect plan," she said. She took a seat in the chair next to the balcony slider. "I haven't been to the States since your mother's funeral. I went home to Mexico and came back this past weekend to attend the baptism of my friend's granddaughter. I would not have been here if the Lord didn't direct my steps."

"Well, I'm glad he did then. Why didn't you talk to me after the funeral?"

"When your mother died, I was afraid and didn't know who I could trust," Maria said, trying unsuccessfully to hold back the tears.

Nick handed her a tissue. "Why were you afraid?"

"Your mother thought someone wanted to hurt her. I told her she needed to tell someone." Maria broke down. "I should have done something," she said through the sobs.

"Don't go there. There wasn't anything you could have done. Do you have any idea who she was afraid of?"

"No, she wouldn't tell me." Her lower lip quivered. "In March of last year, your mother spent the week at the lake house, and I came early Friday morning to clean. She said she needed something from the house in Buckingham for a writing project. She left at about 7:00 am, and got back just before 11:00. When she came through the door, her eyes were red and swollen. She always put her purse on the desk inside the foyer, but that day she squeezed it tight to her chest and went straight upstairs. Later, when I asked her what was wrong, she said she couldn't tell me. After that day, she seemed different, scared, anxious, but mostly sad."

"You don't know what happened at the house?"

"No, Nico, like I said, she wouldn't tell me. I think she wanted to protect me."

"What made you trust me now?"

"I had a dream last night. Jesus had his hand on your head and told me you were his."

Nick smiled. How come he never had dreams like that? He certainly couldn't deny the crazy timing of her trip across the border. He appreciated whatever power brought them together for their brief reunion. They spent the next forty minutes recounting memories of better times.

When she left, Nick called Steve.

Steve had planned to contact Nick at 7 pm, Texas time from a hospital phone, but Nick beat him to the punch. "Hey, buddy," Nick said.

"Well, you're up bright and early."

"Had a surprise guest this morning."

"Let me guess . . . Maria."

"Tell me it came to you in a dream."

"No, why?" Nick chuckled.

"Oh, nothing. My mother told Maria she believed someone wanted to hurt her. I'm not crazy, Steve."

"I never thought you were. We'll talk more when you get home. Let me know when you land."

The words 'when you land' were enough to start the preflight anxiety. Nick swallowed one of his two remaining Xanax tabs as he made the eight-minute drive to Laredo International Airport.

The earliest flight out of Laredo departed at 5:35 pm, into Dallas/Fort Worth, but there were no remaining seats on the connecting flight to Philly. He'd have to spend the night. The first available flight out of Dallas left at 3 pm Wednesday. He could use the rest anyway. The first leg went off without a hitch thanks to the sedative. He checked into the Grand Hyatt at the Dallas/Fort Worth airport and called Steve to let him know of his plans.

Even with the Xanax still in his system a few hours later, he was wide awake. He pulled the old book from his bag, propped a couple pillows behind his head, and read. The minutes turned to hours as the tale by Bunyan grabbed hold of him.

Pilgrim's Progress seemed an odd book, written in old English language, an allegory from start to finish. It told the story of Christian's journey from the City of Destruction to the Celestial City. The characters' names were coincident with their personalities— Mr. Worldly Wiseman, Obstinate, Hypocrisy, and Hopeful.

At first, the reading felt cumbersome but, for some reason, through all the thees and thines, Nick couldn't put it down. It read like his own three-hundred-year-old biography; like somehow Bunyan knew him, knew his doubts, his sins, his burdens, and his fears. He, like the protagonist Christian, wandered through life with a burden upon his back, through a world in disarray, one filled with temptations and dangers. Both knew they needed saving, not from things on the outside but from their own brokenness and failures.

Nick read as his eyelids hung heavy, but still he kept on peering through the two tiny slits at the words on the page. He came to the seventh stage of part I, where Christian and his friend Hopeful meet Giant Despair, the owner of Doubting Castle. Giant Despair throws both men into a "*very dark dungeon, nasty and stinking . . . without one bit of bread, or drop of drink, or light, or any to ask how . . . Now in this place Christian had double sorrow, because it was through his unadvised counsel that they were brought into this distress.*"

Nick closed the book. The last thing he needed was a reminder of his claustrophobia. He wanted to say goodnight to Danielle. He missed her and wished she were lying next to him, maybe in a beachside bungalow in the Bahamas, or her apartment on a lazy Saturday morning. He gave in to his desire and picked up his phone.

"I just wanted to let you know I'll be home tomorrow evening," Nick said.

"I'm glad you called. I miss you."

If those were the last words he ever heard, they'd have been enough. "I miss you too."

They talked until he couldn't keep his eyes open any longer, one of those lying with your head on the phone, you could talk forever, first love kind of talks, but he simply couldn't stay up all night.

He yearned to tell her how he felt but feared it was too much, too fast. What if she hesitated? What if she reciprocated, but the words came out coerced? What if she said nothing at all? Nick had taken risks his whole life, always going for the home run. So, after a small, slow breath, he jumped.

"I love you, Dr. Sorenson," he said, his voice cracked with exhaustion.

"And I you, Dr. Carlotti."

55

MAYBE ANYA DIED ACCIDENTALLY in the throes of rough sex. But if so, Mays sure upped the ante when he hid the evidence and disposed of her body. Rawls tried coming up with a motive that might have enticed Lloyd Mays to make such a foolish, career-ending decision, a choice that might put him behind bars for life. Mays had never married and had never been ashamed of his playboy lifestyle in the past. This little fling shouldn't have ended in the spilling of blood.

One thing seemed off. Before the landlord came forward, no one had reported the girl missing. No friends, no family members, not a single call from a worried boyfriend. A beautiful woman in the music industry wouldn't have been such a recluse, and her disappearance wouldn't have gone unnoticed.

Rawls opened the file and took out the CD that Anya had given the restaurant's manager when she applied for the job. Rawls pulled the insert from behind the plastic cover as Taylor broached the door.

"Do you read Portuguese?" Rawls asked with a hint of sarcasm.

"I barely survived two years of high school Spanish if that helps," Taylor said.

"Doubtful." Rawls tossed the CD insert over his desk toward Taylor. "This might have some information, a bio, a recording studio, names of musicians in the band."

"Good thought. That's why they pay you the big bucks," Taylor said.

"Nope, just bigger headaches. The big bucks go to the slick talkers in three-piece suits who try to negate all of our hard work in court. Have this translated and see what you can find out."

"On it," Taylor said.

"Any progress with your leads in Brazil?"

"Leads? A single lead would be nice. The address she listed on her visa is a hotel in São Paulo, and they have no record of her ever being there. With eight million people in the city and 916 Anyas, it might take a while."

"When and where did she enter the US?" Rawls asked.

"They processed her passport in Dallas/Fort Worth on April 4 of last year — her first and only trip to the States. She came by way of Medellín, Colombia. She traveled back and forth between São Paulo and Medellín every few months before that."

Rawls' phone rang. "Rawls."

"Detective, this is Kyle Henry, a lab tech at the forensic science bureau. My supervisor asked me to call about the case involving Senator Mays."

"Go on."

"Well, when I examined the blood found in the carpet, I noted something that didn't really hit me at the time. We ran the DNA as usual, but something wasn't right. I kept wondering why the blood hadn't coagulated. The red cells and platelets hadn't formed a fibrin clot like I'd expected."

"Does that mean something relevant?"

"I have a hunch, but I'm going to run a gas chromatograph-mass spectrometry to isolate any chemicals in the blood and I'll call when I finalize the results."

"Cut to the chase, Kyle," Rawls said.

"Unless your victim took Warfarin or had hemophilia, someone had to have treated the blood to keep it from clotting. I don't want to speculate what that might mean until I finish the GC-MS. I'll let you know."

"Please do," Rawls said.

"Two more things," Kyle said as Rawls pulled the phone from his ear.

"I found a small amount of residue at the bottom of the martini glass, probably sodium chloride from the olive brine but I want to be sure."

Rawls waited. "You said two more things."

"Oh yeah, probably nothing but when the coroner finished his report on Santini, he noted the right arm loaded with needle tracks and the left arm clean."

"And?"

"And they found the needle sticking in his left arm. Santini was left-handed and probably shot up in his right arm. Not sure why he'd have switched that day."

"Unless maybe someone helped him out?"

"Just a theory," Kyle said.

Rawls hung up and turned back to Taylor. "Forensics is digging deeper into the blood from Mays' boat and some residue in Mays' martini glass."

"What are they looking for?"

"Beats the hell out of me. Something about clots and graphs and chemicals. Speaking about needing a translator," Rawls said.

"It seems all the more likely Carlotti got to Santini."

"Not a suicide?"

"Looking like Collins dropped the ball."

"Your prediction was right on the money."

"I should play the lottery. We need to talk to Dr. Carlotti

again. Just because he's no longer a suspect doesn't mean he's not withholding information."

Taylor smiled. "Agreed." He glanced toward the empty wire-mesh basket. He tipped his head in Rawls' direction, his eyebrows knit together. "Not flying today?"

Rawls hesitated. "No, not today."

"Run out of ideas or paper?"

"Neither." Rawls pulled the glasses from his face, his eyes glassed over. "Forty years ago today, I watched my twelve-year-old brother die."

"Maurice, I'm so sorry." Rawls sighed and shook his head.

"PF Flyers Center Hi."

"What do you mean?" Taylor asked.

"The kid put a bullet through Lester's chest because he wouldn't give up his damn sneakers." Rawls rubbed his wet eyes and slipped his glasses back on. "I wore the stupid things, three sizes too big, for the whole year. My mother said I was as stubborn as her papa's ox."

"Nah, a little determined maybe."

"Probably a little of both," Rawls said as he grabbed his things and headed to the interview room where the bartender from Pier 33 waited. He'd just returned from a cruise when they brought him in for questioning. Officers had met him the minute he'd stepped off the plane at the Philadelphia International Airport.

Rawls entered the room carrying a lined legal pad and a cheap mechanical pencil. The bartender sat in the same chair Mays had occupied only five days prior. The young man, thirty at best, with a smooth, shaved head and auburn goatee, leaned forward, his hands clasped, fingertips pale. Small beads of sweat formed on his forehead. They glimmered like tiny diamonds from the reflection of bright industrial lights hanging from the ceiling. His right foot tapped unconsciously.

"Mr. Laskin, we're looking for information about the singer

named Anya. We're not considering you a suspect in any way. We know she visited your club the night of her disappearance."

The bartender's posture immediately relaxed, and his foot ceased its nervous march.

Rawls pulled up a chair across from the man and clicked his pencil twice. He scribbled on the paper, testing the lead. "Do you know her?"

"Yeah, I know her. From the bar, I mean. She was a regular, over . . . I'd say, maybe three months."

"How regular?" Rawls said.

The man wiped the sweat from his forehead with his right sleeve. "I don't know exactly, maybe once a week, sometimes more."

"Who did she usually come in with?"

"Honestly, she usually showed up alone except for the last time. She came in with the guy you arrested. Other than that, she usually camped at the bar and made guys look like buffoons when she'd blow them off. She had some damn good one-liners."

"She didn't have any friends?"

"I did see her a couple times with some older dude. He'd come in after she'd already been there and stay just long enough for her to grab her purse and leave."

"When was the last time you saw him?" "Two weeks, maybe three before she came in the last time. She must be into gray hair and three-piece suits."

Rawls jotted a few notes. "Tell me about the night she came in with Senator Mays."

The man leaned back in his chair and eyed the video camera in the far corner of the room, then turned back to Rawls. "I didn't notice him at first. Anya ordered a couple martinis while he went to take a piss, I guess. When he came back, they grabbed a table. They had one more round and left. The guy was trashed when they walked out."

"What makes you think so?" Rawls asked.

"He kept leaning on her and had a hard time making a straight line to the door. I'm a bartender, for god's sake, I know drunk, and this guy was wasted."

Rawls put down his pencil, stood, and walked around to the bartender's side. He sat on the table's edge with one leg still resting on the floor. "He had two martinis over an hour or so. Sort of a lightweight, don't ya think?"

"Yeah, but he could have had a six-pack before he came in," the man said. "Who knows?"

Rawls knew that Mays had only one glass of wine at dinner that night. The credit-card statement and receipt subpoenaed from his office confirmed that he hadn't ordered another drink. If Mays left the restaurant a little after midnight and walked into Pier 33 at 12:22 am, then likely he'd had only three drinks from dinner until 1:30 am. Rawls knew Mays well enough to know that three cocktails over that time frame wouldn't have been any more intoxicating than a glass of his mother's lemonade. "Do you mix them on the strong side?"

"Exactly two and a half shots of Grey Goose and half a shot of vermouth for a dirty martini. . . no more no less."

"Is there anything else you might want to add that could help us locate the girl?" Rawls asked, picking up his pad and pencil.

The man paused. "Probably not important, but she was easily the biggest tipper in the bar. I mean, women usually tip me more than the guys do, but Anya usually dropped me a fifty at closing. She called me the perito of mixology."

"Perito?"

"I asked her the same question. It's Portuguese, means master, like a magician with a cocktail shaker. And she'd be right. Hell, with that accent, she could have called me a maggot, and it would have turned me on. I thought she hit on me once, but she made it clear she wasn't interested. Trust me, I tried."

Rawls jotted a couple quick notes and informed him that he'd receive a call to testify if the case moved to trial.

Anya had a sugar daddy. She drove a $35,000 sports car and laid down fifty-dollar tips like they were Lincolns. From what Rawls could tell, she cleared two hundred dollars a night and worked only two to three nights a week. He doubted she got rich on CD sales.

If they found her nighttime visitor, they would have their man. Mays had the financial means to fit the bill, but why not wear her on his sleeve? She wasn't the kind of woman most men would hide, especially a man with Mays' history. Mays would have considered her good for his image. That was his modus operandi. But Anya's lover kept a low profile.

As the bartender got up to leave, Rawls shot him one last question. "Mr. Laskin, is it possible that someone drugged the senator, that maybe the girl slipped him a roofie?"

"I guess so, but a chick like that wouldn't have to drug the dude if she wanted a little action. Besides, isn't she the one missing?"

"Thanks again, Mr. Laskin. If I have any further questions, I'll be in touch."

56

"I WANT THIS DONE RIGHT. No screw-ups," Rock said, drumming his fingers on his desk. The sun hadn't yet broached the horizon Thursday morning as Coroneos put the last of the fifty-five $10,000 stacks of hundred-dollar bills in the suitcase. "The money is clean, Tony. We've divided it, shifted it overseas through Belgium and France, and moved it from currency to hard assets and back again."

"I'm not feeling good about this one. Castillo isn't playing with a full deck," Rock said.

The bastard hadn't seemed too concerned after the lunatic had lopped off Scalise's fingertip. Coroneos put on his game face. "It'll be fine. I'll make the exchange tomorrow and have the product here by early Friday morning. Castillo may be a nut job, but he's sane enough not to blow a good deal."

"I'm counting on you, Peter. A lot's riding on this."

Coroneos nodded and took the chair across from Rock's desk. "Tony, this isn't our first rodeo. I'll verify the merchandise and make the payment just like before. I'll call you when I'm an hour and a half from the Grottos. You can inspect the goods then we can make the transaction with the Paccione brothers as scheduled."

Rock lay his hand on Coroneos' shoulder. "You've been a good friend. This is a hard business, too many egos, and loyalty is hard to come by. We've been through a lot, you and me." He patted Coroneos' hand twice and stood. "Liza's death crushed me, Peter. I've tried hard to let her go, to move on. Hell, I even got hitched, but I just plain miss her." His eye teared up, so he turned away and cleared his throat.

"We all miss her, Tony. She was a good woman."

Rock walked to the window. He spoke without turning back. "Something's been bothering me."

"What's that?"

"Nick is convinced Liza was murdered and I've been brushing it off. Do you think he might be right?"

"Tony, come on, who'd want Liza dead?"

Rock turned. "My enemies are a dime a dozen. Paccione's boys would love to put a bullet in my head, and I wouldn't put it past the Feds to stick it to me."

"The Paccione boys ran with their tails between their legs to Soriano in Brooklyn the day you put the hit on their old man. Aside from their piss poor attempt at payback in '87, they haven't made a peep since."

Rock nodded. "And now we're doing business with them. How fucking ironic."

"Even they know that this amount of dough is worth burying the hatchet. You okay?"

"Yeah, I'm good," Rock nodded, straightening himself. "Just make the damn deal and get back home. Keep me in the loop."

"I've got it covered."

Rock stopped him after his first step toward the door. "You know, Peter, my father was an asshole. He taught me most things with the backside of his hand, but he did give me two pieces of good advice the day I started working for Salvatore. *Don't shit where you eat and don't trust anyone.* I've followed those two rules like they were a command from God. I keep business business, and, aside from you, don't trust a fucking soul."

"It's served you well."

"Yeah, but it's always good to have a backup plan," Rock said with a smile as he patted the handgun under his jacket.

57

Nick landed in Philly early Wednesday night. On the way to baggage claim, he noted a voicemail from Captain Taylor. Probably chastisement for not obeying the stick around town mandate, but Taylor's voice seemed calm and apologetic.

"Dr. Carlotti, please call me as soon as you can. We have new information regarding your mother's accident."

Taylor answered on the second ring.

"Captain, it's Nick Carlotti."

"Dr. Carlotti, thanks for returning my call. We have new information that there was another vehicle involved in the crash."

"No shit! You guys are quick."

"I guess I had that coming, but how about we start with a clean slate."

Nick resisted the urge to let loose a profanity-laced 'I told you so.' "The slate's clean," he said. "Tell me about the second vehicle."

"Until we've completed our investigation, I can't get into the particulars, but if you have any other information, it would be prudent for you to share what you know."

"I would have been happy to do that earlier, had you taken

me seriously. So maybe I'm not sure about getting into the particulars either."

"I thought we had a clean slate."

"Well— it's a process."

"Fair enough," Taylor said. "I'll make you a deal. We'll share with you as you offer us information— quid pro quo."

"Or maybe vice versa," Nick said.

Taylor cleared his throat. "We recovered a black SUV in a pond in Schwenksville. There's reason to believe it was involved in your mother's accident."

Nick's mouth fell open and his knees went weak. He took a seat next to the baggage carousel. "Are you sure?"

"There is ample forensic evidence to link it to her BMW."

"What kind of evidence?"

"DNA and paint . . . Detective Rawls informed me today that paint taken from the SUV's damaged bumper matched your mother's car, granite silver metallic 3 Series. Beyond that, I'm not at liberty to divulge anything more."

Nick caught sight of his bag falling from the conveyer to the carousel, and got up from his seat. "So, where do we go from here?"

"Meet me at the station."

"I'd rather not— doubt all your men are playing for the same team."

"I'd like to think you're wrong, but there's a parking garage on the corner of Walnut and South 12th. Meet me on the roof level. I'll be in a white, unmarked Crown Victoria."

"Give me half an hour," Nick said. He wasn't sure why he felt so compelled, but despite the magnitude of what he'd just heard, he had to make one slight detour.

58

An eight-foot cobblestone wall stood like a sentry along the right side of the narrow alley. It flanked the meager back yards of the historic townhouses; a modest deterrent to burglars looking for easy pickings. Maybe it was pointless to come in from the back alley, but it wasn't that far-fetched to think someone might be waiting for him on the street. Nick hurried along the path's crumbling concrete.

As Nick neared his townhouse, he fumbled for the key to the wrought-iron gate. Why did it feel as if a thousand eyes were on him, like he was being pursued by gremlins in a particularly bad dream? It wasn't outright panic, more like a healthy uneasiness. His hand trembled as he fit the key into the lock. This wasn't the hand of a surgeon who could pass a suture the width of a human hair through the wall of a tiny artery without the slightest hesitation. Get a grip!

Rhino didn't wait for the door to open fully before flying between Nick's legs and relieving himself in the same dead grass corner of the lawn. He came full tilt back again, running in tight circles around Nick until he received his usual reward for not pissing on the living room carpet. With the rawhide chew crunching in his jaws, the dog lay at the base of the armoire while Nick held the music box on his lap.

Staring at the steak knife in his hand, he hesitated. It grieved him to destroy this precious memory. Come on, it's just a box. She's dead anyway and couldn't care less. It would be one last sorrow-provoking object keeping him from healing, but the rationalizations didn't seem to help.

He slipped the sharp edge of the knife between the glossy black lacquered edges of the top and the box just below the brass keyhole. As he put the first bit of downward pressure on the knife, the image flashed before him. It couldn't be. Could it? He'd looked at it every night since he'd brought it home from the salvage yard. He pulled the knife away and sprinted to the bedroom. With the rosary beads in hand, he returned to the living room and placed the tiny key into the keyhole. With a counter-clockwise twist, the top unlocked. Ok, God, I'll give you that one. He smiled.

Her piercing deep-brown eyes stared back at him from a chaotic mess of intertwined gold and silver chains, earrings, and other pieces of jewelry. The driver's license seemed grossly out of place. Nick lifted it from the box and took a closer look. "Oh my god!" It couldn't be. Anya, the Brazilian with no last name, Mays' missing woman! Why in god's name would his mother have her driver's license?

Could this be what had gotten his mother killed? It didn't seem likely Mays would have reached out to Nick if he had something to do with it. Why would he make himself so vulnerable? And what would connect Torello and Mays? Nick's head spun.

He glanced back into the mess in the box. It wasn't like his mother not to take care of her possessions. She wasn't obsessive-compulsive, but she also wouldn't let her jewelry fall into such an unholy mess unless she was under tremendous mental stress.

He shoved the license into his pocket and threw food and water in the dog's bowls. He left the way he came. Maybe he'd show Officer Taylor the license, or perhaps he needed to keep it to himself. He'd make that decision when the time came.

59

Nick made the final turn from the parking garage's fourth level to the roof. He scanned the lot. No Crown Victoria in sight, at least not from his current vantage point. He pulled forward and wound his Porsche through the rows of cars.

The rumble of an engine and the grating of tires on the hot garage floor car sounded behind him. His heart rate shot up. With his foot on the accelerator, he glanced in the rearview mirror. An elderly, white-haired woman sitting way too close to her steering wheel peered at him, barely able to see above the dash. When their eyes met, he slowed and pulled into the first available spot, opting to walk to the end of the row to look for the white Crown Victoria. She drove past him and scowled. Apparently, she'd wanted the spot.

A car honked from the lot's southwest corner. Light from the Crown Victoria's overhead lamp backlit two figures in the front seat. Taylor wasn't alone.

Taylor put down the window. "Get in."

Nick opened the driver's side rear door and slid in. He set his briefcase down next to him. "I wasn't expecting company," Nick said. "Not good for building trust, Detective."

"Nick, you remember Detective Rawls," Taylor said.

"How could I forget?" Nick said. "I'm here against my better judgment, but I'm not sure I had another choice."

"Despite the sarcasm, I appreciate your being here." Rawls turned in his seat. His penetrating eyes exuded a sense of urgency yet still somehow warmth and sincerity. He reached over and extended his hand to Nick. Rawls continued. "We're gathering useful information regarding your mother's murder, and I believe you have as well. If you want her killer brought to justice, I recommend you share what you have."

"Quid pro quo, remember," Nick said.

Rawls gave Taylor a nod.

Taylor answered, "We think Willie Santini may have been driving the vehicle that drove your mother's car off the road."

"You're saying that my father hired Santini to kill my mother."

"I didn't say that," Taylor said. "The fact that Santini was driving the vehicle, doesn't prove your father hired him."

Nick's eyebrows furrowed. "Trust me, Santini was no Einstein, and he sure as hell wasn't stupid enough to double-cross my father."

"Maybe, but we're not taking anything off the table," Rawls said. "Your turn."

"It's a long story . . . but since my mother died, I've been doing some digging. It's clear from a journal she kept that she had information she shouldn't. It put her life in danger."

Rawls made himself a little taller in his seat. "What information?"

"As you know, Danny Torello believed my mom's crash wasn't an accident, that Willie Santini had inside information to that effect. Unfortunately, Willie's indiscretion got him and Torello both killed. Since Willie worked for my father, it seems the old man's connected . . . and I'm still not sure he isn't."

"Who might have wanted your mother dead?" Taylor asked.

"I don't know, but whoever it is isn't working alone."

Rawls cocked his head and narrowed his eyes. "Why do you say that?"

"On July 17, I left the hospital, and some nice men threw a bag over my head and took me for a short ride with a gun to my side. There were at least three men in the car: the driver, the man with the gun, and the guy who did the talking. I assume he's behind this. He didn't care much for my getting too close to the truth, and warned me to back off. They dumped me in the hood where three gangbangers gave me a lift back to my car."

"And where do you think Mays fits in?" Rawls asked.

Nick shook his head. "Lloyd Mays had been after my old man for years, and he was at the art museum the night my mother died. When I heard you arrested him for the girl's murder, it seemed all the more likely he had something to do with my mother's accident."

Nick reached for his briefcase. He hesitated. It might be the only ace in his hand, so he chose not to play it quite yet. He stared for a moment into Rawls' eyes. Not knowing why, he trusted the man. Nick opened the briefcase. "When I received these, I knew Mays wasn't the man," he said, lifting out the letter and the yearbook picture.

Rawls read the letter and glanced at the picture. "No kidding!" He passed them to Taylor.

Taylor's jaw dropped. "So, Mays and your mother were lovers," Taylor said. "That either makes him more of a suspect or less of one. I'm not sure it makes the picture any clearer."

"Then this might muddy the water even more." Nick reached into his pants pocket and pulled out Anya's driver's license. He handed it to Rawls.

Rawls scanned the license. "Where did you get this?"

"My mother had it in a jewelry box. I'm not sure why she had it or how she got it, but I understand she's the woman you've accused Mays of killing."

"If your mother somehow had information about Anya, then maybe Mays wanted her dead," Taylor said.

Nick huffed. "It doesn't make sense. How would my mother have information about some chick Mays picked up for a one-nighter? And why would she care? Besides, the timing is all wrong."

Taylor shrugged. "Maybe she felt jilted."

"For god's sake, she and Mays dated forty years ago," Nick said. "And how do you propose Santini would be on Mays' payroll?"

"We're not supposing anything," Rawls said. "Just putting the pieces together one at a time."

"The girl disappeared four months after my mom died. So, the most my mother could have known about was his relationship with the girl. And who would have given a damn?"

"Like Captain Taylor said, maybe your mother still had feelings for Mays, and they had words," Rawls said.

"Mays may be a prick, and I may be a fool for believing him, but he had no reason to reach out to me . . . "

"Except to try to convince you he was innocent," Taylor said.

"Yeah, but who the hell am I? My opinion isn't worth shit."

"Anything else?" Rawls asked.

"I spoke to Santini's aunt, Rose. She gave me some pretty good reasons for believing Willie didn't commit suicide."

"Such as?" Rawls asked.

"In the note, he addressed her as, Aunt Rose."

"I'm confused," Taylor said. "So was Rose. From the time Willie could talk, he called her Zizzi Rose. It's the Italian version of aunt. He also signed the note Squirrel, his mob nickname. Rose hated that name, and he never used it with her. The note was obviously coerced."

"Wouldn't come as a surprise," Taylor said. "He was dead twenty-four hours after his release from jail and Torello was shot the same night. Someone tried hard to keep their mouths shut."

"It's that someone we need to find," Rawls said. "Be careful who you talk to and where you go, Dr. Carlotti. I don't have to tell you that you're a likely target, especially if you keep on the current track."

"Noted." Nick smirked.

Rawls pointed his finger at Nick and narrowed his eyes. "Don't be a lone wolf. Got it?"

Nick shot him a wink and exited the car. Going back to his apartment again wasn't a good idea, so he opted for a room at a Holiday Inn just over the Ben Franklin Bridge in Camden. He paged Steve, who returned the call from a hospital extension.

"Where are you?" Steve asked.

"New Jersey."

"That's a little vague," Steve said. "Mind narrowing it down?"

"I don't want you or Danielle involved."

"Already am."

"Me too!" Her voice caught him off guard. A flutter of electricity rushed through his body. How did she get to him like that? He wasn't sure, but one thing was certain, he didn't want his desire for her to put her life in danger.

"Nice. Now you two are ganging up on me?"

Danielle grabbed the phone. "Not ganging up on you— teaming up with you."

"That's not the point. This isn't a game, Danielle."

"Reverse the roles. Would you let Steve or me go it alone?"

She was right. Besides, nothing he said would dissuade them from helping him find the answers he sought. They agreed to meet at a South Jersey diner early the next morning, long enough to catch them up on his meeting with Taylor and Rawls.

Without a change of clothes, a toothbrush, or a comb, he would be testing Danielle's volition. If she still seemed interested after seeing him in the morning, this might just be the real deal. He lay his head down on the pillow, a little too soft for his liking, and the faint smell of old cigarettes reminded him of his great aunt's house on Mifflin Street. Aunt Iris had chain-smoked Lucky Strikes while pasting S &H green stamps into books. Said she was saving up for a new electric sewing machine. He missed those days. Life seemed simpler then.

60

"I CAN'T BREATHE! I can't breeeeathe!" The muffled words disappeared in the blackness or maybe just fell on deaf ears. "Let me out!"

Bent over folded knees, arms back and pressed to his side, he pushed upward against the chest's locked wooden top. So dark! Not even a sliver of light passed between the old wooden slats. The caustic vapor of mothballs filled his throat with the first desperate breath. He gasped. From the outside came the laughter and the jeers.

"Hide and seek, that's hysterical!" Eddie cried out.

"What an idiot."

More laughter.

Nick thrashed about in the few spare inches surrounding his contorted body. He tried to scream but didn't have enough air in his lungs to push through his vocal cords. One last arch of his back. He sucked in a long, slow breath. "Help!!!"

"Your mom's gonna be pissed," Jimmy said.

"Nah, she won't be home for a long time, and Nicky won't say nothin' because he knows what'll happen if he does. Ain't that so?" Eddie said, pounding twice on the top of the cedar chest.

"Maybe you oughta let him out!"

"Stop being such a chicken-liver! Come on."

Eddie's laughter faded and then came the muted sound of a door closing.

"I'm going to die! I don't want to die!" Another deep breath. "Mom!" The mothballs smelled like vinegar and smelly armpits. Nick gagged again.

Somewhere in the panic, in the absolute terror, it became apparent that the struggle was futile. The battle only made his fear grow stronger. His heart raced more rapidly, and his breathing felt more like inhaling seawater, not life-giving air. His head fell to his knees, and he sobbed.

In the hopeless desperation, time lost meaning. Maybe an hour had passed, could have been more when the clicking of high heels on hardwood floor quickened his spirit.

"Help! Let me out!"

"Oh, my god Nicholas!" The voice of an angel!

"Mom!"

The lock opened with a clunk as bright light shot through his dilated pupils, so bright it hurt. His mom leaned down to pull him out. She stood backlit by sunlight from the room's picture window, her figure a faceless silhouette.

Nick awoke in a pool of sweat. The dim glow of the back-alley streetlights illuminated the window's thin almond shades. It took a few minutes, but his breathing slowed. He glanced at the clock. 3:47 am.

He closed his eyes and tried to go back to sleep but the memories of that day more than two decades ago would have none of it; how Eddie had opened the cedar chest and convinced him that it was the best hiding spot in the house; how he'd hesitated, but when Jimmy yelled out, "Here I come" he'd jumped in; how Eddie had whispered, "Put your head down," and how the darkness stolen the light as the top came down with a thud.

If Dr. Makos took emergency calls, this might warrant a stat visit. At least he understood why the stupid thing gave him the creeps. Maybe now he could finally "face his demons," but for the time being, they'd have to wait.

The alarm sounded at 6 am, and his head pounded, like the morning after a college frat party. Exhausted, he forced himself out of bed. At least he could take a hot shower before he put on the same underwear and met Steve and Danielle. He didn't want them involved, especially Danielle, but was thankful to see them soon. True friends were a precious commodity.

61

THE WOMAN REACHED DOWN and pulled a menu from behind the hostess stand. "Table for one?"

Nick smiled. "I'm meeting friends," he said, scanning the diner's front room. The Thursday morning crowd bigger than he expected, seemed more like a Sunday after church mob. Their blended voices buzzed with a loud monotoned drone. Steve's red head didn't stick out among those in the packed booths or along the bar. Nick glanced back at the hostess and shrugged.

"You're welcome to check in the back room," the woman said, gesturing with the menu.

"Thanks." Nick walked past her and caught sight of Steve sitting alone in a booth at the far end of the room. Nick's heart sank. "Where's Danielle?"

"She wanted to stop by her house on the way. Don't worry, she'll be here soon."

Nick sighed. "I met with the police and gave them the stuff Mays sent."

"And they gave you what in return?"

"Looks like Santini may have been driving the vehicle that drove my mother off the road."

"Wow." Steve's eyes opened wide. He fell backward in his seat. "So, your old man had her killed?"

"It certainly looks that way, but I'm still not sure how Mays fits in. My mother had the girl's license in her jewelry box, and it may be what got her killed."

"The girl?"

"Anya, Mays' missing girl."

"What in the world! I don't get it."

"Me either. And, by the way, Willie's aunt Rose called me on the way here and said the coroner's report concluded that Willie died from a heroin overdose like the media reported, so less than helpful."

Steve shook his head. "This whole thing is twisted for sure."

The waitress came and poured them both cups of coffee. Nick glanced toward the door. "Where the hell is she?" His stomach sank.

"I'm not sure."

Nick called Danielle but got voicemail. "I thought you'd be here by now. Call me," he said.

Danielle made a habit of being punctual, and given the gravity of the situation, should have been there.

Nick exhaled when his phone rang less than a minute later. He looked at the caller ID. Unknown Number.

"Hello," Nick said.

The voice sounded deep and muffled. "If you go to the cops, you'll never see your little lady again, at least not in one piece."

Nick slammed his fist on the table. "Who the hell are you, you coward? If you lay a hand on her — "

"I'm okay," Danielle said, choking up. Then silence. Her trembling voice nearly stopped his heart.

"You're the reason your girlfriend is in this predicament. You chose to ignore our warning. I'm going to give you an address, so your memory better be good— I'm only going to say this once. 3687 North Delaware Avenue. Go through the main gate and follow the drive to the third building; nine o'clock tonight. Come alone. If you're late, she dies. If you're not alone, she dies." The call disconnected.

Nick gulped. He motioned for a pen and paper. "Give me something to write with!"

Steve patted his shirt pockets, then waved to the waitress for her pen. Nick repeated the address over and over in his head until the waitress arrived. He scribbled the address and time, folded the napkin, and shoved it in his jacket pocket. His head dropped to the table.

"What?" Steve asked.

Nick clenched his fists, his eyes glaring. "They have her. It's my fault."

The worst possible scenarios flooded his mind. His heart pounded in his chest. Oh my god, what had he done? His guilt turned to rage as he raised his hand to smash his phone to the table. Steve caught Nick's arm and held it. When Nick relaxed, Steve let loose his grip.

Steve looked Nick in the eye. "Okay, I know this is serious, but we have to be rational. The first thing we need to do is call the police."

"If we go to the cops, she'll die."

"I don't see that we have any other choice."

"If they're my father's men, they mean what they say. They're using her to get to me so if they have me, maybe they'll let her go."

"Or maybe they'll kill you both."

"I'll call Rawls when I leave," Nick said, though he wouldn't.

"Are you going to tell me what's on the napkin?"

Nick stood. "Nope. You're going to go somewhere safe until you hear from me."

He'd surely be followed. By the police. By whoever had killed his mother. His red Porsche stood out. He needed a diversion, so he concocted a plan. Maybe not a good plan but it was the first thing that came to his mind, and he went with it. Back over the bridge, he headed toward the airport.

Nick parked in the long-term lot, went to the ticket counter, and purchased a one-way ticket to Pittsburgh. After passing through security, he hustled toward the terminal, winding back and forth, doing his best to blend in with the crowd. He paid cash at Brooks Brothers for a navy linen blazer, a Flyers baseball cap, and a pair of Ray-Ban Deco Metal sunglasses. Wearing his new attire, he headed not toward the departing gate, but back out of the terminal and straight to the Avis desk.

Pulling away from the airport, Nick checked his cell phone for messages and found none. The screen flashed *low battery*. "Shit!" He'd left his charger in his Porsche. Going back seemed too risky, so he headed north on Interstate 95 toward North Delaware Avenue. He had time to spare. Way too much time! The ten and a half hours he'd have to wait seemed like a lifetime. He could go now but who knew if they had her there. Besides, if he didn't go along with their directives, they might kill her. What guarantee did he have that they wouldn't kill them both when he arrived? None!

62

AFTER HEARING that the officers following Nick had lost him at the airport, Rawls' mood went south. "What do you mean you lost him?"

The officer cleared his throat. "He purchased a ticket for a flight to Pittsburgh, but he never boarded. We lost track of him between a clothing store and the gate."

"So, you're telling me that he went to the airport for a flight he didn't intend on taking then left undetected?"

"We located his Porsche in long-term parking but not him."

Rawls usual calm demeanor disappeared. "I suggest you un-lose him in a hurry! I want the man found!"

Line two lit up on Rawls' phone. He switched calls.

"Detective Rawls, Kyle from forensics is on the line," his secretary said.

"Put him through," Rawls said. "Mr. Henry, what do you have for me?"

"An update on the results from my analysis of the blood and the residue from Mays' martini glass."

"Let me have it," Rawls said.

"I can tell you with certainty the blood from the boat's carpet didn't come from a live person. Well— it did originally, but it made a temporary detour through a blood-donation bag before ending up on the carpet."

"Are you telling me that someone planted the blood?"

"Like I explained the last time we spoke, the blood hadn't formed the normal clot, or at least as normal as clotting happens outside the body. After running the gas chromatograph-mass spectrometry, I found the reason why— citrate phosphate double dextrose, otherwise known as CP2D."

Rawls waited for the punch line. "Do I need to guess what CP . . ."

"CP2D's a chemical used in blood-donation bags to keep the blood from clotting and to keep the cells viable. Someone spread the blood from a bag. This was a setup."

"I'll be damned. And the martini glass?"

"Benzodiazepines, can't be sure which one, but definitely a Valium-like drug," Kyle said.

"I'm impressed, Mr. Henry. I'll be writing a letter to your boss letting him know you deserve a raise."

"Well, this might seal the deal," Kyle said. "When I determined someone staged the whole thing, I decided to take another look at the other evidence collected at the girl's apartment. The Charvet tie found on the floor— it had no creases. If it came off in the heat of passion, it had to have had a Windsor or double Windsor knot. This tie came out of a box or off a wide hanger, obviously a plant."

"I know a wealthy senator who will be forever indebted to you."

"Just doing my job," Kyle said. "But I wouldn't turn down a little extra in my paycheck."

"You can count on it," Rawls said.

"Thank you, Detective. I'll have the reports on your desk ASAP."

Rawls called the district attorney to inform him of the new

information. He recommended that they drop the charges against Mays but wanted to meet with him before they allowed him to leave the jail. Mays surely knew more than he'd shared. Anya must still be alive and tracking her down rocketed to the top of Rawls' priority list.

Taylor had just picked up the phone when Rawls tapped him on the shoulder and motioned for him to follow along. "Where are we going?"

"To talk to Mays. He's off the hook."

"Off the hook?" Taylor raced to keep up with Rawls as they descended the building steps.

"I'll fill you in on the way. In the meantime, have Nick's credit card and cell phone records surveilled. He's on the lam."

"Why would he be running?"

"You tell me," Rawls said. "But he's hiding something, and I'm going to find out what."

Mays stood in his prison orange looking out a second-floor window of a conference room at Curran-Fromhold Correctional Facility when Rawls and Taylor entered the room.

"Senator," Rawls said.

"Detective," Mays said as he turned and made eye contact with Rawls.

"Nice view?" Rawls asked.

Mays ran his hand through his hair and looked back out the window as if he were gazing into a crystal ball for the answers to his screwed-up life. "If you want to know the truth, I was contemplating the creek's flow down there. It just keeps on keeping on."

"Yeah, streams do that kinda thing," Rawls said.

"Ever wonder where all that water comes from? Why it doesn't just stop, run dry, and give up?"

"No, not really."

"Ah hell— too much time on my hands, I guess," Mays said. He stepped toward Rawls and Taylor. "Not that I'm complaining, but why the change of heart?"

"Considering the newest evidence, you'll be glad to know your story, at least the little you shared, is holding water. It appears that your one-night stand spiked your martinis and staged her own murder."

Mays nearly fell over. "And the blood? It certainly looked like someone died on the Gypsy Rose."

"We think not. It seems the blood that you tried hard to clean up didn't come from a wound but from a blood-donation bag."

Mays closed his eyes and sighed. Tears formed in his eyes and he turned away from Rawls, back toward the window. He nonchalantly wiped his right eye. "Am I free to go?"

"You are, but I'd like you to help me understand the reason for the setup and who might be involved."

"Extortion— cash— sixty-thousand dollars, to be exact. I don't know who, just that they took the money and left me hanging out to dry."

Taylor took a step forward. "Liza Carlotti? How is she involved?"

Mays' forehead crinkled in confusion. "She's not. Why would you ask me that?"

"Can you explain why she might have had Anya's driver's license in her possession?"

"I have no idea," Mays said, turning to Rawls. Rawls cocked his head and peered through slit-like eyes.

Mays continued. "Maurice, you were there the night I met the girl. You know that I left the restaurant, met her at Pier 33, and took her to my boat. That was the first and last time I ever saw her. Liza died four months before I even met the girl."

"We know about your relationship with Liza," Rawls said.

Mays lifted his head, his eyes bloodshot. "A long time ago, Detective — a very long time ago."

"Was it a coincidence that you were talking to her the night she died?"

"My office received a call from the museum board, inviting

me to the event. After I arrived and found out that Liza was on the board, I assumed she initiated the invite. When I spoke with her, she made it clear that wasn't the case so, coincidence? I think maybe not. But it wasn't my doing."

Rawls stared at Mays until he had his full attention. "I don't have to tell you that withholding any other pertinent information could land you back in hot water. As it is, the charges of tampering with evidence and obstruction of justice could still go forward, but the DA assures me that, under the circumstances, if you continue to cooperate, he'll make those charges disappear as well."

"They contacted me by phone from a blocked number on three separate occasions. You probably already checked my phone records. That's all I have."

Rawls called for a guard to accompany the senator to claim his belongings and escort him from the building.

"We'll be in touch if we need anything further," Rawls said, extending his hand.

Mays shook Rawls' hand with a firm grip that lasted as long as his words. "Thank you, Maurice. It'll be good to sleep without one eye open tonight."

"I'm sure it will."

Rawls made it back to the station by 10:55 am. His secretary stopped him as he passed her desk. "Detective Rawls, there is a Dr. VanSlooten in the lobby. He wants to speak with you."

"Do you know what it's concerning?"

"No, but he said it's urgent."

"Send him in."

The young man wasted no time. He spoke fast, his face flushed a shade lighter than his red hair. "I'm a colleague of Nick Carlotti's, and I need to report a kidnapping."

"I'm listening," Rawls said, sitting up in his chair.

The man caught his breath. "Danielle Sorenson, a c — colleague. She was ab — du — du— ducted this morning."

"How do you know that?"

"We wa — wa — were waiting for her at a diner in Camden. She never arrived."

"Slow down and take it easy. Who are we?"

Steve drew in a deliberate, deep breath then let it out between pursed lips. "Nick received a call from her abductor while we were still at the restaurant," the doctor said, seemingly calmed down.

"What did they want?"

"I'm not sure. Nick wrote something on a napkin, an address, I think. I couldn't read it, and he wouldn't show it to me. He did say that if he called the cops, they'd kill her."

Rawls' eyes narrowed. "You did the right thing."

"Not if they kill her because of it."

Rawls rested his hand on Steve's shoulder. "I'll do my best to ensure that isn't the case."

After taking Steve's contact information and as much information about Danielle as Steve could provide, Rawls led Steve to the door. "Call me directly if you receive any new information."

"I will. Thanks."

63

WITH ANYA's driver's license in hand, and possibly a valid address, Rawls made new inquiries with Taylor's Brazilian contact, an officer with the Departamento de Polícia Federal, in São Paulo. The address belonged to the girl's mother, who admitted Anya often used it to receive mail since she spent much of her time abroad. Anya contacted her mother regularly, including a call six days prior. As far as her mother knew, Anya was still in Colombia performing at her usual clubs.

It shocked Anya's mother to hear of her daughter's involvement in the extortion of a Pennsylvania state senator and she agreed to cooperate with the local and American authorities. She wanted her daughter found safely but understood the gravity of the charges against her and the probability of lengthy incarceration if convicted.

Rawls asked his Brazilian counterpart to check phone records and place a trace on any new calls to the girl's mother. Next, the Brazilian agent called ahead to the Detran, the Brazilian department of transportation, to let them know Rawls would be contacting them. This paid off big.

The agent from the Detran gave him more than he expected.

"The woman contacted our office on March 18 of last year requesting a replacement CNH," he said.

"CNH?" Rawls questioned.

"Carteira Nacional de Habilitação. It's what you would call a license to drive an automobile."

"And did she receive one?"

"We issued a temporary card and mailed it to an address in Philadelphia two weeks later."

The address was that of Anya's now vacated apartment in Center City.

Rawls asked Taylor to follow-up with Anya's CD label.

Less than two hours later, Taylor stood at Rawls' desk with a huge grin. "410-555-2498."

"Is that supposed to mean something to me?" Rawls asked.

"It's the phone number Anya used to call her mother six days ago and it just so happens to be the same number registered to the woman renting a PO box in Baltimore where Anya's royalty checks are being sent."

"What is the name on the accounts?" Rawls asked.

"Marisa Fernandez, a Brazilian native living in Baltimore."

"Do we have an address?"

"725 Lancaster St. Tower Three, Apt. 12," Taylor said.

"For now, she's the only connection we have between all the players and maybe our only hope of finding Dr. Sorenson," Rawls said.

Rawls called the deputy police commissioner of the Baltimore Police Department, an old friend from his days at the academy. He explained that Anya was a suspect in an active hostage situation and that time was of the essence. The commissioner called the judge requesting a warrant, and Rawls prepared extradition paperwork for if and when they arrested the girl. Forty-five minutes later, Rawls and Taylor climbed into a police helicopter for a quick flight to Baltimore. They arrived at her apartment just before 3. Two local police officers accompanied them.

Their knocks on the door went unanswered, and her cherry-red Audi convertible was nowhere to be found. The building manager walked them to Tower 3, a twelve-story luxury apartment overlooking Baltimore's Inner Harbor East. He swung open the door.

The spacious penthouse seemed sparsely decorated for a $3,500-per-month apartment. Bamboo kitchen cabinets held a total of four place settings worth of bowls, dishes, glasses, and silverware. The bedroom closets were empty, as were the drawers. Two black suitcases sat in the living room and another, partially filled, lay open on the bed next to a Canali custom men's suit.

"Our girl must be planning a trip," Rawls said.

"From the looks of this apartment, it seems she never planned to be here long," Taylor said.

An eight by ten photo frame lay face-down on the clothes in one of the two pieces of luggage. Rawls turned over the picture. He recognized the gray-haired man with his arm around the young woman at a beachside bar at sunset.

"We've found our man," he said, turning the picture to Taylor. "Peter Coroneos, Rock Carlotti's second in command."

"It seems the shepherd has lost control of his sheep," Taylor said.

"I wouldn't classify Coroneos as a sheep. He and Rock go way back, and I have a feeling the Carlotti family owes its position to the colonel's mind, not the general's."

Taylor lifted the suit. "She wasn't going on this trip alone," he said, showing Rawls the calligraphed initials P.C.

Their search turned up a treasure trove of evidence: a laptop computer found in a carry-on bag, men's clothes, a leather shoulder holster, a Smith & Wesson .38 Special, and a manila envelope containing two passports— one for Peter Joseph Coroneos and the second for Marisa Fernandez Martins. It bore Anya's photo, her smile shameless and carefree.

Rawls put a trail on Peter Coroneos and sent two officers to stake out Rock's house. Rock had entered his mansion Wednesday afternoon and hadn't left since. So far, Nick hadn't surfaced since he'd split from the airport earlier in the morning. Rawls and Taylor wrapped up their search of the apartment and requested surveillance of the building in case of her return. They ducked under the helicopter's rotors and took their seats for the flight back to Philly.

64

THE NUMBER DIDN'T LOOK familiar.

"Hello," Nick said.

"Uh . . . " His heart skipped a beat. It didn't sound like Danielle, but he wasn't sure. "Who is this?" His car veered toward the adjacent lane as his attention waned. Okay, keep it together.

"Uh, it's Delphia." Her voice trembled.

Nick settled and regained his focus. "Del, are you okay?"

"I know where she is."

"Where who is?" Delphia hesitated.

"It's ok, Del. You can tell me."

"Anya."

Nick's hand fell from his ear. For a second, the world stopped. How in God's name did Delphia have anything to do with this woman? He looked up just in time to see brake lights ahead. His Accord screeched to a halt a couple feet from the trailer hitch of a rusted red pickup truck in his lane. He tried to swallow, but there wasn't enough spit left in his mouth to do so. He sighed and spoke in a whisper. The words seemed to barely rise above the pounding of his heart. "How do you know about Anya?"

"It's sort of a long story."

"I have time." Nick pulled to the right and took exit 32. He needed to find a place to park so he could focus.

"Kaleidoscope, a private underground club, you know for people like us, different from the rest of the world?"

"Yes, go on." He turned into the lot of a small strip mall and turned off the car.

"July 27th of last year I met her there, 3:15 am. She was new in town. Said she came from Brazil, wanted to land a record deal or something."

3:15 am? She remembered the exact time? Nick waited for the story to continue. After an uncomfortable silence, he prodded. "Then what?"

"Oh, yeah. Well, I saw her picture on TV last Sunday. The cops said she was missing and the senator from the museum, the guy with the stiff suit, killed her. Well, he couldn't have killed her because I saw her yesterday in the Ritz-Carlton — I'm not a fan."

"Of the girl?"

"No, the Ritz. It's too snooty, but the manager likes my work, and I was dropping off two pieces. When she looked at me, I said, 'Hey Anya,' but she said she didn't know me. Told me her name was Marisa. She said I'd mistaken her for someone else. But that's B.S. because I'm never mistaken. She had spiky blonde hair, but it was definitely her."

If Delphia said it was Anya, it had to have been. But how? Why? And what in the hell did all of this have to do with his mother? One thing was certain: Mays had been telling the truth. "What time did you see her yesterday?"

"7:30 last night. In front of the lobby elevators."

"Was she waiting for the elevator or had she just gotten off?"

"Marisa Fernandez Martins was definitely going up." Her voice came out like Raymond Babbitt's 'Ten minutes to Wapner!'

"Marisa Fernandez Martins?" Nick questioned.

"The name on the tag of her Burberry suitcase— Marisa

Fernandez Martins, but it should have said Anya cuz that's her name. She had a room key in her left hand."

"Delphia, I can't thank you enough."

"Nah, that's what friends do," she said before the call ended.

Ten hours to go-time. But his itinerary had changed. Anya, Marisa, or whatever the hell her real name was had become ground zero and she knew everything. Hopefully, she hadn't left the Ritz. Nick spun his tires as he raced from the lot and headed back to the expressway for Center City.

~

"I'M SORRY, for security reasons we can't give out guests' room numbers, but I'll be glad to ring her room," the woman said.

Nick scanned the lobby. No exotic women with spiked blonde hair. "That's fine, if you don't mind."

The young receptionist dialed the number. Time seemed to slow. Answer already! "Ms. Martins, there is a gentleman here for you."

The woman turned to Nick. "Your name, sir?"

Nick thought quickly. "Tell her it's a surprise."

"He's telling me it's a surprise," the woman said, her up-and-down gaze sizing him up. "Thirties, thick dark hair, and quite handsome." The woman shrugged. "Sure, no problem. Have a good day, Ms. Martins." She frowned and put her hand to her chest. "I'm sorry, she said she wasn't expecting anyone today and didn't want to be disturbed."

He was sure she didn't! He had her pinned down, at least for the moment. The call may have spooked her, but there were only three ways down — the single bank of elevators and two stairwells. On the other hand, if she were afraid of someone finding her out, someone who'd just called from the lobby, maybe she'd hunker down?

From a seat facing the elevators and one of the two stairwell exits, he waited. The first hour seemed like two and the second like three. Either Anya had made her way down the second stairwell and slipped past him, or she was still holed up in her room. He had another idea.

The woman behind the gift shop counter looked up with an amiable smile, her winter-white hair contrasting with her sharp burgundy hotel blazer. "Can I help you?"

"Do you deliver to guest rooms?"

"We sure do," she said. "Something in particular you're looking for?"

Nick walked past the counter and pulled a small vase of roses from a refrigerated cooler. "These are nice. What do you think?"

The woman reached under the counter. She handed Nick a blank card. "If you write something special . . . yes, I think they'll do."

Nick jotted a quick note on the small card and slid it into the envelope. "My fiancée is here on business and doesn't know I'm in town. I want to send her the flowers before I surprise her tonight."

"Her name?"

"Marisa Fernandez Martins. I don't know her room number."

"Not a problem. I'll have them sent to her room." She smiled and attached the card to the vase.

Nick paid cash and positioned himself down the hall with a view of the gift shop entrance. Less than ten minutes later, the bellhop entered the shop and promptly exited carrying the vase. Nick followed. Of course, the guy would be taking the elevator!

The doors closed behind them. Immediately Nick's chest felt tight, but not like impending doom. The bellhop pushed the button for the 37th floor. Would it be too much of a coincidence that he'd be going to the same floor? Probably, so he pushed the button for the 36th. He'd run up the stairs and hopefully not miss the bellhop's delivery.

The elevator ascended quickly as Nick's ears popped. Thankfully no one got on along the way. The magnitude of the situation at hand trumped his brewing claustrophobia, and when the doors opened on the 36th floor, Nick stepped casually from the elevator. As the doors closed, he sprinted to the stairs and raced up one flight. He exited the stairwell and caught sight of the bellhop disappearing down the hall.

The bellhop's knock on the door echoed in the long hallway. Nick peeked his head around the corner as the bellhop knocked again. No answer. Either she fled or just wasn't going to respond. The man slid a key into the slot and pushed open the door. Nick moved past and glanced into the room . . . 3721. Bed not made, Burberry suitcase packed and ready to go inside the door. The bellhop had his back to the door as he set the vase on the desk. Maybe she'd hidden in the bathroom. Nick picked up his pace and made the next turn out of sight.

If she'd left, she'd have to come back for her bag. Should he wait or call Taylor and Rawls? He glanced at his watch . . . 1:32. The woman had staged her own death to extort Lloyd Mays, and her driver's license had somehow ended up in his mother's jewelry box. She knew something, maybe everything. But she certainly wouldn't spill her guts to Nick in a hallway confrontation. He had to trust Rawls. He made the call.

65

"I'D WASTE him right now if I could, the arrogant bastard," Scalise said, taking a puff of his cigar. The bandaged stump of his middle finger rested just above the cigar's label.

Coroneos and Scalise faced each other at a table in a dimly lit room at the rear of the abandoned industrial complex they'd coined "The Grottos," at 4:30 am Friday. The mob had used the site for years as a place to exchange contraband and money, and to carry out other clandestine activities. A series of tunnels and secret rooms lay beneath its expansive concrete floors. Without inside knowledge or a lot of luck, no one would find them.

Coroneos pulled a Marlboro from a sterling silver case and put it to his lips. "We've had a couple miscues that needed rectification. You know I don't like loose ends." He lit the cigarette, and smoke rolled from his nostrils. "They arraigned Mays yesterday morning. There's enough evidence to put him away for life, and given his previous job as DA, I imagine he won't last long in the pen."

Scalise nodded. "I'm sure the scumbags he put away will be glad to have him as their bitch," he said half-laughing. "What about Nick? What if he doesn't play along?"

"Don't worry. He'll come riding in like the Lone Ranger. From what you told me about their little date at Giovani's, he's smitten."

"And the girl? I mean, after the deal."

"I'd rather not have to off her if we don't have to. If you keep her in the dark, we may be able to let her go, but Nick needs to know that if he wants her to stay alive, he'll need to be at the Grottos, alone and unarmed."

"He's been well informed," Scalise said.

"Hold them both until showtime. Tell the boys not to lay a hand on the girl."

Scalise chuckled. "She's a looker. That might be hard for the horny bastards."

"I'm not kidding, Mickey. I don't want her touched. If Nick doesn't cooperate, I can raise the stakes, but for now, she's bait. Got it?"

Scalise nodded. "And Tony?"

"I said I'd call him when I'm an hour and a half out. He thinks he's meeting us here to inspect the goods," Coroneos said. He slid the cigarette case back into his suit jacket pocket. "And Eddie — he doesn't know a thing. The moron thinks his father is still in charge."

Scalise smirked and let out a mocking huff. "Told him we were holding Nick and the girl because they were getting too close. Just teaching them a lesson. That's all, just a lesson, then lettin' 'em go." Scalise paused. He rolled his fingers as his eyes jutted back and forth, unable to look directly at Coroneos. "We still have the same agreement, right? Twenty-five percent?"

The light of a half-moon streamed through a dusty window behind Scalise, casting his shadow on the table. Peter nodded. "Joey and Sal are buying the whole lot. We're looking at four million cash so they can do whatever the hell they want with Tony. Mays' hush money is icing on the cake. You'll clear a little over a mil, and I'll take care of the excess baggage."

Scalise grimaced. "Fourteen years of risking my ass, and him treating me like a fucking slave. The son-of-a-bitch sat and watched Castillo cut off my damn finger."

"It's all business, my friend, just business. I have no hard feelings. Tony's been a good friend, but he'd end my life as quickly if the price were right." Coroneos said. "That's the way this game goes. Old Willie found out the hard way."

Scalise grinned. "The poor bastard screamed like a baby when I rammed the needle through his eardrum."

"He should have just cooperated and saved himself the pain."

"I'd like to do the honors with Rock," Scalise said.

Coroneos shook his head. "As far as pulling the trigger, I think you'll have to leave that to the Pacciones. They've been waiting a long time for retribution and are paying big bucks for the privilege."

Coroneos had indeed been a better businessman. He'd also embezzled an extra eight hundred thousand dollars from Rock's enterprises over the previous three years, a fact that he wasn't going to share with Scalise.

Coroneos' cell phone rang. The sound echoed through the cavernous concrete space.

"Yeah, Joey, it's all set. You'll have the drugs and long-awaited revenge for your pop's death. Just make sure I have my cash. Yes, the Grottos . . . 3 am."

He put the phone back in his suit jacket pocket and patted Scalise on the back. "My flight to Lexington leaves at 6:35 am. I'll pick up the van and should have possession by 1:00 this afternoon. I'll be back here a little after midnight. See to it that Tommy knows what to do."

"Sounds good, boss," Scalise said. "We'll make sure it goes down like we planned."

The men left in separate cars.

66

THE RISING sun shone well above the horizon, its morning rays lighting the underside of the clouds as Coroneos' plane touched down at Bluegrass Airport in Lexington, Kentucky. A white Ford Econoline van with a magnetic sign reading Emerson's Heating and Cooling waited for him in the parking lot, the keys stashed in the driver's side rear wheel well. Fitted with materials germane to the profession, the van held toolboxes, multiple lengths of PVC, copper pipe, and plumbing fittings.

Coroneos slipped on a tan Carhartt coverall with the name 'Al' embroidered over his left chest. He drove down Route 68 to a Motel 6 north of Harrodsburg.

A little after 1 pm Thursday, in a weathered barn along the North Rolling Fork River, Coroneos made the exchange without incident. Castillo's drug runners seemed as eager to count the cash and move it back to Colombia as Coroneos was to move the cocaine back to Philadelphia.

Leeriness and tension permeated the air as they tallied the stacks of bills and tested the cocaine. When everything checked out, both parties were quick to part ways. The $550,000 payment sealed the deal that would soon earn Coroneos and Scalise four million in cash.

Still on edge, Coroneos started the eleven-hour drive back to Philadelphia. No other couriers, as he promised Rock, just him and the 360 pounds of cocaine stashed in multiple compartments under the floor of his van.

He traveled two-lane roads and back street detours as much as possible, stopping only for gas. He relieved his bladder into a hand-held plastic urinal in the back of the van. Coroneos wasn't going to leave his retirement fund sitting unattended while he stood in a rest-stop bathroom pissing next to a trucker from Tennessee.

As he merged onto Route 64 east of Huntington, he caught flashing red lights in his rearview mirror. The siren's wail grew louder as the car sped up behind him.

"Shit!" He glanced at his speedometer. Only three miles per hour over the sixty-five mile per hour posted speed limit. Still, his heart raced as he took his foot from the accelerator and moved onto the right shoulder. He pulled his weapon from the center console and slipped it under his right hip. If the officer asked him to step out of the van, he knew what he had to do. When the Kentucky state trooper flew past him, he took a couple deep breaths. His phone rang. The caller ID— Sarah.

"Oh God, no! Not now. Please!" He couldn't get himself to answer the call. The phone rang a second time. If it was true, if Sam was gone, there was nothing he could do about it now. He slid his thumb over the send but didn't press down. The third ring sounded. He grit his teeth. At least Sam would be free, liberated from a mind and body that had handicapped him for twenty-three years, and Jesus would welcome him at heaven's gate with open arms. Coroneos, however, would never see Sam again, his own fate sealed by a plethora of mortal sins. Not even Purgatory would open its doors for a man like him. The phone fell silent. He wept.

67

SHE DIDN'T PUT up a fight when they made the arrest in her hotel room. Taylor glanced at the card attached to the vase on the dresser. "Nice touch, Doctor." He read aloud: "Anya, Congratulations on your resurrection from the dead, Sincerely, Nick Carlotti."

Rawls smirked and shot Taylor a nod as they led her out.

Back at the station, Anya remained silent, wanting to speak to a lawyer. That was until Rawls presented the evidence against her and her boyfriend.

Rawls stood over her, his voice biting as he spoke. He raised one finger at a time, counting off the charges against her. "Extortion, identity theft, accessory to murder, aiding and abetting, and a few charges we're still working on. You're facing thirty-plus."

Anya kept her gaze to the floor, her head bobbing as she sobbed.

"I'm willing to cut you a deal. But, if the girl he's holding dies, the deal is off the table, so I recommend you start talking."

Rawls handed her a glass of water. She took a sip and looked up, her cat-like eyes bloodshot and swollen, mascara running down her light-brown cheeks. She gripped her eight-carat, pear-shaped emerald between her fingers as it dangled from her neck. Her gaze peered into the translucent green rock.

"What's your offer?"

"Restitution, then permanent deportation back to Brazil. I'm sure the sale of that pretty little gem will more than take care of your financial responsibility."

She wept as Rawls waited for her response. He leaned closer.

"Your window of opportunity is closing quickly."

She nodded.

"How did you meet Peter Coroneos?"

Anya looked up at Rawls. "How do I know you'll keep your word?"

"I always keep my word, but regardless, I don't see you have much choice."

She took a sip of her water. "We met in a club in Bogota in the summer of '94."

"You came to the States last March?"

"Yes."

"And you planned to work gigs, have a covert affair, and then what?"

Strands of her recently bleached blonde hair hung over her face, clumped together and wet. She whisked them aside as tears continued to flow. They dropped one-by-one into a slowly growing pool at her feet.

Rawls slid a box of tissues down the table. Anya took one and held it to her eyes. "Tell me what you know about Liza Carlotti," he said.

She shrugged.

"I believe your boyfriend is the mastermind behind this whole thing, and I'd rather not see you take the fall with him. But I'll do what I have to do. It's your choice. Thirty years in prison is a long time. You'll be a shriveled-up old bag when they set you free and put you on a one-way flight back to Brazil."

She sat back in her chair, her shoulders slumped, and she

spoke between sobs. "Peter had been stealing money from Rock for a couple years, saving for us to start a life together. He said he had one more deal to make."

"How does Liza Carlotti play into this?" Rawls asked, wondering why such a talented and attractive woman would trade it all away for a cheating snake thirty years her senior.

Anya's sleek, dark eyebrows furrowed. "She walked in on us while we were making love. She ruined it. She ruined the whole thing."

"When?"

"March of last year. I'd just gotten to the States. We met at Rock's house in Buckingham. Rock was in Vegas, and she was supposed to be in the Poconos."

"So, you and your boyfriend thought you'd borrow their bed? A little— teenagers home alone, the parents away sorta thing?"

She didn't smile.

Rawls continued. "Coroneos had her killed because? His wife would find out?"

"No, not that she'd find out, but that it would undermine the plan. Peter didn't want to take the chance that Liza would tell her husband or tell Peter's wife, and the whole thing would fall apart."

"So, he threatened her?"

"He said if she talked, people she loved would get hurt. She stormed out, and I heard her tires squealing in the driveway."

"Coroneos didn't think Liza would keep your little secret?"

"If Rock found out about us and the missing money, he'd have killed Peter."

"Liza didn't know about the embezzlement, so what's the point?"

"Peter knew his wife would file for divorce, and when the legal battle started, someone might track down the hidden accounts. I told him we should wait it out, but he didn't want to take any chances."

"And what about Mays?"

"Peter wanted a scapegoat in case Liza's accident became suspicious. He knew Liza and Mays had a relationship in college, so they already had a connection. Peter planned to have Liza killed and then stage my murder on the senator's boat. He thought if Mays was a suspect in one murder and was seen talking to Liza the night of her death, he'd be the main suspect."

"And Peter would make a little money from Mays on the side," Rawls said.

"Yes, and he'd have time to make one last deal before he left his wife."

"One last deal? What does that mean?"

"I don't know exactly." Her expression softened. For the first time in the interview, she looked relieved of her burden. "He told me it would take care of us for the rest of our lives. But not just us, he wanted to make sure Sam was cared for. That boy meant the world to him."

"But you don't know anything about it, the last deal?"

"No."

"And since your staged death you've been living as Marisa Fernandez?"

"Peter knew this guy who set it all up, birth certificate, credit cards, driver's license and . . . " She broke down again.

Rawls directed an officer to take her back to the holding cell. They had to locate Peter Coroneos sooner rather than later. A girl's life hung in the balance.

68

A PUNGENT SMELL like rotten eggs and burnt matches enveloped his car as Nick turned onto North Delaware Avenue on the city's northeast side. To his left, three massive dome-topped petroleum tanks stood side by side in a block-long storage facility. How scared Danielle must have been as she traveled this road. Damn! How could he have risked her life the way he had?

He passed two vacant lots and an abandoned gas station before coming to a poorly lit parking lot in front of an abandoned industrial park. Tall weeds filled the cracks in the lot's pavement.

A rusty, chain-linked gate blocked the entrance to the main lot. The few working floodlights only dimly illuminated the front of the first four-story building. Although most of its windows were shattered, this one wasn't covered in graffiti. Even the gangs didn't feel safe here.

Nick pulled close to the gate and turned off his headlights. Before he exited the car, he took a small pocketknife from his briefcase and slid it between his right calf and sock. It wasn't much, but it was all he had.

The thick, humid air hung still and quiet except for the distant drone of traffic moving along I-95 a few blocks away. A heavy steel chain on the gate draped from one side to the other with an open Master-Lock fitted on one end. Nick lifted the chain from the unattached side and let it fall to the ground. He walked the gate open, then eased the car slowly into the lot and down a dark drive toward the remaining buildings.

He passed the second building and squeezed the steering wheel as he approached the third. It took up nearly three-quarters of a city block. Set back farther from the drive, it appeared industrial in nature, with extensive exterior plumbing and a catwalk that extended from its top floor to the roof of a smaller fourth building farther down.

The kidnapper hadn't told Nick what to do once he got to the address. One car sat in the parking lot at the end of the drive, and aside from the dim orange glow of his parking lights and hazy moonlight filtering through an overcast sky, the place was dark.

Nick turned off the ignition and waited in silence, contemplating his next move. The sudden vibration of his cell phone cut his respite short. His adrenaline surged. He didn't recognize the number and prepared to confront Danielle's captors. He hit SEND.

"Hey, Doc, it's Tyrese. You told me to call if I heard anything."

"Tyrese?"

"Me and my boys tried to jack your briefcase and wallet. Remember?"

"Yeah — yeah, I do now," Nick said. "What do you have for me, Tyrese? Talk fast, I don't have much time."

"You know that Torello dude who got offed in the hospital? He was a dealer— tried once to peddle smack in my territory, and we ran his white ass off. Word on the street is that they wasted him because he knew something 'bout Rock's lady . . . I mean your mother."

"What exactly did he know?" Nick asked.

"I think that's all I want to say. I ain't stupid."

"Tyrese, whatever you say to me stays with me." Nick stared at the blinking battery signal on the screen of his phone. Spit it out already!

"Like, maybe it was an inside . . . "

"Like an inside — what?" The phone's screen went black. "Damn it!" He threw the phone on the seat of his car and eased open the door, listening for any hint of a sound. He stepped from the car and shut the door as quietly as possible. But in the relative hush, he might as well have blasted the horn. The thud reverberated off the brick buildings.

Nick stepped down the concrete walkway toward the front doors waiting for the hammer to fall, for a car to roar in from the side and block his path, or for men armed with assault rifles to order him to the ground. Nothing, just eerie silence. As his hand reached up to try the door, a single blast of a tugboat's horn rang out from the river. He dropped down to the ground and went for the knife in his sock.

"Shit," he mumbled under his breath. When his heart eased, he stood and found the door unlocked. Looking at the broken-out lower pane of glass, he realized that he could have simply crawled through without opening the door.

The moment he stepped through the door, a bright beam of light hit him square in the face.

"On the ground!"

He recognized the voice. "Mickey, you son-of-a-bitch!"

"I said get down on your face, now."

Nick fell to his knees, squinting in a failed effort to see past the blinding light to the face of his adversary.

"All the way down, hands behind your back," Mickey said, his handgun pointed at Nick's head.

Nick lay face down on the dusty floor, his hands stretched behind his back. He turned his head to the side in time to see Eddie step out from around the corner, his gun drawn.

"Scalise, you piece of shit, and you . . . " Nick glared at Eddie standing above him. "You're my brother, man! How could you? And Mom?"

Eddie's smug smile disappeared as his jaw dropped open. "What the hell are you talking about?"

Scalise moved in quickly and stepped on Nick's back. "Tie him up."

Eddie slipped a heavy plastic zip tie around Nick's wrists. Nick clenched his hands tightly, flexing the muscles and tendons of his wrists and forearms to create a small amount of space. Eddie yanked the tie's free end, the plastic digging into Nick's skin. Then Eddie patted him down. He rolled Nick onto his back, repeating the search, thankfully, never making it below Nick's thighs.

"Get up," Scalise said, kicking Nick in the side, his ribs cracking like dry sticks. For a moment he lay, unable to catch his breath.

Straining, he lifted himself to his knees, then to his feet. When Scalise lowered the flashlight, Nick could see his face clearly. A wave of rage coursed through him. His father, his brother, and his father's bodyguard were behind his mother's death. "You murdering bastard!" Nick said as he lunged toward Scalise.

Scalise swung the heavy flashlight, landing a blow across Nick's cheekbone. A searing pain shot through his head, and his knees buckled. He squeezed shut his eyes and shook his head. When the cobwebs cleared, Scalise's imposing figure towered above him in a crimson blur. Nick straightened up and blinked hard to clear his sight. A small trickle of blood dripped down his face. He used his right arm to wipe it dry, but a steady stream continued.

Scalise waved with his gun to his right. Nick glanced back at his brother. Their gazes locked for only a second as Eddie looked away, quite uncharacteristic for him. People used to call him Ice because he never lost a stare down. But in that instant, a hint of remorse showed through. Maybe he wasn't all in. Maybe he actually cared — a little.

Nick followed the flashlight's beam down a long hallway toward the vault's entrance and its dark stairwell. As he descended the narrow flight of steps, the temperature dropped. With each step, the light dimmed. Nick's lungs shrunk in his chest. His throat tightened.

Standing on the last step, outside the big steel door, Eddie took a roll of duct tape and tore off two six-inch pieces. He pressed one against Nick's eyes and the other over his mouth. The metal door opened with the grating of its rusty hinges. Nick tightened the muscles of his legs and leaned back. He wasn't going in. Eddie's foot landed hard against his back. He fell without the aid of his hands to catch him and swung his head to the side to avoiding landing on his face. The impact sent pain like fire from his left shoulder down to the tips of his fingers.

"Hey, darling, your boyfriend's here," Eddie said. "Don't get too attached, though. He's not going to be around long."

"Nick!" Danielle cried out.

She was alive! Nick wanted to tell her how sorry he was for dragging her into this mess. Because of him. Because of his screwed-up family. Because he didn't know when to leave well enough alone. And his own father had orchestrated the whole thing. But to what end? His father had little conscience, but to kill his own wife, and now his son, seemed too heinous. Even for Rock Carlotti.

Scalise grabbed the back of Nick's shirt and jerked him to his feet. He pushed Nick into another room and slammed shut the door. The lock closed with a loud clunk.

69

Rawls scanned the lengthy list of people who'd had access to
Torello during his hospitalization. He chose to eliminate those
who'd been working at the hospital for more than two months.
That narrowed the list to just six people: Nick Carlotti, Torello's
mother and sister, a twenty-three-year-old nurse recently relo-
cated from Denver, a wound-care specialist from Pakistan, and
the police officer assigned to guard the room.

Taylor and Rawls interviewed the nurse and wound-care
specialist. Neither had a criminal record nor did they have a
motive to kill Torello. Although he couldn't rule them out, Rawls'
gut said to move on. The nurse confirmed a fire alarm caused by
burning plastic in the break room toaster oven had sent the ICU
into disarray. She stated that no one on staff claimed ownership
of the plastic container.

The police officer on duty the night Torello died, Luther
Miles, hadn't initially been given the assignment but had volun-
teered to switch with the original officer after that man fell ill.
Miles had joined the force three years prior and had recently
gone through a nasty divorce and a subsequent bankruptcy settle-
ment. He had an unblemished service record but was known to

be a loner, without any close friends in the department, not even his partner of the past eighteen months.

Taylor spoke with Officer Wilcox, the man originally scheduled to watch Torello's room. Wilcox stated that he got violently sick after lunch before his evening shift. He'd eaten Chinese food from a food truck parked outside the precinct and drunk half a chocolate shake he'd received from Miles. Wilcox said Miles offered to take his shift, and their supervisor approved the switch.

Rawls had a warrant issued for Miles' cell phone, bank, and credit card records. Miles' credit card receipt from the day before Torello's death showed a purchase from the pharmacy three blocks from his house, for syrup of ipecac. His bank records revealed a twenty-five-thousand-dollar cash deposit into a savings account on July 9, the day after Torello died.

Rawls brought Miles in for questioning.

"They told me you wanted to see me, Detective," Miles said from the entrance of Rawls' office.

"Yes, Officer Miles, come in and take a seat."

"Is there a problem?" Miles asked as he stepped into the room.

"I want to ask you a few questions about your assignment the day Mr. Torello died."

Miles looked back toward the door and then turned, making eye contact with Rawls. "Sure, fire away."

"How did you come to that assignment? The schedule shows you'd just come off foot patrol in Old City."

"Wilcox was puking his brains out in the locker room, and I told him I'd cover for him. It was a sit-down job, and I wanted to help the guy out."

"Did you eat lunch together?"

Miles bit his lower lip, and his face went pale. "We were both in the break room but not sitting together. Why?"

"Wilcox said you gave him half of your shake. Feeling generous?"

"I was full, and it was a big shake. So?"

"From what I know about you, Officer Miles, you aren't normally the social type. A man died on your watch, and we're just making sure we have all the facts."

"Torello was in the ICU. People die in there every day."

"Anything unusual about that particular day?" Rawls asked.

"The place was a zoo. Fire alarm going off— smoke from some burning plastic in a toaster oven but otherwise, I didn't see anything suspicious."

Rawls pushed his chair back and leaned forward. "Do you have kids?"

"No, why?"

"Any reason why you might want to buy syrup of ipecac?"

Miles' gaze darted around the room, and his hands moved like he didn't know where to put them. He started toward the door. "I don't think I want to answer any more questions."

Rawls stood. "I didn't dismiss you, Officer Miles."

Miles stopped and turned around, his hand moving toward his sidearm.

"Don't even think about it," Rawls said with his gun already drawn and aimed at Miles' chest. "Put your hands behind your head and get to your knees."

Rawls called for backup. He stepped around Miles, cuffed him, and removed the weapon from his holster. "The large cash deposit you made the day after Torello died? Fat payday for a job well done or did a wealthy aunt kick the bucket?"

Miles face was flushed, and he kept his gaze to the floor as he moved to his knees. Rawls got into his face. "Who paid you off? Peter Coroneos?"

Miles stared at Rawls and swallowed hard. "I'd like to speak to an attorney."

Two officers rushed in as Rawls read Miles his rights. The officers led him out to be booked for the murder of Danny Torello.

Rawls called for updates on the location of Coroneos, Rock, and Nick. So far, Rock hadn't left his house, and neither Coroneos nor Nick had been located. Rawls instructed the men watching Rock's house to sit tight. If Rock made a move, it might lead them to Coroneos and possibly Dr. Sorenson. But he likely wouldn't stir if he suspected he was being watched.

Rawls hated the waiting game but had developed steely patience during his lengthy career. Although it often felt like paralysis, waiting for the bad guys to make a mistake almost always won out over jumping the gun. He just hoped Dr. Sorenson didn't come out on the losing end of his wager.

70

WHATEVER MEASURE of calm Nick had gained on the way down the steps all but shriveled when the door slammed behind him. A rush of fear flowed through his veins, and his ingrained response of panic kicked in. He was losing control.

He'd been there too many times before, but this time a bonafide threat existed. It wasn't an elevator, a plane, or a cedar chest. Yet, deep down, he knew, even with duct tape over his mouth, he should be able to breathe. But he couldn't. His brain screamed, "The tape's too tight! The room's too small!"

He hyperventilated, his rapid breaths passing like a rushing wind through his nostrils. Even in the darkness, the room spun, his lips and extremities losing sensation. Then — without self-determination, some magic words, or a slap on the face — it stopped. He had nearly passed out, but he didn't. He just plain quit fighting. Maybe he was dead or only dreaming.

Despondent, he knelt on the cold, damp concrete floor. In the darkness, his arms bound behind him, he cried out to God. "What do you want from me?" His words were garbled through taped lips.

"I'm sorry!" he cried. And he was— sorry for letting down his mother, sorry for being so full of himself, sorry for closing his heart to all of God's gentle and sometimes not-so-gentle whispers. In the darkness of the room and the darkness of his mind, his mother smiled, a sweet smile, a proud smile. She seemed alive to him, and it brought him comfort.

"Nick, are you okay?"

Nick sat upright, Danielle's voice giving him new life. He attempted to acknowledge her with a few muted vocalizations.

She spoke again. "Tap once if you're okay?"

His jaw throbbed, his shoulder ached, and he might have lost a back tooth from his interaction with the working end of a flashlight. He pulled himself toward the direction of her voice, and when he touched the wall, gave it one sharp tap with his foot.

"Thank God," she said.

He tried without success to pull his arms under his backside. With equally poor results, he attempted to peel the tape from his mouth with his good shoulder. The knife in his sock was less than helpful without a hand to wield it.

There had to be something, anything that might be helpful in the pitch-black room. He turned his body sideways with his left shoulder touching the wall and inched forward, one foot and then the other, until his right foot touched the far wall. Finding nothing on his first pass, he made a right-hand turn, left shoulder now against the far wall. He took a few more short, careful steps.

On the fourth step, his left knee grazed a metal post. With the opposite knee, he felt the mattress of a bed. He moved around it, careful to maintain contact along the way. Reaching the second corner post, he turned around to feel the metal with his hands. It felt cold with a smooth, painted surface. As he crouched up and down, sliding his hands along the tubular metal, he noted areas of chipped paint and rust. A bit lower, two smooth bolts protruded from where the bed frame was attached to the post. The bed frame's edge, however, felt sharp, and at the corner, jagged like a knife.

Nick dropped to his knees with his back leaning against the bedpost, his feet extending behind him under the bed. He slid his hands down to where the post attached to the bed frame, and came to the serrated, rusty edge. With a bit of contortion, Nick pushed his wrists backward and tried to catch the plastic zip tie on the corner. When he felt resistance, he let his weight settle. With every pound of weight he shifted to the zip tie, the plastic gouged deeper into his wrists. Please let the plastic give way before the wrists do. As the pain increased, so did the strength of his resolve.

He shifted forward, maintained his downward force, and dragged the plastic against the rusty metal. When the tie slipped off the front edge, he lifted himself, shifted back, and reset. Three times he repeated the maneuver without success. But as he slid forward the fourth time, the zip tie snapped. Nick's butt hit the floor and his head smashed against the bedpost.

Having his hands free mitigated the searing pain in his head and the stinging abrasions on his wrists. He ripped the tape from his eyes, removing a layer of skin and a good portion of his right eyebrow. Thankfully, his stubble made the removal of tape from his lips a bit less like a cheap dermabrasion.

"Danielle," he called, his vocal cords coarse and dry.

"Nick, it's so good to hear your voice." Her words projected low at his feet.

"Keep talking," he said. "I think there's an opening, some sort of ventilation in the wall."

She spoke in a calm, almost matter-of-fact tone. "My mother worried when I took the residency in Philadelphia; thought the city was too dangerous. She would have been thrilled for me to have stayed on our ranch in Kalispell, raised quarter horses, and baked blackberry pies. I don't think even Mom had this in mind."

"When you take me home to introduce me, we won't tell her

about this little misadventure," Nick said as he crouched down toward the sound of her voice, feeling the wall as he went.

"That's a little presumptuous, don't you think?"

"What?"

"My taking you home."

"More like wishful thinking," he said. His hands moved over a metal grate with holes large enough for his fingers. "Down here," he said. "Put your hands on the wall."

Danielle slid her hand down the wall. Their fingers touched.

Like a gentle electric shock, it surged through his whole body. He wasn't sure he'd ever felt like that, not even his first kiss. The subtle caress of her fingers on his felt more intimate, more powerful than all the romantic and sexual encounters of his self-centered past. "I love you," Danielle said.

"I love you too. We're going to make it out of this. But they'll be back, so we need to think fast. Look around. Anything you can use?"

"Nothing, just a bed."

"I have a knife, but you'll need something in your hands too. We'll get only one chance." Nick reluctantly pulled his hand from hers.

He lifted the mattress and took hold of one of the wooden slats resting on the metal frame. The dry wood seemed too light, not likely to make much of an impression even if it hit the mark. It was more apt to piss someone off than knock him out. Nick slid his fingers down the slat and noted an empty screw hole at one end.

"Reach under the mattress and grab a wooden slat. Let me know if it has an empty hole at either end."

A few seconds passed. "Yes, it does."

Nick yanked the necklace from his neck and took the nail in his fingers. "Don't be mad, but we have to be resourceful. Take this," he said, pressing the nail through an opening in the grate.

Danielle groped along the grate, accidentally knocking the

nail from his fingers. It fell to the floor with a ping and bounced once before coming to rest somewhere in the darkness.

Nick suppressed a groan. "It's from the necklace you gave me. You have to find it."

The quiet was interrupted by the shuffling of her hands and knees on the rough concrete floor.

"Got it," she said. "That was a gift, you know."

"I'm sure God will understand. See if you can push it through the hole in the board. Pound it in if you have to."

It was too damn quiet. "Well?"

"Well, what?"

"Did it work?"

"It pressed in but not all the way. Hold on."

The tapping of the nail against the floor echoed off the walls.

"Crap! They're going to hear us," Nick said. "Did it work?"

"Yes, I see what you're thinking," she said.

"I don't know who will be back for us, or when, but as far as they know, I'm still bound and blindfolded, and you're unarmed, so hopefully we can catch them off guard. Don't be shy with that thing when the time comes."

"I'm a cowgirl, remember. I know how to swing an ax."

Nick smiled. "I'm sure you do." He moved carefully in the dark and took a seat on the bed. Now they'd just have to wait.

His eyelids felt like sandbags and his head throbbed like a post-frat-party hangover, but his mind was crystal clear. "I've been thinking a lot about what you've been saying."

"Such as?"

"The whole God thing."

"And what have you come up with?"

"That I can relate to Christian from Pilgrim's Progress."

"I wasn't sure you'd read it."

"Neither was I, but I packed it for my trip and read it on the way home. The part about the uphill climb with the burden on his back— it's the story of my whole stinking life."

"It's the story of all of our lives," Danielle said. "For Christian, the burden fell off at the cross. How about you?"

"Not sure I can trust a God who hurts the people I love."

"Maybe that's the point."

"What, that he's a sadist?"

"No, that it's about faith. Think about the family members of our patients. They sit in the waiting room without control, not knowing what's happening in the OR. They can't see the operation and often don't hear anything for hours. They just have to trust."

"But God still allows people to suffer," Nick said. "And if he is God, he should be able to make things work out."

"Maybe our comfort in this temporary little life isn't the end game. Maybe it's about something much greater, much more eternal."

"So, what are you trying to tell me?"

"That faith comes first, then you will know the author of that faith. Drop the reins, Nick."

She sure the hell sounded calm despite having been abducted by murderous thugs. She was either a lunatic or just plain believing what she was saying. "And how exactly do you recommend I do that?"

"The man on the cross next to Jesus, the one who humbled himself, certainly didn't have control as he hung there to die but he asked Jesus to remember him when he came into his kingdom. Jesus said, today you'll be with me in paradise. It was a personal faith, between Jesus and him, and it has to be personal for you too."

In the silence that followed, Nick contemplated her words. And, with their present situation, doubted God's goodness all the more.

For what felt like a few hours, they talked and even found moments of laughter. He asked her to sing "Somewhere" from West Side Story, and she obliged with a couple lines.

"Wow. I admit I was skeptical when you told me you played Maria, but I'm impressed."

"You should hear me do Shania Twain."

"You are a country girl," Nick said. "When we're out of this jam, I know a rockin' country bar in Jersey where they do karaoke and line dancing."

Danielle chuckled. "When have you ever gone to a country bar?"

"There's a lot you don't know about me. I'm multifaceted."

"You can say that again."

A loud knock rang out from metal pipes in the ceiling. Nick sprang to his feet. "I'm scared," Danielle said.

"It's okay, I am too."

71

CORONEOS MADE the call to Rock at 1:02 am. "I'm an hour and a half out."

He called Scalise immediately after. "Meet me at the drop zone in half an hour. It's go-time."

"Good. I'll send Tommy to grab Nick and the girl after we unload the goods. He'll bring them up from the vault when Rock arrives," he said.

"I've reconsidered," Coroneos said. "We don't need any loose ends."

"I've got it covered."

When Coroneos arrived, he pulled the van around the back to the loading dock. The large door opened slowly. He drove into the massive warehouse where Scalise and Eddie stood waiting with four empty aluminum cases.

Coroneos exited the van with a change of clothes. He didn't waste any time barking orders. "Start transferring the goods. Rock will be here in less than an hour and the Pacciones forty minutes later," he said. He scanned the loading dock, uneasy. He'd schemed, risked, and sacrificed for months for this moment, yet now it seemed he'd just received his own dose of bad karma.

Somehow, the sweetness of the payoff tasted bitter, in light of the loss of his boy. He contemplated making a quick call to Anya to give her the news, but no, she didn't need to know. She'd find out soon enough.

As Scalise, Tommy, and Eddie removed floor and wall panels from the van, Coroneos changed from his coveralls and work boots to street clothes and loafers. He moved his Glock from the center console to the shoulder holster under his sports coat. When he finished changing, he joined the others in removing the goods from the van.

The men transferred the cellophane-wrapped packages of cocaine from the van to the four metal cases. As they neared the end of the task, Coroneos sent Tommy for Nick and the girl. "Hold them there until we let you know Rock has been secured, then bring them here."

Tommy puffed up his chest. "Will do, Boss."

$\approx$

THE VAULT DOOR's handle clanked, bringing a quick end to their conversation.

"Get ready," Nick said.

The outer door opened. The beam of a flashlight passed under Nick's door, allowing just enough light for him to see. He gripped his knife at his side as he positioned himself for one clean strike. He hoped Danielle stood locked and loaded with her makeshift weapon.

The light under Nick's door, initially bright, faded to black. Heavy footsteps passed in Danielle's direction.

Damn it. Come here, you son-of-a-bitch.

The turning of the lock's mechanism rang crisp and clear. Danielle's door creaked open.

Crack! The board splintering against the man's head coincided with the shriek he let out. The high-pitched chime of keys hitting the floor preceded Danielle's yell. "Oh my god, it's stuck in his head, and he's trying to pull it out!"

"Tell me it's not my brother."

"It's not."

"Then hit him again!"

A guttural groaning and the shuffling of feet sounded, and dim light passed through the grate in the wall.

"Danielle?"

The sound of a blow to the body preceded the thud of a body hitting the floor and the sickening crack of skull against concrete.

"I think he's dead," Danielle said.

"Are you okay?"

"Yeah, I'm looking for the keys. I think they're on the floor, but I don't see them."

The flashlight's glow waxed and waned through the metal grate. It was taking too long.

"Well?"

"I'm looking."

"Look faster!"

"I see them. They slid under the bed." The bed's metal feet scraped across the concrete floor. "Got 'em!"

"Get me the hell out of this room," Nick said.

When she opened his door, Nick threw his arms around her and pressed his lips against hers. As much as he wanted to stay locked in the embrace, he pulled away. He slipped the knife into his back pocket. Danielle held a gun in her right hand and a flashlight in her left. Nick grabbed the flashlight and dashed into the adjacent room. Tommy lay face-up, the board stuck to his head, the nail's full length driven into his left temple. His eyes stared wide open; the terror of death frozen in time. A small pool of blood congealed next to his head, and a slow trickle dripped from beneath the board.

"Nice shot. I hope you don't mind me leaving the nail here," he said.

"Not at all. I'll buy you a new one." She handed Nick the gun.

Before Nick left the room, Tommy's cell phone vibrated. Nick pulled the phone from the dead man's pocket and pushed shut the door.

"We need to move. If Tommy doesn't answer, Mickey will be back," Nick said, securing the lock.

Finding their way out proved no easy task. The complex lay shrouded in darkness and every hallway looked the same. The direction they chose could lead them directly to Scalise. The flashlight was a double-edged sword, light to show them the way, but at the same time saying 'here we are.' Nick took the lead with his finger on the Glock's trigger.

He turned the corner, holding Danielle's hand. A bright light shone from behind as their distorted silhouettes projected on the wall directly in front of them. Nick spun his head around. The beam hit his eyes.

A shot rang out with an instantaneous high-pitched zing inches from Nick's head. Wind from the speeding bullet lifted the hair above his ear. As Nick turned back, Danielle ran forward. The two collided. The flashlight crashed to the floor. Scalise ran full stride as Nick reoriented and yanked Danielle's arm, positioning her behind him. Nick fired a single shot down the hallway. Scalise froze, took cover, and returned fire.

Nick picked up his flashlight.

"Run!" he shouted.

As they flew down the hallway, Nick searched for an open door. The first didn't budge. The second on his left swung open when Nick gave it a shove. He tugged Danielle's arm in the direction of the opening. "Get in and keep quiet."

"No, I'm going with you."

"Just do it. I'll be okay." Nick pulled Tommy's cell phone from his pocket. "Take this. You can use it for light but sit tight as long as you can."

Danielle warily let go of his hand as the door shut. Nick continued down the hall, the steady pounding of footsteps in his wake.

When the footsteps ceased, Nick heard the multi-toned beeping of a cellphone dialing. Scalise's hushed voice resonated in the eerie silence. His words were unintelligible and brief. Nick inched his way around the next corner and tucked himself into a small alcove. He aimed his gun down the dark hallway.

As the light from Scalise's flashlight grew brighter, Nick pulled the hammer back slowly until it clicked into position. Scalise didn't emerge around the corner. Nick tried to slow his breathing. Steady. Scalise's gun-hand appeared first. Nick tightened the grip on the gun, his finger squeezing shy of the point of no return. Scalise stepped into view.

"Drop the gun, Nick. The party's over."

The hard, cold, steel barrel of Coroneos' silenced .44 Magnum pressed against the back of Nick's head.

Nick let the gun fall to the floor.

Scalise stepped up and took the gun. "Hey, Doc, you and your girlfriend saved us some work. Not quite how we planned to take care of Tommy, but it'll do."

Nick glared at Scalise. "I'd rather it would have been you, Mickey, but we didn't have a spike long enough to penetrate your thick skull."

Mickey looked past Nick to Coroneos. "The boy has his old man's sense of humor," he said, then landed a right cross to Nick's jaw.

Nick straightened and turned toward Coroneos and the barrel of his gun. "My mother trusted you. She loved you, you son-of-a-bitch!"

"Tie him up," Coroneos said to Scalise. "We need to get back."

Nick glared at Coroneos. "Where is my father?"

"Don't worry. He's on his way."

"I'll end you!" Nick said. His gaze was like a laser-beam burning a hole through Coroneos' head.

Mickey yanked Nick's hands behind his back and bound them with a zip tie. The sharp plastic dug into the already raw wounds. The two men led Nick toward the loading dock. Nick's heart raced as they neared the door where Danielle hid, but they continued without slowing down. Nick exhaled. If only she were safely out of the building. Her moxie with the bed-board-nail contraption gave Nick confidence in her ability to survive. God, please protect her.

When they made it to the loading dock, Eddie stood guarding the metal containers. Nick knew that look. The pulling in of one corner of his lip between his teeth. He wasn't all in. Their gazes locked, and for the first time in decades, Eddie seemed sorry. He looked away.

Scalise replaced the duct tape across Nick's mouth and leaned him against a metal dumpster. "You get a free front-row seat. Enjoy the show." Scalise said.

Nick's heart hadn't slowed but it wasn't pounding out of his chest either, just strong and steady. He wasn't sure why. Maybe out of recent repetition and desensitization, or maybe Danielle's prayers had reached heaven. Regardless, Nick's mind remained sharp, and he had little fear for his own life. He mostly regretted Danielle's involvement in his mess. Just lay low, please!

72

RAWLS GOT word that Rock had just received a call from a cell phone registered to Peter Coroneos. The call originated from a cell tower near Upland, about twenty miles southwest of Philadelphia. Minutes later, undercover detectives let Rawls know that Rock's car had pulled out of his winding driveway. They kept Rawls informed as they followed Rock down I-95 south from Buckingham.

Rawls and Taylor pulled onto the ramp at exit 40 and joined the pursuit, keeping Rock's car in full view. Thirteen miles later, Rock exited the highway toward Delaware Avenue.

"Don't follow too closely," Rawls said.

Traffic was light at this time of the night, so the two trailing cars might stand out. Taylor eased off the accelerator.

Rawls sent the other officers three blocks farther south to approach Delaware Avenue from the opposite direction. He instructed them to pull onto the street, park, and turn off their lights. "Sit tight until I give you further word."

～

Rock's car slowed as it neared the Grottos. Rawls and Taylor followed a block behind with their headlights off. When Rock pulled through the gate and down the drive, Rawls and Taylor got out and advanced by foot.

As the car stopped in front of the third building, Rawls and Taylor crept close to the wall and weaved their way amidst the overgrown shrubs and weeds. When they reached the corner, they crouched low. Rawls peered through his binoculars. Three vehicles sat parked in the lot— Rock's Jaguar, a silver Mercedes, and a dark-colored Honda Accord, presumably the one Nick had rented at the airport.

The plates on the Honda and the Mercedes were clearly visible, illuminated by moonlight filtering through thinning clouds. Rawls radioed the station, ran the plates, and confirmed the Honda was Nick's rental. The Mercedes belonged to Mickey Scalise, a man known to be Rock Carlotti's bodyguard. Nick and Danielle had to be somewhere inside.

Rawls wanted to act, but his hands were tied. He called for his backup to move to within a hundred yards of the first lot with their lights off while Taylor obtained blueprints of buildings three and four. In close communication with Rawls, Captain Simms, commander of the SWAT team, prepared two teams to move once they had the building's layout.

～

Inside the loading dock, Coroneos greeted Rock with a handshake and a hug. "It went off without a hitch," he said.

Rock eyed the four cases sitting outside the van. "That's good, very good. Let me take a look." He patted Eddie on the shoulder as he moved closer.

"It's all there," Mickey said, opening the first case. "Three hundred and sixty pounds of white gold."

Rock surveyed the room. Eddie nodded and lifted the barrel

of his Russian AK-74 assault rifle. "Where's Tommy?" Rock asked, glancing back at Scalise.

"Went to take a leak," Scalise said. "He should be back any minute."

Rock sat on his haunches and pulled a five-pound bag of coke from the case. He flipped open his pocket knife and made a one-inch slit in the bag. A small amount of white powder fell to his finger. Touching the cocaine to his tongue, he smiled. He turned to give his approval to Coroneos, but instead met the working end of a sawed-off double-barrel shotgun. "What the hell are you doing?"

Scalise smirked. "Sorry, Boss. I'm submitting my resignation."

Rock turned his head and glared at Coroneos, who had his pistol jammed against the back of Eddie's head. The AK-74 hung in Eddie's right hand, the barrel aimed at the ground.

"What is this, some kind of fucking joke?" Rock said.

"No, Tony, it's no joke, just business."

"You lousy, backstabbing son-of-a-bitch! Forty-five years we've been friends!" Coroneos shook his head.

"Forty-five years you've been thinking you were one rung above me, using me because you weren't smart enough to run this show yourself. We both know who kept this ship afloat."

The veins of Rock's temples budged and his hardened face turned beet red. "Peter, you ungrateful piece of shit!"

Coroneos tapped his pistol on the back of Eddie's head. "Drop it." The AK-74 hit the concrete with a metallic clang. With his foot, Coroneos slid the rifle backward, picked it up, and slung it over his shoulder. Scalise reached inside Rock's sports coat and removed his pistol.

"You think you're different from me?" Coroneos said. "Sal Paccione saved your business from bankruptcy, gave you a job, and promoted you through the ranks. And how did you repay him? With a bullet to the face. No, Tony, we're the same, you and me, businessmen. I'm just better at it."

Scalise glanced down at the stump of his finger and shot Rock a smirk. "Yeah, Boss, just business, like killing Liza. Such a shame."

Rock lunged at Scalise. Scalise jerked backward, lifting the shotgun's barrel into the air beyond Rock's outstretched hand. A single deafening shot rang out from Coroneos' pistol positioned an inch behind Eddie's left ear. The bullet passed clean through Rock's left thigh. It ricocheted off the floor and hit the far wall.

Eddie pulled away from Coroneos and sprinted to his father's side. The back of Eddie's head seemed an easy target but not yet. Perhaps the Carlotti men should all die together— a grand finale of sorts. Rock, the top prize, should go last. Eddie, because he'd be dangerous. He'd become what the Paccione boys had become after their father's assassination, a ticking time bomb, revenge waiting for payback. And Nick, because he was too damn smart. He'd gotten too close. Coroneos actually liked Nick, but he had no other choice.

Rock slumped to his side, clutching his leg with both hands. Eddie caught him before his head hit the floor. For the first time since Coroneos knew him, Rock looked afraid.

Scalise rammed the barrel of his shotgun into the side of Rock's head. "Damn, I was so close to ending you."

Coroneos patted Scalise on the shoulder. "Tie them up and drag them to the trash." He motioned with his head toward a large steel dumpster adjacent to the van.

A steady trail of blood flowed behind Rock as Scalise lugged him across the floor toward the dumpster.

Eddie followed, his hands tied behind him. As he crawled to his feet, with the gun to his back, he took a seat on the ground next to his dying father. "It's going to be okay, Pops," Eddie said.

Coroneos holstered his pistol in the small of his back then lit a cigarette. A casual smile formed around the cigarette as it hung loosely from his lips. The white smoke hung in the still air above the Carlottis. "You didn't really think you were going to retire and earn a gold watch, did you, Tony? You knew you'd either get bloody or live out your last days in the federal pen. I'm doing you a favor."

Rock struggled to lift his head and whispered something unintelligible.

Scalise kept his weapons aimed at Rock as Coroneos bent over. "What is it you want to say? Might want to make it good because they may be your last words."

When Coroneos drew near, Rock threw his head forward and spit in his face, the thick wad landing across the bridge of Coroneos' nose. Coroneos wiped his face with his sleeve. He shot Rock an arrogant smirk and walked to the back of the van.

Nick looked past his father. For a brief moment, he locked gazes with his brother. Eddie shook his head slowly, his eyes red, the corners of his lips turned downward. Nick couldn't recall ever seeing his brother so pathetic — broken and remorseful, somehow asking Nick for forgiveness. They'd never been on the same side. Ever.

Coroneos approached again and lifted Rock's head by his hair. "Sorry you got Nick tangled up in your filth? You should be. His blood will be on your hands."

"Leave my boys out of this Peter, please," Rock said.

"I told you to deal with him. You failed. Now he gets to see how the family business works."

Rock's face dulled. Beads of sweat gathered on his forehead, and the pool of blood around him grew. Nick pitied him. He looked weak and helpless, not the unbreakable Rock whom Nick had known for three decades. Rock had just become the recipient of the same brand of evil he'd been dispensing for years.

Nick's mouth remained taped, but he wanted to say something, to say how his anger boiled over his father's greed and callousness, for indirectly causing his mother's death, but some insane part of him wanted to say, "I love you," before it was too late. Deep down, he did love him.

Despite his pain and bondage, his position couldn't be better, on his knees, his feet behind him. If he could just grab the knife, both his wrist and feet ties would be accessible without being visible to Coroneos and Scalise. He struggled to reach into his back pocket with his right hand. With his hands bound, he could only slide his index and middle fingers into the pocket only far enough to touch the top of the knife. Every time he squeezed the two fingers together, the knife slipped back into his pocket. God, please help me.

Coroneos moved toward an overturned wooden packing crate a few yards from the van. He glanced at his watch. "Ten minutes."

Scalise nodded and unzipped two navy blue leather duffels. "I hope these are big enough."

Coroneos grinned. "I'm sure they'll be fine."

73

THE SINGLE GUNSHOT escalated the situation, but still, Rawls needed to hold tight until his units were in position. Moving too early could prove risky for both the hostages and his men.

At 2:55 am, Rawls received a call.

"A black Lincoln Town Car just turned onto North Delaware Avenue a block south of your location," the detective said.

Seconds later, the car's headlights went dark before it slowed and turned into the main lot. It continued around to the back of building number three. Rawls and Taylor crept tight to the brick wall as they followed the car and watched it pass through the overhead door. The massive door closed as the car disappeared into the loading dock.

Rawls called for a helicopter to get airborne but stay for enough away to remain silent. He called his backups to watch the remaining exits to building number three. Taylor stayed in contact with an officer Simms back at headquarters who reviewed the building's blueprints. He determined the catwalk connecting the two buildings and the loading dock door to be the best portals of entry for his two three-man SWAT teams.

Unless all hell broke loose, Rawls wanted to make contact with Coroneos once they'd secured the building on the outside.

~

THE LINCOLN, with its dark, tinted windows, inched toward the middle of the room. Coroneos stood next to the overturned crate, his feet spread apart, his shoulders pulled back, and his hands resting on the small of his back. Even from a distance, he looked different, older and more haggard. The large, dark bags under his eyes were out of character for a man who always looked like he was heading to a photoshoot. This wasn't the same man Nick had seen at the wedding. Maybe the guilt of betraying his best friend had gotten the best of him.

Fifty feet away, the car came to a stop, the engine still running. The four aluminum cases sat aligned in a row behind Coroneos. Scalise moved to Coroneos' side, pistol in hand, glancing at the Carlottis every few seconds. The crimson pool swelled at Rock's side.

Nick's knife remained elusive, an agonizing two and a half inches from his fingertips. Yet with his wrists bound, it might as well have been a mile. He repositioned himself ever so slightly so as not to alert Scalise. He strained to stretch his arms downward, the plastic ties again cutting into his already shredded skin. He forced his fingers as deep as they would go, the index and middle fingers sliding along the knife. The blistering pain in his wrist seemed like an insurmountable barrier to the freedom that lay so close. Just a bit more. The flesh pulled away from the bone as the tie sliced deeper, but it seemed his fingers gained ground. A trickle of blood rolled down his fingers. He squeezed them together and found purchase. For every half inch the knife moved upward, it slipped a quarter inch away, a precarious balance of give and take.

A minute later, the knife's edge inched above the rim of his pocket. He breathed a sigh of relief before flipping it open. He turned the blade toward the plastic tie.

Three men exited the Lincoln. Two approached Coroneos and Scalise. The third man, larger in stature, stood alongside the car, holding a compact assault rifle. The two men walked toward Coroneos, each carrying a large brown briefcase in one hand and a handgun in the other. They stopped about twenty feet short.

"Mr. Coroneos," Sal Jr. said.

"Good to see you, Sal. You've grown."

Salvatore Junior, the older brother, stood six foot nothing, lanky, with a white t-shirt and a black leather jacket. A sizable gold cross hung from his neck. His brother Joseph, a few inches shorter and considerably thicker, stood by Sal's side, his gaze darting around the room.

"I was eighteen when I watched them bury my old man," Sal said. He turned his head toward the van. "My, my, isn't this our lucky day." He stepped in the Carlottis direction before Peter stopped him.

"First things first, Sal," he said. "We have business to do."

Sal turned to Coroneos. "Show us the goods," he said, then grimaced and pointed his gun at Rock. "I'll get back to you maggots in a while."

Coroneos motioned for Scalise to carry the cases closer. With shotgun in hand, Scalise dragged the cases over one at a time, setting them at the Paccione brothers' feet.

Joseph Paccione took a couple steps back.

Sal tapped his pistol on the first case. "Open it up," he said to Scalise, who exposed the neatly stacked bricks of cocaine.

Sal squatted down and began counting. At the eighteenth brick, he sampled the product. He asked to see the remaining three cases.

As Scalise opened the second case, Nick's knife passed through the zip tie. His hands fell apart and the pain eased. The plastic pulled away from the gash on his wrist, but the blood seemed to flow a bit faster, covering the palm of his hand. The knife's handle felt wet.

He remained as still as possible as Sal's inspection continued. One by one, Sal examined the goods, counting as he went, randomly checking packages for quality.

The operation proved to be tedious and held the men's attention. It provided Nick with enough time to loose his feet. Once the knife sliced through the tie, Nick quietly cleared his throat. Eddie turned his head slowly and the two made eye contact. Rock didn't flinch. His face bore a dusky pale color with a grim look of impending death. His eye remained closed. The pool of blood hadn't grown much over the past couple minutes, either because the wound had begun to clot or because he had no more blood to lose.

Nick leaned forward and flashed the knife behind his back. How could he pass it to Eddie? Eddie nodded slightly and turned away. Rock remained slumped over in a heap between them, his eye now opened to a slit, its luster fading. He tipped his head slightly in Nick's direction. Nick moved his hands enough to let his father know he was free. Rock blinked hard, maybe with all the energy he had left in his failing body, but at least this might give him a glimmer of hope. Thank God their task at hand kept the men preoccupied, confident they had their hostages well contained. For the time being, Nick opted to sit tight, waiting for what might be his one opportunity.

After Sal finished the inspection, Joseph placed the first briefcase on the crate. Scalise carried a small battery-operated money-counting machine from the van and set it next to the briefcase. He flipped the switch. The device started with a whirl, its pitch increasing as the motor got up to speed. Stack by stack, Coroneos ran bills through the machine. He visually scrutinized random bills for evidence they might be counterfeit. The cash flew through at light speed, but even so, the first case took a little more than twenty minutes. As they counted the bills from both briefcases, Coroneos rewrapped them in stacks of one hundred, placing the first million dollars in Scalise's duffle. He filled his own with the remainder.

When they'd counted the final bill, Coroneos shook hands with both brothers. "It's a done deal, boys. The goods are yours, and so is the Carlotti family." He picked up the smaller duffle and tossed it at Scalise's feet.

Scalise, still holding his shotgun, grabbed the duffle and smiled. "Thanks, Boss." He threw the bag over his shoulder and turned toward the door.

While Sal and his brother loaded the four cases of cocaine into the Lincoln's trunk, Coroneos lifted his duffle from the table and stepped toward Scalise. "Hold on, Mickey, you might want to stick around for the show. You've been waiting for this day."

74

"THE MIGHTY ROCK HAS CRUMBLED," Sal said, grinding his heel into Rock's wounded thigh. "Don't you look like a pathetic lump of shit, dying in a pool of your own blood."

Rock struggled to talk. With one deep breath, the words came through his dry lips, weak but every word clear. "Like your good-for-nothing father did when the nurses had to wipe his ass and change his diapers."

Sal pumped another round into Rock's opposite thigh, the blast echoing throughout the complex. Rock recoiled and groaned in pain. A spray of blood hit Nick in the face. Everything went red. Nick wanted to move, but it would be suicide. He blinked a few times to regain his sight and squeezed his right hand around the handle of his knife. He glared at Sal.

Sal pointed the gun at Nick and sneered. "Who's this?"

Scalise yelled, "It's little Nicky, all grown up into a fancy doctor!"

Sal's sneer turned to a grin. "Doctor, huh? Didn't have big enough balls to go into the family business?" He ripped the tape from Nick's mouth. "I want to see if you cry like a baby."

Nick bit his tongue. He'd be useless with a bullet to the leg, so he settled for a stare-down. Sal blinked first.

$$\sim$$

AFTER THE SECOND gunshot rang out, Rawls radioed Simms. "Captain, status please."

"Bravo team ready. Alpha team nearing the dock."

Without eyes on the inside, Rawls had no way of knowing where the hostages were, who fired the shot, or if anyone inside lay injured or killed.

Alpha team had crossed the catwalk and made its way toward the loading dock. Bravo team poised outside the loading dock, readied to storm the room when Alpha team breached the inside doors.

"Captain Simms, as soon as Alpha and Bravo teams are a go, you're in command?"

"Roger that."

$$\sim$$

THE SHARP CRACK of something hitting the ground interrupted the party, the sound emanating from beyond the inside door. Coroneos gave Scalise a gentle elbow to the side and whispered in his ear. Scalise hurried to the far wall sneaking toward the door.

"Don't tell me we're not secure, Peter," Sal said with a scowl.

"It's not a problem," Coroneos said. "We'll handle it."

Scalise reached the door in less than a minute and yanked it open with his shotgun ready. Danielle let out an abbreviated shriek as her cell phone hit the floor. Scalise towered over her.

"Hey, Doc," Scalise said with a sneer. "What's that saying about curiosity killing the cat?"

"Get her over here!" Coroneos said.

Danielle looked toward Nick and silently formed the words

'I'm sorry,' her lips quivering. Still, she looked resolute. Nick shook his head, wishing with all his heart she'd stayed hidden. At least she was alive.

"I hope we won't have any more problems," Sal said.

Coroneos took hold of Danielle. "No, we're good," he said, slapping Danielle hard across the face with the back of his hand. "I should kill you here and now, sweetheart, but I'm feeling generous."

"You're a coward, Peter!" Nick yelled.

Coroneos pushed Danielle back in Scalise's direction. "Put her in the van. She's our insurance policy."

Scalise pressed his shotgun into Danielle's back and led her to the van with Coroneos following close behind.

Please, Lord, don't let them hurt her. Nick needed to act, but the moment wasn't right.

Scalise had taken no more than five steps when Peter raised his gun and fired two rounds from his silenced .44 Magnum straight into Scalise's back, dropping him to his knees. The shotgun hit the ground.

Danielle covered her head and screamed.

Sal and Joseph drew their weapons, and their guard put his rifle to his shoulder, but all three eased them down when they understood Coroneos' intention. Scalise's head dropped and his body tipped, slowly at first, then accelerating like a felled tree as gravity took over. He landed face first, his forehead smacking the concrete with a dull crack.

"Sorry for the interruption," Coroneos said.

"Well, it seems you just got a raise," Sal said.

"A little earlier than I'd planned, but I like to adapt."

Coroneos shifted his pistol's aim toward Danielle. He pulled the duffle from the dead man's shoulder and picked up the shotgun. He led Danielle to the back of the van.

"Let her go, Peter!" Nick yelled.

Danielle's fearful gaze locked on to his for a split second before she disappeared into the van.

Coroneos opened the van's driver's side door and tossed in Scalise's duffle before scrounging for more zip ties.

Joseph stood next to his brother and stared down at Rock, who lay slumped beneath him, his gray-pleated pants bullet-ridden and soaked with blood. "We've been waiting a long time for this day," he said. "Sal and I promised each other when the time came, we wouldn't kill you right away."

Sal chimed in. "That would be too easy. We'd want you to suffer as much as our father did." He turned to his brother. "What do you think, Joe? Break his back?"

"I think maybe cut out his tongue, then break his back."

"Sounds like a plan, but since Mr. Coroneos has been so kind as to deliver up the brothers Carlotti, I say we let Rock watch his sons die first."

"Perfect, like an appetizer to the main course," Joseph said.

"May I have the honors?"

Sal smirked and nodded. Coroneos kept his handgun on Danielle as he grabbed the ties from a small wooden box.

Joseph bent over, clutched a fist-full of Nick's hair, and yanked him to his feet.

In a flash, Nick seized Joseph's wrist and swung the knife from behind, thrusting the blade deep into the stunned man's abdomen. The silver revolver fell to the ground between Nick and his father. Rock snatched up the gun, his arm weak and trembling. He and Sal raised their guns simultaneously, but Rock beat him to the trigger and set off two quick rounds. The first grazed Sal's right shoulder but the second caught him in the middle of the forehead, the entrance hole the size of a dime. Before a single drop of blood flowed, he collapsed in a pile at Rock's feet.

The Pacciones guard lifted his assault rifle to respond as Nick spun Joseph around and wrapped his arm around Joseph's neck, using him as a human shield. The guard, with his assault rifle still aimed in Nick's direction, stood by helpless, unable to return fire.

Joseph pressed his hands tightly to his stomach as blood seeped between his fingers. His eyes wide open and bulging with fright, he looked pleadingly toward his guard. The color drained from his face and his lips were nearly white, as he turned his last dying gaze down to his blood-soaked hands.

Rock struggled to keep his head upright. With an unsteady arm, he turned his weapon toward Coroneos and fired three rounds above his head, sending him diving into the back of the van.

"Run!" Nick yelled to Danielle.

The door of the van flew open and Danielle leaped out, diving behind a row of metal shelving units. Rock shot three more evenly spaced rounds into the van's side.

Coroneos tried unsuccessfully to exit the van as Rock let loose his last round but kept pulling the trigger. The falling hammer's rhythmic clicking continued as the echo of the final shot faded. The room fell silent.

Nick leaned forward, trying hard to keep Joseph's body, now completely limp, between him and the guard. With an outstretched foot, he slid Sal's pistol back in his direction, dropped to his knees with Sal in tow, and grabbed the gun with his right hand.

Rock's arm weakened and sank to the ground. His fingers loosened their grip on his gun's handle.

"Hold on, Pops," Nick said as he pivoted his hand around Joseph's arm and took two rapid shots at the guard. The guard leaned out and returned a flurry of shots. The "crack" of the supersonic bullet passing by Nick's ear preceded a lightning-like burning of his left shoulder.

"Shit!" He tested his arm, and everything seemed to still work. He let go another round, the shot catching the guard in the upper body. He disappeared behind the Lincoln, his assault rifle crashing to the floor still in plain sight.

Nick wasn't sure how badly he'd injured the guard or if he still posed a threat. Either way, Nick's shot had taken the man's rifle out of play. Joseph was dead or near dead. Peter, however, wouldn't hesitate to shoot clean through Joseph. Nick dropped Joseph's body and slipped behind the dumpster. He reached around and attempted to pull his father to safety. Even with two working arms and leverage, it would be a difficult task. Today— impossible. The shoulder hurt like a mother but still seemed to move, just not well enough to drag two hundred and forty pounds of dead weight.

"Let me go," Rock said, his voice faint and raspy.

"Don't you die on me!" Nick pleaded, pulling harder but unable to haul his father's body around the corner. "Breathe, Pops — just keep breathing."

"Nick, the knife!" Eddie shouted out.

From Nick's vantage point, he couldn't see his brother, who had been sitting to his father's left. "Hold on," he answered, still unsure how to pass him the knife.

"Can you get to me?" Nick asked.

"I think so." Eddie's head peeked around the corner.

A shot rang out from behind the van, the bullet careening off the dumpster between Nick and his brother. Eddie dropped to his knees at Nick's side. Nick reached behind Eddie and slit the tie binding his hands. "I need a piece," Eddie said.

"Sorry but you'll have to settle for this," Nick said, handing him the knife.

Eddie took it from Nick's hand. Both men squatted low, keeping the dumpster between them and the van.

Nick glanced around the corner. The contours of Danielle's body stood out as she knelt behind the empty shelves. Coroneos had to be able to see her from the van. "Peter, let her go and take the damn money," Nick said.

Coroneos eased open the passenger door and slipped from the van. He walked straight toward Danielle, his pistol drawn. "Stand up, sweetheart," he said, his words calm but firm.

"Get your hands off of me!" The frightened tone in Danielle's voice shot like a burning spike in Nick's gut.

"Shut the hell up," Coroneos said, yanking her to her feet. They appeared from behind the rusted, green metal shelving unit. He led her out into the open.

"I'm so sorry, Nick," she said, tears rolling down her face.

Nick stepped from the dumpster. His gun hand hung at his side. "You know she's not part of this thing, Peter. Don't dig yourself a deeper hole."

"Too late for that, Doc. I'm leaving here with her and the money. If you make a move, I'll drop her, so help me." Peter eased toward the van, keeping Danielle between them.

As Peter continued back-stepping, Nick lifted his hand, aimimg the sight of his pistol aimed above Peter's head. Danielle's gaze locked on Nick in silent, stoic pleading for him to find a way out. She held her head high, her eyes refusing to shed a tear.

The Lincoln's engine fired up with a deafening roar in the closed space of the dock. Thick white smoke poured from the tires as the car raced toward Nick. It happened so fast. Eddie bolted from the side of the van and hit Nick broadside. Airborne, Nick caught a glimpse of the speeding car's left front fender as it passed. Then a sickening thud. Eddie's body flew through the air and struck the ground.

Nick rolled at least twice, ending up on his stomach, the pistol still clenched in his hand. He spun his head back toward the van as Peter pulled the side door shut, the fair skin of Danielle's legs visible for a split second. The Lincoln came to a stop. The car's door swung open. Nick lifted his right arm and fired a single shot at the guard rushing toward him. The man froze as the bullet hit just above the belt. He stumbled. His eyes wild with rage, he surged ahead. Nick emptied his magazine with a rapid "pop, pop, pop, pop." The man's legs collapsed beneath him, and he crumbled to the floor in front of Nick.

Still on his belly, Nick peered under the car toward the dumpster. Eddie's body lay face-down, motionless a few feet away, one leg twisted at an unnatural angle. A jagged shard of his femur protruded from a tear in his pants.

Was his whole family dead? The empty gun in his hand might as well be a toy. But Coroneos didn't know that.

Nick jumped to his feet, his left arm numb and dangling to his side. The van hadn't moved. Where was that son-of-a-bitch? Not in the driver's side seat. With the empty gun held out in from of him, he crept closer to the van. Something moved to his left. Coroneos stood next to the expansive main garage door, his hand reaching for the red push-button switch. "Peter! Stop!"

Coroneos didn't flinch. His gun gripped in his right hand lay against his thigh. "Well done, Nick. I'm wondering one thing, though."

"What's that?"

"Do you have the guts to kill me?"

"In a heartbeat, if you don't take your hand off the switch."

Both men stood frozen. Nick took a step forward. Coroneos pressed the button and spun while dropping to one knee. He fired a single shot as the massive door began to open. Nick hit the ground.

Deafening explosions and flashes of light filled the warehouse. Tear-gas canisters hit the floor and spun wildly, sending thick clouds of burning fumes into the air. Officers yelled commands from behind their gas masks.

Nick struggled to breathe as he climbed to his knees. He ran blindly through the fog toward the van. A blurred figure appeared to his right. "Danielle?" Someone drove Nick to the ground, the gun ripped from his hand. Two officers held him down.

"Hands behind your back!" one yelled.

Nick's eyes burned as he blinked hard to make out the blurry, vague figures before him. His throat felt like he'd swallowed battery acid. In between coughing fits, he succeeded in getting the words out. "Where is Danielle?"

One officer restrained him and the other placed cuffs on his wrists. The cloud of gas dissipated. Nick lifted his head and, in the distance, made out her silhouette. She stood between two officers, backlit by floodlights. What a beautiful sight! His heart eased. Two more officers knelt by his father.

"Is he dead?" Nick asked, still trying to clear his throat. The percussive chakk-chakk-chakk of a helicopter's rotors hovering above the warehouse added to the confusion.

"Uncuff him," a muffled but familiar voice said. "He's clear."

The cuffs came loose, and someone lifted Nick to his feet.

Rawls removed his gas mask. "Your father's alive— barely. We have paramedics on the way, but I don't think he has much time."

Nick rushed over. He dropped to the cold concrete floor next to his father. Rock's head leaned back against the dumpster, his face ghost white and his skin draped from his bones. The blood around his legs had thickened to a gelatinous mass.

"Pops," Nick said softly.

Rock remained motionless and silent.

"Pops, please hold on," Nick said as a hand came to rest on his shoulder. He turned to see Danielle. Her eyes welled up with tears as she crouched beside him, her hand never leaving his shoulder.

Rock strained to peek up at his son through the narrow slit of his eyelid.

"Dad, I love you. I'm sorry," Nick said, not sure what he was sorry for. Maybe that he'd never really had a father, but if Rock could survive this, perhaps he'd change, and they might get a second chance.

Nick scooped up his father's hand and Rock squeezed hard;

not like he was in pain, but instead, a silent act of remorse, a voiceless, "I love you too, Son." It was the first time Nick remembered his father holding his hand.

He pulled his father's head to his chest. Rock's lips moved as he struggled to form words, but none would come.

"It's okay, Pops. You don't have to talk."

Rock nodded as if to say, "Yes, I do." But, still the movement of his mouth produced only a raspy flow of air. He stared deeply into Nick's eyes and squeezed his hand even harder.

"I know, Pops. I know."

A subtle smile came to Rock's face.

Rock took a few short, spastic breaths. His hand fell limp. Nick wept with Danielle's arms around him, holding him close. Eddie still hadn't moved as a paramedic leaned over his contorted body. Sirens wailed in the distance and the helicopter's rotors faded. Nick closed his eyes and rested in Danielle's embrace.

EPILOGUE

(The Following Spring)

IT WAS like being raised from the dead, emerging from the womb with that deep, miraculous first breath. It wasn't that Nick felt his first baptism "didn't take," but he knew that he'd never owned it. He had been dead in his spirit for so many years. Thanks to the love of his future wife, the encouragement of his best friend, and a little prodding by the Holy Spirit, Nick made this baptism personal. It was something he had to do, something he wanted to do.

Even before the pastor lifted him up, before he rose, the sun emerged from the clouds, and its light shone through his closed eyelids, as if God said, "Awake! Awake!" And, when he broke the water's surface, a burst of emotion caught him like a tidal wave. He thrust his hands in the air. Tears and sparkling drops of river water merged as they cascaded down his face.

Amidst clapping, cheers, and a few wet cheeks, Nick waded toward the bank of the Blackfoot River, just upstream from where

Bear Creek flowed in. The pastor stayed back, watching as a handful of Nick's friends waited on a grassy hill above the clear mountain river. Danielle ran into the cold water, knee-deep, and threw her arms around him. They held each other for a few moments and clasped hands, Danielle's engagement ring glistening in the bright sunshine.

"No hug for me?" Steve said, meeting them at the stream's edge.

Nick pulled his best friend close and gave him a couple firm slaps on the back. "I love you, man," Nick said, leaving the wet imprint of his shirt on Steve's.

"Love you too, Brother."

Summer 2000
(Two Years Later)

THREE YEARS after his father's death, much had changed for both Nick and the Carlotti crime family. The jury had convicted Peter Coroneos on multiple counts, including conspiracy to commit murder in Liza's and Danny Torello's deaths, murder in the first degree for the assassinations of Mickey Scalise and Willie Santini, extortion, racketeering, drug smuggling, money laundering, and a host of smaller charges.

Three weeks into a mandatory life sentence, they'd found Coroneos dead in the laundry room of the Supermax Prison in Waynesburg with multiple stab wounds to his chest and most of his broken teeth spread out on the floor around him.

As part of her plea deal, Anya served a six-month sentence for extortion and paid her restitution with money she made from the sale of her emerald necklace and Audi. They deported her back to Brazil in March 1998.

Nick's brother Eddie survived a severe concussion and a broken pelvis and femur. He spent a week in intensive care and two months in rehab. After taking a plea agreement in exchange for information related to Peter's role in smuggling cocaine from Colombia and other illicit business activities, he served eighteen months in a minimum-security facility in Somerset, Pennsylvania.

Nick visited his brother twice. The first visit was an emotional purging of three decades of animosity, resentment, and loss. They shared stories of better times with their mother and the few memories they had of their father with his guard down, times when they'd resembled a typical family. This was a humbled Eddie, a broken man who seemed ready to start anew, set on making things right. Two months later, at their second meeting, it was back to business as usual. Eddie's face had hardened and his tone was flippant and brash. The visit lasted only fifteen minutes before Nick laid his open hand on the glass separating the two men and bid his brother goodbye.

Jennifer moved to the Jersey shore with her sister while she waited out a plethora of legal battles over Rock's estate. Civil lawsuits from Willie's aunt, Danny Torello's parents, Senator Mays, as well as the IRS seeking years of back taxes made it likely she'd walk away with no more than she came in with. Nick kept in touch with her regularly. After all, she was his only surviving parent.

The judge cleared Senator Lloyd Mays on all counts. He chose to resign his seat in the Pennsylvania Senate and gave up his bid for the US Senate, telling the press he needed a clean start. He passed the South Carolina bar and started a lucrative personal-injury firm on Hilton Head Island, where he lived year-round on his ninety-two-foot Hatteras, the Carpe Diem. He sold the Gypsy Rose to a retired real estate broker from Atlanta. He was currently single and not dating.

Steve continued on staff at the hospital of the University of Pennsylvania for another year then he took a job in Grand

Rapids, Michigan, about half an hour from where he grew up. Two months later, he met a witty and irresistible barista at an eclectic cafe a block from the hospital. Aside from her looks and sense of humor, a tattoo of Galatians 2:20 on her right forearm sealed the deal. They planned a small wedding in the fall. He and his best man remained the closest of friends.

Mayor Rendell approved Rawls' appointment to First Deputy Police Commissioner in 1998. Behind his desk sat a grand mahogany bookshelf, its shelves lined with books, plaques, and a few assorted knickknacks, but most notable, Lester's yellowed PF Flyers Center Hi. In the farthest corner, in a wire-mesh basket, lay a black and white paper airplane.

Dr. Danielle Sorenson-Carlotti finished her fellowship and took a job on staff in a hospital in Missoula, Montana with her husband, Dr. Nick Carlotti. Both were thankful to leave the big city behind. With their dog Rhino, they relished the beauty of the Bitterroot Valley from the deck of their log home overlooking the sparkling Clark Fork River. Nick learned to tie flies, and his brother-in-law taught him how to keep a tight loop with his eight-and-a-half-foot five weight Winston fly rod. Nick caught his first cutthroat trout as his pregnant wife watched from the river's bank.

A month after moving West, Nick received the first of many royalty checks from Blue Heron Press. His mother had named him the beneficiary with the legal rights to all of her works including *Rebecca's Box*.

Nick and Danielle cherished bedtime the most. They prayed, talked, laughed, and cried. They made love and dreamt sweet dreams, but one ritual held a most special place in their hearts. Nick read a little from the book each night. He did the math. At the proper pace, he'd reach the book's last page in exactly forty weeks.

It went like this — Nick picked up the old leather book from his nightstand, slid down in the bed, and put his head close to

Danielle's growing belly. He read from *Pilgrim's Progress* in a voice just above a whisper:

"The hill, though high, I covet to ascend; The difficulty will not me offend, For I perceive the way to life lies here. Come, pluck up, heart, let's neither faint nor fear. Better, though difficult, the right way to go, than wrong, though easy, where the end is woe."

The End

~

ABOUT THE AUTHOR

David Dalrymple is a retired oral surgeon, wildlife photographer, and writer living in North Carolina. He has written for surgical textbooks, professional journals, and a Christian blog. When he's not hiding in a blind with his camera or pounding the keys of his laptop, you'll find him on a river with a fly rod or in the mountains looking for elk. Carlotti is his first work of fiction.

If you are interested in his nature and wildlife photography, you can follow him on Instagram or visit his website.

www.daviddalrympleauthor.com
www.instagram.com/wildlifeshooter
www.daviddalrymplephotography.com

Made in the USA
Columbia, SC
03 December 2022

72648586R00233